Praise

LIE
IN
WAIT

'An exciting, twisty read that **had me hooked from the first page** . . . a brilliant summer read'

Lisa Hall, bestselling author of *Between You and Me*

'This is one clever novel . . . a crime thriller with an ingenious plot and vivid characters . . . It is **a really gritty, dark novel. I am hugely impressed with this**, only Minett's second novel, and I think it sets him up as **a writer to watch out for in the future**'

Bibliomaniac

'A psychological thriller in the purest sense . . . **Deeply satisfying**'

Cleopatra Loves Books

'Deserves to be read in one sitting . . . **His books are some of the best I've ever had the pleasure to read**'

The Quiet Knitter

'**Intriguing characters, a clever plot and another gripping opening**. I shall look forward to book three!'

Buried Under Books

'Long after you have turned the last page you will still be thinking about *Lie in Wait* . . . this **dark and twisted journey of a book**. A great read, this book will keep you turning the pages long into the night'

Nudge Book Reviews

G.J. Minett studied at Cambridge and then spent many years as a teacher of foreign languages. He studied for an MA in Creative Writing at the University of Chichester, and won the 2010 Chapter One Prize for unpublished novels with the opening chapter of *The Hidden Legacy*.

Also by G.J. Minett

The Hidden Legacy

LIE
IN
WAIT

G.J. MINETT

ZAFFRE

First published in Great Britain in 2016 by
Zaffre Publishing

80–81 Wimpole St, London W1G 9RE
www.zaffrebooks.co.uk

A CIP catalogue record for this book is available from the British Library.

ISBN: 978-1-785-76058-7

also available as an ebook

1 3 5 7 9 10 8 6 4 2

Typeset by IDSUK (Data Connection) Ltd

Printed and bound by Clays Ltd, St Ives Plc

Zaffre Publishing is an imprint of Bonnier Zaffre,
a Bonnier Publishing company
www.bonnierzaffre.co.uk
www.bonnierpublishing.co.uk

Ronald John Minett
03.11.22 – 16.01.16
With all our love

PROLOGUE

NOW: WEDNESDAY, 1ST OCTOBER

OWEN

'How long now, would you say?' she asks.

Out of the roundabout, up into third and accelerating away, engine screaming like a harpy till he manages to slam the mule of a gear stick into fourth. Gently doesn't seem to cut it anymore. Gearbox nearly shot to pieces. Probably got another five, ten thousand miles left in it, according to Vic at the garage. Then he's going to have to start looking for a replacement. New truck altogether would be nice but a couple of years away at least. Even stumping up for a reconditioned gearbox is going to leave him a bit stretched.

Willie says it's his own fault for never showing any ambition. *Brain the size of a planet – why the fuck are you pissing around with lawnmowers for a living?* Swears a lot, does Willie. You can pick him up on it as much as you like but it never does any good. Straight back at you – effing this, sodding that.

'Twenty minutes,' he mumbles. 'M-maybe less.'

'What . . . Worthing or the hotel?'

'Don't know the hotel.' He's told her this already, wishes she'd listen. Like he's got nothing better to do than answer stupid questions.

Engine starts to shudder as the needle creeps up to fifty. In the headlights he can make out the number plate of the car in front: GR02 ZMM. Total = 79, the calculation automatic, the irritation instantaneous. *Prime number*, he thinks to himself. So . . . overtake or drop back, one or the other. Anything as long as he doesn't stay too close. Quick check to see what's coming the other way and it's non-stop headlights, so he eases his foot back on the accelerator and watches as the car in front starts to pull away despite itself.

Stupid, he thinks. You wouldn't drive a car with faulty brakes or with tyres that were almost down to the rim. Why is it that people will happily pour their faith into so many leaky vessels in life – looks, dress code, personality – and yet ignore the certainty of numbers? People lie – they lie all the time. Only numbers are constant.

'OK,' Julie says, holding up her iPhone. 'Just shout when we get anywhere near Worthing and I'll switch on Google Maps.'

They're heading out into open countryside now, Yapton and Barnham away to their left. Street lights racing off into the distance in his rear-view mirror. He risks a quick sideways glance. Can't really see her face – not clearly. There's the glow from the dashboard and the oncoming headlights that strafe across her features, causing the lenses of her spectacles to flash for an instant. Otherwise, nothing. Darkness.

Not pretty exactly, he thinks to himself. Wrong word altogether. Pretty is Abi. Always has been. And he can accept it's maybe not ideal to be using her as a yardstick even now but there you go – you don't get to choose these things. No, Julie's not *pretty*. Pretty suggests petite and she's a good few inches too tall for that. Loose-limbed, athletic. Something of a swagger in the way she holds herself, he's noticed, as if she's ready for a scrap if it comes to it. At least she's here. It's not like people are queuing round the block to help him right now.

Fuckable is Willie's assessment of her. Tells you all you need to know about Willie.

Past the Climping turn-off. Away to the right, Littlehampton golf course and the seaside resort itself huddled down beyond it, dimmer switch turned right down and a strange, murky haze hanging over the lamps which have reappeared at the roadside.

'We getting near yet?' she asks again. Another stupid question.

'Quarter of an hour or so.'

She sighs, wriggles around in her seat. 'Look, I'm really sorry about this but do you think we could stop somewhere for a few minutes? I'm bursting for the loo.'

Tesco has just flashed past on the other side of the dual carriageway. He maps the next couple of miles in his head. Picks out the Body Shop roundabout. Zeroes in on the Shell station on the opposite side of the road.

'About two or three minutes,' he says.

'That's great. Sorry about this,' she giggles. 'Small bladder.' He blushes, hoping she can't see his face any more clearly than he can see hers.

New traffic lights up ahead, turning amber. He brakes and rams the truck into neutral. Glances in the rear-view mirror again as they roll to a standstill and sees the headlights of the car immediately behind, which seems to be taking an eternity to close the gap. There's a blast on the horn from further back and as the lights turn to green, the car stutters forward as if the driver has been woken from a daydream.

HK12 RCA: total = 53. *Prime number*. His heart skips a beat as he moves through the gears and pulls away once more. *Same car*. He trawls back through the journey so far, pinpoints the locations exactly. Traffic lights near the Martlets roundabout. Then just after they left Bognor seafront, as they went past the beach entrance to Butlins. Now here.

And here comes the rocking – he's moving back and forth, back and forth in his seat, mumbling the number plate to himself, over and over.

> *Oi, how many times d'you have to be told? Cut it out.*
> *Owen, dear . . .*
> *You gonna sort him out or you want me to?*
> *Owen, don't do that, there's a good boy.*
> *Like living with a bloody half-wit.*

Out of the corner of his eye he can see Julie's watching him closely, puzzled rather than alarmed. 'You OK?' she asks, and she reaches forward, placing a hand on his knee. He recoils as if she's holding a taser, forces himself to calm down, concentrate. Pushes himself back in the seat, shoulders taut, neck muscles braced against the headrest. Needs to ride this out.

'What is it?' she asks again.

'Car behind – no, don't turn round,' he says, catching her arm as she twists in her seat.

'What about it?'

'I think it's been following us.'

She pauses before replying, allowing time for this to sink in. 'Why?'

'It's been there since we left. Keeps letting other cars get in between, then closes the gap when there's no choice.'

She shakes her head. 'No, I mean why would it be following us?'

No answer to this. He's told no one about Worthing or the Burlington. Unless she's let something slip, no way anyone can know about it.

'Dunno,' he says.

She laughs, tells him he's been watching too many films.

'Let him go past if he's bothering you.'

Hand on his knee again. Slight reduction in voltage this time but he wishes she wouldn't do that. He doesn't know her well enough for that level of intimacy. Says nothing. Takes three deep breaths. One . . . two . . . three. The frantic impulse to rock back and forth is still there but it's starting to ease off a bit and he's able to relax his shoulders a little. Runs a finger across his damp forehead. Evenings starting to get cooler now but he can feel a trickle of sweat working its way down his neck and into his T-shirt. More deep breaths. Perhaps she's right. Maybe he's imagining it. All the same, he's not about to take his eyes off the rear-view mirror, watching every manoeuvre made by the car behind.

New housing estate coming up on the left, tucked away in the shadow of the sprawling Body Shop complex. One more roundabout and he'll know for sure. She's seen the petrol station up ahead and waves a finger at it.

'That any use?' she asks. 'They're bound to have a loo there, aren't they?' He nods and realises as he does so that he'd rather they went somewhere else. In his mind's eye he can still see Callum filling the car while his fancy woman disappears inside to pay. Doesn't see how he can say no though, not with her squirming around on the seat next to him.

'You need any petrol?' she asks. He shakes his head. 'Do you mind popping in and getting me some mints or something while you're waiting? I could do with something to freshen my mouth up a bit.'

He nods but in truth he's only half listening. His eyes are on the mirror the whole time, staring a hole in it. There's thirty metres between the two vehicles when he signals right and pulls across into the outside lane. Two seconds later, he winces as he sees the other driver do the same. Huge Norbert Dentressangle lorry coming from the right. Just time to get out ahead of it and accelerate into the roundabout; then *no* to the Body shop entrance, *no* to the A259, *yes* to the third exit. Copycat has to wait for the lorry and a couple of cars to pass and his headlights are no longer in the mirror as Owen turns left again almost immediately to pick up the access road to the Shell station. He slows for a second or two, half-turning in his seat to get a better look. Watches with some satisfaction as a large estate car drives straight over the top of the mini-roundabout, heading off towards Rustington. He can't see the number plate from here but he's pretty sure it's the same one that was following them. He relaxes, his heart beating a little less insistently.

'Can you let me out here?' she asks. As he pulls over towards the rear of the building, she points out of her window. 'That tyre-pressure thingy – if you park over there I'll just go and find the loo. I'll only be a second, I promise.' She flashes him a rueful smile. 'Really sorry about this.'

He waves away her attempt to give him the money and she jogs off past the red Biffa bins before disappearing into the darkness at the rear of the building. He turns in his seat, more interested in whether the driver's going to realise they've turned off and double back. Wouldn't surprise him one bit. You don't shrug off prime numbers that easily. 53 is one he's always had trouble with. Year his father was born? 1953. Callum's mobile? 07977 642452 – total: 53. These signs are there for a reason. You don't just ignore them.

Gives it a few more seconds, then drives round to the front and parks next to the tyre-pressure gauge as she's suggested. *Mints*, he thinks to himself. Checks he's got his wallet, then gets out of the truck, leaving it unlocked in case she's first back. Nothing in there worth taking anyway. Smart thing would be to leave the keys in the ignition and hope someone drives off with it.

Busy inside. Gum-chewing lad at the checkout, serving a queue of people: girl in a white blouse and black jeans, holding everyone up while she tries to get her credit card to work; woman holding the hand of a small boy and making a point of keeping herself between him and the row of sweets and chocolates; middle-aged man in oil-stained overalls, tapping his feet and mumbling about his chances of getting out of here before Christmas. He joins the queue and looks through the choice of mints while he's waiting. He hasn't any idea which sort she'd prefer. Decides to get several different packs. Can't go wrong that way.

The girl finally leaves and they all move forward one place. The boy has noticed him now and is staring at him. Little children can't seem to help themselves. Jack and the Beanstalk. Hagrid. Shrek. Stares back at him and the boy toughs it out for a second or two, then clutches his mother's leg. She nudges him away with her knee, too busy tapping in her own credit-card details to take much notice. The boy's not so interested in the sweets and chocolate anymore.

Front of the queue at last. Puts the five packets on the counter and rummages in his pocket for the right money. The lad serving him makes a sort of snapping sound with the gum in his mouth, looks at all the mints and grins.

'Worried about your breath?'

He frowns, shakes his head – *no*. Such an odd thing to ask. Counts out the coins . . . carefully. The lad shrugs his shoulders and asks *any fuel?* Shakes his head again, pushes the exact sum across the counter. Then he picks up the mints, turns and walks back to the pickup truck. A Toyota drives past and the little boy turns to stare out of the back window, bolder now he knows he's safe.

She's not there when he reaches the pickup. Thought she'd be back by now. He was in the shop long enough. Throws the mints onto the passenger seat and decides to stay outside, leaning against the bonnet while he waits for her. Five minutes crawl by. Six. He thinks this is a bit odd. Doesn't see how a simple trip to the toilet could take this long. He pushes off from the truck and walks round to the rear of the petrol station, eyes adjusting to the darkness as he seeks out where he assumes the toilets will be. Nothing. He completes a full circuit of the building. Still nothing. No outside toilets at all. Inside, then – she must have gone in while he was parking the truck.

Different people in here now. The lad behind the counter doesn't look up. Too busy laughing and joking with two women who won't see forty again but are dressed as if they think they will. One other customer – man in a suit, tie tugged loose, checking the sell–by dates on a range of sandwiches left over from this morning, bottle of Irn-Bru dangling from one hand.

The toilet must be in the recess in the far corner. He fakes an interest in the crisps aisle and then, when he's sure no one is looking, walks through the alcove and knocks on the door. Calls her name quietly. Knocks again, a little more insistently this time. Still no reply. Tries the handle and it's locked so he calls a third time and bangs on the door with the flat of his hand. Everyone's awake now.

'Oi. 'Scuse me.' The attendant has managed to tear his attention away from the women at the counter. Seems to think he ought to be doing something about this. Owen bangs again, shouting now, calling Julie's name.

'Is there a problem here?' the lad asks, a little more politely once he's emerged from the other side of the counter. He's less sure of himself out in the open. Thinks maybe aggressive isn't the smart option here as he sizes Owen up.

'She won't c-come out.'

'Can you not do that, please?' the lad asks as Owen slams his hand against the door again. 'There's no one in there, OK? It's locked.'

'JULIE.'

'It's *locked*, OK? The key's behind the counter.'

The man in the suit is there now and the two women have clattered their way over on heels that border on suicidal. He's not happy about the audience.

'She c-came in to use the toilet,' he says, aware that the pounding is starting up again in his temples. The rocking won't be too far behind.

Everyone's joining in now, trying to help the attendant get the message across. She can't be in there. It's locked from the outside. It's only unlocked if someone wants to use it and to do that they have to get the key from the counter. No one's done that in the last couple of hours or so. Does he understand? They're talking very slowly. He hates it when people do that.

He turns to face the wall, pressing his forehead into it. Tries to concentrate, squeeze out all the distractions – the growing audience, the stupid questions, the clucking expressions of concern. One of the women catches hold of his arm and tries to lead him back towards the till but he shrugs her off. He just needs a few moments on his own, a chance to think this through. If she's not in here and never came in at any stage, where did she go? And why? And what's he meant to do now – drive off and leave her? If they'll just leave him alone for a few minutes . . .

He can hear them whispering among themselves, pushes past them, knocking over a display stand of chocolate bars in the rush to get outside. Runs over to the pickup truck – she's not there. Mints still on the front seat. And next to them . . . a brown A4 envelope that's materialised out of nowhere. He whirls round suddenly, hoping to catch sight of whoever left it here. Reaches in and picks up the envelope. Tears it open, watching as its contents spill out onto the seat.

Photos. Four of them. He turns on the interior light and examines them, one by one. And as the attendant calls out to ask if he's OK, he barely hears him. He's already in the driver's seat, fingers fumbling with the ignition key as he tries to ram it into the slot. The engine's reluctant to catch, takes three attempts before it finally fires up. Then he puts his foot to the floor and races out of the forecourt, working his way through the prime numbers, shouting them at the top of his voice to drown out their insistent gloating and strip them of any powers they think they might have over him.

He's reached 317 – 66th number in the sequence – before he realises he hasn't fastened his seat belt or even turned on the headlights.

PART ONE

1

EARLIER: FRIDAY, 22ND AUGUST

ABI

'Oh my God, Abi.'

Mary stepped back to get a better view, one hand to her mouth.

'You like it?'

'*Like* it? Are you kidding? It's . . .' She broke off, apparently lost for words which, for a novelist, seemed anomalous enough to pass for a compliment. Abi busied herself with the empty box, head bowed. Replacing the lid, she carried it over to the draining board and placed it next to her car keys.

Her motives for doing so were baked from a complex recipe of disparate motives: one part practical (this way she'd remember to take the box with her), one part tactical (always allow the customer to provide the soundtrack) and maybe just a sprinkling of embarrassment. It wasn't like this was her first cake and yet here she was, tongue hanging out for approval. Mary hardly needed a nudge of any kind. Even allowing for her hyperbolic tendencies, the glistening at the corner of each eye was testimony enough to how impressed she was.

'Honestly, Abi – you're so talented. I wouldn't have the faintest idea how to go about something like this. You really ought to do it professionally.'

'You haven't forgotten that you're paying for it, have you?' she joked.

'No, seriously. I mean full-time. Why waste your time working in a bookshop when you could be doing this for a living? Oh Lord, look at that!' She pointed to the upper tier – a model of a huge book with lines of print running across the open pages. 'That's . . . those pages are taken from the new novel.' She traced the title at the top of the page with her finger – *The Hard Way by Mary Kowalski*. 'How on earth did you manage to reproduce the pages?'

'Photocopied,' said Abi, pleased to have a chance to explain. 'You can copy onto edible printing paper nowadays if you have the right printer. You'd be amazed what you can do.'

'And is it all edible?' asked Mary. 'I don't know why I'm even asking. I can't imagine cutting this up. It would be like . . . I don't know, slashing a Vermeer or something.'

'Well, you can keep the models if you like,' explained Abi, checking an arm here, a leg there to make sure they were still adequately supported. 'They're just sugar paste. Everything else, I'd cut it up if I were you. You've probably got a week or so to eat it unless you decide to freeze it. Just don't keep it in the fridge, OK? It'll make the sugar paste go all wet and shiny.'

Mary took one more lingering look, then turned to hug her.

'I'm not paying you enough,' she said. 'This must have taken you hours. I'm going to parade it round the garden and make you take a bow. You are coming tonight, aren't you? Both of you?'

Abi picked up the nuance – the last three words carried about them more than a whiff of reluctant afterthought. 'Of course. Callum might be a bit late but I can be there to help you set it up if you like.'

'If you're sure you don't mind,' said Mary. She raised one finger to suggest a light coming on. 'You're not in any hurry, are you? Have you got time to come and look at something?'

Abi checked her watch: 'I'm OK for five minutes or so.'

Mary took her by the arm and led her to the back door. 'You're not going to believe this,' she said, opening the door and stepping outside onto the patio. 'You saw this place when we first moved in, right? Remember what a shambles it was out here and how Max promised he was going to get it all sorted by the end of the summer? Well . . . tell me what you think.'

They crossed the patio, tiptoed their way along a path littered with gardening tools and half-empty compost bags and turned left into what, only four months ago, had been little more than an overgrown, weed-ridden, bramble-infested jungle. Now it was completely transformed. For one thing, the whole area had been cleared and flattened which was no small achievement in itself. Bushes had been uprooted, trees cut back and years of neglect by the elderly couple who had lived there previously had been reversed in a matter of months. Then borders had been dug and planted on either side of a footpath which led to a brand new summer house, perfectly positioned at the end of the garden to catch the early afternoon sun. It was a different garden altogether.

'I'm not even going to ask if Max did this,' Abi said, shaking her head in amazement.

Mary laughed. 'As if. No, it's this guy I came across a while ago. Found his card in the post-office window, believe it or not.'

Abi looked again at the summer house and thought how bland their own back garden was by comparison. Drab. Uninspired. It needed a radical overhaul, nothing on the scale of what had been done here maybe, but if someone who knew what he was doing were to take hold of it and devote some time and imagination to the project, the potential was definitely there.

'His name's Owen,' said Mary. 'Owen Hall. I can give you his number, or he's got his own website if you prefer. Just Google *Hall Gardening Services.*' She paused, noticing the quiet smile on Abi's face. 'What?'

'No, nothing,' said Abi. 'It's just I used to know an Owen Hall, years ago. We were at school together.'

'An old boyfriend?'

'Owen,' Abi chuckled. 'God, no.'

'Well, this guy's six foot six and absolutely ripped. Don't tell Max but I've been spending hours sitting at my writing desk on the off chance he might take his shirt off, so if it's the same boy you went to school with I'd have to ask how come you didn't nail him there and then. That sound like him?'

Abi smiled again, shook her head. 'Not really. No.'

DANNY

The first he saw of the girl was when she was about a hundred or so metres away. She'd come to a halt in the middle of the cycle path and was peering anxiously at her front wheel. There was room for him to pass on either side if he wished but as he drew closer she threw him a beseeching look and spread her arms to make it clear she needed help. He braked hard and stopped a few metres in front of her, his rear wheel swinging round in a satisfying skid.

'Everything OK?' he asked, lowering the bike to the ground and walking over to her. 'Can I help at all?'

The girl thanked him for stopping and explained that the wheel felt as if it might be coming loose. 'I'm worried it's going to send me flying over the handlebars or something.'

'Here,' he said, squatting next to her and checking the wheel carefully for excessive play. 'Let's have a look.'

While he was doing so, a black Mercedes pulled out of the queue of traffic and came to a halt on the grass verge. The rear door opened and a shaven-headed youth, probably a couple of years younger than Danny himself and dressed in wife beater and joggers, walked over to them. Danny looked up, grateful for the implicit offer of help, and was surprised when the supposed Samaritan walked straight past them both and picked up Danny's bike. He swung his leg over the crossbar and bounced his backside off the seat two or three times as if checking it out for comfort.

Danny climbed slowly to his feet and walked over to him.

'You mind?' he asked, fairly pleasantly under the circumstances. 'That's my bike.'

'Piece o' shit,' mumbled the youth without even bothering to look at him. 'Wanna get yourself some decent wheels.'

'Well, thank you for that,' said Danny. 'You think you could get off now? I'd like it back.'

The youth tugged at the brakes and pushed hard, causing the back wheel to lift into the air. 'Get in the car,' he said.

'What?' Danny turned to look at the Mercedes. The back door was still wide open but he couldn't see clearly enough to make out who else might be inside. He wondered what the girl was making of all this and was surprised to see that she'd remounted her bike and was now leaning on the handlebars, watching closely, as if intrigued by what would happen next. She mouthed the word *Sorry*, and flashed a quick smile which conveyed all the sincerity of a game-show host. *What the hell was going on here?*

'I said, get in the car, Danny.'

'You serious? I'm not getting in any car.' He stopped suddenly, his brain only now catching up. 'And how come you know my name anyway?'

The youth stopped playing with the brakes and looked Danny in the eye for the first time. No hint of a smile. No hint of anything. He got off the bike and lowered it to the ground with exaggerated care.

'I'm asking you nicely. Want me to say please?'

'No,' said Danny, stepping forward and trying to reach past him. 'I don't want you to say *please*. I want you to give me back my bike before I –'

The speed of the assault was what did for him, although there was something about the slickness of the move that suggested the outcome would have been no different even without the element of surprise. One minute they were brushing shoulders, the next he'd slumped to the ground and was lying across the rear wheel of his bike, struggling desperately to suck air into his lungs. The punch had slammed into his kidneys, just below the ribcage, with stunning force. He hadn't seen it coming, had made no attempt to protect himself, so the aftershock was immediate and excruciating. He wasn't sure where his next breath was supposed to come from.

'There you go,' said the youth, bending over him as he struggled to find anything resembling a comfortable position. '*Please* . . . get in the fucking car.'

'Thank you, TJ. I think we'll take it from here.' The voice, cultured, measured, utterly incongruous under the circumstances, came from somewhere deep inside the Mercedes. 'If you could just help Mr Locke into the car, that would be excellent.'

Danny was still gasping for breath and in no position to offer any resistance worthy of the name as the youth grabbed him under the armpits and, with a strength which belied his slender frame, hauled him into an upright position. He slumped forward again, clutching his ribs, and a second man stepped from the Mercedes to offer assistance. Between them they half-carried, half-dragged him over to the car and tossed him into the back seat where he landed next to a sharply dressed middle-aged man who clearly bought and applied his aftershave by the vat. The second man climbed in next to him; the youth in the wife beater hovered by the door.

'How long do you and Sonia think you'll need?' Mr Armani Code asked him.

'Arun Leisure Centre? Twenty minutes, maybe.'

'I'll ask Trevor to take a bit of a detour and we'll meet you there. You might like to take off your cycle helmet, Mr Locke,' he added, turning to address Danny directly for the first time. 'I think TJ's need will be greater than yours for the next quarter of an hour or so.'

'He's broken my ribs,' he managed to gasp.

'Oh, I very much doubt that,' came the reply. 'For a young man, TJ has a lot of experience of this sort of thing and if he'd wanted to break your ribs, I think we'd know all about it. There could well be some bruising there in the morning though. I'd get some ice on it when you get in tonight, if I were you. And you might like to sit up a little straighter and take a few deep breaths just now. Get a bit of wind into your sails, yes?' He clicked his fingers. 'Helmet, please?'

Danny briefly weighed up his options and decided there were none. He unfastened the helmet and peeled it slowly from his head, thinking that sitting up straight might be easier said than done. He retained enough of his wits to wonder why no one was coming to his assistance. There was so much traffic around – surely someone had to have seen what was going on.

He watched as the youth took the helmet and started cycling off down the path with the girl alongside him. They were both laughing.

'Where's he going with my bike?' he managed to ask, each word spent like marked currency.

'Don't worry – it's quite safe, I assure you. It'll be waiting for you at the leisure centre when we drop you off. In the meantime, Trevor here will take us for a little drive along the seafront. Much nicer than sitting here on this grass verge. Don't want to draw attention to ourselves, do we?'

The indicator started to tick quietly as they waited for a chance to pull back into the stream of traffic on the A259. Then they set off towards North Bersted and Bognor, barely managing to keep pace with the cyclists for the most part. They certainly weren't gaining on TJ and the girl who had long since disappeared.

'I don't understand what's going on here?' he groaned. 'Who are you? What do you want with me?'

'I apologise. You're obviously alarmed, which is not that surprising under the circumstances. Perhaps if I were to introduce everyone?' If this touch of civility was intended to come across as reassuring, it somehow missed its mark. 'The gentleman behind the wheel is Trevor,' he continued. 'He's the perfect chauffeur, really – safe, steady and hears only what he's supposed to hear, don't you, Trevor?'

'What was that, Mr Cunningham?'

'Very good, Trevor. Very droll. And next to him is Marshall . . . that's his Christian name incidentally, not his surname. Parents obviously had an off day. He's a bit of a whiz with all matters pertaining to finance, is Marshall. Don't pretend to understand any of it myself. He could be cheating everyone left, right and centre for all I know but somehow I very much doubt it, don't you, Marshall?'

Marshall smiled and said nothing.

'And the gentleman sitting next to you is Mick. Big lad, isn't he? I probably don't need to tell you what he does. As for me, my name is Ezra Cunningham. You won't have heard of me. I'm not anyone important. Just a sort of . . . well, factotum really, I suppose you could call me. You know what a factotum is, Danny? You don't mind if I call you Danny, do you?'

He shook his head, a response which Cunningham interpreted as covering both questions.

'So . . . factotum. Dogsbody, really – yes, that would be the best way to look at it. I like to think of myself as a bit of an all-rounder, jack-of-all-trades, but I'm probably flattering myself. Anyway, I digress. The point is, I'm employed by Mr Bellamy to keep an eye on things – Mr Freddie, that is. Mr Joey isn't around much at present owing to an unfortunate misunderstanding which we're hoping the authorities will put right very soon. Maybe you've heard of them both?'

Danny most certainly had – and the temperature in the car dropped by several degrees in a matter of seconds. There weren't many people in the Bognor area who hadn't heard of the Bellamy brothers. He'd never had any direct contact with them but he knew plenty of people who had and, even allowing for a certain amount of exaggeration, he was more than happy to stay off their radar.

'I still don't understand what you want from me,' he said. It sounded horribly like a whine and he wished he could try again. 'I'm nobody. I've never met you – any of you. I'm not looking for trouble.'

'. . . which is what we like to hear,' said Cunningham. 'There's nothing for you to worry about here, Danny. All this . . .' he spread his arms wide to take in the situation as a whole '. . . just look upon it as Mr Freddie's way of introducing himself. He likes to establish contact with all those he does business with. To break the ice, so to speak.'

'What business?'

'Always important to make sure everyone's singing from the same cliché, don't you think? And in your case he wants to be absolutely clear about the repayment structure.'

'What repayments? I don't know what you're talking about!'

'The loan you took out a while ago for . . .' He snapped his fingers.

'Five hundred pounds,' said Marshall.

'Five hundred pounds. Exactly. With a repayment plan for . . . ?'

There was a brief rustling of papers as Marshall searched for the exact figures. 'The loan was taken out over three months at an APR of 345 per cent which means Mr Locke is due to pay £643.75 on the fifteenth of next month.'

'Which, unless I'm very much mistaken, is just over three weeks away?'

'Three weeks on Monday.'

'But that loan was with Arun Readies,' protested Danny. 'It never said anything about Freddie or Joey Bellamy on any of the documents I signed.'

'Indeed. Unfortunately, however, Jimmy Vince, who set up that particular company, has decided to sell up and move into other more profitable and, dare I say, less hazardous corners of the business world. As a result, all of the loans already agreed by said Jimmy have now fallen under Mr Freddie's remit and he has asked us to speak individually with every one of the good people concerned to establish ground rules and make sure there are no misunderstandings. All we need from you just now is some idea as to your intentions when it comes to repaying the loan. He's more than happy for you to settle with us this evening if you have it and that will mean our business relationship is terminated – at least until such time as you need to call on us again. But we do understand that immediate repayment may be neither convenient nor even feasible, in which case we have Mr Freddie's authority to let you have until the agreed date of the fifteenth of September to settle the debt in full. You have to understand however that this will incur additional costs and the original loan will have increased to . . .'

'One thousand and four pounds –'

'What?'

'And forty-five pence.'

'A grand?' gasped Danny, and this time the pain in his ribs had nothing to do with it. 'You're joking!'

'Danny –'

'I'm only meant to be paying six hundred quid. I never signed up for a grand. Jesus, if I could lay my hands on that sort of money at a moment's notice, I wouldn't have needed to take out the loan in the first place.'

Cunningham tugged at each of his cuffs in turn. 'I'm sure you'll understand that *how* you go about reimbursing us isn't really any of Mr Freddie's concern.' He couldn't have come across as less interested in Danny's dilemma if he'd tried. 'I'm sure you'll find a way if you put your mind to it. Just keep reminding yourself of the important things in life. Like Evie, for example.' Thin air again. Cunningham had a way of sucking the oxygen out of the car with no apparent effort.

'Evie? What about her?'

'Barely out of her teens and a second baby on the way already? Early December, isn't it?'

'How do you –?'

'And little Kayla,' continued Cunningham. 'Such a sweetie, I'm reliably informed. But she can't be more than about eighteen months old. That's a lot for a young mum to be coping with and you all the way out here at work all day. She must be desperate for company half the time.'

'Leave my wife out of –'

Again, the blow seemed to come from nowhere. This time it took the form of a short, sharp slap to the face, delivered with the open hand. It stunned him momentarily and when his senses unscrambled themselves, his initial reaction, oddly enough, was one of relief that he hadn't taken another blow to the ribs. Neither did he want to think about the damage this slap would have done to his face, had it been delivered with a closed fist.

'That's unfortunate,' said Cunningham, in the same measured tones that were definitely starting to get on Danny's nerves. 'Mick does get a bit concerned when voices are raised. I think he sees it as threatening. Anyway, as I was saying, I really admire your Evie. Nice girl, if a bit too trusting. I mean, leaving all the family finances in the hands of someone who thinks there's such a thing as a system that will allow him to win big on Betfair – I mean, I ask you. You'd have to say that's asking for trouble. Does she know you maxed out the credit cards recently?'

'How in God's name do you –?' This was like a subtle variation on the old Chinese water torture – one piece of information after the other, working away at his defences, drip, drip, drip.

'Or that you squirrelled five hundred pounds out of the savings account which is why you had to go to Jimmy V in the first place? I mean, maybe she thinks the world of you but there have to be limits, wouldn't you say? What's the plan, anyway? Have you already blown the money you borrowed from us?'

'No.' *None of your business* is what he wanted to scream but he wasn't sure which part of his body Mick might work on next and wasn't keen to put it to the test. 'I used that to get the savings account back to where it was before.'

'Ah . . . did we know that, Marshall?'

'No.'

'No. Well, that's good news anyway. Nice to know you're finally embracing a modicum of financial responsibility, Danny – even if it is rather late in the day. And you're still working at Estelle Roberts, I take it. That's something, I suppose. Fancy jeweller like that – pity they don't pay you a little more, isn't it? Ah, the sun-drenched holidaymakers wending their weary way home,' he sighed, turning away as the lights at one of the innumerable pedestrian crossings on the seafront brought them to a temporary halt. 'You ever had a Butlins holiday, Danny? Can't imagine anything more ghastly, can you?'

Danny interpreted the question as rhetorical and said nothing.

'Anyway, I assume, since you say you've topped up your savings account and presumably don't have any other cash to hand, that you won't be going for option one and paying off your debt this evening. Am I right?'

Danny nodded, shoulders slumped in defeat.

'And just out of interest, on a scale of one to ten, how likely do you think it is that you'll be in a position to settle your debt in full on the fifteenth?'

He shook his head.

'The original deal, I might have come close. A grand? I don't know.'

'We'll call that a two then. Ah well, it's not a problem from our point of view if you need another month,' said Cunningham, 'but I'm sure you'll understand that it's not going to come cheaply. These APRs . . . never can get my head round them but Marshall here just laps it up and he'll be happy to let you know exactly what that would mean. Could probably do it without even using a calculator.'

'I'll get the money, OK?' snapped Danny, careful not to raise his voice at the same time. 'You'll have it.'

'Maybe a six then? Yes, well, I think that would be your best bet . . . if you'll excuse the unfortunate choice of words. Ah, here already,' he said, with all the cheerful bonhomie of a tour guide announcing that they'd reached their destination. 'And there are TJ and Sonia with your bicycle, just as I promised. You see, Danny – we always keep our promises. It's always worth remembering that.'

Mick slid out of the back seat to allow Danny out of the car.

'You mind how you go now,' said Cunningham. 'And make sure you look after that good lady of yours, yes?'

TJ held out the helmet for him to take and kept hold of the bike while he fastened the strap under his chin. All smiles. So helpful. No way anyone passing could possibly imagine what he'd been through in the last quarter of an hour.

'Enjoy the ride home, fuckwit,' whispered TJ before clambering into the Mercedes with a smirk that simply begged to be scraped off his face.

Danny watched as they drove away, the girl pedalling furiously after them.

PHIL

Quarter past nine in a deserted Arun Valley Shopping Centre, empty corridors echoing to their footsteps. Two hours done and dusted, another ten to go before the end of their last evening on nights. Seven o'clock couldn't come soon enough – there was something intensely liberating about stepping out of the twilight zone and back into the real world for a few weeks. He could almost imagine he was connected somehow.

'Your turn,' Anna said, as he held the door open before stepping through after her. He started to climb the stairs, switching on his lapel mic as he did so.

'Sierra 5 to Mic 2, Sierra 5 to Mic 2 – over.'

Pause. Click.

'Mic 2 here,' came the tinny reply in his earpiece. 'Go ahead Sierra 5 – over.'

'Ground Floor clear. Moving to Level 1 – over.'

'Roger that, Sierra 5. Over and out.'

'Roger that,' she mimicked, shaking her head. 'Dick!'

Phil grinned. 'You really don't like him, do you?'

'Nice work, Sherlock.'

'Any reason in particular?'

'You want a list? The guy's like . . .' She gave an exaggerated shudder. 'I dunno, he's . . .'

'Oh. Well, that clears that up.'

'He's a dick.'

'So what's he done to upset you – apart from getting promoted?'

'Got nothing to do with it,' she said, slapping his arm. 'He was a dick before. Sticking a badge on him isn't going to change anything. Just makes him a dick with a badge. If they're stupid enough to make him Assistant Head of Security, why should I care?'

'Yeah, well, you sound like you've taken it pretty well.'

She rattled the door to one of the clothing outlets, a little more vigorously than she needed to.

'Some people, you know? They get a bit of responsibility, mainly because there's no one else prepared to take on the shitty job in the first place, and all of a sudden they're off on some power trip like Hitler or something. It's pathetic.'

'You didn't go for it yourself, then?'

She stopped in her tracks and glared at him.

'Ha ha. No I did *not*, thank you very much.'

Pushing open the door to the women's toilets, she peered inside to check no one was in there while he did the same next door.

'You know he tried to friend me the other day?' she said as they continued to work their way round the shops on the first floor.

'Tried to *what* you?'

'*Friend* me.'

He shook his head. 'I thought friend was a noun.'

'Not on Facebook, it isn't.'

'Ah. Facebook!'

'And don't start on that old dinosaur routine. You're on Facebook like the rest of us.'

'Nope.'

'Seriously?' She stopped and looked up at him, shining her torch into his face to check whether this was another of his wind-ups.

'Seriously.'

'Jesus,' she said, pausing in a doorway as he held the door for her. 'Your social life must be something else.'

'I have my moments. Your turn.'

She switched on her lapel mic.

'Level 1 clear, Shaun. Moving up to Level 2.'

Pause. Click. Then the tinny voice started up again.

'Please identify yourself, Sierra 2. Over.'

She rolled her eyes and gave a deep sigh. 'Shaun, you know who it is. You just identified me yourself.'

'I know it's you, Sierra 2, but you're supposed to use the proper call signs. Over.'

'It's the night shift, for f—' She took a deep breath. 'We've been doing this for the past three weeks. There's only you, me and Phil on duty and only one of us is female. That's not a big enough clue for you?'

'Sarcasm's not cool, Sierra 2. Doesn't matter how many people are in the building. You have to follow the correct procedures. I've told you before. Over.'

'It's Arun Valley Shopping Centre, Shaun. It's not the Pentagon.'

'You follow the correct procedures or I'll have to report you. Is that what you want? Over.'

'Trust me, you don't want to know what I want.'

'I'm still waiting, Sierra 2. Over.'

She rolled her eyes.

'Sierra 2 to Mic 2 – over.'

'Mic 2 here. Go ahead, Sierra 2 – over.'

'Level 1 clear. Moving up to Level 2 – over and out.'

She held up one finger and began to count. She'd reached four when the tinny voice returned.

'OK . . . ah, roger that, Sierra 2. Over and out.'

'Jesus,' she said, switching off the lapel mic. 'Are you seriously telling me that doesn't piss you off?'

'Clearly not as much as it does you.'

'Seriously – it doesn't bother you at all that he's in a position of authority over you?'

Phil smiled, his head tilted to one side. 'Well, maybe it's not the most convincing argument in favour of natural selection.'

'I don't know how you just accept things like that. I'd be spitting bullets if I was in your shoes. You had how long with the police – thirty years? He's barely had thirty days on solids. You should have put yourself forward for the job. With your experience you think they wouldn't have bitten your hand off? All the contacts you've got as well? They'd have begged you to take it.'

He shook his head. 'Yeah, well, thanks for the vote of confidence but I'm still the new boy around here, remember? Besides, I'm happy doing what I do now.'

'What, patrolling round a shopping centre day and night? Taking orders from someone who thinks UNESCO is one of the stores on the ground floor? How can you be?'

'Oh, I don't know. You get to fifty, maybe it takes a bit of the edge off your ambition.'

Anna snorted. 'Your problem is you don't push yourself forward enough,' she said. 'Anyone ever tell you that?'

There was a long pause – long enough for her to wish she could snatch the words back before they really dug deep. The silence seemed to amplify their footsteps as they echoed down the empty corridor.

'Yeah . . .' he said eventually. 'Sally used to say it all the time.'

And the clang as the shutters came down was loud enough to shake the building to its foundations.

CALLUM

And it had all been going so well.

I'll get badges made up, he thought to himself, as he kicked a stone into the gutter. *Story of my life.*

So much for good intentions. The best joke was, he hadn't really wanted to go to the Kowalskis in the first place. He'd got a totally legitimate excuse for once and this arty-farty sort of affair usually bored the pants off him, so he was pretty sure Abi would have been relieved rather than annoyed if he'd tossed in his Get-Out-Of-Jail-Free card and left her to go on her own.

But this business of doing things separately was happening more and more lately – in danger of becoming the norm. He knew most of the blame for that lay at his feet and maybe that was what brought on these random impulses to do something that would take her by surprise. So he'd changed his mind at the last minute, taken a rain check with the Lannier group, caught an early train back from Victoria and arrived home in time to walk with her to the book launch. And he'd felt good about himself, even if it was just for the one evening. It was nice sometimes to imagine they might somehow drift back to those uncomplicated times when their first thought was always for each other.

So he'd been on pretty good form for most of the evening as he wandered from group to group, turning on the charm which had always come as naturally to him as breathing. Whatever else he did with his life, he'd always have that to fall back on. He'd even managed to win over Mary Kowalski for once by pledging a couple of grand to some charity for refugees she was heading up. *A couple of grand!* He suspected he'd probably regret it like a hangover the next morning but what the hell – Nick would find a way of writing it off and besides, the way Abi squeezed his arm and rested her head on his shoulder made it more than worthwhile. For a moment there, it was like the old days – only with money to burn.

It hadn't lasted.

Now they were walking home and she'd retreated into one of her distant moods. Lovely evening, warm enough to let you imagine you were in the Med somewhere rather than strolling through the lanes of Bosham. All it needed was a few cicadas and a zither playing in the background. There was a time when they'd have been all over each other during the ten-minute walk back to their four-bedroom detached house in Walton Lane; only it wouldn't have been a ten-minute walk – one of them would have dragged the other off into a field somewhere, they were that horny for each other back in the day. But tonight they'd barely brushed hands since they left the Kowalskis.

And all because of Owen Hall. *Owen Fuck-all*, the ultimate in ugly ducklings if Mary Kowalski and her sex-starved ramblings were anything to go by. Not that long ago – twelve, thirteen years, maybe – he was a big, fat numpty everyone took the piss out of at school. Retard of the first order. King Blobby. Used to sit there in class with his thumb in his mouth and saliva dribbling down his chin. Bright enough – Christ, what he couldn't do with numbers. Obsessed or what? The maths teachers used to get him to recite all the prime numbers and he could keep going into the thousands. Wasn't bullshit either. They never caught him out once. And that thing with turning letters of the alphabet into numbers: $a = 1$, $b = 2$, etc. He could take any word and tell you the total before you'd got past the first couple of letters. Nowadays they'd probably say he was Special Needs, on the autistic spectrum or some such crap. Back then it was simple – he was just a complete and utter mong. Never should have been in a school with normal kids in the first place. His mother wised up eventually and took him out altogether – home schooling, they called it. One big doss, more like.

And now, if the country's greatest living novelist, in her own mind at least, was to be believed, Owen Fuck-all had somehow transformed himself into Monty Don, turning wastelands into the Garden of Eden, like water into wine wasn't good enough. Well, he might just about buy into that, as it happened, having seen the evidence for himself. Everyone at the book launch had been practically press-ganged into wandering round the Kowalski estate and he'd oohed and aahed along with the rest of them because he had to admit, it did look pretty good in a kitschy sort of way. So if she was to be taken at her word and it *was* all his own work, then maybe Owen Fuck-all had made some sort of progress along the food chain, in which case fair play to him.

But all that crap about Owen the Stud, Owen the Hunk? He wasn't having any of that. Max must be some letdown in the bedroom if Mary had been reduced to drooling over someone who, not so long ago, was drooling over himself. The guy was a freak. Could you really go from that to a normally functioning member of society? Could you fuck!

And now, best joke of all, Abi was talking about hiring him to do their garden. He'd laughed out loud when she suggested it at the party, hence the stiff, slightly remote Stepford Wife who was sharing the walk home with him now. Because there were rules governing that sort of thing – he could say what he liked to her, behave like a bigoted arsehole of the first order in the privacy of his own home, but God forbid he should say or do anything to embarrass her in public. There were no histrionics – exaggerated displays of emotion weren't her style. But that didn't mean you got away with it. She had a way of withdrawing that was like a work of art. Perfectly pleasant, even bordering on affectionate at times and certainly not offering anything substantive you could hang your hat on and use as evidence against her, but you knew somehow that however much appearances might suggest the opposite, she just wasn't there anymore. Not for you. Not in any way that mattered. And that was how she'd been for the last hour or so.

Well, to coin a phrase . . . *fuck you, Abi.* He'd gone out of his way to make this evening all about her and this was how she thanked him. OK then! If she wanted to do her bit for Care in the Community and free up a bed for some other basket case by keeping Owen Fuck-all meaningfully occupied, good luck to her but she'd better start making a helluva lot more cakes in the next few weeks because he sure as hell wasn't about to throw hard-earned moolah at someone who would probably start chewing it. And if she wanted a bit of distance, she could have that too. *No one-way streets here, lady.*

Monday night couldn't come soon enough as far as he was concerned.

OWEN

He goes to bed around ten o'clock. Gets up again at midnight. Can't sleep. Two hours lying there, thinking about the phone call. Figures flashing through his head the whole time.

Abi: total = 12, multiple of 3. Owen: total = 57, multiple of 3.

Safe. Happy.

Abi Hall: total = 45, multiple of 3 and 5. Owen Hall: total = 90, multiple of 3 and 5.

Safe. Happy.

Abi Green: total = 61.

Prime number. Keep away. How many times has he tried to tell her?

He decides in the end to make a cup of tea and take it into the conservatory. No need to turn the light on. Cloudless night, moonlight, lots of stars. Fox slinking across the middle of the lawn – fifteen yards away and he can see it, clear as day.

Might as well get it over with.

You're going to do it, aren't you? says Willie.

'Do what?'

Do what? Do what, he says. Think I'm stupid or something? You're going to say yes. Sort their garden out for them.

'Don't know yet.'

Like fuck you don't know. You've already decided. The moment you realised it was that bitch on the other end of the phone –

'She's not a bitch, Willie.'

She's a bitch and you know it. Stop making excuses for her.

'You don't even know her.'

I know you're well shot of her. I know she did squat to help you when everyone else was treating you like shit. You think she couldn't have put a stop to it if she'd tried hard enough? You think for one minute she gives a toss about you? Ask yourself, who did she marry, eh, this so-called friend of yours? Who did she marry?

'Please don't swear. It's not necessary.'

Callum FUCKING Green, that's who. Christ, how many times did you come home either bawling your eyes out or with sopping wet trousers where you'd pissed yourself? How many times did he take your lunch off you and hand it out for everyone else to chuck around the playground? Have you forgotten how he used to bark in your face when he heard you were terrified of dogs? Really loud. Close up. WOOF WOOF! You remember that? WOOF WOOF! WOOF WOOF! Till you started crying? That's the person she married, this sweetheart of yours.

'She's not my sweetheart. And she was nice to me.'

She was not *nice.*

'She used to sit and talk to me.'

Only when she was damned sure the others wouldn't notice. Moment anyone else came along she was out of there like shit off a shovel.

'Please don't swear.'

It's all gonna start up again, you know that don't you? All those years are gonna come flooding back . . . just as you've started to turn a corner.

'You're wrong.'

I'm not wrong and you know it. She's gonna twist you round her little finger all over again. I'll bet you've already told her you'll do it.

'I haven't.'

Yeah, right.

'I said I'd go and have a look. I didn't promise anything.'

No . . . course you didn't. Fucking joke. You might fool yourself half the time but you don't fool me. I know you too well.

'I know why you're doing this.'

You don't know squat.

'I know why you never liked her.'

FUCK ALL is what you know.

'If you're going to keep using that sort of language –'

Yeah, I know. You'll piss off back to bed and leave me here. Well, before you do, let me tell you this, OK? You allow her to sneak back in, don't come crying to me when it all goes tits up. You hear me?

'I'm going back to bed now.'

That bitch is your weak spot and some day you'll wish you'd listened to me. You mark my words.

'Goodnight, Willie.'

You mark my words.

2

NOW: THURSDAY, 2ND OCTOBER

HOLLOWAY

At 10.25 Andy Holloway was sitting at his desk, catching up on paperwork and wishing he could turn back the clock, just an hour or so. Specifically, he'd have welcomed the chance to rewind to a few seconds before he tore into DC Andrew Walker, giving him the sort of bollocking that he undoubtedly deserved and which had been coming for quite some time but which, on reflection, might have been more appropriate if delivered in private, rather than during morning briefing with the rest of the squad looking on. Thirty seconds of sustained vitriol, bordering on spite, might clear out a few cobwebs, but that wasn't exactly textbook procedure for dealing with a subordinate with an attitude problem.

It would have been nice to be able to airbrush those thirty seconds from the record and find a better way of dealing with the arrogant little turd but you don't get second chances in life, he'd learned. You have to live with your mistakes. There was no point in worrying about it now. It was done.

He suspected that if it had been anyone but Walker he'd probably have cut him some slack, and the double standards implicit in that flash of insight didn't sit easily with him. The plain and simple truth was, he just didn't like the kid. He'd seen his sort before – nepotism on legs, naked ambition shining out of his arsehole, career plan already mapped out, future promotions underwritten by influential family connections, the whole process delayed only by the need for a touch of plausibility in the timeline of the narrative. Walker wouldn't be stopping at plain old DI, a fact he made clear with his body language every time he entered the squad room. For young Master Walker it would be a case of onwards and upwards, *per ardua ad astra,* only with as little of the *ardua* as he could get away with. The only consolation for Holloway was the knowledge that by the time the wunderkind got an office of his own and started looking around for a little payback, he himself would be long gone and out of harm's way. Four more years. He could do that.

He read through another sheet, scribbled a few notes in the margin, scrawled his signature at the bottom and transferred it to a much smaller pile in his out tray. In a different context, with much less at stake, he might have laughed at the futility of it all. *Catch-22* had nothing on the Major Crimes Team. The harder they worked, the more paperwork they generated and the less time they then had to do the groundwork which might bring some sort of breakthrough with the crimes they were so busy cataloguing. It was like slapping the custard pie in your own face. You spent days setting yourself up, producing all the evidence needed to confirm your own failings. And much as he hated that word, no more appropriate alternative sprang to mind because that was how it felt right now. By any yardstick you cared to choose, they were failing.

Young Jamie Barrett had disappeared a week ago now – and a week was too long. Forget the first-forty-eight-hours myth that TV shows were so keen to peddle under the guise of authenticity. The first six hours were what really mattered. If you hadn't turned up anything by then, you might as well accept that you were in this for the long haul, and this was very much where they all found themselves right now. Deep in it.

So now they were going to have to start over, go back through every piece of evidence, re-examine every lead, challenge every assumption in the hope that shaking the dog for long enough would work a few fleas loose. It would require huge levels of commitment and team work from everyone in the room. What they most definitely did not need were exaggerated sighs and muttered asides about what a waste of time it was from DC Walker or anyone else.

Add to that the South Mundham murder case, which appeared to be going absolutely nowhere at present, and you'd have to say the past couple of months hadn't shown him in a very good light. He'd heard on the grapevine that eyebrows had been raised upstairs and questions asked about his handling of these two high-profile cases. He knew his worth, was confident he still had an open line of credit in the bank of professional credibility, but he was relieved none the less to have someone with the integrity of Marie Loneghan watching his back. Move it along ten years and imagine newly promoted DCS Andrew Walker sitting in the office along the corridor . . . Didn't bear thinking about.

He reached for another sheet of paper as Neil Horgan knocked and poked his head round the door.

'Boss, you got a minute?' he asked.

Holloway held out both hands to indicate the imposing piles of documents on the desk before him.

'Depends whether it's good news or bad.'

'Not really sure to be honest, but I think you're going to want to hear this.' Horgan stepped into the office and closed the door behind him. He walked over to the desk and waited to be asked to take a seat before doing so, a touch of deference Holloway always appreciated. There was no sense of entitlement with Horgan but neither was there the slightest hint of sycophancy. He was the model DS: loyal, hard-working, intelligent, dependable, a family man whose devotion to his wife and two small children somehow never made him a target for the more cynical members of the squad. He was also immaculately turned out without being remotely showy about it. He wasn't one to splash out on a different suit for every day of the week and expensive shirts and shoes from up-market stores in Chichester and Portsmouth, but whatever he wore he always managed somehow to look as if he were ready to step straight into a photo shoot. Old school. Bit of a throwback. Holloway had a lot of time for him.

He told him to take a seat, putting his pen on the desk and leaning back to ease some of the stiffness out of his shoulders.

'So,' he said. 'What have you got for me?'

'It's a flag.'

Holloway folded his arms and made a moue with his mouth. A flag was interesting.

'Jamie Barrett or South Mundham?' he asked.

'South Mundham. Littlehampton have been in touch. Seems there was an incident last night at a petrol station on the A259. You know, the Shell garage opposite the Body Shop?'

Holloway nodded. 'What sort of incident are we talking about?'

Horgan rested his notebook on the edge of the desk, confident that he had the DI's attention.

'Bit of an odd one, really. There was a report of a disturbance: a man hammering on the door of the toilet and insisting that some girl – *Julie,* apparently – must be inside.'

'And this Julie was . . . what? His girlfriend?'

'Didn't say. But he was getting worked up because she wasn't where he thought she'd be. He was adamant he'd driven up only a few minutes earlier and that she'd nipped in to go to the loo but never come back out again. The person on duty was equally adamant no one had used the toilet for at least a couple of hours. You need to get the key from the desk.'

'And the girl had disappeared?'

'Right. Assuming she was there in the first place. I'll come to that in a minute. Anyway, one of the customers decided to call the police – either because he was concerned for the girl or just scared that the situation was getting out of control – at which point the guy causing all the fuss promptly dived into his truck and drove off like a bat out of hell.'

'Without waiting to see what had happened to her . . .'

'Exactly. By the time the patrol car got there he was long gone. They thought it was probably someone's idea of a practical joke but decided they might as well take a look at the CCTV while they were there. And the weird thing was, the cameras picked up this Mitsubishi truck as it came round the front and parked away from the petrol pumps, and you can see the guy get out of the truck, but there's no sign whatsoever of any girl. He goes inside for a few minutes, comes back out, waits around for a while, then goes back in and starts kicking off.'

'But no sign of the girl during all that time?'

'Right.'

'So he came alone.'

'Looks like it.'

'What about cameras at the rear?'

'None there – no need. There's nothing out back, just a few bins. The cameras just cover the forecourt and the entrance to the store itself, and then there are the ones inside of course. They checked all of them, working on a description the guy had given while he was kicking off, and there was no one who even vaguely resembled this girl, either inside the shop or out.'

'So he . . . what? Made it all up?'

'Who knows? All they could say for certain is that there's no visual of her at any time while he was there.'

'So what's he up to then? Why invent something like this and kick up such a fuss that the police are called in and then disappear before they've arrived?'

'I agree it doesn't make a lot of sense. And here's the good part.'

'Oh, I think I can guess the rest. It was a big guy, right?'

Horgan smiled. 'Right.'

'The Mitsubishi truck . . . I notice you slipped it in there without drawing attention to it. Testing out the old man, are we?'

'Wouldn't be so presumptuous, sir.'

'And I'll bet the truck's a red one – even if it's lost a bit of colour over the years.'

'I said you'd like it.'

'I do indeed. Owen Hall,' mused Holloway, steepling his fingers and tapping the bridge of his nose. 'Now what do you suppose that's all about, eh?'

3

EARLIER: SATURDAY, 23RD AUGUST

ABI

The first thirty seconds of their phone call the previous evening had been enough to confirm that this was indeed the same Owen Hall. Not exactly the same, of course – the voice was a couple of octaves lower and twelve years had eroded all but the merest hint of the stammer which had been the bane of his adolescent life. But the pauses were still there, the same interminable gap between question and response while he formulated his reply, as if testing it out mentally before committing himself. The delivery, although nowhere near as robotic and unnatural as before, was still hesitant, almost diffident. Clearly in the darkest recesses of his mind there lurked the suspicion, even after all these years, that anything he was about to say was bound to meet with derision or worse.

But as she watched him step out of his truck this evening, she wondered in all seriousness whether she would even have recognised him if they'd passed in the street. He was a good eight or nine inches taller for one thing, and the soft, almost flabby teenager she remembered had disappeared beneath several layers of muscle. If Mary's description of him as *ripped* was a little wide of the mark – he was too bulky, his movements laboured and bearing none of the lithe athleticism she always associated with the word – he nevertheless cut an imposing figure as he walked up the drive towards her front door. Whatever scars might still be there on the inside, it was clear he no longer had anything to fear from the adult equivalent of playground bullies.

After a few awkward moments – a nod from him, an effusive *hello* from her and a hand on his elbow that served as a halfway house between a hug (surely a bit OTT) and a handshake (too formal) – she suggested they get down to business right away. Then maybe they could catch up on the last dozen or so years over a cup of tea. She was looking forward to it. She'd always felt sorry for Owen at school and had taken Callum to task as much as she'd dared for the way he and his friends were always picking on him. When he didn't return at the end of Year 9, it was assumed he'd simply transferred to another school and it was a good while later that she learned he was being home schooled by his mother. She'd felt bad about that and it would be nice to know he'd come through it all and was doing well for himself.

She led the way down the path at the side of the house, through a gate whose hinges were betraying the first signs of rust, and into the area at the back of the house, on which she hoped he might be able to bring a little imagination to bear. It would be intriguing to see what he might come up with. At Mary Kowalski's he'd had a virtual ground zero to work with. Here it would be different and she wasn't sure whether that would make it more difficult for him than starting from scratch.

The garden had definable areas for one thing; the lawn was mown every three weeks or so and she'd managed to keep flower beds and borders pretty much under control. But lately it had begun to feel more like fire-fighting than maintenance – keeping things vaguely tidy and functional fell a long way short of what she and Callum had envisaged when they'd first viewed the property. She remembered walking through it, his arm around her waist, as they talked enthusiastically about its potential. What they'd had in mind – and she was sure it applied as much to Callum as to her – was a shared interest, a joint venture with an end product they could show off whenever friends came to call, or Callum brought home business clients for dinner.

The reality however had proved to be very different. Network marketing was a demanding mistress and before he was headhunted by ACI, neither of them had any way of knowing he would be spending quite so much time away from home. Even on those weekends when he wasn't travelling the length and breadth of the country, delivering keynote speeches at a never-ending succession of conferences, it wasn't easy for him to forget work entirely. There was always a presentation to prepare here, markets to analyse there, important phone calls breaking into what was supposed to be their time together.

As a result, their ambitious plans for a shared labour of love had inevitably been downgraded over a period of time to little more than routine upkeep, for which she was almost exclusively responsible. He might come out occasionally for half an hour and pull up a handful of weeds to show willing, but that was pretty much the extent of their collaboration nowadays, and in her more negative moments she couldn't help seeing this as representative of a much wider picture.

She took a few minutes now to explain to Owen some of the original features she and Callum had been keen to incorporate into the overall design and they talked briefly about possible budget constraints within which he might work. Then she left him for a moment to go inside and put the kettle on, watching through the window as he strode around the garden, pacing out measurements and jotting them down in a small notepad. When the tea was ready, she brought it outside with a plate of biscuits and sat at the garden table while he finished off what he was doing.

The business side of things was dealt with relatively quickly. He offered to draw up a number of plans based on different budgets she'd given to him. He'd start in the morning as Sunday was usually the day he set aside for designing anyway. He still had other work which would keep him from starting here for a few days but he could bring the plans round on Monday evening after he'd finished work if that was convenient. They agreed on a time and she was just wondering how to work the conversation around to his life away from work when the patio doors slid open and there was Callum, stepping out onto the path, squash racquet dangling idly from one hand.

'Well, well,' he said, a wry grin sketching an unconvincing welcome as he walked over to join them. 'If it isn't Owen Hall.' He kissed the top of Abi's head and placed what felt like a proprietary hand on her shoulder. Laying the racquet on the table, he reached across and held out his free hand which Owen shook as he hauled himself to his feet.

'Jesus,' said Callum, craning his neck in exaggerated fashion. 'Mary Kowalski wasn't kidding, was she? How tall are you for Christ's sake?'

Owen shrugged.

'Six-six? Six-seven?' Callum continued, tilting his head in Abi's direction as if inviting her to guess along with him. 'You at Fitness First?'

Again Owen said nothing, merely shook his head.

'You must be working out somewhere. You can't tell me you got those guns from lugging a lawnmower around.'

'G-got some weights at home.' He wasn't one for eye contact at the best of times and smiling had never been part of his make-up but at least he'd seemed fairly composed until then, with just the two of them there.

'Well, you look good on it, doesn't he?' said Callum. 'You two been catching up on the good old days?'

'We were just about to,' she said, wincing inwardly. She wasn't sure Owen would recall any of his schooldays with a warm glow of nostalgia. 'We've been talking about the garden mostly.'

'Well, good luck there, that's all I can say. I'll leave all that to the two of you,' said Callum, casting a doubtful eye around him. 'Kind of got away from us a bit, didn't it, babe? Don't think these hands were meant for manual labour. Tell you what though – do half as good a job here as you did at the Kowalskis' and you won't get any complaints from me. The difference you made there – couldn't believe it when they said it was you.'

Abi shifted uncomfortably in her seat, reaching for her cup as a cover for removing his hand from her shoulder. She wondered whether Callum realised he was talking more loudly than usual and slowing down his delivery. He couldn't have sounded more patronising if he tried.

'You need a shower,' she said, plucking at his sweat-stained sports shirt. 'Did you win?'

'Do bears shit on the Pope? Three–one; let him have the first to make it interesting. Mind you, it *was* Alfie. Speaking of which, I'll need your car tonight.'

'Tonight?' she asked, looking up and shielding her eyes from the early-evening sunshine.

'I got him to drop me off here and he's taken mine with him. He's sorting out the brakes tomorrow so that it's ready for Bournemouth on Monday.'

'Sorry,' she said. 'You can't have mine, I need it. Book Club, remember?'

'Ah, Jesus . . . you're kidding, right?' He linked both hands behind his head, squeezing the elbows forward.

'No. It's on the calendar.'

'You know I never look at that. You might have told me.'

'I did. Several times.'

'Well, can't you get a lift or something?'

'I don't need to. I've got a car. Can't you?'

'I'm having dinner at Woodies with the MD of Heseltine's and two of his associates,' he said, his facial contortions making it quite clear just how ridiculous a suggestion this was. 'You know how important it is. You seriously think I'm going to ask him if he can come out here and pick me up?'

'So take a taxi,' she suggested. 'I think we can probably afford it.'

'Why can't I just drop you off at your book chat thing? Where is it?'

'It doesn't matter where the *book chat thing* is. I need *my* car, OK? Why give yours to Alfie when you know you're going to need it?'

'Because a), I need to get the brakes done before I drive to Bournemouth on Monday and b), I didn't think for one minute you'd be so possessive about yours – which I seem to remember buying for you.'

And there they were – it always came back to this. It was a favourite tactic of his. He was the big success story; she was merely clinging on to his coat-tails as he flew through life. He was generous to a fault, happy to provide her with anything she asked for, as long as it was on his terms. The slightest bump in the road was all it took to bring out the child in him.

'Look, we're meeting in West Dean,' she said, trying to broker some sort of compromise. 'How about I drop you off in Chichester on my way through? Is quarter to eight any good?'

'No, it's not – I'm meeting them at seven. Forget it – I'll get a taxi.' It was his ball and he was taking it home with him.

He paused as a thought occurred to him.

'Unless . . .' He turned to face Owen, who had been pretty much forgotten for the past minute or so. 'I don't suppose you'd be able to drop me off around then?' he asked. 'You going anywhere near Chi centre?'

'I d-don't know – I s-suppose so.'

'There you go then – problem solved.'

'Are you sure, Owen?' she asked, annoyed that Callum should presume to ask. Getting a taxi wouldn't have presented any problem at all. She wasn't sure what point he thought he was scoring here.

'Said so, didn't he?' said Callum, picking up his racquet and striding back across the lawn. 'Cheers, mate – give me ten minutes to shower and get changed and I'll be back in no time. Tell you what, make it fifteen. You two can do some catching up while you're waiting, right? And help yourself to some of those biscuits. You've probably lost a pound or two while you've been sitting there, ha, ha.'

She watched as Owen picked up his spoon and slowly stirred his tea before taking a biscuit from the plate.

As instructed.

HANNAH

The text came through as she stepped out of the bath:

> Change of plan. No car. Have to take yours. Pick me up
> 7.15 outside Woodies in Chi

Hmm, she thought. *No kisses.*

She wrapped the towel around herself and let the water out before texting back:

> Front or back? Xxx

The reply was almost instant.

> Car park at back? Explain l8er

She wrapped a second towel around her hair and secured it as she padded her way through to the bedroom.

> Everything OK? Xxx

A slightly longer delay this time, then:

Wots with all the questions ffs? Said I'll explain l8er

Ouch! She flipped the phone shut. *Terrific.* Not exactly the start to the evening she'd been hoping for. *Whatever's upset him,* she thought, *please don't let it be Abi.* Anything to do with work and she might just get away with it. He'd grumble all the way there, get it out of his system and then they could enjoy the dinner party. If it was Abi though, it wouldn't be just the journey. He'd spend the whole evening complaining about her and it would spill over into the sex afterwards, staining everything. Her time alone with Callum was limited enough as it was – taking Abi to bed with them didn't feature high on her list of preferred options.

She dried herself quickly and searched frantically for several minutes for her hair straighteners. It wasn't until she thought to check Izzy's room that she spotted them resting on the dressing table and decided, not for the first time, that she was going to have to speak with her about this. Renting a room was one thing – it didn't mean you could act as if you owned the place, helping yourself to other people's things without even asking. *Soon as she gets back*, she promised herself . . . not for the first time.

She checked her watch. If she was going to pick Callum up rather than the other way round, that left her a bit pushed for time and if the tone of his texts was anything to go by, keeping him waiting for any length of time wasn't an option. Just as well she'd already decided what she was going to wear. She'd spent half the afternoon trying on different outfits and changing her mind every few seconds, taking advantage of the fact that Izzy was visiting her family. She'd have been merciless – *haven't you got anything better to do with your weekend than worry about what he thinks?* Then again, Izzy had never liked Callum. She didn't approve, not that it was any of her business. Sometimes you'd think Victoria was still on the throne to listen to her. She was never openly critical – too fond of her room to risk losing it – but she certainly knew how to slip in the sly look here, the snide remark there and a constant downturn of the mouth whenever his name was mentioned.

Yes. It was definitely time she had a word.

She checked herself in the mirror, changed her mind about the bag and tried two others out instead. One more look in the mirror, a quick fluff of the hair at the back and she decided she would do. *Knock him dead, girl. Still got it.* Then she looked at her watch again and realised it was nearly seven already.

Damn!

That wasn't going to improve his mood one bit.

OWEN

Thoughts rattling around inside his head as Bosham becomes Fishbourne.

Should've said no. Should've told him to . . . to get lost. *You want a favour? From me?* Who did he think he was, asking for a lift like that?

What did he do instead?

I s-suppose so.

As if they were still fourteen years old and the minutes till the end of break were crawling past like a snail through treacle.

I s-suppose so.

Luckily there's not much in the way of conversation now they're in the truck. Obviously feels he can drop the act now Abi's not around. Just sitting there, stinking the cab out with his stupid hair gel and checking his phone every ten seconds for messages. No need for any more pretence about *the good old days* because there's just the two of them. And they both know.

Fishbourne roundabout, joining the A27 – traffic coming at him from all directions. He makes a couple of attempts to dive into the flow – no luck. Then a gap, only for a black Honda Civic to change its mind at the last moment despite having signalled left. Quick slam on the brakes as he realises what's happening and Callum flies forward, using both hands to stop himself from hitting his head on the windscreen. Hadn't fastened his seat belt . . . of course. The Callums of this world don't need seat belts. Nothing touches them.

'Please don't swear,' he says as Callum screams through the passenger window at the driver of the Honda, who's already taken the Portsmouth turn-off.

Spots a gap. Pulls into the traffic, ignoring the look of disbelief coming from his left.

'You know,' Callum says eventually. 'I'd forgotten how you used to do that. Always asking people not to swear. What's that all about?'

'I d-don't like it.'

'So you don't swear, right?'

'No.'

'Never?'

'N-never.'

'So . . . you're opening a cupboard door and it smacks you in the face. You don't swear then? You don't yell *shit* or something?'

'No.'

He thinks about this for a moment. Shakes his head.

'Bullshit. Everybody swears. The Pope, Kate Middleton . . . The Dalai Fucking Lama. They all do it. It's human nature. Instinct.'

'I d-don't like it.'

'Yeah well . . . there are lots of things I don't like, but I don't go around nagging people about it. Suck it up, you want my advice. Make things a bit easier for yourself.'

Stockbridge roundabout – keep straight on. Better to go left at the Bognor Road one, past the Peugeot dealer, over the bridge. Avoid the level crossing that way. Gates are always shut round about this time. So many trains.

Not much longer now. He can do this.

'Hey, can you still list all the wotsit . . . prime numbers?'

He doesn't see what business it is of Callum's but finds himself nodding anyway.

'What about that code thing? You know, where you used to take someone's name or a long word or something and work out the total? You still do that?'

'Seventy-one,' he says, and waits.

'You gonna give me a clue?'

'The black Honda Civic back there.'

'What . . . the one that carved us up at the roundabout?' Looks over his shoulder as if he expects it to still be there.

'GN09 DLY. Total's seventy-one.'

Callum frowns, then throws his head back and laughs.

'Jesus, you're something else, you really are. Some guy almost totals us, you slam on the brakes and come close to sending me through the windscreen and you've still got time to take the number plate and do all the calculations?'

'Prime number.'

'I don't get it, I really don't,' he says, flicking at a fly which has come in through the open window. Probably the hair gel. 'I mean, anyone else would be like, *What the fuck*, life flashing before their eyes, brain turned to mush and you're sitting there cool as anything, going a = 1, b = 2 . . . how do you do it?'

'I don't d-do anything. It just comes to me like . . . like a p-picture.'

'Wow,' he says, as they turn into The Hornet and take the right filter for St Pancras. 'Rain Man.'

Owen pulls up outside Woodies. Callum gets out, makes a point of wiping imaginary dirt off his trousers.

'Thanks for the lift, big man,' he says. Checks his hair quickly in the wing mirror. Two bangs on the roof of the pickup. Cheese-eating grin. Then he disappears inside.

Peace.

Two minutes later, just going back over the bridge, Owen hears a buzzing sound, then tinny rock music coming from somewhere. He pulls over, reaches across the passenger seat and his fingers locate something down between the seat and the door. Lifts it up and looks at the display but the call ends almost immediately. The name *Alfie* lit up for just a brief moment.

Must have slipped out of Callum's pocket or maybe fallen to the floor when they had to brake so suddenly. He wonders what to do now, whether he should take it back to the restaurant and interrupt his business dinner. If he had a die, he could try a probability test. Three or six means safe. Two or five danger. Knows what Willie would do. Willie would stand on the bridge and wait for the next train, then drop the phone onto the roof and watch it sail off into the distance. Or stamp on it and throw it under the wheels of a passing lorry to make sure. *Think you're such a big shot now, Mr Callum Green?*

He's not Willie. He starts the engine again, turns into a side road and heads back towards the restaurant. If he hurries, he might get there before the important guests arrive.

He has to drive past Woodies because there's nowhere he can leave the truck in St Pancras. Next left, then left again takes him into a packed car park at the rear of the restaurant. Finds a space and gets out, slipping the mobile into his pocket. He's weaving his way in and out of the rows of parked cars when he sees him. Callum's not inside with his business clients. He's walking over to a yellow Mazda sports car and stepping over the door rather than opening it. Then he's leaning across and kissing a woman who looks a bit older than him and who may be attractive enough in an obvious sort of way but who definitely, most definitely is *not* Abi.

She adjusts the mirror so that she can check how she looks, then puts the car in gear and drives round the far side of the car park, heading for the exit. And there's a pause, just a moment or so while he wonders exactly what he's supposed to do now, before he runs back to the pickup, starts the engine and sets off after them, keeping just enough distance between them to remain undetected.

And he's not sure what he's doing exactly but he's pretty sure he's not returning any mobile.

PHIL

By eight o'clock, near as damn it, the last few stragglers had left the gym and Baz was standing at the door, waggling the keys to let him know he was ready to lock up. Phil looked around, picked up a couple of towels that had been left lying on the floor, then walked over to join him, taking a swing at the speedball as he passed it. Old habits.

As he drove Baz home, they swapped notes on Jimmy Fernandes, the young lightweight Phil had been working with all evening.

'He's not ready for the Areas,' he told Baz. 'Way too soon. He falls apart the moment you pressurise him. The height and reach advantages he's got, all he needs to do is keep it long but there's no snap to his jab, you know? Just paws at opponents which means shorter guys are always going to get inside and he hasn't got a clue what to do when that happens.'

'I think it's the Prosser kid from Crawley he's fighting.'

'No chance. He'll walk right through him.'

Baz nodded. He wasn't about to dispute any of it.

'Pisses you off, right?'

'Don't like to see natural advantages go to waste like that,' he said, directing the air stream onto the windscreen which was starting to fog up. 'Tell him as often as you like, it goes in one ear and straight out the other.'

'You ever wonder what you might've done if you'd had his height and reach?' Baz asked.

He nodded. *All the time.* Went without saying.

Baz asked if he wanted to come in for a drink, maybe something to eat – Marcie would always rustle something up. He thanked him for the offer and took a rain check. 'Things to do,' he told him, as he did most weeks. Baz never asked what these things might be. Probably didn't need to.

The moment he'd dropped him off he pulled over and rang through to the China Garden. When the girl told him the order would probably be half an hour or so, he decided he might as well stroll along the seafront for a while. It was a warm evening and even though the light was fading so much more quickly now with August drawing to a close, he figured that would be better than waiting at the takeaway, reading yesterday's paper or watching some game show on the TV tucked away in the corner.

He worked his way through the back streets and into Victoria Drive, then crossed the Aldwick Road and headed down to Marine Drive West. Just past the Waverley, he pulled into the first parking slot on the left and locked the car before stepping through the bushes and onto the start of the promenade.

He wondered whether there would ever come a time when he'd be able to walk here and not think of Sally. It was hard to imagine somehow. Right where he was standing, for instance, was where they used to bring Callum in his pram – God, twenty-six years ago. It was only a ten-minute walk from the flat they'd been renting in West Street in those days and when no amount of cajoling and rocking would induce the baby to sleep they used to wrap him up and push him from here to Felpham and back. As often as not, it took up to an hour before the motion of the pram worked its magic – Callum was a stubborn little beggar, even as a baby – but they were in no hurry. They had the whole evening ahead of them. Their whole lives.

And a little further on from here, just after the Yacht Club, was where they used to bring him with his first two-wheeler bike, encouraging him to cycle without the training wheels. Sally would stand 75–100 yards away with her arms outstretched, offering reassurance, while he ran along behind Callum with one hand on the saddle, trying to judge the right moment to let go. Always ended in tears somehow.

And down there on the pebbles just before the pier, was where he'd sat one lunchtime with Sally and a couple of her friends, watching the gaily coloured yachts drift past, desperate for the others to leave the two of them alone for a few seconds so that he could ask her if she'd go to Dave Freeman's twenty-first with him. And then, when the chance did present itself, he'd been too tongue-tied and nervous to go through with it and she'd gone with someone else instead. Seven months it had taken him to make up the lost ground. She'd almost given up by then, she told him years later.

A lot of history.

He walked back to the car, arrived at the Chinese a good while after the stipulated half hour and took the spare ribs and yung chow special fried rice back to Blondell Drive, trying not to think what it would do to his weight. He searched for a clean plate and threw the meal into the microwave to warm it through. Then he sat in front of the TV, channel-hopping on the off chance there might be something worth watching, settling finally for *Casualty* which was just running through the opening credits. He stuck with it for as long as it took him to eat the meal, then flicked lethargically through the channels once more before giving up.

He carried his plate through to the kitchen and dropped it into the sink along with the others which had accumulated there for the past week. Then he shuffled back into the lounge, sifting through the mail he'd picked up earlier that afternoon when he'd first got up. Two household bills, two letters urging him to switch energy providers, ah . . . his *Boxing News* magazine. He unwrapped the latter and read the first few pages but couldn't get comfortable as he lay there, sprawled on the sofa, so he put it to one side and went back into the kitchen to get himself a Heineken.

Maybe a DVD, he thought, tugging at the ring pull, having decided against looking for a clean glass. He took the can back into the lounge and got down on his knees next to the TV to look through the collection that had been lying there for some time, gathering dust . . . literally: a number of sports compilations; a box set of *The Sopranos* that Callum (Abi, more like) had bought him for his birthday more than nine months ago and which was still in its cellophane wrapper; *Fawlty Towers* which he'd picked up in a charity shop near the Regis Centre a while back. Sally had loved it when it first came out. She thought Manuel was brilliant – loved the cruelty shown towards him by Basil which he always found odd, given that she never had an unkind thought in her life.

He took the DVD out of its case, turned on the TV again, slipped the disc into its slot and clambered to his feet. As he reached out and grasped the shelf for support, he knocked the photo frame, just managing to grab it as it toppled over the edge. He tottered for a step or two to regain his balance, his knees protesting that they deserved to be treated with a little more respect. *Like a bloody old man,* he berated himself. Fifty-four and falling apart at the seams.

He moved to put the photo frame back on the shelf, then changed his mind and held it out in front of him. Sally and him – Puerto Banus – 2010. Only four years ago. She was squinting slightly, not because of the sun but because a stiff breeze was making her eyes water. He looked fifteen years younger than he did now and a couple of stone lighter. Still had that shirt and those cut-offs upstairs somewhere although God only knew why – he wouldn't be slipping into them any time soon.

In one of the drawers of the cabinet next to the TV there was a rack of DVDs of most of the holidays they'd had – more or less every trip since she'd bought the video camera, in fact. He pulled them out from time to time, when the need to see her smile and hear her voice again became too strong to resist, even though an hour or two of such self-indulgence came with an emotional price tag he wasn't sure he could afford too often. The very fact that nearly two years had passed and her clothes were still in her side of the wardrobe told him all he needed to know about how much he'd been able to move on. Closure? Nice word.

He switched his attention away from the photo frame to the lounge itself, taking in the general air of neglect that had been creeping in over the past few months. When he'd first come back here after the funeral, he'd thrown himself into a frantic spring-cleaning session, determined to keep the place as immaculate as Sally had done. He'd managed to maintain it for more than a year but eventually things had started to drift. He had to admit it didn't look so much like their home anymore.

He placed the photo gently back on the shelf and walked round the room, plumping up cushions on the settee, as if that was going to make much of a difference. Then he decided *what the hell*. He wouldn't be going to bed much before three anyway. It was always the same, the first day after a four-week spell on nights. If he was going to be up that late, he might as well do something useful.

So he grabbed a bin liner from the kitchen and went round the lounge, picking up empty cans, wrappers, old newspapers. Then he rummaged around in the cupboard under the sink and found a rag and an old can of Mr Sheen which coughed and spluttered just long enough to enable him to make the shelves and the bookcase look a little more presentable.

When he'd finished in the lounge, he went into the kitchen, filled the dishwasher and turned it on. He ran a bowl full of hot water, squirted soapy liquid into it and set about cleaning the rest of the plates, dishes and cutlery which were dotted around the kitchen, scrubbing away with the brush as if scouring away at something else entirely. Something you could scour away at for the rest of your life and barely leave a mark.

Two years ago he hadn't known what an aneurysm was. Oh, he knew the word, knew it was something to do with blood vessels in the brain and that if they burst . . . Now he knows more than enough about aneurysms. Knows exactly what they are. An aneurysm is a cheat. A bastard. A sneak thief in the night that doesn't announce itself – just creeps up and takes her away from you while you're not looking. Makes a complete farce of all the plans you've been making, like maybe a villa in Spain when you've both retired and can afford it. Ha bloody ha. It doesn't allow for any last-minute farewells or expressions of undying love. It loves the prosaic in life. Feeds off it. You can be sitting in the armchair one minute, watching *X-Factor* and she can get up and go into the kitchen to make you a cup of tea during the adverts, calling out to you while she's in there, asking if you want a . . .

Want a . . .

Only you'll never get to know what was on offer – a piece of cake? A couple of biscuits? – cos while you're waiting for her to finish the sentence, she's whisked away and when you hear the crash you think, *oh no, sounds like another one of our mugs gone for a burton,* like that's the worst thing that can happen because you, knowing nothing about aneurysms, can't imagine for one moment that your life's just altered beyond all recognition. That's what aneurysms are.

Yeah . . . that's what aneurysms are.

OWEN

Oh my God, he's fucking her.

Willie and his language again.

'Please don't do that.'

Oh come on, Owen. Lighten up, will you? It's a perfectly genuine Anglo-Saxon word. What else would you want me to say? He's tupping her? They're having . . . carnal relations?'

'We don't know they are.'

I thought you said the bedroom light went on right after they got home.

'I don't know if *he* went upstairs.'

No, you're right. He was probably making fairy cakes in the kitchen. This . . . is . . . fucking . . . fantastic. I can't believe you followed him all night. How cool is that! Did they stay long at this place in Wick?

'About three hours.'

And you sat outside in your truck all that time? What if someone had seen you and phoned the police?

'There was this lane down one side of the house. You couldn't see the truck from the main road – I got out and checked.'

And from there to her place, they still didn't know you were following them?

Shakes his head.

You're sure?

Nods.

'I was a bit worried when they pulled in to fill up with petrol but once we were back in with all the traffic it wasn't difficult to stay a few cars behind them.'

Willie's thinking now, trying to find a flaw somewhere.

So . . . when he came round just now to get his phone back. You didn't give anything away then?

'I wanted to hit him.'

Well of course you did. But you didn't say anything to tip him off that you knew about this woman of his in South Mundham?

'No.'

You're absolutely certain?

Nods. He likes it when Willie is happy. You don't often see him this excited. He'd like to share in it but there's one thing bothering him. Feels he needs to get this out of the way first.

'Do you think I should tell Abi?'

Willie bursts out laughing.

You are kidding, right? Ah . . . let me think about that for a moment. N-o-o-o.

'But she needs to know.'

Again . . . N-o-o-o. You hear me? Trust me on this one. If she's got anything about her at all, she knows already. Even if she doesn't know the who, the where or the when she'll have a pretty good idea as to the what. And if you think she's going to thank you for being the one to fill in any gaps for her, you couldn't be more wrong. She'll hate you for it. Probably take your eyes out. Any time she thinks of you, she'll remember you as the person who took the blindfold away. Trust me, telling her is the last thing you want to do.

'But –'

You're still not listening, are you? People like your sweet little Abi – deep down they want their men to be bastards. They like the whiff of danger. Why the hell d'you think she's been with him all these years? It's like Everest: the ultimate challenge. Every woman always thinks she can be the one who finally clips Casanova's wings and makes him appreciate the attractions of a life of domestic bliss. At the moment she thinks she's the one, right? The moment you open your mouth, you're taking all that away from her, reducing her to the same level as everyone else. You think she'll thank you for that? Trust me – you do NOT want to go there.

He's not convinced. 'It's just . . . it doesn't feel right, keeping secrets from her.'

She'll know soon enough, don't you worry. If he's sloppy enough for you to find out – no disrespect – someone else will join the dots before too long and they'll be quick to let her know. But until that happens, it gives you something a bit special.

'What?'

Power, Owen. Power over Callum Fucking Green. Something you've never had in your life. A hold over him. A chance to get your own back after all these years. The moment you tell her, you've got squat. Say nothing for now and maybe, just maybe you'll have a chance to make him squirm a bit. Have a bit of fun at his expense for a change. Watch him twist in the wind. You'd like that, wouldn't you? Well ... wouldn't you?'

And he would.

Has to admit it.

Maybe he shouldn't, but he *would* like that.

4

NOW: THURSDAY, 2ND OCTOBER

HOLLOWAY

This was their third visit to Hall's bungalow in Pagham in the past five weeks. The first time had been a mere formality, a simple alibi check – in and out in five minutes, 'Thank you for your co-operation, Mr Hall'. The other, a few days later, had been just as brief because they'd picked him up and taken him to the station for a more formal interview with an AA present.

Holloway decided, without clearing it first with Marie Loneghan, that this morning's visit wouldn't require an appropriate adult. He knew it was a fishing expedition, based on a gut feeling more than anything else, but if anyone chose to take exception to it later, he was confident he'd be able to pass it off as nothing more than a routine follow-up call. There was nothing to link this incident at the petrol station to the South Mundham case other than Hall's involvement and, as links went, that was tenuous at best. Chances were, Hall would have a perfectly innocent explanation for his odd behaviour and they'd be in and out of there in no time. You didn't need an AA for that.

He and Horgan didn't disagree on much as a rule but Owen Hall was a rare exception and each saw it as a bit of a blind spot in the other. The one thing on which they did find common ground was his status as a vulnerable adult. Bright as he was, and no one seemed to be in any doubt about that, the lack of eye contact, the strange rocking back and forth and the seemingly random muttered asides were all cast-iron guarantees that they would have difficulties introducing potentially crucial evidence at a later stage unless they proceeded with due caution and provided him with all the support he might need at a formal interview. Any defence team worthy of the name would drive a lorry through their case otherwise.

But when it came to making sense of South Mundham and more specifically Hall's involvement in it, they agreed to disagree. Horgan liked straight lines and Occam's razor. To his way of thinking, Hall was big and unpredictable enough to have carried it off, had a motive that no one would have trouble understanding and an alibi that wasn't anywhere near as watertight as it seemed – not when you took into account the fuzzy edges around the time of death. And he'd not been straight with them, which always counted for a lot in Horgan's assessment of anyone. As far as he was concerned, you don't lie without good reason and he wasn't sure he bought into the explanation given for all the evasiveness. In short, in a small field of poor quality, he was odds-on favourite; and if he had his way, they'd be leaning a lot more heavily on Owen Hall right now.

Holloway on the other hand was more inclined to proceed with caution and accept Hall's explanations at face value until such time as they were presented with solid reasons for supposing them to be false. He was as relentless as ever in checking everything down to the last detail but drew the line at putting excessive pressure on a vulnerable adult until such time as the evidence warranted it. He accepted this wasn't a courtesy he extended as a matter of course but wasn't about to apologise for any influence the Adrienne Lasalle case might still be exerting on him, even after all these years.

He'd been a young DC back then and had been swept along with everyone else in the all-consuming desperation to find the killer of a pretty French tourist whose body had been found in an alley behind the beach huts on Felpham seafront. The pressure had been intense and seemed to be coming at them from all sides. The French police were keeping a close eye on developments, itching for an excuse to get involved. The local MP had decided this was the perfect peg on which to hang his hat and demonstrate to his local constituents that he had his finger on the pulse. As for the media, his superiors had done their best to strike a balance between keeping the public informed and preserving the integrity of the investigation but it was clear almost from the outset that the two sides had very different ideas as to where that particular line should be drawn. So after a few days with no real signs of progress they were desperate for a breakthrough. And Derek Rafferty had come along at just the right time, like an answer to a prayer.

Everyone knew within minutes of bringing him into the station for initial questioning that he was two fries short of a Happy Meal and if anyone had sat down for long enough and asked serious questions about the so-called evidence that had brought him to their attention, they might just have taken things a little more slowly and made sure of their facts. They certainly might have thought harder about just how much pressure they were entitled to exert on him during his brief stay in custody.

But time was of the essence and the need for an arrest almost unimaginable. And when Derek Rafferty had hanged himself in his Rustington bedsit within twenty-four hours of his provisional release, the general consensus of opinion had been: well, these things happen. Terrible, of course, but what can you do? Can't make an omelette without cracking a few eggs. And anyway . . . innocent people don't kill themselves, do they? Not when they haven't even been charged as yet.

But when incontrovertible new evidence emerged six months down the road that Adrienne Lasalle had been killed much earlier than originally believed and at a time when Rafferty had been visiting his mother in hospital, that had hit Holloway hard. He could rationalise it, tell himself that hindsight makes fools of us all, fall back on reminders of just how small his own role had been in the whole wretched affair, but it made no difference. Collectively they'd failed the poor boy – as the subsequent public inquiry had made abundantly clear.

So no, he'd never forgotten Derek Rafferty. And no, he didn't see a few oddities in someone's behaviour as a good enough reason to start piling on the pressure. He had an open mind about Owen Hall and was determined to go where the evidence might lead him, rather than nudge it in a pre-determined direction. Once burned . . .

They turned into Harbour View Road and pulled up outside a red-brick bungalow with a tile-hung roof and a built-in garage. The sight of the red Mitsubishi truck in the driveway was reassuring. Holloway shaded his eyes as he peered into the cab and smiled to himself while Horgan tried the doorbell. When no one responded, they walked round the other side of the house and opened a wooden gate leading to the back garden. Here they found Owen Hall working at a bench that had been set up on the back lawn, apparently disembowelling an old mower. He looked up at the sound of the gate opening, then returned to his work, head bowed in concentration.

'Hello Owen,' said Holloway, nodding at the entrails of the mower which littered the grass at his feet. 'You sure you know how to put that back together again?'

Hall said nothing and Holloway accepted the implied rebuke with a nod. Patronising at best. Served him right.

'We weren't sure you'd be here,' he continued. 'Half expected you to be out on a job somewhere.'

Hall picked up a rag and started rubbing furiously at one of the blades.

'Things are a bit quiet at the m-moment,' he mumbled.

'Really? I'd have thought autumn would be a busy time for you gardeners. All those leaves to rake up, trees to cut back . . . that sort of thing?'

'Yes. Well, w-word gets around.'

'Word?'

'I've l-lost a few customers. Thanks to you.'

'I'm sorry to hear that.'

'Then stop c-c-coming round to my home. It doesn't help.'

Holloway nodded by way of apology.

'OK. I'll get to the point, then we can get out of your hair as quickly as possible.'

'I've got an appointment with a ph-physio in a f-few minutes.'

'OK, I'll make it quick. We just need to ask you a couple of questions. First of all, can you tell us where you were last night?'

'Home.'

The answer was so instant it almost overlapped the question and it was obvious to both of them that he'd known what was coming.

'All night?'

'Y-yes.'

'But you must have gone out sometime during the day, surely?'

'I w-went to the c-cinema in the afternoon.'

'And what time did you get back?'

'Dunno.' He'd dropped the rag now and was standing almost to attention, the fingers of both hands pointing downwards. Every so often he looked up, as if daring himself to face them but within seconds he would be staring at the ground again. Holloway felt for him, wondered what it must be like to be constantly on the defensive.

'Roughly,' he said. 'What time did the film end?'

'About five.'

'And you came straight home?'

He nodded.

'So that would make it about half five you got back here, right? And you're saying you didn't go out again all evening?'

He nodded again. Holloway and Horgan exchanged a meaningful glance, taking care to make sure he noticed.

'Well, that's a bit confusing,' said Holloway. 'You see, we've got CCTV footage of your truck at a petrol station near Littlehampton a good two hours after that.'

'N-n-not my t-truck.' The words were barked out – came out like soot from a blocked exhaust. Again it was difficult to escape the impression that neither question nor response had come as a surprise.

'You can see the number plate very clearly, Owen. And then there's footage of you inside the shop. Not only can we see your face close up, we can even make out what you're buying – the mints are still on the passenger seat of your truck, by the way. So we know you were there. What we don't know is why you couldn't just say so when we asked.'

Hall suddenly folded his arms across his chest and started the curious rocking thing they'd seen the last time he was interviewed. He was mumbling to himself – it sounded like a series of numbers. Holloway flashed a quick glance in Horgan's direction and could tell his colleague wasn't in any way impressed.

'Are you OK, Owen?' he asked.

'I d-d-don't have to answer your questions,' he said after a few moments.

Holloway pursed his lips.

'Well, technically that's true of course. But you need to understand something here. You always have the right to say nothing but if we decide there are questions we need to ask, you do at least have to listen to them, and the only reason we're here is because we thought you'd prefer it that way rather than having to come down to the station. If we're wrong about that, you only have to say.'

'You can't ask me questions without Mr Mitchell.'

'If this ever gets to the stage where we need to make it a formal interview, then no one does anything until your friend Mr Mitchell is there to support you. But we were hoping this might be just a friendly two-minute chat between the three of us. Save bothering him.'

'I'm not saying anything without Mr Mitchell.'

Holloway could sense Horgan bristling next to him. His body language left no doubt as to what he felt the next move ought to be but he wasn't ready to up the ante and take Hall in for questioning just yet.

'Look, put yourself in our position for a moment, OK?' he sighed. 'We've got CCTV that puts you there and also witnesses who say you were upset about some girl who'd gone missing. Now, you don't expect us to ignore that, do you? We can't just sit back and do nothing or we wouldn't be doing our jobs, would we? Help us out here. Either it's true, in which case we need you to be a bit more co-operative so we can find out what's happened, or it's not and you made it all up for some reason. If it's the latter, Owen . . . you need to tell us now.'

This seemed to bring Hall to life again. Suddenly he seemed very animated.

'No one's b-been abducted,' he said, a touch of anger creeping into his voice. He'd picked up a large adjustable spanner, which immediately put Horgan on the alert. 'You know no one's been abducted!'

'Are you saying you made it up?'

'No!'

'Then I don't understand. Have you spoken with this girl Julie since last night?'

'It's a trick. All of it.'

'A trick?' Holloway frowned. 'I don't understand. What do you mean?'

'You think I'm stupid and you're all so c-c-clever. But I've checked.'

'Checked what?'

He shook his head.

'Are you saying this girl . . . Julie . . . is OK?' Holloway persisted. 'You know where she is?'

'I'm not answering any questions without M-M-Mr Mitchell.'

It was clear from his posture that he wasn't about to back down from this position, which meant Holloway had a decision to make. He knew what Horgan would do. An hour or so alone in an interview room, left to think things over for a while, was often all it took to persuade an inexperienced suspect to be a little more co-operative.

But Holloway wasn't about to take any chances. He apologised to Hall for disturbing him, thanked him for his time and told him he was free to go to his physio appointment. They would go back to the station and would expect to see him at 3.30 that afternoon. Did he want them to contact Mr Mitchell in the meantime to see if he was available or would he prefer to do it himself?

Hall seemed surprised, opting for the latter as if approaching a package he regarded as suspect. Holloway reminded him again: 3.30. Non-negotiable. Then they left him and made their way back to the car.

'So what do you think?' Holloway asked, as Horgan started the car and pulled away.

'You know what I think, boss.'

'You think he's playing us?'

'You saying you don't?'

'So this business with the girl . . .'

'What girl? All due respect, sir, but I didn't see one on the security tapes. Did you? The people at the petrol station didn't see one. What we *did* see was him arriving on his own and leaving the same way.'

Holloway scratched an itch behind his ear and gave this some thought.

'She could have got out of the car somewhere else. Round the back, maybe? There are no cameras there, remember.'

'But why? Why stop the car and let her out, then drive another thirty metres to park it? Wouldn't she just get out when he did?'

'Maybe she thought the toilets were round the back.'

'But they're not, so she clearly didn't know, in which case why assume they were? Wouldn't she try inside first? That's where public toilets are most of the time nowadays.'

'OK,' said Holloway, keen to explore Horgan's theory further and put it to the test. 'Let's say you're right. There never was a girl. This Julie is someone he's invented. Why? Why would he do that? I mean, if she doesn't exist, that means he's driven from Bognor to Littlehampton, which is what . . . twenty-five minutes? Maybe half an hour in that clapped-out truck of his. Then he's gone inside and kicked up a fuss about his girlfriend having gone missing and when the police are called in he drives off like a scalded cat before they get there, even though he must know his truck will be identified and that we'll be calling on him before long to ask what he's playing at. That make any sense to you?'

'OK,' said Horgan. 'Look at it the other way. There *was* a girl and they were on their way somewhere and she's genuinely disappeared. Vanished into thin air. What does he think? She's been abducted? If so, why not hang around and tell the police what's happened? But what does he do? He drives home and forgets all about it. He doesn't phone it in, explain what's happened. How does that work?'

Holloway smiled.

'Doesn't make a lot of sense either way, does it?'

'Smoke and mirrors, boss. He's up to something.'

'Up to what exactly?'

'Don't know yet but I think he's messing with you. I know he's an oddball but that doesn't make him stupid. Difference between you and me. I think he's devious. You know the first thing everyone who knows him has said to us? How clever he is. Really clever. They've all gone out of their way to say so.'

'You don't think he is?'

'On the contrary – I'm *sure* he is. So someone that clever . . . we turn up and ask where he was last night and he says he was at home, like it hasn't even occurred to him there's such a thing as CCTV cameras and we're going to trip him up at the first hurdle. Really?'

Holloway smiled. 'So what do you think?'

'It's a double bluff. *We* know he was there; *he* knows he was there. Only a simpleton would try to make out he was at home. So that's exactly what he does, then falls apart at the seams when he's found out. It all helps to reinforce this idea of him as some sort of helpless victim who needs to be protected from himself, like all this barking at things that aren't there and the number chanting and the Weeble impression and all the rest of it. Do I think he's clever? Yes – I think he's clever enough to play on these things to throw us off balance, stop us pushing as hard as maybe we ought to.'

He paused for a moment. 'You mind if I speak honestly, boss?'

Holloway waved the question away. 'Go ahead.'

'He's disturbed, yes. He's vulnerable, yes. I'm sure he's had a hell of a time of it in the past. But he's not Derek Rafferty, boss.' He turned to face Holloway briefly before concentrating on the road ahead once more. 'He really isn't.'

They drove for a while in silence.

5

EARLIER: MONDAY, 25TH AUGUST

ABI

The plans were fantastic. Way beyond what she'd expected. He'd done four separate drafts, one for each budget range she'd suggested. So much attention to detail – not to mention imagination and creativity – had gone into each design. He must have spent the whole of Sunday working on it. She was amazed and told him so. And as she might easily have predicted, his face turned a brighter shade of crimson in a way that instantly brought back some of their conversations as children. It was touching somehow that there was still a connection of sorts, even after all this time – just a little incongruous though to see such embarrassment and self-consciousness in a man of his size.

She'd called round as soon as she'd finished work at the bookshop. This wasn't her first visit. She'd been here once before, to a birthday party when she and Owen were both at the same primary school. But that had been twenty years ago and she'd needed her sat nav this time.

The bungalow had aroused vague stirrings in her, shards of memory pricking at her consciousness as she walked through the front door and stepped into the tiny lounge. She had no clear recollection of how it had been furnished back then but imagined that things probably hadn't changed a great deal in the intervening years. The furniture had a dated and worn feel to it. The mantelpiece still had an old mahogany clock that looked as if it had been passed down through several generations and was flanked by a number of family photographs from years gone by. There was also a solitary birthday card, which she assumed must be for Owen until she peeped inside while he was making tea.

To Willie
From your loving brother
Owen.

She'd bitten her lip at that.

It had been fun catching up with him. She'd enjoyed the conversation a lot more than the tea and the stale Swiss roll in all honesty but it was touching that he'd made the effort. For the first few minutes he was as shy and withdrawn as ever but, as had always been the case with her, he'd opened up a little once he started to relax. Even in those early years at secondary school, when things had been so tough for him, she'd always had the ability to draw him out of his shell and she found it reassuring that she still could after all this time.

He even talked about his mother whom she herself remembered as being a kind but sickly woman, always coughing her lungs up and dabbing at her lips with a handkerchief. It turned out she'd lasted a lot longer than might have been expected, finally succumbing to lung cancer just over fourteen months ago – on his twenty-fifth birthday, he mentioned as a casual aside, as if the awful poignancy of such a thing hadn't even occurred to him. She had to admit that he'd adjusted fairly well to his loss considering that, when she'd known him before, he and his mother had been just about joined at the hip.

They were still poring over the plans when her mobile started ringing. She apologised and fished it out of her bag. *Callum,* she mouthed, offering a reassuring smile. She wondered whether the twitch near his eye was anything more than coincidence.

'Leaving in the next few minutes, babe. Thought I'd ring and say goodbye since you're not here.'

'I'm at Owen's remember?' she said, half-turning away from him. 'We're going over the designs he's drawn up. I told you this morning.'

'Right. Forgot. Anyway, I'll ring later, OK? Probably won't be till ten or elevenish cos I think we're all meeting up for drinks first and then going out for a meal.'

'Maybe texting would be better if it gets too late,' she said. 'Do you know where you're staying yet?'

'Not till I get there. Bill Shawcroft's set it all up – his secretary at any rate. I'm picking the keys up from him so I'll let you know later.'

'Make sure you do . . . just in case your mobile packs up and I need to get hold of you. When are you back on Friday?'

'Late afternoon, I'd have thought. Maybe we can go out to dinner. I'll book somewhere.'

'That would be nice. Drive safely. And look after yourself, OK?'

'It's Bournemouth, babe, not Baghdad.'

She laughed and ended the call, her thumb lingering on the *End call* icon for a moment. She tried to summon up a modicum of regret that they would be spending the next four days apart and was only mildly disturbed to find that she couldn't do it. They needed a break, she felt bound to admit. Things had been tense of late. Maybe a few days away from each other would do them some good.

Owen seemed a little subdued after the call. It wasn't as if he'd shut down exactly but some of the spontaneity that had just started to ease its way into their conversation appeared to have seeped away. She had no illusions about why – it was sad that Callum still had this effect on him after all this time. Under different circumstances she'd have happily stayed a little longer to make sure everything was OK but after a few minutes he got to his feet and told her he needed to get ready. He'd booked a ticket online for Cineworld and would have to leave soon.

She gathered her things together and asked if it was OK to take the designs with her. If she had a good look at them later that evening, she'd be able to ring him in the morning and let him know which looked the most likely. He told her he'd be working but would have his mobile with him.

As she got to the front door and turned to say goodbye, he surprised her by putting one hand on her shoulder and leaning forward. Then, just as quickly, he pulled away sharply and gave her a clumsy pat to cover his obvious confusion.

She said goodbye and started to walk away. Then, on an impulse, she turned and came back. Going up on tiptoe, she gave him a quick peck on the cheek, smiling to herself as she walked back to her car.

CALLUM

'Designs,' he chuckled to himself. Owen Fuck-all and his grand designs. Some bloody joke that was. She seemed to forget sometimes that he knew the guy almost as well as she did and if there were two words that would never belong in the same sentence in this life, they were *Owen* and *design*. Couldn't plan his way out of a cardboard box. He hoped she'd bring these masterpieces home for him to have a look at as soon as he got back from Bournemouth. He could do with a laugh. He could remember when a design for Owen Fuck-all involved a crayon in a grubby fist and a square house with square windows and stick people. *Oo, Owen, that's really good. Well done.* Yeah . . . for a fucking two-year-old.

He didn't bother to text Hannah to say he was on his way. She wouldn't be ready in any case. He could send a team of liveried servants round to help her pack and she'd still find some excuse to keep him waiting. Woman's prerogative was how she saw it. No worries though. He wasn't in any great hurry. It wasn't like they needed to be in Bournemouth by any specific time. They could take it easy, stop for a meal on the way if they saw somewhere they fancied. He knew where to pick up the keys when they got there.

He turned off the A27 at the Whyke roundabout, picking up the Selsey road before branching off left again towards Pagham. He found himself caught in a stream of vehicles behind a pony and trap whose two occupants were either oblivious or utterly indifferent to the problems they were causing. In different circumstances he'd have been leaning on the horn and yelling at them through the open window the moment he got within striking distance but today he was happy to sit back and just drift along the back road. No hurry. No worries. A week of good business, better food and unbelievable sex stretching ahead of him. The two pikeys in the cart up ahead, no doubt smirking at the hold-up they were causing, obviously thought this was as good as it gets. They had no idea.

When the procession reached the Walnut Tree, he stopped to book a table for Friday night. It wasn't so much an act of penance. He'd probably quite enjoy it after a week away but Jesus, was he ready for a bit of a break from Abi. There was no specific thing he could put his finger on. She just seemed to be on his case all the time. This needs doing, that needs fixing, did you remember to put such and such away? A thousand varieties on the theme of *How many times have I told you . . .* All with a smile on her face but nothing much else there to prop it up. Maybe a night out together would go some way towards pulling the stick out of her arse.

Having booked the table, he turned into Brookside, then followed a series of back roads until Honer Lane came into view. All open countryside and single-track road now. Pagham Harbour somewhere up ahead. The clouds were starting to roll in with a vengeance, and even though it was still warm enough to have the hood down he thought he'd probably have to sort it as soon as he reached Hannah's place. Didn't need Carol Kirkwood to tell him a downpour was on its way.

He heard another vehicle approaching from the opposite direction before he saw it, hidden as it was by the hedges and the bends in the road. Someone was going to have to back up here and although usually he'd be quite happy to sit there and wait till hell froze over before giving way, he found himself taking note of an entrance to a field he'd just driven past. If it came to it, he could always reverse into it and let the vehicle pass – amazing what he was prepared to do when all was right with the world.

He laughed at how he seemed to be full of the joys of spring all of a sudden. In August, ha ha! Laughed, that is, until he saw who it was coming the other way.

And then he thought: *what the fuck?*

PHIL

He leaned back against the wall and smiled to himself as he watched her at work on the speedball. Amazing, really. He could see one or two others were watching with interest too. Most newcomers found it hard just to keep their hands in the air for that length of time and even before their arms gave out they'd have been struggling to find the co-ordination and timing needed to hit it every time.

She was as comfortable with the speedball as she had been just now on the heavy bag. He'd corrected her slightly crouched stance, which probably owed a lot to her beloved mixed martial arts, and offered a few tips designed to improve her leverage, but by and large she'd punched well, hitting through the target and pivoting to get maximum force into the shot. And as for the fifteen-minute warm-up – she'd sailed through it, even though he hadn't been able to resist the temptation to make it a little bit more demanding than usual. Came up with a big grin on her face as if to say, *Is that all you've got?* He was impressed.

Anna had turned up out of the blue. She'd often threatened to come along, usually when they were out on patrol at Arun

Valley, teasing each other to pass the time. He'd reached the point where he didn't really believe she was serious about giving it a go and had been surprised to see her saunter through the door as if she hadn't a care in the world. She'd drawn her fair share of compliments already and seemed to have been well accepted by hardened regulars, who were not easily impressed. He couldn't help feeling pleased for her, even though he suspected he was in for a rough few days on patrol with her chirping in his ear about how easy this boxing lark was.

She finished the session on the speedball and grabbed a towel, wiping the sweat away from her face and the back of her neck. As she tugged at the scrunchie her hair fell forward, partially covering her face, and it occurred to him that at Arun Valley it was always tied back – he'd never seen her like that before. This was Anna the athlete, the girl who'd been area cross-country champion as a schoolgirl and claimed she could probably go out and run a sub-five-minute mile even now if she put her mind to it. Looking at her, he felt inclined to believe it.

'So how did I shape up?' she asked him, the grin there again.

'Not bad.'

'For a beginner?'

'For someone who does MMA.'

'Thank you, kind sir. I suppose you could do better?'

'Doubt it. Back in the day, maybe.'

She unfastened her shoe and removed one training sock so that she could have a closer look at a blister that had been troubling her.

'So just how good were you?' she asked. '*Back in the day*.'

'He was shite,' said Baz, as he walked past.

Phil smiled quietly to himself. The two of them had sparred each other often enough when they were younger and he couldn't remember Baz ever getting the better of him. No one knew it better than Baz himself.

'I had my moments.'

'What does that mean?' she asked, feeling the inside of her shoe.

'ABA quarter-finals. Had to pull out then – broke my hand.'

Anna's eyes widened. 'ABAs. That's pretty good, isn't it?'

'Like I say, I had my moments.'

She sat down on one of the benches to put her sock and trainer back on and he slid alongside her. She slipped the extended fingers of one hand inside the scrunchie while the other tugged her hair back from her face.

'What about your boy?' she asked. 'He ever try boxing?'

'Callum? Not so's you'd notice.'

'Not for him?'

He pulled a face.

'It was OK till they started hitting back. Then it wasn't quite so much fun anymore.'

She wiped her face again, then wrapped the towel round her shoulders.

'Disappointed?' she asked.

'Not really,' he said, remembering Sally's relief when Callum announced he was giving up. 'I've never been one of those dads who want to live their lives through their kids' successes. I just wanted him to be happy, that's all. If I'm disappointed about anything, it's the fact that there are so many good lessons to be drawn from boxing and somehow he's managed to pick up the wrong ones every time.'

'Oh . . .'

She couldn't possibly know about the times he and Sally had been called to the school to discuss Callum's behaviour, especially the bullying he always tried to pass off as standing up for himself. Couldn't possibly know – but she seemed to get the general drift of what he was hinting at without him actually saying it.

'What does he do now?' she asked.

'Oh . . . couldn't really tell you,' he said with a self-deprecating chuckle. 'Way over my head. Something to do with marketing is all I know. The rest of it – not a clue. He's making a fortune out of it though, I know that much.'

'So he turned out OK then,' she said, nudging him in the ribs. 'Even though you still beat yourself up about it.'

'I guess so.'

'Well, at least you care. Wish I could say the same about my old man.'

Phil sat upright and looked at her. This was probably the first time in the three months they'd been working together that they'd strayed over into more personal territory. It occurred to him just how little he knew about her family.

'You don't get on?' he asked.

She shook her head. 'Not really. I'm still expected to turn up every week for Sunday lunch and we do our best to keep things civil for Mama's sake but it's never really comfortable. We're probably too alike. I'm different from what he expected in a daughter, I guess. I should have been like Lucia.'

'Your sister?'

She nodded. 'She did everything right. Grew up the way a bella bambina ought to: pretty smile, loves her poppa, married at nineteen and had already given him two grandchildren by the age of twenty-three.'

'You don't think you've got a pretty smile?' he asked.

'Wouldn't matter if I did, but thanks for the thought,' she said. 'No, I was the rebel, the tomboy. More interested in running and getting sweaty than parading around in frilly dresses and ribbons. *Conduct unbecoming*, I think the phrase is. Don't suppose the fights helped either.'

He laughed. 'Sounds like you and Callum would get on well.'

'Yeah . . . or beat the crap out of each other.'

She picked up her sweatshirt – the first indication she was about to leave.

'You haven't told me how much the subs are,' she said.

'On the house.'

'No, seriously.'

'Seriously. No charge for first-timers.'

She slapped his knee as she got to her feet. 'OK. In that case I'll pay for you when you come to MMA for the first time.'

He laughed.

'Why not?' she urged him. 'Go on – live a little.'

'MMA? At my age?'

She tutted and turned to head for the door, waving goodbye to Baz as she went.

'You know how often you do that?' she asked, as he caught up with her. 'Put yourself down? What happened to *you're only as old as you feel?*'

He held the door open for her and walked outside. It didn't seem in keeping with the rest of the evening somehow to point out that alongside her he felt every second of his fifty-four years.

He offered to drive her back to her place but she demurred.

'Think I'll go for a run,' she said. 'See if I can turn this into a proper workout.'

She went up on tiptoes and gave him a quick kiss on the cheek. Then she was off, heading down towards the beach, hair bobbing behind her, so relaxed and easy it was difficult to imagine her ever running out of energy.

He walked a few yards to the end of the road, avoiding the temptation to lift a hand to his cheek, and watched the retreating figure until she disappeared from view.

HANNAH

She tried his mobile again. The '9' in brackets after his name laughed back at her, reminding her how many times she'd tried it already.

Nine calls.

Three voicemail messages reflecting increasing levels of concern and frustration.

At least half a dozen texts laced with the same potent mix. And still no reply.

Damn you, Callum Green. Damn you!

He should have been here ages ago. She hadn't worried at first. He'd probably been delayed – some problem at work or maybe Abi had thrown some last-minute obstacle in his way. He'd be there soon enough, that was all that mattered. She even wondered whether he might be having a joke at her expense, deliberately keeping her waiting as some sort of payback for all the times she'd left him kicking his heels downstairs.

But as the minutes ticked past, she started to wonder what was going on. Was he OK? If he'd been taken ill, he'd have got a message to her somehow, wouldn't he? And the same applied to any change of plan. She was quite capable of driving to Bournemouth and meeting him there if the need arose. All she needed was a call to explain – anything so that she knew where she stood.

Because there was a third possibility that had dawned on her just a few moments ago, and that was that he might have changed his mind about the whole thing. She hadn't reached the stage where she thought this was *really* likely because things had been so great lately. Even as recently as Saturday night he'd almost had to peel himself away from the bed, so she didn't see how things could have changed substantially in less than forty-eight hours, but then again you never knew, did you? Being the third party always meant being on the outside and if the freedom that bought her was appealing for the most part, there were definitely times when it was anything but.

So at 9.30, with her patience running on fumes, she decided on what she'd promised herself she would *never* do – to ring his home. She worked out a cover story: a colleague from work who needed him to sign off on some documents. Did Abi know where he was at the moment and when he'd be back? Then, having got her side of the conversation straight in her head, she dialled his home number, hoping against hope that he would answer instead of her.

Again . . . no reply. After eight rings it cut to voicemail, both of their voices reading out a message in a sing-song voice which she could easily imagine giving way to fits of giggles the moment they'd finished recording. Happy families. It felt like more than just a slap in the face.

'DAMN YOU', she screamed as she cut the connection. 'WHERE THE HELL ARE YOU?'

6

NOW: THURSDAY, 2ND OCTOBER

HOLLOWAY

Edmund Mitchell was a diminutive retired accountant with a comb-over that bordered on the ridiculous and halitosis that surely ought to have come with a government health warning. He and his wife had been neighbours and close friends of Laura Hall, nursing her through the final stages of her illness and acting as surrogate family to Owen ever since his worthless wastrel of a father had upped sticks and left the two of them to fend for themselves. As such he'd been the obvious person for the boy to turn to whenever he needed a father figure and today was no different.

They sat next to each other, across the table from Horgan and Holloway. In preparation for the interview, Mitchell removed his rimless glasses and began polishing them on his tie. In front of him on the table a small notebook had been opened and a monogrammed fountain pen lay alongside it, primed to record any minor deviation from the correct procedure. Even though he was no more than five-feet-six-inches tall and probably hadn't weighed more than eight and a half stone dripping wet at any stage of his entire life, he nevertheless had a presence that was in inverse proportion to his size. Until he opened his mouth to speak, it was easy to dismiss him as a nonentity, just one more humble employee worn to work every day of the week by the same suit, spending his lunchtime breaks feeding the ducks in the park from the sandwich he'd meticulously wrapped in greaseproof paper the night before.

Holloway opened proceedings which, he advised them both, would be tape recorded and videoed. It was not a formal interview as such, he pointed out. Its purpose was merely to ascertain exactly what had happened on the evening of Wednesday, 1st October 2014 at a service station on the A27 just outside Littlehampton and, specifically, to determine whether any follow-up action needed to be taken. Did he understand?

Owen nodded and when reminded that he needed to speak for the benefit of the tape, mumbled: 'Yes.'

'Might I make an observation here, Inspector, before we get started?' asked Mitchell. *Here we go,* thought Holloway, preparing himself mentally for an afternoon of paragraphs and sub-sections.

'By all means.'

'When Owen came to see me earlier, he explained in detail everything that had happened. I advised him it was very much in his best interests to get down here and explain it to you himself so that you would then be free to get on with doing your job.'

'I'm very pleased to hear it,' said Holloway, smiling to show his appreciation before turning his attention to Hall. 'Owen?'

Hall leaned forward, hands clasped, both elbows resting on the table. He looked a lot more comfortable than he had done in his own garden earlier in the day.

'I'm sorry I l-lied earlier,' he said, looking directly at the table. 'I p-panicked because I d-didn't understand what was happening. I'll answer all your questions now.'

'OK,' said Holloway, loosening his tie and undoing the top button of his shirt. 'Let's start with a few basics, shall we? You are now saying that you were there at the service station at the stated time?'

'Yes.'

'Was there anyone with you in the car when you arrived?'

'Yes.'

'And this was the girl Julie whose whereabouts were causing you some concern?'

'Yes. Well . . . I d-don't know if that's her real name but it's what she t-t-told me.'

Holloway paused for a moment. 'OK,' he said. 'We'll come back to that. So, this Julie . . . we'll call her that for now, shall we? How long have you known her?'

'A f-few days. She rang me. Last week sometime. S-said she was a freelance reporter from Brighton. She wanted to meet me.'

'Did she say why?'

'Not then. She just said she had something I'd want to know about – something I'd find really interesting. I gave her my address but she said it was better if we met somewhere else in c-case she was being watched.'

'Watched?'

'Yes. She suggested the seafront outside Butlins would be best. Lots of people. We'd be safer in a crowd. She said she'd find me . . . knew what I looked like.'

His right index finger started tracing imaginary circles on the surface of the table as he spoke.

'She said she knew all about the case. She'd t-taken an interest in it, been d-doing a lot of investigating of her own and the m-m-more she looked into it the angrier it made her cos she thought you were all coming at it from the wrong angle.'

'What did she mean by that? Did she explain?'

He shook his head. 'Doesn't matter. She was lying anyway. Making it all up. But I believed her. She said she was c-c-close to working out exactly what had happened and that if she was right everyone would get off my b-back and leave me alone. There was this woman who was meant to have some sort of p-proof that I couldn't have been involved and she'd been trying to get her to c-come forward with what she knew. She was expecting to hear from her any time.'

'And did she?'

'Couple of days later. She phoned me, said she'd arranged to meet this woman on Wednesday night at the B-Burlington Hotel in Worthing and I could come with her if I liked but I mustn't tell anyone in case it scared her off. So I didn't . . . not even Mr M-Mitchell.' He looked apologetically at his AA who patted his arm to let him know it was all right.

'So that's where you were heading last night?'

'Yes.'

'The Burlington, you say?'

'Yes.'

'And whose idea was it to stop?'

'Hers,' he said. 'She said she needed to go to the t-toilet. I went inside to buy her some m-mints and –'

'No, no. Let's back up a little. Where exactly did you stop?'

'Just past the petrol pumps. Over by the tyre-pressure gauge.'

'Are you sure? Only, we've seen footage of you getting out of the car. There's no sign of her.'

Hall stopped and thought about it for a moment. 'No, that's right. I d-dropped her off first, on the way in and she pointed over to the p-pressure gauge and told me to p-park over there.'

'So you're saying she got out somewhere round the back?'

'Yes.'

'And that was her suggestion or yours?'

'Hers, I think. Yes. Hers.'

'OK. So what happened then?'

Hall told them about the queue at the checkout and the long wait until he decided it was time he went to look for her.

'So what did you think when you couldn't find her?' Holloway asked.

Hall bowed his head and ran his fingers through his hair.

'I d-didn't know what to think. I looked everywhere and she'd just v-vanished. Then I remembered this car.'

'What car's that?' This was new. There had been no mention of any other vehicle before now.

'I thought it was f-following us all the way from Bognor. I t-told her about it and she said I was probably imagining it and when we stopped at the petrol station it k-kept on going so I thought she must be right. But then, when I couldn't find her anywhere, I thought . . . what if the car d-doubled back while I was inside? What if it *was* someone f-following us and they'd taken her?'

'This car . . . tell me a bit more about it. What sort was it?'

'Dunno. I'm not very g-good with cars. And it was dark.'

He shrugged apologetically.

'I got the number plate though.'

Holloway looked up in surprise. 'You did?'

'Part of it anyway. The last three letters were RCA. I remember because of the record label – RCA Victor.'

'You're sure of that?'

'Yes. And it was a p-prime number. Fifty-three.'

'Fifty-three. So that makes it September 2003, right?'

'No – I mean the total's fifty-three.'

'I don't understand,' said Holloway, looking to see if Horgan was any the wiser. His eyes were locked on Hall as they had been since the start of the interview.

It was Mitchell who stepped in to explain. Horgan took this as an invitation to take over the questioning for a while.

'So let's see if I've understood how this works,' he said. 'You noticed this car behind you and did all the calculations in your head, right?'

'Right.'

'Even though you think you're being followed and you're worried you might be in some sort of danger, you find time to sit there and do all these calculations.'

'I don't do calculations. It just comes to me.'

'It just comes to you. Like some sort of epiphany, you mean?'

'I don't know what an epiphany is.'

'A revelation.'

'I suppose so.'

'OK. So if we take my car, which is HN61 NRT, that would mean –'

'One hundred and thirty-five,' said Hall, before Horgan had even finished writing it down, let alone started the calculations. 'Multiple of three and five. Safe. Happy.'

Horgan paused and looked at him, then continued transcribing the numbers and letters. H = 8, N = 14, 6, 1 . . .

'No,' said Hall, putting his finger on the offending digits. 'Sixty-one. Not six plus one.'

Horgan nodded, crossed out his mistake and continued. He finally came up with the total. A good twenty seconds later. One hundred and thirty-five.

'How do you do that?' he asked.

Hall merely shrugged his shoulders. 'I just do,' he said.

'And what did you mean just now when you said safe and happy?'

'Owen takes comfort in numbers that are a multiple of three,' explained Mitchell. 'Either three on its own or in combination with five. Conversely, he is easily distressed by prime numbers. You and I are influenced by a number of factors when we look for patterns in life. With Owen it's numbers.'

'I thought three *was* a prime number. So is five for that matter.'

'Apparently Owen takes comfort in the way they interact,' said Mitchell, a quiet smile playing at the corner of his lips. 'I'm not sure we need to become unduly concerned with the logic underpinning it all.'

Holloway had been watching this exchange closely, leaning back in his chair, tapping his front teeth with a biro as he processed this new information.

'So what you're telling us is that this car, whatever make it was, had a number plate where the last three letters were RCA, and when the numerical value of those three letters is added to that of the other two letters plus the two numbers, they'll come to a total of fifty-three? Have I got that right?'

'Yes.'

'So we can rule out September-registered cars altogether, can't we? They all start with fifty or sixty something and the total will be too big.'

'Yes.'

Holloway and Horgan looked at each other, wondering just how much help that would actually be in practical terms. It didn't do much to narrow down the number of possible combinations.

'And you can't help us out with the car itself? Make? Colour?'

'It was dark,' said Hall. 'And I told you – I'm not good with c-cars. I like trucks.'

Holloway decided to leave it and get back to the one point that was still niggling away at him.

'OK, Owen,' he said. 'I need to ask because this is what we're having difficulty understanding here. You think you're being followed and this Julie disappears so you understandably think she might have been abducted, right?'

'Right.'

'And yet you drove off instead of waiting for the police to arrive. Why? I mean, if that happened to me, my first thought would be to get as many people out there looking for her as possible. Why didn't you stay there and report it if you thought she might be in some sort of danger?'

And here comes the rocking again, he thought as Mitchell got out of his seat and put an arm on Hall's shoulder to reassure him. In other circumstances it would have been difficult not to laugh at the strange juxtaposition. Even when sitting, Hall seemed to tower over his mentor somehow.

'I didn't want to b-be there cos I knew how it would look,' he said eventually. 'The only reason we were g-going to Worthing in the first place was to meet this woman who was supposed to help me c-clear my name. The last thing I n-needed was to get caught up in another m-mystery. It would be in the papers and you'd think it was my fault just like before. I knew I didn't want that so I panicked and d-drove off.'

'But you didn't even call it in when you got home, did you?' Holloway said. 'You still haven't. If we hadn't got your registration details from the CCTV footage, no one would know the first thing about it. This girl could have been in serious trouble. You want to tell me why you just left her to it?'

This time, Hall sat upright and looked him in the eye for the first time, as if challenging him in some way. He looked on more solid ground now than at any stage of the interview so far.

'Because I knew it was a trick,' he said. 'Even before I got back home, I'd worked it out.'

'Worked what out?'

'She was lying. Had to be.'

Holloway shook his head. 'You'll have to explain that to me, Owen,' he said. 'I don't see how you . . . reached . . . that . . . conclusion.' The last three words came out hesitantly – even as they were leaving his mouth he realised he knew where the problem lay, although the calculations buzzing around his head were still in inchoate form. It was the timing. The timing was all wrong.

How long would it have taken the girl to walk round the back and find there were no toilets? Fifteen seconds? Twenty at most. The moment she realised her mistake, she'd have come round the front and checked inside the store, because that was the only other place they could be. And *that* meant she'd have been in there at more or less the same time as he'd been buying the mints. In fact, they'd probably have bumped into each other on the way in.

But she didn't go inside – everyone was adamant about that. And given that she couldn't possibly have been snatched outside on the forecourt, in full view of everyone, it meant she had to have been taken in those twenty seconds while she was out of range of the cameras . . . where she herself had arranged to be. But for that to happen, the car would have had to follow them in and it hadn't because Hall had seen it drive straight on. And yes, it could have doubled back but that would have taken at least a couple of minutes or Hall would have seen it. The maths simply didn't work. Unless . . . unless she'd walked back out the way she came in while he was parking the truck. And why would she have done that unless she'd arranged to be picked up?

Hall had worked it all through in his own mind and come up with the same conclusion. He'd been set up. He slipped his hand inside his trouser pocket and produced a small rectangular card. Holloway took it from him, holding it by the edges as he opened a drawer in the desk. *Julie Mowbray,* it read in bold print. *Investigative journalist.* An email address and a mobile number.

'I rang the m-moment I g-got home,' he said. 'The mobile doesn't exist. The e-mail b-bounced back.'

Holloway slipped the card into an envelope he'd taken from the drawer, then looked at Horgan. He merely sat there, his expression giving nothing away.

'So tell us what you think,' Holloway said after a while. 'You said you thought it was a trick. What did you mean by that?'

Hall flashed a glance at Mitchell who nodded his encouragement. Then he reached into a bag he'd brought with him and pulled out a brown A4 envelope which he placed on the table. Holloway opened it and spread the four photos out on the table in front of them.

The first was of a tall Georgian house with a number of expensive-looking extensions that had been added over the years. Holloway turned it over to see if there was any clue as to where this was or when the photo had been taken but there was nothing. Parked in the drive was a flashy-looking car – BMW maybe – but there was a stone wall obscuring the number plate.

The second showed the forecourt of a petrol station which Horgan immediately recognised as the one where Hall had been the previous evening. This photo was taken during the day though and there were several cars dotted around.

The third was easiest to place but no less mysterious. He had countless variations on the same theme in a file on his desk, taken from every conceivable angle. There was no one in this particular shot although, if he looked closely, he could just make out the crime-scene tape in the far corner of the field, the car itself having been removed.

And the final photo, just in case the link had not already been established, was a full-length shot of a good-looking man in his early twenties, holding a trophy in one hand and a squash racquet in the other.

Holloway looked at each photo again, then slid them back inside the envelope.

'What are these?' he asked.

Hall shook his head. 'I don't know,' he said. 'They were in my t-truck.'

'In your truck?'

'Last night. At the petrol station. Someone must have put the envelope through the window while I was trying to find her.'

Holloway and Horgan exchanged a quick glance. They'd watched the CCTV footage a couple of times and had commented on the fact that Hall had leaned in through the window and rummaged around inside the truck for a few seconds before driving off. They'd dismissed it as unimportant.

'How?' asked Horgan.

Hall took a handkerchief from his pocket and blew his nose.

'How what?'

'If someone walked up to the truck and lobbed an envelope in through the open window, we'd have seen it on the CCTV. No one came near the truck at any stage.'

'That was my initial reaction too,' said Mitchell. 'But if you look closely at the photo of the petrol station . . .' He reached inside the envelope and carefully removed the one he was referring to. '. . . you'll see that just the other side of the tyre-pressure gauge there is a bush which separates the petrol station from the A259. Now if someone were to come at the car from that direction . . .'

He spread his hands to invite the detectives to join the dots.

'It was dark so I don't imagine it would be very easy for you to see from the opposite side of the forecourt whether someone stepped out of the bush and slipped the envelope through the open window.'

'They'd have needed to know the window was going to be open.'

'. . . which would have been easy to arrange if they were in league with the young lady in the car.'

Holloway looked again at the photo and conceded reluctantly that Mitchell had a point. It *could* be done. And they wouldn't have picked up on it when looking at the CCTV footage. Their focus then, understandably, had been Hall and the missing girl. There was no reason to look for someone trying to leave a calling card. One thing was for sure though – they'd be all over that video like a rash first chance they had.

'The house in the photos,' he asked Hall. 'Do you recognise it?'

He shook his head.

'You've never seen it before? Don't know where it is?'

Another shake of the head.

'So when you saw these photos, what did you make of them?'

'I didn't know,' he said. 'I couldn't m-make any s-sense of it. I thought maybe it was you.'

'Me?'

'The police. I wondered if maybe you were trying to make things d-difficult for me. Stir things up a bit.'

'I explained to him the police aren't allowed to do that sort of thing,' offered Mitchell. 'It's called entrapment. There are codes of behaviour they have to abide by.' He looked meaningfully at Holloway in a way that suggested he wouldn't be entirely disappointed if it turned out they *had* tried something underhand.

They called the interview to a halt a few minutes after that. Hall gave a detailed description of the girl for the record and agreed to come back in the following morning to put together a photofit image. He didn't sound too hopeful though. 'Not that good with faces,' he explained.

Holloway thanked them both for coming in 'voluntarily' and asked if he could keep the photos. He didn't imagine for one minute that he would find any prints other than those belonging to himself and Hall but you never knew – sometimes Lady Luck decided to smile on you. He escorted them to the front desk, then came back to rejoin Horgan who hadn't moved.

'You ever see anything like that?' asked Holloway, taking his jacket from the back of the chair and slipping it on. 'That number-plate business?'

'One–nil to him,' said Horgan with a rueful smile. 'Thought I was going to score a point or two there and he shoved it straight back down my throat. With interest.'

'So what did you make of it? Change your mind at all?'

Horgan shook his head.

'Nope.'

'You don't think what he said makes some sort of sense?'

'On the contrary. I think it makes perfect sense. I just don't buy it.'

'Because . . .'

'Smoke and mirrors, boss . . . remember? I told you he'd have a cover story – he's too clever not to. But if you pare it all back and focus just on the things we know to be true, what's he actually given us apart from a shedload of work? The photos? He could have taken them himself. This card he gave you – we'll send it off to forensics and I'll bet you what you like any other prints we find on it will belong to people who have nothing to do with this. And the card itself is one of those DIY jobs – he could have knocked it out himself on one of those machines in town.'

'What about the girl?'

'What girl? We still don't have anything other than his word for it that she even exists. There's nothing that puts her in the car or anywhere else for that matter. So on his say-so and with naff all else to support it, we're going to sink valuable man hours into canvassing his neighbours to find out if anyone else has seen her and he's already prepared us for that by saying they met outside Butlins . . . And all the time we're doing this, not to mention sorting out photofits and working our way through every number plate ending in RCA and adding up to fifty-three, who's going to be working the South Mundham case and trying to find ways to tie him to that? Like I said, we're being played – big time.'

'You ever think there might be a touch of the sceptic in you, Neil?' asked Holloway, pushing his chair back under the table.

'Except I shall see in his hands the print of the nails,' quoted Horgan.

Holloway sighed and picked up the envelope from the table.

'If I've got my Bible straight, Doubting Thomas got it wrong, didn't he?' he said.

Horgan smiled wearily.

'No. He just needed convincing, that's all. And at least he got off the fence, boss,' he added. 'No splinters in his backside.'

7

EARLIER: TUESDAY, 26TH AUGUST

HANNAH

She was woken by the alarm at 7.00 – an alarm she had absolutely no recollection of setting. Flapping a hand in its general direction, she missed completely with her first attempt to shut it off, then succeeded only in knocking it to the floor, where it continued to gnaw its way into her brain like a buzzsaw through knotted wood. She rolled over and snatched it up from the floor, seriously contemplating hurling it across the room until sanity prevailed. It wasn't the clock's fault her head hurt like hell and her throat felt like a furred-up pipe.

She'd held off the alcohol for as long as she could. Even after the first unanswered call to his home number, she hadn't grabbed the nearest bottle just yet because there was always a chance he'd ring any minute and suggest she get into her car and pick him up somewhere. How could she do that if she was totalled?

Blind, desperate optimism had held sway until getting on for midnight, at which point she'd decided, *what the hell!* Opening the first of two bottles of Château Altimar 2009, which she and

Callum should by rights have been drinking that very moment in Bournemouth, she told herself she wasn't going anywhere now, even if he *did* ring. *Too bad, sunshine. Missed your chance.* And after the first few glasses, having alternated between blubbing like a lovesick teenager and turning the air blue with a volley of imprecations that would have shamed an Alaskan trucker, she'd taken the second bottle to bed and drunk herself into a stupor, finally checking out altogether at some ungodly hour.

So no, maybe it wouldn't be fair to take her frustrations out on the alarm clock. On the other hand, if she didn't manage to find the right button in the next few seconds to stop the infernal row it was making, all bets were off.

She checked her mobile to confirm what she already knew: no messages. Whatever he was doing, it was obviously more important than picking up the phone and keeping her in the loop. She spent an eternity in the bathroom, doing her level best to put right the damage wrought by the excesses of the previous evening. It wasn't just her hair but her eyes, her mouth, her complexion – in fact, pretty much anything on show, that needed to be teased back into shape – and if she was moderately pleased with the eventual outcome, it was more akin to the relief experienced by a hurricane survivor who's managed to erect a makeshift shelter with a tin roof.

Convinced there was no way she'd manage to keep anything down, she skipped breakfast and made do with a coffee so strong the spoon almost baulked at entering. As soon as her head began to clear a little, she made a stab at weighing the pros and cons of another call, not to his mobile – if he still hadn't answered any of the calls, it was either disabled in some way or he was ignoring it – but to his home. Phoning seemed like the most productive option available to her. She wasn't exactly spoiled for alternatives and if there was one thing she was *not* going to do, it was sit around all day, waiting for some sort of explanation. Whatever the risks inherent in phoning, including having to talk to Abi in person, it was time to get onto the front foot and be proactive for a change. She'd had enough of supine last night. She hadn't been stood up since God knows when and no one was going to walk all over her now, not even Callum Green. Whatever the reason for last night, he was going to have some major-league sucking-up to do.

She rang just after 9.30 and was just about to give it up as a dead loss again when someone picked up and gasped 'Hello', before apologising for being out of breath. 'Was upstairs – only just made it to the phone in time.' She recognised the same sing-song tone from the voicemail message. Chirpy. Not a care in the world; default position set at friendly. She hated her already.

The cover story was in something like its fifth or sixth incarnation by now. Judith Price, conference secretary, phoning from Bournemouth, wondering if she could speak with Mr Green to confirm what he'd need for his keynote speech in the way of IT support and admin services. Hoping to catch him before he set off in case he wanted any photocopying done. Any chance of a quick word?

Abi regrets: her husband – and isn't it strange how a simple possessive adjective in conjunction with the wrong noun can just get up and grab you by the throat like that when you're at your most vulnerable? – *her* husband is already there in Bournemouth. Left sometime yesterday evening and no, she's afraid she doesn't have a contact number for him other than his mobile.

She suggests maybe contacting someone named Bill Shawcroft – he'll know how to get hold of him. If Abi knows him at all though, she's sure Callum would have let them know well in advance if he'd needed anything done.

If she knows him at all . . . ha!

Something slightly unnatural in the voice. No discernible accent but the rounded vowels didn't quite ring true. A telephone voice, cultivated to make her sound better educated and more upwardly mobile than she probably was, redolent of dinner parties and afternoon tea at Bailiffscourt. Did she talk that way with Callum? Somehow Hannah very much doubted it. Would she talk that way if she knew what her husband had been up to recently? Yeah . . . right. A few vowels might just lose some of their shape when that day dawns.

She thanked Abi, akin to chewing a wasp, and sat at the kitchen table for a few moments, tapping the mobile against her chin. *Already there in Bournemouth. Left sometime yesterday evening.* Pretty much as they'd planned, if you were to overlook the apparently minor detail that she was supposed to be going with him. For some reason he'd left without picking her up and spent the first night there on his own. For presumably the same reason he was knocking back her calls and texts. She had absolutely no idea why that might be. If this was the big brush-off, it had come out of nowhere as far as she was concerned. If anything had been wrong the last time they saw each other – it was only Saturday, for Heaven's sake! – he certainly had a strange way of showing it. He'd even texted her several times since then to say how much he was looking forward to the two of them going away together and not having to creep around like criminals.

No, she told herself. Whatever it was that had caused such a major deviation from the original plan, it had to be something to do with his work, which she knew to be unpredictable and subject to last-minute changes, even if she didn't really understand quite what it was he did. She had no idea why it should prevent him from keeping her updated but one thing was for sure – she wasn't going to sit around here waiting for someone to enlighten her, even more so now she remembered Izzy was due back sometime later that afternoon. God, could you imagine how that conversation would go?

No. The answer was in Bournemouth.

So was Callum.

And in a couple of hours or so, she would be too.

ANNA

'Shame about that Attenborough dude.'

Back on days again. Sunday and Monday off to let the body clock readjust. Then straight back into it.

'You mean that *Lord* Attenborough dude, right?' he said.

'That's the one. Only heard about it this morning. So sad . . . makes you think, doesn't it?'

'Apparently.'

'I mean, right out of the blue like that.'

'I dunno – he *was* ninety-something.'

'*Shut . . . up!*'

'Why? How old did you think he was?'

'Dunno. Not that old though. God, he was so active. So . . . *alive*, you know? My parents will be upset.'

'They big fans of his?'

'You kidding? It'll be like losing a member of the family. Every time one of his series came on, it was like the biggest event of the year. We all had to be there.'

She let it hang there, wondering how much further she'd need to nudge it before he'd bite.

'That one with the frog,' she added mischievously. 'How do they do that?'

'The frog?' Nibbling now.

'And the polar bears. We all cried . . . even Poppa, although that's not saying much. He cries at the drop of a hat. Latin temperament.'

He stopped. Looked closely at her, trying to make up his mind.

'You do know it's *Lord* Attenborough who's died, right?'

'What I said.'

'Only it's his brother who does all the natural world films. *Life on Earth*? *Planet Earth*? *Frozen Planet*?'

'Good with titles, isn't he?'

'This is a wind-up, isn't it?'

She sighed dramatically.

'Lord Attenborough, formerly Richard. Actor, director, President of BAFTA, darling of the nation, all-round clever Dickie, really. Won eight Oscars for *Gandhi*, probably should have picked up another for *Brighton Rock*. Yeah . . . it's a wind-up. What took you so long?'

He smiled, shook his head before walking on.

They went through the automatic doors and out into the fresh air which was more than welcome after the succession of hot days they'd had. The storm in the night had woken her around 3 a.m. and threatened to mess with the readjustments her body clock was still in the process of making but it had died away soon afterwards. All that remained now were a few puddles which the intermittent sun and a stiff breeze would hoover up before long.

They headed towards the car park to make sure that the unlicensed breakfast van they'd moved on half an hour ago hadn't sneaked back. Later they'd probably be butting heads, metaphorically at any rate, with the local goths who, for some unaccountable reason, seemed to have taken a liking to the fountain near the car-park entrance and had to be encouraged to find somewhere else to mooch around and look weird. She had nothing against them herself – live and let live as far as she was concerned, although quite why anyone would want to look like a corpse was beyond her – but there had been concerns expressed that some of the customers might find them intimidating. Personally, she thought anyone who might be intimidated by a Goth probably shouldn't be allowed out but what did she know? Dispersing them every so often was all part of the rich pageantry of day patrol.

'You do that a lot, I've noticed,' he said.

'Do what?'

'Joke. Fool around.'

'Oh, you've noticed, have you?'

'I have. Why d'you do it?'

'Does it bother you?'

'No. Just curious.'

She picked up a plastic bag which was skipping across the car park and dropped it in a bin.

'You want the serious answer or the flippant one?'

'The serious one.'

'OK,' she said, and paused to work out exactly what her answer might sound like. Just how serious did he want her to be? 'It's a confidence thing, I guess,' she said at length, brushing a few specks of dirt away from her trousers to give her hands something to do. 'I figure if everyone's going to be laughing at me anyway, I might as well make it look like it was my idea in the first place.'

He pursed his lips as he digested this.

'You *did* ask,' she continued.

'You think everyone's laughing at you?' he asked.

'Hello . . . have you met the Keystone Cops upstairs?'

'I thought you didn't take them seriously.'

'Yeah well . . . like I said, confidence thing. And I've been here a few years now. Starts to wear you down after a while. I've shown zero interest in any of them, so that makes me a dyke. I do MMA, so I'm an aggressive dyke. I like to talk about things other than football and sex, so I'm an uppity dyke. There's a bit of a pattern in there somewhere.'

'I don't laugh at you.'

'No, you laugh *with* me which is why I like patrolling with you and not them. We've got the same sense of humour.'

'You trying to upset me now?'

'See? That's what I mean. We're on the same wavelength. We make a good team.'

She tried to synchronise her footsteps with his as they walked on, weaving their way through the hordes of shoppers heading for the main entrance. *Go on,* she urged him silently. *Say something. You can do it.*

'We do,' he said eventually. And the sun edged its way out from behind the clouds, its reflected glare dancing off the rows of cars ahead of them like fireworks.

OWEN

A buzzing in his pocket. Takes out his mobile and lowers the shears to the ground while he answers it.

Abi.

Good news. She's looked closely at the plans and more or less decided which one she wants to go with. Just needs to check with Callum when he gets back to make sure he's on board. Would it be OK if she left it until the weekend before confirming with him?

And speaking of Callum, she wonders if he could do her a favour. Just a small one. She doesn't think for one minute it will ever come to this but if Callum ever asks what time she left his place last night, would he mind saying it was sometime around nine rather than whenever? She's sorry to sound so mysterious. Feels bad about asking him to lie, even if it's just a tiny white one, but it would mean a lot to her. She'll explain why next time she sees him. Does he think he can do this for her? As a special favour?

He says yes and she goes over it again, making sure he's got the time straight. Like he's doing her some massive favour. The way he's feeling right now she could ask him to do just about anything and he would.

So now he knows – Callum and Abi lie to each other. He has a mistress, which is about as big a lie as there is, and now he knows she lies to him as well. And if she really loves him, she wouldn't do that, would she? He knows *he* wouldn't. If he was married to Abi, they'd never, ever lie to each other. They'd never need to.

There are cracks in the relationship and the thought of it, plus the memory of the way she kissed him as she left his house yesterday, send him back to his work with a spring in his step and a song in his heart.

PHIL

'Mic 1 to Sierra 5, Mic 1 to Sierra 5, over.'

He switched on his lapel mic and responded. Langford, the Chief of Security, was in the Control Room today which at least meant some sort of respite from Mic 2, whom everyone assumed to be his idiot love child. Even so, he still had to listen to the apparently obligatory lecture and offer assurances that he understood the company policy on personal calls before Langford got around to telling him, almost grudgingly, that Abi had rung. She'd asked if he could ring her back and stressed that it was urgent but he knew that didn't necessarily mean anything. Both she and Callum understood that was the only way they'd ever get a message through the practically impermeable membrane that was the Control Room.

He left Anna to continue patrolling the ground floor on her own for a few minutes while he went outside to make the call. Abi answered on the first ring and apologised immediately for disturbing him at work. 'I know they don't like you taking calls there.'

'Don't worry about it,' he said. 'What is it?'

'I don't know,' she replied. 'It's probably nothing, only . . . have you heard from Callum since yesterday?'

'Callum? Why? Where is he?'

'I don't know,' she said, a level of exasperation coming through loud and clear. 'Well, Bournemouth, in theory, giving this talk at some conference or other. Only they rang a few minutes ago in a bit of a flap because he hasn't turned up and they can't get hold of him on his mobile. They've just rung home to see if I've heard from him or have any idea where he might be.'

'Well, he's probably just misjudged it and got caught up in traffic. You know what the M27 can be like.'

'No, the thing is, he was already there,' she said. 'In Bournemouth. He rang me just before he left last night.'

'OK,' he said, processing this. 'So you've tried his mobile too, I suppose.'

'Just now. It goes straight to voicemail.'

'Where was he staying last night? Have you tried there?'

'I can't,' she said, and he listened while she gave him the gist of Callum's call just before he left. He leaned against the rail that separated the trolley area from the car park and tried to think of what to suggest. It wouldn't be out of character for Callum to change his plans at the last minute. And much as it grieved him to think such a thing about his own son, the boy could be supremely selfish at times. Letting his wife know where he was and what he was doing wouldn't necessarily have rated high on his list of priorities. But if he could be said to be utterly dependable in any one respect, it was professionally. His reputation mattered greatly to him and missing the start of any conference was not like him. Not like him at all.

'Do you know who this friend is?' he asked. 'The one who booked the apartment?'

'Yes. Bill Shawcroft. He's leading one of the seminars, I think.'

'And do you have a number for him?'

'No. But the conference people will.'

He asked her if she knew where the conference was taking place and she read the phone number to him from her calls list.

'It's the Royal Exeter,' she told him.

'Is that a hotel?'

'I think so.'

He wondered why Callum would have wanted an apartment away from the conference centre but decided he didn't want to wonder too hard. And if Abi hadn't had the same thought, he didn't see it as his place to nudge her in that direction.

'Where are you now?' he asked her.

'I've been in town,' she said. 'Just on my way home in case he's left a message on the answerphone.'

'And you'd know if he rang last night?'

There was a slight pause at the other end.

'I was out for a while but I wasn't late back. And anyway he'd have rung me on my mobile – he knew I was out. Phil . . . what do you think I ought to do?'

He thought he could hear genuine concern in her voice now. Until then he'd picked up on exasperation and bewilderment in equal measure but this was the first time she'd sounded worried, as if other possibilities were only now beginning to occur to her. He did his best to reassure her, told her she was doing the right thing in going home to check for messages. He suggested she stay there while he tried to get a number for this Bill Shawcroft. If they hadn't heard from Callum by the time he finished work, he'd ask a few of his mates on the force to look into it. For now, the best thing she could do was to make herself a nice cup of tea and sit tight. A bit of patience.

'It's Callum,' he said, trying to inject a lighter note into the conversation. 'You know what he's like. At some stage he's going to come waltzing in through the front door with a bunch of flowers in his hand. He's probably there right now.'

'Yeah . . . you're right,' she said, sounding about as confident as he felt.

And he didn't feel confident at all.

PETER WILKINSON

The field was off to the left, deep into Honer Lane, not far short of the halfway point of his afternoon walk. He'd taken the same route more or less every day for just shy of twenty years since he'd retired: turn out of Punches Lane and into Honer Lane, then up towards Pagham Harbour. Thirty minutes one way, turn around, thirty minutes back. Same route, several different dogs over the years.

For most of that time, he'd had Linda for company. It had been an established part of their daily routine – have lunch, load the dishwasher, quick cup of tea and maybe a brief nap, just to recharge the batteries. Then Nelson – or Pixie before him – would pick up his lead and come pottering into the lounge, nudging at their feet until they got the message.

For the past five years, it had been just him and Nelson. He didn't consider himself a particularly sentimental man and would have laughed at the suggestion that he was sticking to the same route every day as some sort of memorial to Linda, but the plain and simple truth was that he couldn't quite bring himself to walk anywhere else. He felt closer to her now on sunny afternoons, with the sun dipping behind the trees and the shadows stretching across the road, than he'd ever felt while she was actually there in person. She'd always been a compulsive chatterbox. He would have been quite happy to stroll along the country lanes and exchange no more than a few words the whole way, just soaking up the scenery, but she was uncomfortable with any sort of silence and could talk the hind legs off a donkey. Now he had all the peace and quiet he could wish for and no one with whom to share it. The silence stretched out ahead of him like Honer Lane itself.

He sighed and used the ball launcher to send Nelson scurrying along the road. The retriever skidded to a halt, sweeping the ball up into his mouth in one flawless movement before trotting back towards his master. Then suddenly, for no apparent reason, he stopped dead, pricked up his ears and shot off through the entrance and into the field.

Rabbits, thought Peter, stepping off the road in pursuit of his dog.

PART TWO

8

EARLIER: THURSDAY, 11ᵀᴴ SEPTEMBER

DANNY

If he was going to go through with it, he told himself, it was going to have to be today. It was too good an opportunity to miss. Monday the loan would have to be repaid to the Bellamys which left him with just three working days to pull it off. He'd managed to snatch a few moments at the end of work yesterday to do a quick search through cash sales over the last few weeks – *just in case*, he'd told himself. *If there's nothing in there that fits the bill, forget it.* Knowing all the time there would be.

He'd picked out a transaction for an item he knew they had in stock, which was in the right price range. Then he'd made a note of the customer's details and spent most of Sunday batting the whole thing back and forth, even though he was pretty sure deep down he was going to do it. He had to come up with the money somehow. Had to.

And today was the day. D-Day. Decision Day. Danny Day ha ha. The reason was simple. Yvonne, his manager, was on her way to Croydon for a training seminar and it was Jenny who would be acting manager for the day. Yvonne was as sharp as a tack, great to have in charge as long as you were doing all the right things but a nightmare if you were trying to slide something past her. The thought of those few seconds while he waited for her countersignature was so daunting, he wasn't sure he'd be able to go ahead if she was there.

Jenny, on the other hand, had fallen out of the stupid tree and hit every branch on the way down. Whenever she'd stood in for Yvonne in the past, the difference between the two of them had been appreciable. She was a compulsive worrier who started to come apart at the seams whenever the pressure was on. Normally they all dreaded it when she was in charge because she had such a way of adding to the stress of the day, you could almost comb it out of your hair by the time you got home. Now however it seemed for all the world as if the gods had given their blessing: *go ahead, son. Do it.*

As soon as he arrived at Estelle Roberts, he checked again to make sure the necklace was still in stock. It was priced at £474.99, which was just about perfect. In the event of refunds for anything in excess of £500, it was company policy that the manager would try to persuade the customer to exchange it for an alternative item around the same value. Under that figure, it was left to whoever happened to be serving to process the refund and simply get the manager to sign off on it. For such a relatively small sum they preferred not to place any more obstacles than necessary in the customers' way, so as to encourage them to return in future.

He already had £490 of the £650 he'd been expecting to pay back, which meant he'd have £964.99 by the end of the day if his nerve held. The other £35 or so wasn't even worth worrying about. He'd get that from somewhere, even if it meant tapping up his parents. And with Jenny in charge for the day, his chances of success had improved immeasurably. It was just a matter of picking the right moment.

For the first couple of hours business was maddeningly slow. Then, shortly after eleven o'clock, as he was about to sneak out the back and scream at the gods for toying with him, things picked up significantly. Not only were there several people inside the store, there was even the added bonus of a particularly awkward woman who was insisting that another customer had been served ahead of her out of turn. Jenny was called over to appease her and was starting to look flustered. He knew that if there was going to be an opportunity, this was it.

He was in the process of serving an elderly couple at the time. While they were looking at a selection of rings in the display case, he asked if they'd excuse him for a moment – he'd be right back. Then he walked over to the window, removed the necklace and brought it over to the till. He quickly tapped in his four-digit operator number, trying not to think too much about what he was doing in case it made him change his mind at the last minute. He tapped in -1 plus the stock number, remembering to look up and smile at the elderly couple as he did so.

The till recognised his entry and came up with -1 necklace at £474.99. He pressed Total and when asked for the customer details he pulled the slip of paper from his pocket and entered the name, postcode and house number of the original purchaser whose order he'd pre-selected on Saturday evening. Then he hit the address button.

While the returns form was printing, he counted out the notes in fifties and twenties, casting a nervous glance across to the elderly couple who, to his intense relief, were still undecided. Then he picked up the printed form and jotted down *Faulty clasp* as the reason for returning the item, scrawled an utterly illegible signature and took it over to Jenny as soon as he was ready, trying desperately not to remind himself that there was still time to back out if he wished. He might well be wading in it up to his thighs but the river hadn't been crossed just yet.

He hovered just out of Jenny's eyeline, taking huge encouragement from the anxious look on her face as she tried to appease two customers at once, each equally unwilling to back down. At an appropriate moment he slipped a pen into her hand, smiled apologetically and placed the form in front of her, asking her to sign for a refund. Barely taking in what was happening, Jenny checked the total, scribbled a quick signature and turned back to the customers. Danny walked away, his heart pounding like a marching band at Mardi Gras, and replaced the necklace in the window.

'Now then,' he said, returning to the elderly couple, the ultimate professional. 'Have we seen anything we like?'

He patted his trouser pocket to reassure himself that the money he'd taken from the till was still there. The worst, he knew, was over. At the end of the day, the tills would be checked against the refund forms and everything would match up. Jenny would countersign all the forms and they'd be filed away, never to see the light of day until the auditors decided it was time for a visit, which could be months away. They would discover then that they were a necklace short but it wouldn't be the only thing missing – there was always a stock deficit of some sort and any items unaccounted for were assumed to be the result of shop-lifting. As long as losses weren't significant, they'd not lose any sleep over it. Natural wastage was how they viewed it.

He knew this had to be a one-off. Others had tried similar schemes in the past and had come unstuck because they'd been too greedy, going to the trough too many times. If this was going to work it would be because he'd tried it just the once, left no trail for them to follow. A one-off, in and out quickly, was always in with a chance. And he felt good about this, as if somehow by taking such affirmative action when it was needed, he'd managed to turn around his fortunes.

Suddenly the sun was shining and anything seemed possible.

HOLLOWAY

'You'd think they'd let me have my own parking space here by now, wouldn't you?'

'Boss?'

'Special customer privileges? I was working it out on the way here. This is the sixth time this year. You don't think that ought to qualify me for a little "Reserved" plaque of my own?'

He backed up to allow the first group of mourners from the previous ceremony to pass through on their way to the car park. One down, plenty more to go. The place really was like a conveyor belt.

Tired of squinting into a refulgent sun which seemed unwilling to acknowledge that it was now September, Horgan removed his sunglasses from his top pocket and put them on.

'Goes with the territory, I suppose.'

'And what territory would that be?' he asked. 'The job or my age?'

Horgan smiled.

'Wish it *was* just down to the job,' Holloway sighed. 'Two of them have been family. Two others were friends. I've got to that stage in life where you start looking over your shoulder.' He thrust the tip of his tongue at the hole in the Polo mint he'd been sucking since they got out of the car. 'By the way, son,' he continued. 'You can leap in any time you like and tell me I'm not *that* old.'

'You're not *that* old, boss.'

'He said with conviction.'

More and more people were now using the footpath in either direction. They exchanged sympathetic nods with each other as they passed, total strangers united for a moment in time by shared misfortune. He glanced at his watch and decided they might as well move along and join the others who had been waiting for the past fifteen minutes or so for the funeral cortege to arrive. Until now he and Horgan had made a point of maintaining a respectful distance. It was important to be there in order to reinforce the message that they were all in this together. At the same time Holloway never lost sight of the fact that this was an intensely personal moment for the family. A little distance was needed to allow privacy and show respect.

'Did you and Phil Green ever work together?' Horgan asked, jiggling the keys in his trouser pocket.

'A bit . . . back in the day. Started more or less the same time as each other. We were at Littlehampton back then. I mean, we're talking more than thirty years ago now. Haven't really kept in touch since then . . . not like we should have.'

'He OK?'

'Phil? Yeah. One of the good guys. Steady Eddie, you know? Never showed any interest in CID or promotions or anything like that as far as I'm aware. Not one of your glory hunters. Quite happy to plod along doing the same job year in, year out.'

'He got out early though, didn't he?'

'Family reasons. Don't think his wife was ever very happy about him being in uniform. You know she died not that long ago. Couple of years, maybe?'

'Jesus.'

'Yeah. First his wife, now his boy.'

'Has he got any other children?'

'Nope.' They stood in silence for a few moments, each lost in his own thoughts. Holloway himself was divorced and almost totally estranged from his ex-wife. If they spoke at all, they maintained an appropriate degree of civility but there was always an edge to it, as if recriminations were lurking just around the corner, waiting to pounce. As for his two children, they had lives of their own now. They did their best not to take sides but he suspected any sympathies they had would be with their mother if it came to it. Irrelevant anyway – they'd both moved far enough away to make visits difficult to co-ordinate and contrived when they did take place. Even so, he wouldn't trade places with Phil Green for anything. No one should have to do what he'd be doing today.

As he and Horgan approached, some of the mourners started to make a move from the waiting room into the chapel, prompting others, who had been guiltily enjoying the sunshine, to do the same. Holloway watched as they shuffled forward, collecting an order-of-service programme from a woman just inside the doorway and leaving the front row vacant as they took their seats. He'd already interviewed many of them during the first few days of the investigation; the others he'd be seeing in due course. Logic and experience told him that someone in there was harbouring a piece of information, however inadvertently, that might give them the impetus needed to drive the case forward and as far as he was concerned, that couldn't come soon enough.

The facts of the case were easy enough to establish. Callum Green had been battered to death with a large wooden implement (presumed to be his own baseball bat which was missing from the boot of his car) on the evening of Monday, 25th August. It was his wife – widow – who'd told them about the bat. She'd always been unhappy about it being there but he'd insisted on having it to hand – *because you never know*.

He'd been found in his BMW convertible in a dip that was hidden from view unless one walked into the field itself. A half-hearted attempt had been made to delay its discovery even further by dragging loose branches across it, but whoever was responsible had clearly given this up as a bad job, either because there were too few branches available or for fear of being disturbed.

The elderly man who discovered the body the following afternoon had walked back towards Manor Lane before eventually flagging down a passing car. Unfortunately (the ultimate in Sod's law as far as Holloway was concerned), there had been the mother of all rainstorms on the Monday evening which had turned the field into a quagmire, all of which meant that by the time the occupants of the car had also waded across the field and had a good look, any physical evidence had been either washed out or sufficiently compromised for it to count as useless.

An approximate time of death at least had been quickly established. The scene-of-crime guesstimate of sometime between 7 and 10 p.m. on the Monday evening was borne out by the autopsy and was narrowed down still further by the phone call, logged at 7.28 p.m., from Green himself to his wife to say he'd be leaving for Bournemouth in due course. It wasn't immediately clear what his car was doing in South Mundham if he was meant to be driving in the opposite direction but the calendar app in his mobile revealed that he had a dinner reservation for Friday evening at the Walnut Tree. A quick follow-up call established that he'd been there sometime between quarter to eight and eight o'clock to make the booking in person. And the reason why he might have driven ten miles in the wrong direction rather than just phone it through became clearer when they checked his text messages and voicemail. A woman who lived in Honer Lane had been expecting him sometime around eight. He'd been found no more than 400 yards short of Hannah Reid's cottage.

So they were clear about the *when*. The *who*, on the other hand, looked like being a different proposition altogether. Green, it seemed, had been the antithesis of his father. It didn't take long for a picture to emerge of an arrogant, confrontational, opinionated young man with more money than sense and an inability to look beyond his own interests that strayed into the pathological.

He'd already come to the attention of the authorities on two separate occasions. In April 2007, at the age of nineteen, he'd been questioned about an affray at 2 a.m. outside Liquid in Portsmouth in which two Polish youths, having been subjected to a series of racist taunts, had then been assaulted by half a dozen lads who'd followed them out of the nightclub. Three years later his name had surfaced in an investigation into a revenge attack at a party in Barnham which Green and a handful of friends had gatecrashed and subsequently been asked to leave. Even though neither incident had resulted in criminal charges being brought, his name was out there and it told a story.

Professionally, at a superficial glance at any rate, he'd been bounding from one roaring success to the next. Although relatively young, he'd already made a name for himself in network marketing and had been headhunted by a large American corporation with offices in London and several other European capitals. Employers and colleagues alike had been fulsome in their praise, describing him as energetic, enterprising, sharp as a razor. Gift of the gab, by all accounts. He was a man who was going places – no one was in any doubt about that.

The moment Holloway's team started to look more deeply into his financial dealings however, it was like stepping out onto Spaghetti Junction wearing blinkers. Or, as Horgan put it, like tugging at a nest of cable wires. Just as you thought you'd managed to isolate one of them, it dragged a host of others out with it and tracking back through the various knots to the junction box was a nightmare.

There were donations, loans, down payments, multiple transactions involving transfers of large sums of money, both into his various accounts and back out again via intermediaries to financial institutions in a number of different countries. Complex didn't come near. It was going to take quite a while to unravel it all sufficiently to get a better idea of what he'd been up to but one thing was clear: there was an awful lot more money passing through than could possibly be accounted for by his income from ACI, substantial though that was. Callum Green's hands were looking distinctly grubby and, judging by some of the names that were already starting to emerge, he hadn't been too fussy about where he'd been putting them. Wading through a directory of that calibre was going to present a host of problems.

Holloway was jolted out of his reverie by a gentle nudge to the ribs from Horgan. Away to his left he could see the funeral cars as they made their sedate, respectful way through the shade thrown by a row of trees and neatly trimmed hedges, before drawing to a halt in front of the chapel. They were preceded by a tall man in full mourning regalia, complete with black top hat and gloves, wing-collar shirt and Ascot tie, Oxford shoes polished to within an inch of their life.

Holloway and Horgan watched from the doorway as the cars emptied and other formally attired employees moved into dignified action. Holloway caught his first glimpse of Abi Green, dressed simply in a knee-length black dress, looking at once attractive and vulnerable. At her side was a tall, square-shouldered man whom Holloway assumed to be her brother – he was meant to be flying in from Lyon when he'd last spoken with her. No sign of her parents though, which told a tale.

Phil Green came round from the other side of the car and joined her briefly to check she was OK, then walked over to join the other pall-bearers, taking his place at the head of the coffin. Together they hoisted it onto their shoulders, steadying themselves to make sure everyone was ready before the procession made its way indoors. Holloway and Horgan lingered for a moment, waiting until everyone else was seated before stepping inside.

At the entrance Horgan took hold of his colleague's elbow and nodded in the direction of the footpath where a woman was hurrying towards them, head bowed. As she drew closer Hannah Reid looked up and nodded without saying a word, then walked past them and took a seat at the rear of the chapel. Her arrival seemed to go unnoticed by everyone else.

'Jesus,' whispered Horgan, as one of the attendants offered her an order-of-service sheet. She thanked him with a smile that barely made it to her lips before dying away, exhausted.

Holloway watched her for a few seconds, then switched his attention back to Abi Green who was taking her seat at the very front, waiting for Phil to join her. Two women, both grieving for the man they'd lost, neither able as yet to come to terms with what had happened. Two lost souls with so much in common. And no way on this earth of making the connection.

ABI

She hadn't looked at the coffin since they got out of the car. Not once. Not even on the short walk down the aisle to the front of the chapel. Instead, she'd looked resolutely at the floor, avoiding the well-intentioned but no less intrusive looks of sympathy which would inevitably be coming her way. She didn't want to know who was or was not there. Didn't want to speculate as to what they might be thinking. Just wanted to get to her seat and block everything else out. Grit her teeth. Get it over with.

Having taken her place between Phil and Richie in the front row, she couldn't bring herself to look up from her shoes other than to consult the order of service. Phil had designed a split-page front cover, bearing two photos of Callum. One showed him at the age of six, straining to go higher and higher on a swing in his grandparents' back garden. Higher and higher. Pushing it just that little bit further every time. The other was more recent, a favourite of hers. She'd taken it herself at a party to celebrate his twenty-sixth birthday and she'd caught him unawares, managing to capture that sly, enigmatic grin she'd never been able to resist, the one that hinted at secrets she'd always believed herself to be a part of. *Us two against the world. You and me, babe. Cross my heart and . . .*

She wouldn't look at the coffin. Refused to invest in it any meaning it didn't merit. It was a box – expertly crafted but still just a box. There wasn't a single level on which she was prepared to accept that it was Callum in there. The Callum she'd known almost all her life no longer existed . . . if indeed he ever had. At some stage the curtains were going to draw slowly across as the rollers took the coffin on its way, but even then she wouldn't dignify it with as much as a glance. This wasn't the end. The life she and Callum had known had been blown apart long before she arrived at this soulless place – she just hadn't known it. She'd been feeding and caring for a corpse all this time.

Alongside her Richie held out a tentative hand as they stood for the first hymn. She grasped it, clinging on for dear life. She was so glad to have him there; so grateful he'd made the effort. When her parents had bought a farmhouse in Bourg-Saint-Andéol, they'd taken her younger brother with them and she'd seen very little of him since. They'd tried blackmail, threats, everything short of kidnap to force her to go with them, just as they'd gone out of their way to try to break up her relationship with Callum. So overt and virulent was their disapproval of him that right up until the last minute they were convinced she'd give way, to the extent that they'd even bought a ticket for her. But they'd misjudged her – she was eighteen and stubborn. She'd stood firm, moved in with Callum and his parents for the remaining weeks of her A levels and married him three years later.

Her parents had been implacable in their response. They'd contacted her just twice in the eight years since they left for the Ardèche: once to decline the wedding invitation in the most formal and hurtful tone imaginable and then, shortly after her twenty-first birthday, to inform her that they were handing over to her responsibility for a savings account, which they'd set up for her when she was very young (subtext: before she became damaged goods) and which was now worth something in excess of £12,500. It had felt at the time like a pay-off, a ritual washing of the hands, but in case it was actually intended as an olive branch of sorts, she'd written to thank them and asked how they both were. Neither had replied.

In such an atmosphere it had been difficult for her and Richie to maintain the sort of contact they would have liked. She could only guess at the emotional blackmail to which he'd been subjected because, even at the age of twenty-two, he still found it hard to shake off the feeling that any move towards her was a move away from them. But she'd been sure, when she phoned to tell him what had happened, that he would be there if he could. Just as she'd known her parents would not. She just hoped the price Richie would have to pay for this show of solidarity wouldn't be too exorbitant.

The hymn came to an end and they took their seats again. Behind her she could hear Alfie making his way to the front to deliver the tribute. He'd offered to do it and she'd been happy to accept. Neither she nor Phil would have been up to it and Alfie had known Callum at least as long as she had – and probably better, if recent revelations were anything to go by. Any tribute would be better coming from him. She'd spent half an hour or so with him, providing a few key dates he'd asked for and filling in blanks. He'd asked if there were any little anecdotes she'd like him to work in and she'd said no.

So now, eyes still glued to her shoes, she squeezed Richie's hand once more and did her level best not to listen to the sanitised, expurgated version of the life of Callum Green, which was starting to sound like one of the all-time great works of fiction. Easier to tune out, she suspected, than to suspend disbelief.

OWEN

He remembers the policeman. Not the two who were in the car park when he arrived, although he knows them too. They're the ones who came round to check what time Abi left his house. No, he remembers the other one, the one at the front – knew who he was the moment he walked past, carrying the coffin. Looks a lot older now but he'd recognise him anywhere.

First time he saw him, he was marching through the school playground, taking Callum out through the school gates. Everybody was buzzing, saying, 'Callum Green's been arrested', until they realised it was just his dad come to collect him. Three-day suspension for persistent bullying. No wonder his dad looked so cross.

He remembers pressing his head against the railings as he watched the two of them walk off down the road: the big, angry policeman walking two paces ahead of his son. Callum didn't look quite so full of himself now. His turn to be scared to death for once. He wished he could have been there when they got home – would have loved to watch Callum getting his come-uppance. Now that his dad knew the sort of things he'd been doing every day at school, maybe that would put a stop to it. He *was* a policeman after all.

But the moment his suspension was over, Callum was back at school and things were just as bad as before. Worse, if anything – cornered him in the playground first chance he got, accused him of dobbing him in – and it was obvious after the first day back that Callum's parents had no more influence over him than the teachers. He was free to do what he liked.

Then, not long after that, same policeman on their doorstep. No uniform this time. Wanted to speak to him with his mum there. Off the record, he said. Just a friendly word, although that wasn't true – nothing friendly about it. Didn't smile once.

He said he wasn't about to excuse his son for the things he'd done in the past but neither was he going to let him be blamed for things he *hadn't* done. Callum had come home upset because he'd been accused of locking Owen in the drama store cupboard during the lunch interval. The school would have sent him home again if another teacher hadn't stuck her nose in and said it couldn't have been Callum – he'd been with her all lunch hour.

The policeman had leaned forward in his chair until he was really close to him; said being bullied was a horrible thing but so was making up lies about other people and if it hap-pened again there would be consequences. And his mum had got really cross – asked him to leave. Slammed the door after him. 'Blooming cheek,' she'd said. 'Telling me how to bring up my own child.' Next day she went to the school and told them

Owen wouldn't be coming back. She could do a better job of teaching him on her own.

So no, he hasn't forgotten the policeman. He can see him now, sitting next to Abi, while Alfie Parker tells everyone what a wonderful person Callum was. He wishes someone would stand up and say that this is all lies. He can't be the only person here who knows what Callum was really like. But this is what you do at funerals, he's learned. He remembers some of the things Mr Mitchell said when they buried his mother. How she'd been unlucky to die so young – no mention anywhere of the cigarettes that stank the house out. Two packs a day, even when she knew they were killing her. That's not bad luck. That's just stupid and selfish. But everyone had nodded and dabbed at the corners of their eyes when he said it. 'Wonderful mother', he'd called her. So wonderful she spent the last two years of her life sitting around the house in the same dressing gown she wore to bed. Went months without having a decent wash, let alone a bath. Smelled like sick most of the time. Nothing wonderful about that. But you don't say that sort of thing at funerals because people don't want the truth. It will make them sad. And the point is, they're already sad enough.

He looks at the other person next to Abi, the one who keeps holding her hand. This must be her brother who's come all the way from France. She doesn't know him very well and he knows whose hand she'd rather be holding if she could choose. He hasn't seen her since that night, the one he had to lie about – 8.52, he'd told the police, just like she asked him to. One of them, the older one, said that was very precise, but he knew they'd say something like that so he'd already worked out what he was going to say. Told them he'd noticed because he was supposed to be at the cinema at nine and he was going to be late. They asked what film and he was even able to show them the ticket receipt which shut them up pretty quickly.

She's been busy since then so she hasn't had a chance to thank him for helping her but maybe once this is all over she'll come round and see him again. And when she sees the surprise he has for her, he knows she's going to be thrilled. He hasn't forgotten that she kissed him on the cheek last time.

PHIL

The funeral director suddenly materialised alongside them and asked if they were ready to accompany him. He escorted them out through a side door and into a small courtyard, where they waited like society hosts to receive everyone's condolences: Abi self-conscious but stoical, her brother slightly bewildered by the sea of unfamiliar faces. Not that he was alone in that – Callum's life had exploded in so many directions in recent years, it was difficult to keep up. There were a few of his old school friends from way back and a number of others Phil vaguely recognised but for the most part he was dependent upon each person offering a few contextual words of introduction.

Holloway and Horgan were last in line. He thanked them for coming and asked if they needed to dash off. If not, Abi had organised an open bar and some food (he'd always hated the word *wake*) at the Chichester Park Hotel just around the corner. There was a moment's hesitation, which felt a little like reluctance giving way to a sense of propriety, before Holloway agreed.

Half an hour later he found the two of them in a corner, clutching plates of sandwiches and mini sausages and looking about as inconspicuous as a cow in a wedding photo – runaway winners of any Spot-the-Policeman competition. Horgan he barely knew but Andy Holloway was someone he'd worked with a long time ago and for whom he'd always had a sneaking regard. Not a friend exactly – their career paths had gone in very different directions and they'd seen too little of each other – but nevertheless someone he'd viewed as a kindred spirit. Everyone said Holloway was a safe pair of hands. Inasmuch as he could take consolation from anything under the present circumstances, that was something at least.

Both of them turned to balance their plates on the window sill as they saw him approach. They all shook hands and he thanked them again for coming. When Holloway asked how he was bearing up, he offered a grim smile.

'You see the flowers before you came over?' he asked. 'The wreaths?'

'We did. Pretty impressive display.'

'Read the cards by any chance?'

Holloway returned his look without blinking.

'Most of them.'

'Yeah, thought you would,' he said. 'Always worth a look, eh? Never know what you might find in there.'

There was a pause and Holloway and Horgan exchanged a quick glance.

'I *did* notice, in case you were wondering,' he continued.

'Phil –'

'Only I was just thinking to myself on the way over here . . . twenty plus years on the job, I don't know how many names

I came across in all that time. Must run into the tens of thousands, I'd have thought. And some of them you wouldn't believe, you know? The things people call their kids nowadays, no wonder they turn out the way they do, poor sods. But tell you what – all those names, you know how many Ezras I came across?'

There was a crash from the far corner where a plate had been knocked from the table, sending vol-au-vents spilling to the floor. A couple of bystanders quickly stooped to retrieve them and share a joke with the guilty party.

'Fingers on one hand,' he continued. 'That's how many. And you know how many of those were arrogant enough to feel they didn't even need to put their surname on a card cos everyone would know who they were anyway?'

'I was hoping you might be able to offer an alternative explanation,' said Holloway.

'You and me both,' said Phil, wiping a thin film of sweat away from his forehead. 'Then again, what do I know? It's not like I ever made much of an effort to get my head round what Callum was up to. Network marketing, portfolios, trust funds … *motivational speaking*,' he said, wrapping speech marks around the words. 'Way over my head. You want the honest truth, I haven't got a clue what he did on a day-to-day basis or who he mixed with. Sad or what?'

Holloway, he realised, hadn't taken his eyes off him for a moment. Not even when the plate fell to the floor.

'You don't know for a fact that there's any connection there?' he asked.

'For a fact? No. I was kind of hoping you'd tell me it's a different Ezra altogether. You saying this is the first you've heard of it?'

Holloway pursed his lips before answering.

'His name hasn't surfaced in all of this before today.'

'What about the Bellamys?'

He shook his head.

'You wouldn't lie to me, would you?' Phil asked, watching closely for the slightest hesitation. He sensed they were both on the defensive for some reason. 'Not about something like this?'

'No. I wouldn't lie to you.' Holloway's reply was decisive and convincing. He turned to lift his cup from its precarious perch on the window sill and took a sip from it. 'There are things I might not tell you – you know that.'

'Yeah, I've had the lecture.'

'I can't let you play any sort of active part in the investigation. You've got to leave it to us to do our jobs and trust us to get it right. We're not going to be able to keep you updated on every detail that comes across the desk. But if you ask me a direct question, I'm not going to lie to you, OK? If I can't answer, I'll say so.'

Phil took a deep breath and ran his fingers through his hair. For what it was worth, he believed him. It chimed with everything he knew of the man.

'But you're not that surprised,' he said, more an observation than a question. 'Are you?'

'This isn't really the place,' said Holloway, looking around as if expecting to be interrupted at any minute. 'Or the time.'

'So is this one of the things I'm not supposed to ask about?'

And the lack of response told him all he needed to know. He'd been given as clear an answer as he was going to get.

OWEN

Willie thinks he's crazy. Says he's got no chance. Total waste of money – he ought to sell it and get whatever he can for it. Does he really think she's going to be interested? Has he looked in the mirror lately?

Then again, Willie always feels threatened whenever he thinks his own circumstances might be about to change. And besides, he wasn't there earlier. He didn't see the way she kept her eyes fixed on the floor, as if forcing herself not to turn round and look at him. She knew she couldn't do that without others noticing and that would look bad. You can't ask someone else to come and sit next to you at your husband's funeral, can you? Even if it *is* what you want more than anything else.

But he's not fooled for one minute.

He knows she would have if she could.

9

NOW: MONDAY, 6TH OCTOBER

HOLLOWAY

Detective Superintendent Marie Loneghan was a cold, calculating, ambitious bitch with an eye for the main chance and legs she was happy to spread for anyone in a position to enhance her career. Alternatively, she was a calm, perceptive professional who did not suffer fools gladly and had high expectations of everyone in her team, to which she herself measured up at every turn. In short, she polarised opinion without seeking to do so and which camp anyone belonged to was a matter of personal preference.

Minor considerations such as actually having worked with her counted for very little. Indeed, Holloway suspected some of her loudest critics would have had trouble picking her out of a line-up but that wasn't going to stop them having their say. He'd always defended her in the strongest terms but was no longer under any illusion that her detractors might be converted. The only weapon he had at his disposal was first-hand experience – her critics were armed with prejudice and personal grudges, a far more pernicious and persuasive combination.

She was sitting across the table from him now, looking sharp and alert in a dark grey trouser suit and open-necked blouse. She often asked for a quick word before they joined the rest of the team for the morning briefing and today's promised to be one of the more positive sessions in recent weeks. Any arrest was always good news, even if grim satisfaction sometimes seemed more the order of the day than high fives and fist pumps. The Jamie Barrett case had finally broken open and even though his body had not as yet been recovered, his mother's live-in boyfriend had been charged with his murder. He was still screaming his innocence from the rooftops but CCTV footage had come to light which blew a hole in his previous statements. A wedge had been driven between him and Jamie's mother, who had been covering for him out of misguided loyalty and a refusal to face reality. Without her crucial support, everyone was confident he would fold in the next twenty-four hours. Maybe then they'd have some idea what he'd done with Jamie's body and the whole sorry episode would be brought to a close.

It wasn't the unqualified success they'd been hoping for at the outset but they were used to dealing in cold realities and the plain and simple truth was that they'd known for some time that they weren't going to find the boy alive. It was a result of sorts though, and a much-needed one which might earn them a welcome brief spell out of the firing line. If nothing else, it meant their attention could now focus solely on Owen Hall and whether his strange tale of a disappearing girl might have anything at all to do with the murder of Callum Green in South Mundham.

The interviews with his neighbours had unearthed a few surprises. Neil Horgan wasn't the only member of the team with doubts about whether the girl in the car even existed. The general consensus of opinion was that Hall had invented her and was throwing up some sort of smokescreen in an attempt to run them ragged. He'd even disowned the photofit he'd helped them to put together, claiming he wasn't very good with faces. It was 'sort of like her' was as far as he was prepared to go, which struck almost everyone as hugely convenient.

Holloway was reluctant to dive head first into the pool of common consensus just yet but even he hadn't expected much joy to come from canvassing the neighbourhood, given that Hall was adamant she'd never been to his house. He'd viewed it as a box they had to tick before they could move on, but then again, ticking boxes was how they'd managed to close the Jamie Barrett case. Good, honest plodding.

For most of the previous morning, their suspicions had been confirmed. The photofit, for what it was worth, had been shown to everyone living in the same road as Hall and not one of them could remember having seen the girl. They described him as a strange lad, polite enough but almost pathologically shy. Didn't go out much apart from when he was working. No social life they were aware of. He did have the occasional visitor but they were presumed to be business callers. The elderly couple next door remembered a girl leaving his house just a few weeks earlier but they insisted that she hadn't looked anything like the photofit.

They might have left it at that but Holloway had instructed them to cast the net a little wider just in case, and that had eventually brought their first piece of good news. A woman serving in the local fish-and-chip shop had been on the point of handing back the photofit when she took another look and said, 'It's not

Julie, is it?' She pointed out that it wasn't a brilliant likeness but it looked a bit like young Owen's girlfriend. The woman knew Owen well because he came in every Saturday evening, regular as clockwork – same order every time: large cod and chips and a battered sausage.

A couple of times recently a girl had come in and bought it for him midweek – Tuesday and Thursday, maybe? The first time she'd referred to herself as his girlfriend. 'Nice girl, very chatty.' The woman remembered thinking she'd be a good person for Owen to be around as she'd probably bring him out of himself. And then the second time she'd come in, the girl had been much more subdued, her face badly bruised. She'd tried to make out a cupboard door had swung back and caught her just below the eye but that didn't explain the red marks on the other side of her face as well. 'Not many doors come back and take a second or third swing at you, know what I mean?'

Once they'd added the facial bruising to their description of the girl, they soon found other people who remembered her. She'd posted a parcel for Owen in the local post office; bought a box of After Eight mints from the sweet shop because they were Owen's favourites; called in at the chemist's for some lozenges because her boyfriend Owen had a sore throat. Not everyone knew this Owen she was talking about but they remembered her, all right – especially the bruising. So one thing was settled, that was for sure. The girl was no figment of Owen Hall's imagination.

And then his version of events at the petrol station had been further supported when DC Walker – *it would be him!* – had called Holloway over to look at the CCTV again. When they'd first viewed it their focus had been entirely on the truck and on the inside of the store where Hall had queued for the mints before kicking off outside the toilet. Walker had used footage taken from a different angle and identified a blurred figure, hovering on the edge of the shot, heading away from the forecourt towards the grass verge which separated it from the main road. The figure disappeared behind a parked lorry, then reappeared for a second or two before being swallowed up by the bush at the back of the tyre-pressure gauge. Seconds later the same figure re-emerged, scuttling back in the opposite direction before disappearing for good from the edge of the screen, presumably heading for the rear of the petrol station.

They had done what they could with the image but there was no way of making the figure any clearer. It was almost certainly a male but beyond that it was impossible to determine anything for certain. The only inference to be drawn from it was that his movements were strange to say the least. It was difficult to imagine why he would have chosen to wander off in that direction unless he wanted to use the bush as a screen.

They'd gone back to the footage of the truck, synched the timelines on the two cameras and identified the five-second slot when the figure would have been at the far side of the bush. They'd run it several times, stared so intently at the screen that their eyes hurt, but the images were so grainy and dark that it was impossible to make anything out for certain. Some of Holloway's colleagues were adamant they could see something near the window on the far side of the truck but he couldn't be sure it was anything more than wishful thinking.

There was enough there though to add at least a shred of credibility to the version of events Hall had been peddling.

'I'm not sure whether this is good news or bad,' said Loneghan, making a note on her iPad.

'It's just news, Ma'am,' he replied, forgetting himself for a moment. In front of everyone else Loneghan always insisted on the appropriate form of address but when they were together like this she usually preferred to keep things on a less formal basis. 'It's another piece in the jigsaw, that's all. The more we've got, the clearer the picture.'

'But if we could have proved she *doesn't* exist, at least we'd have known for sure Owen Hall isn't being straight with us and must have something to hide.'

Holloway sniffed.

'Always difficult to prove a negative. The best way to look at it now is that we've answered one question and can move on to the next.'

'Which is what?'

'Take your pick. Was she in the truck? If she wasn't, why is Hall trying to make out she was? And if she was, what happened to her? Where is she now?'

'How about: who is she?'

The phone on her desk rang. She checked the caller ID, then lifted and replaced the receiver.

'Yeah. That too,' said Holloway. 'We're not getting anywhere as yet with *Julie Mowbray, Investigative Journalist*, that's for sure, so we're assuming it's fake.'

'So this could be someone messing with Owen Hall's head, right?'

'Could be. Assuming he's not the one who set it all up.'

Loneghan frowned. 'But why would he do that?'

'Exactly. Brings us back to was she in the car or not,' said Holloway, sketching a loop with his forefinger. 'If you ask Neil, and most of the others for that matter, she never was. They'll tell you Hall is either in league with this girl for some reason we haven't identified yet or he's done something to her and is blowing smoke up our collective rear end to cover himself in case we ever connect him to her.'

Loneghan smiled.

'Wasn't Neil equally adamant that she didn't even exist?'

'He was,' said Holloway, 'but to be fair, the fact that we now know she does makes very little difference to his argument.'

'But you're still not convinced by it?'

'No.'

'Why not?'

Holloway absent-mindedly played with his mobile, turning it end over end on her desk as he marshalled his thoughts.

'Because Owen Hall is not an idiot. It's ironic really – that's about the only thing we all agree on and yet, for their theory to work, he'd have to be just plain stupid.'

'Explain?' Loneghan pushed her iPad away from her and leaned back in her chair.

'OK. What's the one thing more than anything else that makes Owen Hall look iffy? I mean, we've got one person saying a girl has disappeared and a handful of witnesses at the petrol station saying they never saw her at any stage. And the two officers sent to check it out decided in all probability it was a hoax. What made them think that?'

'Owen Hall's connection to South Mundham?'

Holloway shook his head vigorously. 'They didn't know who he was at that stage. And the name probably wouldn't have meant anything to them anyway.'

'The fact that he ran off?'

'Could have been any number of reasons for that. Back up a bit.'

Loneghan thought about it, fingering the silver cross on her necklace. 'The CCTV,' she said.

'Right. There's no sign of her getting out of the car. So this elaborate scheme of his is in danger of coming apart right from the outset, which begs the question: why try to pull this stunt somewhere they've got security cameras? I mean, if I wanted to make up a story, the last thing I'd do is act it out with someone filming what's really going on. He could have chosen anywhere, told us they'd met in a car park in Eartham Woods or on the beach at West Wittering or in Pagham Harbour. Why in God's name would he drive all the way to Littlehampton and pick out a petrol station where there was bound to be CCTV?'

'Maybe he didn't realise there were cameras there.'

'So now he's stupid all of a sudden? I thought the whole idea underpinning this theory was that he's the exact opposite, that he's capable of putting together a complex scheme which is making us chase our tails. I don't see how it can work both ways.'

The phone rang again and this time Loneghan snatched it up and cut the call without even checking who it was. She rested the receiver on the desk and Holloway could hear the dialling tone buzzing away in the background.

'And then there's the way this girl was behaving before she disappeared,' he continued. 'I go into a chip shop, I'm there to buy chips, not trot out my life story. How many people do *you* know who introduce themselves to everyone they meet in shops and tell them they're so-and-so's girlfriend? Does that sound right to you?'

'No, but that could have been something she and Hall had worked out between them.'

'It could – but again, why? He could have taken her round to a few neighbours to introduce her himself, paraded her up and down the street if he wanted everyone to notice her. Why would he ask her to do it in such a bizarre way?'

Loneghan pushed a stray lock of hair back behind her ear.

'So you're saying she had to do it that way because she didn't want it to come to Owen's attention, right?'

'Not before she'd had a chance to disappear, no. Again, the only way he can be making all this up is if he's stupid.'

'Or very, very clever and working a double bluff?'

Holloway pinched the bridge of his nose, using thumb and forefinger to massage away an ache that had been developing since he'd woken that morning. He wished he'd thought to take a couple of paracetamol before setting out.

'That would be a real gamble,' he said, pulling back from the involuntary *Ma'am* at the last moment. 'And I know I'm no expert but I really don't think that's how his mind operates. This whole business of him plotting away and coming up with a scheme that Machiavelli would have been proud of – I just don't buy it. It's not him. You know about this numbers thing of his?'

Loneghan nodded.

'Well, *that*'s who he is. He's a numbers man. Thinks in straight lines. And even if he *was* that imaginative, even if he was capable of weaving an intricate web of lies to keep us all wrong-footed, there's still one thing that doesn't make sense.'

'Which is?'

'Why bother? I mean, why would he imagine for one moment that we needed wrong-footing? It's not like we've been swarming all over him. We had to question him about Abi Green's alibi and the fallout from that but we haven't hauled him in here and put him through the wringer. What on earth would make him think he needed to go to such lengths to throw us off a scent we hadn't even picked up in the first place? He's gone from insignificant bit-player to chief suspect in some people's eyes in one jump. Again, how can he be that stupid and so devious at one and the same time?'

'So you think he's being set up?' she asked.

'Not necessarily. But it makes at least as much sense to me as what we're being asked to believe. We need more answers.'

'More of your little boxes ticked,' she said with a smile.

'It's how we get there.'

'So what's next?' she asked, replacing the receiver on the phone.

Holloway picked up his mobile and put it in his pocket, taking the hint that the briefing was due to start any minute.

'I want to start by impounding his truck.'

10

EARLIER: SATURDAY, 13ᵀᴴ SEPTEMBER

PHIL

The day after the day after. One day at a time. Still on compassionate leave until Monday, although a part of him wondered if he might not be better off back at work where Anna's wacky conversation would have taken his mind off things. Then he remembered she'd booked the day off anyway because she was having her first competitive MMA bout that afternoon in Sittingbourne of all places. It was a hell of a way to go for a fight but he wondered even so about turning up to surprise her, see what all the fuss was about. Problem was, he didn't know exactly where the event was being held and ringing her to ask felt a bit iffy. He wasn't sure how it would look.

So instead he decided he might as well get started on painting the front of the house. It had been crying out for attention for some time now and he'd been putting it off, half-hoping the wet weather would arrive and put paid to laudable intentions for another summer. The sky was still clear though, the weather set fair for a few more days yet, so he was fresh out of excuses.

With the day stretching ahead of him, he took his time over breakfast and thought it all through. He'd need to pick up the paint and brushes which he'd been meaning to buy since the end of May. Then he'd have to drive over to Callum and Abi's . . . to Abi's place in Bosham to pick up the ladder which Callum borrowed last Easter to clear some of the gunk out of his gutters. He had to take her birthday card and present over anyway – nothing much, just a book about Amy Winehouse and a DVD of series 1 and 2 of *The Inbetweeners* which she'd missed on TV. Nice cup of tea and a chat there with Abi for an hour or so, as long as she wasn't too busy. Just to make sure she was bearing up, he told himself. Then he could pop down to the Anchor Bleu and have lunch on the terrace overlooking the quayside. Ploughman's and a pint of lager. If he took a paper with him, he could probably drag it out until two or three o'clock by the time he got back home. Paying homage to the god of procrastination, if there was such a thing, he told himself it probably wouldn't be worth getting started that late in the day. Might be better if he left any actual painting till the following morning. No problem either way. His time was his own. And he had lots of it.

It was 10.15 by the time he arrived at Homebase in Chichester. If he'd been thinking straight he probably would have chosen another DIY store, rather than one within spitting distance of the crematorium, but he was almost there before it dawned on him. And besides, if he was going to go out of his way to avoid anything with the slightest connection to Callum, he might as well pack up now and move out of the area altogether. *Suck it up,* he told himself.

Shortly after eleven he was heading down Walton Lane into Bosham. He followed the road round to the right, past the primary school, and pulled up outside Hedge End, the expensive four-bedroom detached house Callum had bought which was so much larger than they'd needed. Typical Callum extravagance. Playing to the galleries. The first property he and Sally had bought outright was a two-bedroom bungalow with a postage stamp for a back garden. It had been more than big enough, not just for them but for Callum too until he was three or four. They'd have rattled around inside Hedge End, never managed to find each other. That bungalow had set them back £21,250 – Callum had spent twice that on his car.

In the driveway was a dusty red Mitsubishi pickup, *Hall Gardening Services* and two phone numbers emblazoned on the side. He remembered Abi mentioning that she and Callum were getting someone in to turn their garden into something more presentable. More extravagance, he'd thought at the time. The garden had always looked OK to him. He wondered how much the decision owed to this mania nowadays for outdoing everyone else. Bigger, faster, flashier – anything, as long as it screamed out how much it had cost.

He could hear a chainsaw droning away in the back garden, so rather than ring the doorbell he walked down the path and in through the side gate, which he noticed had been given a fresh coat of paint and no longer creaked like something out of a Hammer horror movie. At the far end of the garden, driving a wedge into one of the birch trees which had always robbed the garden of much of its sunlight, was a tall, powerfully built man wearing a logger's helmet and earmuffs which presumably did their job effectively because there was no response at first when Phil called out. When he eventually caught sight of him out of the corner of his eye, he stopped what he was doing and pushed up the protective visor to get a better look. No smile.

No attempt at a greeting. Something wary, mistrustful in his expression.

'Abi here?' asked Phil. He put her present and card on the metal shoe scraper just outside the back door and watched as the gardener removed his heavy gloves. Slow, deliberate movements. Big boy this. Phil's first instinct was to wonder if he'd ever boxed. The protective glasses he'd been wearing beneath the visor were peeled off and a flash of recognition carried him back to the small courtyard at the side of the chapel – a long line of well-wishers filing past, offering meaningless words of comfort, and then suddenly there's this odd-looking lad, head and shoulders above everyone else, built like a brick shithouse and obviously uncomfortable in a suit, who shuffled past with his head down. A quick handshake, a few mumbled words and he was gone.

'I'm her father-in-law,' he explained.

'I know. We've m-met.'

'Is she in?' asked Phil.

'In Ch-Chichester.'

He'd shown no interest in moving from where he was, so Phil picked his way through several branches which had already hit the deck and were piled up in the centre of the lawn. 'Phil,' he said, holding out his hand. 'Phil Green.'

There was a moment's hesitation before the offer was reciprocated. When it was, Phil was impressed by the strength of the grip.

'Owen.'

He picked up the name, added it to the logo on the side of the truck and made the connection. A picture swam into focus, a dimly lit front room with a three-bar electric heater offering no more than a vague glow. A timid dumpling of a boy and his wheezing, overprotective mother. A vague sense of discomfort on his part because he hadn't really wanted to be there but Sally would have gone round and sorted it out herself if he hadn't and she wasn't always at her most rational when it came to defending Callum. And the kid *had* lied after all. He looked more closely now at the fully grown man standing opposite him and tried to find the boy within. It wasn't easy.

'You were at the funeral,' he said.

'Yes.'

'And you were one of Callum's friends at school, right?'

'I was Abi's f-f-friend.'

The stammer, maybe. That was the only real indication – that plus the little dig at Callum implicit in his last remark. He looked at the branches strewn across the lawn and the chainsaw propped up against the birch tree.

'Well, you certainly seem to have done all right for yourself. Your own business and all.' He looked around him. 'Got your work cut out here though.'

Hall looked at him for a moment, then turned his back.

'You c-came to our house,' he said.

'I'm sorry?'

'You c-came to our house. C-called me a liar.'

He put the helmet and safety goggles back on and picked up the gloves. Phil did his best not to take offence at the tone of voice. Some people, you have to make allowances for their lack of social skills. And besides, what he'd said was true. It was exactly what he *had* done.

'That was a long time ago, son,' he said, flicking one of the loose branches back into the pile with his foot. 'A lot's happened since then.'

'I wasn't lying.'

'Fair enough. I didn't come here for an argument, OK?'

'I wasn't lying.' He was facing Phil now, no more than three feet away. Everything in his posture oozed hostility and resentment.

'You really want to talk about this?' asked Phil.

'Your son was a b-bully.'

'Yes . . . yes, he was. But, as I recall, the reason I came to see you that night was because you'd accused him of something he hadn't done.'

'He was a b-bully. He used to p-pick on me every day.'

'I know, and I'm sorry about that. But that time it couldn't have been him because he was in a detention with another teacher.'

'How many times did you c-come round to our house and apologise for what he was doing?'

'Listen, Owen –'

'Not once. You didn't come round once. And the one time I g-got it wrong, you c-couldn't get there quick enough. You upset my mother.'

Phil held his hands up in apology.

'That's not what I intended. Look, let's just calm down a bit, shall we? I just came round to see Abi and drop off her birthday present. Any idea when she'll be back?'

His eyes narrowed as Hall suddenly started rocking back and forth, arms straight down by his sides and eyes screwed tight shut behind the goggles.

'Are you OK?' he asked. It looked for all the world as if he was about to have some sort of seizure. Hall mumbled something – it sounded like 'Please don't swear', although that didn't make a great deal of sense. Then his eyes sprang open and he reached down and picked up an adjustable spanner from a tool box which was on the ground next to him.

'Whoa,' said Phil, taking an involuntary step back, raising both hands, as a defensive measure this time.

'It's not his funeral,' Hall said, his voice almost a drawn-out groan.

'Excuse me?'

'I don't have to say nice things about him. I can say WHAT I LIKE!'

'Owen. I think you'd better put that down now, OK?' Phil was aware of a touch of apprehension for the first time. Ten, fifteen years ago this wouldn't have produced in him much more than a burst of adrenaline. He'd faced this sort of situation plenty of times at work and had never worried about the outcome. The instincts from his days in the ring were still there even now – without even thinking about it, he'd already calculated the arc in which the spanner would be swung, knew if he stepped inside and threw a straight left followed by a right hook somewhere in the groin area, Hall would collapse like a sack of potatoes, big as he was. But he wasn't sure instinct was enough. He knew he could handle himself better than most people his age but he *was* fifty-four. Much as he'd have liked to take the spanner from this kid and put him on his back, he was out of condition, his reflexes probably shot to pieces. There had to be better ways of dealing with the situation. He took another couple of steps back. Damn, he was big.

'I want you to g-go.'

'OK, look . . . I'm going. No problem.'

'I don't want to talk to you.'

'That's fine by me, son. Let's just put the spanner down, shall we?'

'I'm not your son.'

'No, you're not,' he agreed, taking another couple of steps towards the gate. To his relief Hall had stayed where he was and made no attempt to follow.

'Look, I'm sorry if I upset you, OK?' he said. 'That's not why I came here. I just wanted to call round, give Abi her birthday present and go. I'll leave it here, shall I?' He pointed to the package and card on the metal shoe scraper just outside the door. Hall still hadn't moved, the spanner still clenched in his fist. 'You tell her it's there, right?'

He turned and walked away, keeping an eye on Hall's reflection in the conservatory window – just in case. He watched him drop the spanner and pull on his gloves as if nothing had happened.

The chainsaw started revving up again even before he'd reached his car.

And he was the other side of Fishbourne before he remembered the ladder and pub lunch.

ABI

Phil's car was almost upon her before she realised who it was, travelling in the opposite direction. Instinctively she flashed her lights but he was already past her, much to the confusion of the three drivers behind him who all wondered why the pretty blonde in the flash car was trying to get their attention. She guessed that he'd probably been over to see her and tried not to feel guilty over her reasons for having missed him. It was just a latte. What was so wrong about having a coffee in town with a friend? Then again, she'd told Owen when they crossed in the driveway earlier that she had shopping to do in Chichester, so who was she kidding?

She let herself in, walked through to the conservatory where she opened a window to let Owen know she was home, put the kettle on and asked would he like a drink? He told her a glass of water would be fine. She noticed the package and card on the doorstep and he confirmed it was Phil who'd left them there before turning straight back to his work. She got the impression he was annoyed about something and wondered if she'd offended him by setting off for Chichester the moment he arrived or whether he'd brought the mood with him. He'd always been such a strange bundle of neuroses; even given their shared history, she still found it hard to identify predictable patterns in his behaviour.

She went to the back door and brought Phil's presents inside. Then she ran the cold tap and held a glass under it before filling another with lemonade and lime for herself, throwing in a couple of ice cubes for good measure. Her mobile beeped at her and she checked the text, smiling to herself when she saw who'd sent it. She tapped out a quick reply – Zizzi's would be just fine by her. She loved Italian and had been denied it more often than not because Callum had always preferred more traditional English cuisine. This would be a real treat, even though she felt obliged to remind herself of the need for a little perspective. It was just a birthday treat. Nothing more.

She called Owen in rather than taking the drinks out into the garden, which looked like a bomb had hit it. She sat on one of the stools at the breakfast bar and opened Phil's card. It was a picture of a girl in a broad-brimmed sunhat and flowery dress, sitting on a sun-drenched beach somewhere exotic. There was no printed message inside. Instead, he'd written:

Happy 27th Birthday

And underneath it:

Still our daughter ... always.
Phil.

Our. She blinked rapidly – Phil was such a sweet, sweet man. She was saddened by the thought of him driving all the way out to see her and then heading back to that house, which had been empty enough for him for the past two years and must seem even emptier now. The uneasiness kicked in again and she wondered whether she ought just to come clean about everything. She wasn't sure how much he'd worked out for himself about the way things had been with Callum in recent months. For a man who was pretty perceptive in any other context, he'd always had a bit of a blind spot where his son was concerned, possibly influenced by Sally, who'd worshipped the ground her boy walked on. She wondered whether it would be better to fill in a few gaps now or leave him with any illusions he still preferred to cherish. He would have to know sometime – and it would surely be better coming from her.

She reached for the parcel, which looked and felt like a DVD attached to a book. Owen came in, washed his hands at the sink and sat opposite her as she opened it. She smiled ruefully as she realised what was inside. She already had the Wine-house book – she'd bought it last Christmas with money Phil had given her. As for the DVD, she could have downloaded that for free any time she liked. Even so, she was touched by the gesture. It was the thought that mattered. In the absence of her own, he was like a father to her. She hoped nothing she might have to tell him would ever change that.

Owen was watching her over the rim of his glass. He seemed restless, his eyes skittering every which way, his foot tapping out an insistent beat on the tiled floor. Grumpy to excited in the space of five minutes.

'I've got you a birthday present too,' he said.

'Really?'

He nodded and started picking at his nails.

'That's really sweet of you,' she said, as surprised as she was touched. 'I didn't think you'd remember.'

'Thirteenth September. M-mine is thirteenth June. Nine months exactly.'

'Multiple of three,' she laughed.

'Multiple of three.'

'Well, you didn't need to – really. I honestly wasn't expecting anything.'

He stood up. 'I left it in the truck. I was going to give it to you tonight but I c-can get it now if you like.'

'Tonight?' she asked.

He blushed, eyes fixed on the breakfast bar where his fingers were dancing to an arrhythmic beat all their own.

'I was wondering if I you'd like to c-come round for d-dinner,' he said hesitantly. 'F-for your b-birthday.'

'Oh, Owen –'

'You're p-probably b-b-busy, I 'spect,' he said, and it was clear from his body language exactly how much it had cost him to ask in the first place. The likely need for retreat was firmly imprinted in every gesture.

'No, really Owen. That's such a lovely thought,' she said, clutching at his sleeve. 'Really it is. And I'd love to take you up on it, only –'

'That's OK,' he said, hurriedly.

'No, honestly. It's just that I've already got something arranged for tonight. A friend from work – you know, the bookshop? We're going out for a meal, otherwise I'd have loved to come round.'

'It's OK.'

'You're sure?'

He nodded. 'I just didn't want you to have to spend your b-birthday on your own . . . you know.'

'It's such a kind thought. Thank you.'

There was an awkward pause, during which she let go of his sleeve and thanked the Lord she hadn't said something crass like, *maybe another time.* She was genuinely fond of Owen and hadn't managed as yet to absolve herself entirely from blame for what he'd gone through at school but she had to admit that in emotional terms he was high maintenance – there was no escaping that. And, however cruel it might sound, she wasn't sure she was up to spending a whole evening with him.

'Do you still want me to g-give you the present though?' he asked apprehensively.

'Of course,' she said, grasping a lifeline, and that appeared to galvanise him once more. He disappeared through the conservatory and out into the driveway, returning a minute or so later with a small package and a card which he placed carefully on the breakfast bar in front of her. She opened the Forever Friends card with the trademark picture of a bear on the front, this time blowing a dandelion clock. Inside he'd signed it simply, *Owen*. She made all the appropriate noises, told him how sweet it was and put it to one side.

Then she lifted the package which felt like a long, thin box: some sort of confectionery, she told herself, like wafer-thin mints or chocolate toffees. Owen knew all about her sweet tooth. She shook it gently and held it up next to her face.

'How many guesses do I get?' she asked playfully.

He shook his head. 'Open it.'

'Nice wrapping,' she joked, trying to find a way through the multiple layers of Sellotape. It seemed disrespectful to dig a nail in and simply tear the wrapping apart so she picked away at it until eventually she managed to prise one of the pieces of tape loose and ease the paper back over the gift. His eyes, when she looked up, were gleaming like fireflies and her heart sank even before she saw the jeweller's name engraved in italics. Already she suspected this was going to need levels of diplomacy she feared were beyond her.

She lowered the dark blue box to the breakfast bar, then slowly opened it to reveal a white-gold necklace curved into a wishbone shape in which a number of small diamonds were embedded. Mouth agape, she lifted it oh so gently from the box and held it out in front of her, where it picked up the sunlight flooding in through the kitchen window and sang to her like a cathedral choir. It was perfect – there were probably more imaginative words for it but they escaped her for the moment. Perfect would have to do. It reminded her of the sort of gift

Callum had sprung on her from time to time, soon after the money had started pouring in. He'd come home from work with a smile on his lips and a gleam in his eye, put his arms around her waist and tell her to close her eyes. Then he'd produce something not unlike this necklace and look on with amusement as she shrieked and dashed off to the nearest mirror so that she could see what it looked like. The way it whispered seductively to her now as she held it up in front of her, she knew it was a case of back off right away or dig an even deeper hole for herself.

'Owen,' she said, lowering it carefully back into the box.

'Try it on,' he urged her.

'Owen, I can't. I'm really sorry. It's a beautiful, *beautiful* present and I'm so touched. But I can't possibly accept this.'

'Here ... let me help you,' he said, seemingly oblivious to what she was saying until she reached out and closed the box with a snap that was sharper than she'd intended.

'No, really,' she said. 'I can't. It's – it's too much, Owen. It must have cost you an absolute fortune.'

'No –'

'Please. I need you to take it back.'

He sank back onto a stool, incomprehension writ large across his features.

'I d-don't understand,' he said, and for one awful moment she feared he might be about to burst into tears. 'It's for your b-birthday. D-don't you like it?'

'Like it? I *love* it. It's stunning.'

'So why won't you try it on? I d-don't understand.'

She could see the confusion and hurt in his eyes and wondered how best to deal with this. The one thought that screamed out to her was that she couldn't accept the necklace. This was just wrong. Too inappropriate for words.

'I know you don't,' she said, raising one hand to his cheek. 'And it's a beautiful present, Owen. I don't want you to think that I'm not grateful, but something like this . . .' She took her hand away, concerned that an incorrect signal now would only confuse things further. 'Listen,' she continued, 'you and I are really good friends, right? We've known each other for a long time now.'

'Twenty-one years and three months.'

'Right,' she laughed, happy for an excuse to lighten the mood for a moment. 'Twenty-one years and three months.'

'Multiple of three.'

'Right. And because we're such good friends it's fine for us to buy each other a little something when birthdays and Christmas come round. Like Phil for instance,' she said, picking up the DVD and book. 'He came to see me and drop off these presents, right? They didn't cost a lot of money but they didn't need to because it's the thought that counts. That's what friends do. But this necklace – it's just not the sort of thing friends give as birthday presents. It's something a husband might buy for his wife or a man would think of getting for his girlfriend if they were involved in a serious relationship. It . . . it's on a different level. Do you understand what I'm trying to say?'

A cloud passed over his face and she began to realise that he understood only too well. First the offer to cook dinner for her and now the necklace. She was the one who'd been slow on the uptake.

'If C-Callum had bought it for you, you'd have t-tried it on,' he said, his breathing coming now in short, sharp bursts.

'Yes. Yes, I would. Because he was my husband.'

'But I lied for you,' he said.

'You what?'

'When the p-police came round to ask what time you left, I t-told them it was later than it really was.'

She picked up her glass and took a sip, then swirled what was left of the ice cube around inside the liquid and drained it. She rose and walked over to the sink where she rinsed the empty glass before opening the dishwasher and placing it inside. She'd always suspected this moment would come, although it was usually Phil she'd imagined sitting opposite her. Now it was here, she wondered how best to approach it. Maybe honesty was the best solution. Maybe she ought to come clean and tell Owen first as a dummy run. Then tell Phil. Then the police. Maybe then, last of all, she could start being honest with herself.

'I didn't mean for you to lie to the police,' she said, sitting down opposite him again.

'You told me to,' he protested. 'You s-said on the phone.'

'I know. But what I meant was for you to cover for me if Callum happened to say anything to you. I didn't mean the police. How could I? If you think about it, there *were* no police at that stage. It was before we knew anything had happened to Callum.' She picked up the two birthday cards and started fanning herself with them as she picked her way through the route ahead. 'Look, I need to tell you something, OK? Only you can't tell anyone just yet. It's our secret, right?'

He thought about it for a moment, then nodded.

'The thing is, that evening when I came round to see your plans for the garden, I didn't go straight home afterwards. I'd arranged to meet someone from work, just for a quick drink, and I didn't . . . I didn't want Callum to know about it, because he could be funny about things like that. You know what he was like, right? Then, when I got home there was a missed call on the home phone and I was worried it might have been him, trying to get hold of me there because my mobile had run out of battery. I knew he'd want to know where I'd been so I asked you to say I'd stayed with you for a bit longer in case he asked. It was only an hour or so. I didn't see what harm it could do.'

'But why didn't you t-tell the police the t-truth?'

She sighed, dropped the cards onto the breakfast bar and leaned back too far, almost overbalancing on the stool.

'Because I didn't want to drag my friend into it if I could help it. He was just being kind. And, like I said, I didn't think it would matter.'

Owen's eyes narrowed.

'He?'

She nodded. 'Adam. He's someone I work with at the bookshop. He's just a friend, like you. There's nothing, you know . . . *going on*. Nothing like that. He's got this girlfriend, Freja – she's a medical student and she's doing voluntary work for twelve months in Africa somewhere so he gets a bit fed up with his own company, same way I do. He's just a good friend. Someone I can talk to.'

'T-talk about what?'

'I don't know. Anything. He's a really good listener. I can sort of bounce ideas off him, you know? He helps me think straight. And he knew things weren't going well with Callum so we agreed we'd meet up for a drink and I could get a few things off my chest and he could talk about how he was missing Freja. That's all it was. And then, when they asked me where I'd been that evening, all kinds of things started buzzing round in my head like how would it look if I'd been having a drink with another man while my husband was being killed. Because I felt like I should have been home, you know? And I'd already told Phil I was with you, looking at plans for the garden, so I didn't want to go back on that if I could help it. And then there was Adam – I didn't want to cause any difficulties between him and Freja, if she came to hear about it somehow. So I just blurted out that I was with you, seeing as that's what we'd agreed earlier. I know I shouldn't have but I wasn't thinking straight. It just seemed easier that way and I didn't think that an hour either way made any real difference. But you're right – maybe it's time I went to the police and told them the truth.'

'No. You c-can't do that.'

'It's OK – I'll tell them it was my fault. You didn't know what time it was and I misled you into thinking it was later than it was. I'll make sure they understand.'

'No,' he said, shaking his head vigorously. 'No, it won't work. I t-told them I looked at my watch and it was eight fifty-two.'

'OK. So we'll tell them the truth. I asked you to say it was later because I didn't want to drag Adam into it. Maybe they'll agree to keep it just between us if I explain.'

'They'll be angry.'

'Not with you, they won't,' she said, anxious to reassure him. 'I need to do this, Owen. I don't like the fact that I've lied to Phil and to the police – it makes me look as if I've got something to hide and if they're going to find out sometime it's much better if it comes from me. Don't worry – you'll be fine. And Adam says he's cool with it.'

There was a silence, interrupted only by the insistent buzzing of a fly which smashed repeatedly in kamikaze fashion into one window pane after another in its frantic search for a way out.

'How long have you known him?' he said eventually.

'Adam? Oh, I don't know. A couple of years, maybe.'

'You've known me f-for twenty-one years and three months.'

'Yes.'

'I'm a g-good listener.'

The implication dug its heels in and refused to budge. She understood that it was up to her to shift it but knew instinctively that she couldn't. How was she supposed to explain different levels of friendship to someone who saw the world in such simplistic terms that longevity was all that mattered? As far as she was aware – no, for God's sake, as a matter of indisputable fact – Owen had never had a relationship with anyone in his life other than his mother. What did he imagine might qualify him as someone she could have turned to for comfort when things started to go pear-shaped with Callum? And, more to the point, what on earth could she say to make him understand her reasons without giving offence?

'Yes,' she said, side-stepping the issue altogether. 'You're my oldest friend. And that's why you were the first person I thought of when it came to sorting out the garden. And I was right – I can see that already. I can't believe the progress you've made even this morning. There's so much more light.'

He hauled himself to his feet, nudging the necklace back towards her as he did so.

'I'd better be g-getting on,' he said.

He didn't look as if he'd bought a word of it.

And he looked anything but appeased.

PHIL

The first thing he did when he got back from Abi's was check the text that had announced its arrival with a beep while he was driving. It was from Anna:

> Fight cancelled. Other side of Horsham before
> they phoned. Took day off work for nothing.
> Bummer. You OK?

He texted back straightaway to say he was fine – she was welcome to come and paint his house for him if she was bored, ho ho. His finger was hovering over the *Send* key before he thought better of it and deleted the draft. Trying again, he simply told her that was how he would be spending *his* day. Casual conversation. Bit of a hint but much less presumptuous. That way she could decide for herself without feeling any pressure.

The second thing he did was phone Baz to check whether it was OK to borrow the ladder that was kept in the maintenance store at the rear of the gym, given that he'd forgotten to pick up his own. By the time he'd driven round to collect it, the morning had just about dwindled away with next to nothing to show for all his good intentions. Determined to make a start at least, he decided to sugar soap the walls now, break for lunch at around 1.30 and then start the actual painting an hour or so after that. If he could just make sure he got the first coat out of the way today, it would provide him with the incentive to finish the job tomorrow.

When he came in for lunch, he checked his mobile and found two texts and a missed call. The texts were from Anna again. He read the first one, sent just after midday:

> Need an extra pair of hands for a couple of hours?
> Pretty good with a brush. Can help out till 2.30ish
> if that's any use. Just let me know x

He looked at his watch and cursed under his breath, wishing he'd taken the phone up the ladder with him instead of leaving it inside. A bit of company would have brightened up the day. The second text had been sent nearly an hour later:

> No worries. Guess you're busy. See you Monday x

He started to text a reply to explain what had happened, but gave up after three or four attempts. He'd explain when he saw her on Monday. Make a joke of it. Much better that way.

The missed call was from Abi. He rang the home number and there was no reply so he tried her mobile which she answered immediately, the tinny quality and background traffic suggesting she was on hands-free. He apologised for not answering earlier and asked if it was anything important. There was a pause before she told him it was.

'Actually I'm on my way round to see you,' she said. 'About ten minutes away. Is that OK?'

'Of course,' he told her. 'Is everything all right?'

'Yes . . . no,' she said. 'I'll explain when I get there.'

The ten minutes were just long enough for him to wash and tidy a few things away while he waited. When she pulled up outside he went out to meet her and gave her a hug. She noticed the ladder propped up against the wall and the scrubbed exterior and joked about how he could make a start on hers when he'd finished. They laughed and swapped silly throwaway comments for the next few minutes, but even if she hadn't phoned to tip him off in advance he'd still have known something was up. It was one of the things Sally had always loved about her daughter-in-law, even when she was just a teenager – 'Wears her heart on her sleeve, that one,' she'd said. 'Couldn't keep a secret if her life depended on it.'

It turned out Sally was wrong.

He sat across from Abi and listened while she told him everything – or what he had to assume was everything: where she'd been the night Callum was killed, how she'd left Owen's an hour or more earlier than she'd claimed, not just to him but to the police as well, all about this friend of hers she'd met for a drink and a heart-to-heart. Someone from work. Someone who only turned out to be male about five minutes into the explanation – no actual name mentioned until he made a point of asking. She was dry-eyed throughout; red-faced, but clearly past the stage where tears solved anything.

Nothing she had to say about her relationship with Callum came as a great surprise. He might not have been privy to any of the detail but he did know his own son and harboured no illusions about him. It had been one of life's great mysteries that someone as grounded and self-possessed and downright likeable as Abi should have seen enough in him to want to extend their relationship beyond the teenage years when image is everything. Sally had always thought of them as the perfect couple but he'd never subscribed to that. Callum was only ever governed by the dictates of his own whims and any relationship with him was wholly dependent upon the extent to which others were prepared to let the dazzle outweigh the substance.

So no, he hadn't been surprised earlier to learn about Callum's woman in South Mundham and he had no problem now in believing Abi when she told him that she was just the tip of the iceberg. And, under the circumstances, it was entirely understandable if she felt the need from time to time to let off steam or cry on the shoulder of a friend who might be able to help her find perspective.

But the fact that it was a male friend did surprise him. And, if he was honest, it did more than that. It bothered him. It shouldn't have but it did. He didn't like the thought that Abi was involved in a friendship that needed to fly under the radar. He didn't like the deceit – knew how much it would have hurt him if he'd ever discovered Sally had been doing the same thing at some point in their marriage. He felt no outrage on the part of his son who deserved nothing better, but there was a level of disappointment that Abi had not been above that sort of thing. She could swear on a stack of bibles that it was all entirely innocent and she might conceivably mean every word she said but even she wouldn't know for sure. The moment you felt the need to keep any sort of relationship quiet, that always told you something, didn't it? Whether you knew it or not. Why else the need for secrecy?

'I'm sorry I misled you about that evening,' she said. 'I don't know how it happened. I just sort of drifted into it. Embarrassment as much as anything.'

Misled. Interesting choice of word. So much more innocent than *lied*, he thought. But then the tears came. Or tear, to be precise: a solitary pearl gleaming as it tracked its way down her cheek, hovering for a moment before falling from her chin – and he was out of his chair, knees protesting as he squatted down next to her and pulled her head into his chest.

'Don't worry,' he said, patting the back of her head while trying to shift as unobtrusively as possible into a kneeling position. 'We can ring the police now, go in and see them if necessary to straighten it all out. It's no big deal.'

He wondered, even as he said it, whether Andy Holloway would agree with him.

And he also realised that the house wasn't going to get its first coat that afternoon either.

11

NOW: MONDAY, 6TH OCTOBER

HOLLOWAY

Owen Hall was upset. And Holloway for one thought it was entirely understandable. The man needed his truck for work and to be asked to give it up for as long as it took the lab technicians to check it over, with no guarantee as to how long that might actually be, was never going to go down well. They'd gone out of their way to appease him, stressing that this was intended as a supportive measure. If the check for fingerprints produced a match somewhere in the system, they would know at last who this Julie Mowbray really was, which was in everyone's best interests. If it didn't, what had they lost? Long shot or not, surely it was worth a go?

Edmund Mitchell, who had been scribbling notes in his small notebook since the start of the interview, raised a finger and asked if he might establish a point of order here for the record. Holloway asked him to go ahead.

'Is it fair for Owen to assume that this search for fingerprints will be confined to the cab of his pickup truck only?' he asked.

Holloway looked at Horgan who raised one eyebrow to express his surprise.

'I'm not sure I understand what you're asking, Mr Mitchell,' he said.

'Oh, I suspect you do, Inspector. Owen has been one hundred per cent consistent in his version of what happened and has made it quite clear from the very beginning that the only time this young lady was anywhere near his truck, she was in the front passenger seat. This means there would be no reason for you to waste valuable time examining any other part of the truck for fingerprints that cannot possibly be there.'

'Why would that be a problem?' he asked.

'It would be a problem because it would be tantamount to what I believe you call a fishing expedition.'

'Mr Mitchell,' said Horgan, who was clearly not enamoured of this puffed-up little man and would have welcomed nothing more than the chance to put him in his place. 'I believe you may be misinterpreting your role here as Appropriate Adult. It's not for you to offer legal advice to Mr Hall.'

'Indeed,' answered Mitchell with a quiet smile. 'That would be the responsibility of any legal representation to which Owen is entitled but which you're more than happy for him to waive for the time being – in the interests of clarity and expediting things, I believe you said. Well, thank you for reminding me of my duties as an Appropriate Adult but I think I have them fairly well established in my own mind. You've made it clear that you would rather not simply impound Owen's truck because you know that would change the basis on which this interview is being conducted. He would have to seek legal advice on it. As it happens, Owen is prepared to co-operate with your request, despite the considerable inconvenience it will cause him in his work, because he has nothing to hide and is as anxious as you to identify this woman. If you want to do anything more than that however – if you're going to start examining the truck in its entirety – it does rather suggest that you're not being entirely honest with him and I'm afraid I'd have to take legal advice on it. I'm sure you understand my position here.'

Holloway smiled. 'I always think co-operation is the best way forward, Mr Mitchell,' he said. 'So do we have your permission to take your truck, Owen? On the understanding that this is a gesture of goodwill and that we will only be checking inside the cab for fingerprints?'

Hall looked at Mitchell who nodded. After a pause, he agreed.

'OK,' said Holloway, 'moving on. Tell us about the fish and chips, Owen.'

Hall and Mitchell looked blankly at each other.

'You have fish and chips – large cod and chips and a battered sausage, to be precise – every Saturday evening. Would that be right?'

'What's that got to d-do with anything?'

'Always from the same fish-and-chip shop? Always on Saturdays?'

'N-nearly always. Yes,' he added cautiously.

'And you say that this Julie never came to your house?'

'That's right.'

'So where did she take the cod and chips she picked up for you?'

'I d-don't understand. She d-didn't. I d-don't know what you mean.'

'The lady in the chippie says she did. Are you saying she never bought cod and chips for you?'

'No. N-never.'

'What about the After Eight mints?' Horgan chipped in.

Hall turned to face him, his expression reflecting his confusion. 'What d'you m-mean?'

'She bought a box of After Eights for you. Told the shopkeeper it was a surprise – they're your favourite, right?'

'No,' said Hall and it occurred to Holloway that if he was faking his amazement here he was a very accomplished actor indeed. 'I don't like mints. And I d-don't eat chocolate very often. It's bad for me.'

'Did you ask someone recently to post a parcel for you at the post office in Rose Green?' he asked.

'What parcel?'

'Take your time.'

'No,' Hall repeated. 'I d-don't need to think about it. I haven't sent a p-parcel for ages.'

'Then you see why we're anxious to find out who this woman is, Owen. Because if what you say is true, that means she spent a week or so before she disappeared, passing herself off as your girlfriend and inventing stories to support her version of events.'

'I haven't got a girlfriend,' he said, colouring up. 'She's lying!'

'In which case, we need to know why. I apologise for asking this but it *is* important. Did you ever hit Julie at all?'

'Hit her? No!' He looked taken aback by the suggestion.

'The reason I ask is because for most of that week she had a badly bruised face which suggested she'd been struck by someone.'

'I d-don't hit ladies. I d-don't hit anyone.'

'Did her face appear bruised to you when you met her that evening?'

'No. I'd have n-noticed. I was n-next to her in the truck.'

'So you're saying the bruising must have been fake, right?'

'I'm saying I never t-touched her. And she's not my g-girl-friend. I d-don't even know her. Why's she saying these things?'

He was becoming increasingly agitated and Holloway, able by now to read the signs as well as Mitchell, called the interview to a halt almost immediately. He watched as the two of them walked off down the corridor, the little man taking two steps to his partner's one, looking more than ever like something from a Steinbeck novel. Then he turned to Horgan, who had thrown his biro onto the table and was leaning back in his chair, hands locked behind his head.

'Well?' Holloway asked.

Horgan shook his head.

'I hate to say this, boss,' he said.

'Oh, go on. Make my day.'

'I think you may have been right all along. He's being set up.'

'Did we have a little side bet here?' asked Holloway. 'I think we did.'

'I know better than that,' said Horgan, staring at the ceiling as he tried to bring his thoughts into some sort of order. 'OK, so where does that leave us? If someone's playing games with him, why? I mean, what would be the point?'

'Well, at a guess I'd say someone thinks we should be looking more closely at Owen Hall, wouldn't you? The question is who.'

'Someone who's feeling the heat a bit from South Mundham, maybe? Wants to deflect some of the attention elsewhere?'

'What heat?' asked Holloway. 'What attention? We're back to the same problem we had when you were sure Owen Hall was trying to mess with our heads and throw us off track. We've never really been *on* track. We haven't had anyone in our sights. I mean, we've looked at the Reid woman's ex-husband but if he's behind all this I'm retiring right now cos it means I've learned nothing in all these years in this job. We're knee deep in all the shady financial dealings Green was involved in and we may get something out of that eventually but we're a million miles from pointing the finger at anyone in particular. So who exactly would think he was in our sights?'

'What about the Bellamys?'

'No way,' laughed Holloway. 'We're nowhere near them.'

'Doesn't mean they weren't connected in some way.'

'Doesn't mean they were either. We haven't got within spitting distance of the Bellamys. And even if we had, they're not exactly virgins are they? D'you think they'd be even remotely bothered to hear we're sniffing around their financial records and any possible links to Callum Green? We've had them almost bang to rights before now and they haven't even blinked. I don't buy it.'

'Me neither.'

'So if it's not someone trying to wrong-foot us, it must be personal. There has to be someone out there with a real grudge against Owen Hall. In which case this whole petrol-station business could be just a sideshow. It may have nothing to do with South Mundham at all.'

Which, he realised, would leave them right back where they'd started.

12

EARLIER: WEDNESDAY, 17TH SEPTEMBER

OWEN

He's on his own today. She's working at the bookshop. All day. She said something about it yesterday but he forgot, otherwise he could have made today a work-at-home day. When she's not here, it's not the same. Doesn't feel like something they're doing together.

He hasn't seen much of her recently, not since Saturday. He wonders if it's because she feels embarrassed about the fuss she made over the necklace. He's confused about what happened – doesn't understand why she can't just accept it. It's a present. People give presents all the time for birthdays. You don't hand them back and say they cost too much. He can't see her doing something like that to Callum. She admitted as much. He also thinks her reaction would have been very different if it was this new friend of hers – this *Adam* – who'd bought it for her. Why is she like that just with him? Saying that he needs to take it back is just stupid. What would he want with a necklace? Who's he supposed to give it to if not her?

He doesn't want it back. He'd rather she sold it and bought something else with the money. And more than anything else he wishes things could go back to how they were before the weekend because it's not the same when she's not here. He needs to be able to show her what he's done in the garden, have her come out from time to time and tell him what a difference he's making. It's not fair to leave him here on his own. It feels like he's being punished.

Willie's very unhappy about Abi's reaction. He was against giving her the necklace anyway, but the least she could do was show a bit of gratitude. He also suspects there's more to her friendship with this Adam than she's letting on. Says she's lying. *Just like Mum lied when she said she'd always be there to look after us.* Just like Mrs Winstone lied when she said she'd never allow any bullying in her school. It's what women do – they can't help it. It's part of their make-up. *Ask Dad* is what Willie says. *He'll tell you.*

Owen thinks that's a bit harsh but it does feel as if something's broken somehow and he wishes someone could tell him how to mend it. When he and Abi do get a few minutes together, she always manages to slip in some reference to the necklace, trying to persuade him to take it back. Maybe Willie was right after all. Maybe he shouldn't have given it to her. But now he's done it he can't undo it. He keeps clinging to the idea that one day she might try it on in a moment of weakness, see how lovely it is. Then she'll be glad she kept it.

As for her new friend, he doesn't know what to think. He doesn't like the idea that she might lie to him but, as Willie pointed out, it wouldn't be the first time. She'd met this Adam in secret . . . and you don't do that without a reason, do you?

He wishes he understood more about women and how their minds work. Things would be so much easier if you could believe what they said. It's bothering him, taking all the enjoyment out of his work this morning.

He breaks for lunch around 12.30, letting himself into the house with the spare key that Abi keeps in a hiding place in the back garden so he can get in when he needs to. He pours a glass of water for himself and is about to tuck into his hard-boiled egg, pork pie and chicken sandwiches but he can't settle down to eat just yet. His stomach feels funny and he decides it's probably all the uncertainty. This whole business has ruined his morning; he's not going to let it spoil his lunch as well. If there's something he ought to know about Abi's new friendship, there must be signs of it somewhere around the house. It's just a matter of knowing where to look. She won't be back for several hours yet. It's the perfect chance for him to set his mind at rest and show Willie that he doesn't know *everything*.

So he takes his shoes off, picks up the glass of water and the lunch box and climbs the stairs. There won't be anything downstairs, he tells himself. Not where anyone can see. The best place to start will be her bedroom. His heart is hammering in his chest as he turns the handle and pushes the door open, only to discover that he's in the bathroom. There's more than one toothbrush and various men's toiletries lying around but those could easily be Callum's, he tells himself. He doesn't think she'll have moved his things out just yet.

The next room looks like a guest one – neatly made bed, no personal items of any sort. Down the corridor, three more doors: one to an airing cupboard, another to what looks like it might have been another small guest room at some stage but has been converted into an office. Writing desk, expensive-looking chair with adjustable arms and lumbar support. Space for a laptop . . . maybe the police have taken it. Photo of Abi – he wonders if she'd notice if he took it with him. Decides she would.

Into the final bedroom – large double bed covered by a pink quilt with an oriental floral print. Huge wardrobes. En-suite bathroom. Large window looking out onto the back garden. He takes a sip of water from his glass and puts it on one of the bedside tables next to a Michael Connelly novel. Then he opens the lunch box, takes the egg from it and bites into it as he wanders around the room in search of clues.

It takes him ten minutes to find what he's looking for, even though he's been hoping he won't actually find anything incriminating at all. Two things actually. The first is in one of the wardrobes, tucked away on a shelf containing half a dozen neatly folded jumpers. Out of sight, out of mind. He knew it wasn't in the jewellery box on her bedside table because he checked that only a few minutes ago and he's been talking himself into believing that this might mean she's actually wearing it today. She tried it on and just couldn't resist it. But no – it's here, still inside its case, not even out in the open where she might see it every day and be tempted by it.

He picks up the box and carries it over to the window. Places it on the window sill and puts alongside it the pork pie, from which he's just taken a bite, in order to free up both hands. Then he lifts the lid and gently removes the necklace, holding it up to the light pouring in through the window. It's so pretty. It doesn't belong in a dark wardrobe. He carries it over to her pillow and lays it out there. He'd like to leave it that way so that it's the first thing she sees when she comes home but he's not sure how he can do that without giving away the fact that he's been searching through her bedroom. He puts it back with a heavy heart, taking great care to leave it exactly where he found it.

His other discovery comes almost by accident, just as he's getting ready to leave the room. He picks up the book, wondering what sort of things she reads. He prefers to watch television himself but if he knows what sort of books she likes reading, it will give him a few ideas as to what he can buy her for Christmas. He rests it in his lap and opens it at the bookmarked page. Only it's not a bookmark. It's a birthday card – a long, thin one. He picks it up and looks at a photo of a peaceful, rural setting, a pale sun dragging itself over a hilltop to signal the start of a new day. The message on the front says:

Some things you just know you can rely on.

Inside it continues:

… some people are just the same.

And it's signed *Adam* with one small cross after the name. Adam with a kiss.

That's not good. Doesn't sound to him like a friend who's just a good listener. It sounds like someone who's a bit more than that. And he's just trying to process this when suddenly there's a loud ringing sound throughout the house to signal that someone is at the front door. It startles him and he leaps to his feet, forgetting the book, which falls to the floor and shuts. He's standing there, holding the card in one hand and wishing he'd made a note of the page she was on because now he doesn't know where the makeshift bookmark is supposed to go. In his desperation he picks the book up and slides the card somewhere in the middle – it's the best he can do.

He needs to get out of there. He knows it won't be Abi – if she'd forgotten her keys, she'd just go round the back and use the spare. But what if it's her father-in-law – the policeman? What if he knows where the key is kept? What's he going to think if he finds him wandering around upstairs?

He straightens out the quilt, grabs his lunch box, remembering the empty glass at the last moment, and races across the landing. Then he tiptoes his way downstairs as quickly and as quietly as he can and dashes into the lounge, where he peers around the curtain just in time to see the postman turn away from the door and start walking back down the path. Relieved, he bangs on the window to get his attention, then goes to the front door and signs for a parcel in Abi's name. His breathing's just about back to normal by the time he's returned to the kitchen and started eating the remaining chicken sandwich.

His mouth is dry, probably from all the excitement of the last few minutes, so he pours himself another glass of water and resumes his place at the table. His mind is clearer than it was a few minutes ago. He might not like it but at least he knows where he stands.

He has a rival now.

ANNA

'Got a joke for you,' she said. 'Good one this time.'

'Is it better than the last one?'

'Which one was that?'

'The one about the morris dancer.'

'Yep. Even better than that.'

'Go on then.'

'OK. Duck walks into a baker's shop and goes up to the baker and says, "You got any matches?" The baker says, "No – sorry," so the duck walks out. Next day, duck comes back in again and says, "You got any matches?" The baker says, "No. I told you yesterday. We don't sell matches. This is a bakery – we sell cakes, bread, pastries . . . no matches." Duck says "OK" and walks out. Next day . . .'

'Don't tell me – I'll bet the duck walks in again.'

'Aaah, you've heard it,' she said sarcastically. 'No, listen. It's a good one. So . . . next day, duck walks in again, goes up to the baker and says, "You got any matches?" This time the baker loses it, reaches over the counter and grabs the duck by the neck and says, "Listen – I keep telling you this is a bakery. You come in here once more and ask if we've got any matches, I'm gonna take a bloody great hammer and nail that beak of yours to this counter. Do you understand?" The duck nods and walks out.'

'And next day –' he says.

'Next day, duck comes in, goes up to the baker and says, "You got any nails?" And the baker's all surprised like, so he says, "Nails? No, we haven't." So the duck says, "Right. Got any matches?"'

She was already giggling during the lead-up to the punchline, at which point she burst into laughter. He liked her laugh – it was uninhibited, genuine. Infectious too, to the extent that an elderly couple coming towards them felt obliged to smile along with them, as if wanting to be included as well.

'Good one, eh?' she said, dabbing at the corner of one eye with her finger.

'Yeah. Good one.'

'Better than the morris dancer?'

'Anything's better than the morris dancer.'

'Well, it got a smile out of you at any rate,' she said. 'I told it to Lucia . . . my sister? Nothing. Not a hint of a smile. Know what she said? "Why would a duck need nails?" Seriously,' she added, when he shot a disbelieving look in her direction. 'God's honest truth. *Why would the duck ask for nails?* I really worry about her sometimes. Stand close enough to her, you can hear the sea.'

He smiled and they walked on a few paces, nodding at passers-by.

'You're talkative this morning,' she said at length.

'Sorry.'

'Barely get a word in edgeways. You OK?'

'Yeah, I'm fine,' he said, turning to apologise to a shopper with whom he'd inadvertently collided. 'Bit preoccupied, I suppose.'

'Callum?'

'Sort of. Yeah.'

'Well, if you want to bend someone's ear about it all, feel free cos we've got another five and a half hours of this and I'm just about out of jokes here. And you know what they say?'

'What's that?'

'A problem shared is a . . . isn't a problem anymore. That's not right, is it?'

'Not quite.'

'Something like that anyway. So, come on then – I like moody and magnificent as much as anyone else but you can get too much of a good thing.'

He stopped near the entrance to Estelle Roberts, the jeweller's on the second floor and nodded to Danny, one of the assistants working inside. Anna leaned against the shop window next to him, waiting him out.

'It's nothing in particular,' he said at length. 'It's just –'

'You miss him.'

'Yeah. I do. Stupid, yeah? I mean, it's not like we were living out of each other's pockets or anything like that. In fact, I used to go weeks without seeing him. Weeks. And I probably spent more time moaning about him than anything else.'

'It's what dads do.'

'Yeah, well . . . he wasn't the easiest kid you'll ever meet, you know? Always in trouble, one scrape after another. I hoped he'd grow out of it some day. Thought maybe there was a better Callum inside, struggling to get out. But if there was I never really got to see it. Pretty awful thing to say about your own son, right?'

'I dunno,' said Anna, rubbing distractedly at a mark on her uniform. 'I've always felt my dad doesn't love me enough. Maybe you and Sally loved Callum just a bit too much. I guess it's a pretty difficult balancing act most of the time.'

'Spoiled him, you mean?'

'Whoa,' she said, holding up two hands in an exaggerated defensive gesture. 'Not for me to say. I just don't see why you should be beating yourself up about it, is all. If you're going to get it wrong, loving him too much is the better way to go, trust me.'

He said nothing as he stared vacantly at the jewellery in the window. Anna was prepared to bet he couldn't describe a single item he'd been looking at.

'What about the investigation?' she asked, more to break the silence than anything else. 'How's that going?'

'Bit of a mess, if you ask me,' he said. He told her about Abi's visit on Saturday afternoon and their subsequent interview with Holloway, who had not been best pleased to learn about the inaccuracies in her previous statement.

'How about you?' she asked, picking up on an edge to his voice when he was talking about Abi. 'You sound a bit annoyed with her.'

'A bit. Maybe.'

'Because she's been seeing this other guy?'

'She says he's just a work colleague. Nothing to it. Just a friend she wanted to confide in.'

'And you think it's more than that?'

'I don't know. I mean, I know Callum had been cheating on her but two wrongs don't make a right, do they?'

'No. They make you human though. Not sure how many saints I've ever met.'

'I know. None of my business anyway . . . not really. I just –'

'You thought better of her.'

'Yeah. I guess. Stupid.'

Anna asked him for more detail about the investigation and he told her what he knew, which was precious little.

'It doesn't feel as if they're getting anywhere,' he said. 'I keep ringing and they're all polite and everything, say all the right things. But if they're going after anyone in particular, they're not letting me in on it, that's for sure. They've made it quite clear I'm to stay out of it. Be a good boy. Leave them to do what they're good at.'

'Only you don't think they're doing that good a job, is that it?'

'I don't know,' he said. 'I know they're stretched to the limit with that kid who's disappeared. They say there's a key period in every investigation and I just worry maybe they took their eye off the ball and missed it with Callum. And I'm not very good at sitting back and staying out of things at the best of times but when it's your own son –'

'So don't,' she said.

He stopped and looked at her.

'Don't what?'

'Don't stay out of it. Why not do a bit of digging around, see what you can come up with?'

He shook his head. 'I've been well and truly warned off,' he said.

'So be discreet about it. Who's going to know? If you need a volunteer to help out, you only have to ask. I've always fancied myself as a bit of a sleuth. Stake-outs. Following people. Anna Castrogiovanni, private eye. It's got a ring to it, don't you think?'

He laughed.

'I'm serious,' she insisted. 'Instead of sitting around all day, brooding over it all, why not get off your backside and do something? I'll help. It's not like either of us has got a social calendar that's about to explode. We can do our own interviews, see what we can dig up. It'll be fun. You remember fun, don't you?'

He draped an arm across her shoulder and gave her a quick hug which came across as appreciative but no less dismissive for all that. He wasn't taking her suggestion seriously.

'Come on,' he said. 'I'll buy you a coffee. My treat.'

'Just think about it,' she said. 'If you don't want to do it, I may just go ahead and do it on my own. Ten years from now I'll have my own PI business and you'll be wondering why you didn't get in on the ground floor while you had the chance. Give it a go. The proof's in the pudding.'

'In the eating,' he laughed.

'The what?'

'The proof of the pudding is in the eating.'

She stopped and stared at him.

'I swear to God, you say the weirdest things.'

OWEN

He's cooking his dinner, turning sausages in the pan and checking that the potatoes don't boil over, when the phone rings.

It's Abi.

'Owen,' she says. 'Have you been in my bedroom?'

Oh.

He turns the sausages and the potatoes down to a low heat. He'll need to concentrate.

'No.'

'I'm going to ask you again,' she says, and she sounds very cross with him. This is not good. 'I found a half-eaten pork pie on the window sill. It certainly wasn't there when I left this morning and you've had one in your lunch box just about every day you've been here. There were also a couple of those sticky burrs that cling to your clothes – I found them on the floor next to the bed. So I'll ask you again – have you been in my bedroom?'

He vaguely remembers putting the pork pie down so that he could open the box and hold the necklace up to the light. Can't believe he was so stupid as to leave it there. He needs an excuse. Badly.

'I'm sorry,' he says, almost a whisper.

'Why were you in my room? What were you doing in there?'

'I was looking for the necklace.' He's pleased with this reply. Turn the responsibility back onto her. If she'd been wearing it like she was meant to, he wouldn't have been in there. She doesn't need to know the real reason.

'So you ask me, Owen. You want it back, you ask me. You don't go nosing around in someone else's bedroom without their permission. It's private!'

She's still angry. He thinks that's a bit unfair. If she didn't keep trying to hide things from him, like her friendship with Adam, he wouldn't have to go anywhere near her bedroom. He'll explain this to her some day when it's not such a big deal but maybe now's not the right time.

'I'm sorry,' he says again, because this is what she wants to hear.

'Yes, well I'm sorry too, Owen, but if you're going to be working here while I'm not around I've got to be able to trust you. I think we're going to have to sit down and go over a few ground rules. I certainly don't think it's a good idea for me to leave a key out anymore. If you're going to carry on working here, it will have to be while I'm at home. Either that or you'll have to make do like any other contractor would, but I'm not having you wandering about the house. My bedroom, Owen? Really? My *bedroom?*'

Any other contractor? He's still stuck on that part of the conversation, can't believe she could possibly be that hurtful. How can he be just any other contractor? So he went into her room – it's not that big a deal. He's heard that women can be irrational at times. She's certainly not making sense just now.

'And as for the necklace, I'll give that back to you tomorrow morning,' she says.

'I don't want it b-back.'

'I thought you said that was why you were in my bedroom?'

'I . . . I was just looking,' he says, trying desperately to improvise. 'I wanted to see if you still had it. I was worried you m-might have sold it already.'

'Then you should have asked me,' she says, and there's still no sign of her backing off from this. He can't remember her ever being cross with him before. Maybe he needs to be there with her. If she could see his face, she'd realise how sorry he is. Then she'd take his hand and tell him it's OK – *just don't do it again*. He wonders whether it might be better to tell her about the bookmark but doesn't see how he can do that right now without making her angrier still.

She's still harping on about the necklace. Saying things he doesn't think she can possibly mean. Not deep down. She's going to give it back to him tomorrow. If he doesn't accept it, she's going to take it round to a charity shop and give it away. Up to him. Take it or leave it. He knows she doesn't mean it and is about to say so when she puts the phone down on him. Just like that. No goodbye or anything.

She's never done that before.

And Willie's sitting at the kitchen table watching him, a smug grin on his face, the words *told you so* stamped across his forehead.

PHIL

He hadn't really taken Anna's suggestion seriously at the time. Maybe it was a legacy from all those years on the force but the idea of going against clear instructions from a superior officer was something that just didn't sit comfortably with him. If you were told to back off and leave it to others, that's what you did. Sharpish. It was deeply ingrained in you, a code of conduct that removed the need for complex calculations and reduced everything to one simple, incontrovertible rule: *because I say so.*

But he found it niggling away at him throughout the afternoon. Maybe it was the tiny but insistent voice that kept reminding him he was his own man now, no longer bound by their rules and regulations. Or perhaps it was just his growing frustration with an investigation that seemed to have come to something of a standstill or might just as well have done for all the feedback that was coming his way. And besides, he reasoned with himself, it wasn't as if he was asking to work alongside Holloway and Horgan. He wasn't stupid – he could see how inappropriate that would be.

Still, the more he thought about it, the more aggrieved he felt at being ... well, marginalised, for want of a better word, because that was pretty much what was happening here, wasn't it? When you stripped away all the sympathetic handshakes and expressions of support. Even if it was just a case of fiddling around in the background, he couldn't see what harm it would do if he were to ask a few questions here and there. Nothing high-profile. Nothing intrusive. Just satisfying his curiosity on a few details. If he did no more than rattle a few cages, who was to say that wouldn't turn up something useful? When it came down to it, who could blame a father for wanting to get off his backside and *do* something as Anna put it?

So by the time he left work, he'd managed to persuade himself that she had a point, even if she was probably just pulling his leg. This was the way to go. He owed it to himself.

And as soon as he got home, he started making a few phone calls.

Which is why, barely an hour later, he was standing in the entrance to the dining room at Bognor Golf Club, making a deal with himself: if he's already left, I'll forget it; if he's still here . . .

It took him no more than a few seconds to pick out Ezra Cunningham. He was sitting alone at a table in the centre of the room, transferring his salad from a side dish onto his plate, arranging it precisely around fish of some description. Phil threaded his way through the diners and stood facing him across the table. Cunningham paused briefly, then helped himself to another spoonful without looking up.

'Can I help you?' he asked eventually.

'I need a word.'

'Excuse me?'

'I said, I need a word.'

Cunningham looked up at him, frowning as if trying to place him.

'Yes, I heard you well enough. It's just that you have me at something of a disadvantage here. I'm afraid I don't have the faintest idea who you are.'

'My name's Phil Green.'

Cunningham tossed the name around for a second or two.

'Is that supposed to mean something because for the life of me –'

'I'm Callum's father.'

'Ah.' He slowly lowered his cutlery to the table, then half-rose from his seat. 'In that case . . . would you care to join me?'

'I'm not staying.'

'Even so, can I offer you a drink, perhaps? You're welcome to share this bottle,' he said, fingering a spare wine glass, 'but if you'd prefer something from the bar –'

'This isn't a social visit.'

Cunningham smiled.

'It is however a visit and I'm sure you'll feel more comfortable sitting down. For what it's worth, I'd certainly prefer not to have to crane my neck to look up at you. Please.' He gestured towards the seat opposite him. Phil hesitated, then decided to accept the offer. A waiter appeared at his elbow and he waved him away.

'Now,' said Cunningham. 'You say this isn't a social visit, so that rather begs the question . . . what sort of a visit is it? How can I help you?'

'I'm here to talk about my son.'

'Of course.' Cunningham's expression clouded over, dignified sympathy personified. 'My condolences, Mr Green. I wish we might have met under less difficult circumstances. Callum always spoke of you with the utmost respect and no little fondness.'

He leaned forward and linked his hands on the table in front of him, pausing as if expecting some sort of response from Phil. When it became clear that none was forthcoming, he picked up the salt cellar and began sprinkling salt over his tomatoes and lettuce.

'I don't have children of my own,' he continued undaunted, 'so I've no idea how you must be feeling right now, but you have my deepest sympathies. I trust you received the flowers.'

'I did. They're the reason I'm here.'

'Yes, well . . . it's the very least I could do. I feel bad about staying away from the ceremony itself. I hope you'll understand.

It's just that putting in an appearance might easily have engendered, shall we say, unwelcome levels of attention from the authorities. I find they generally need very little encouragement to leap to inappropriate conclusions where I'm concerned, and turning up at the funeral of a murder victim didn't seem like the wisest course of action. Not to mention the distress it might have caused you and the rest of Callum's family.'

'Your concern for us is very touching.'

If Cunningham picked up on the sarcasm he gave no sign of being offended by it.

'But you wanted to talk about your boy. So tell me – how can I help?'

'You can start by explaining how the hell he managed to get himself mixed up with the likes of you.'

Cunningham paused in the act of spearing a tomato.

'The likes of me?' He shook his head, then raised the fork to his mouth. 'Mr Green, we seem somehow to have got off on the wrong foot. If it's something I've said or done, I can only apologise but I suspect the reasons for a certain brusqueness in your manner lie elsewhere and that you've made up your mind about me before we've even had a chance to get to know each other. Perhaps if I were to disabuse you of some of the more fanciful notions you seem to be harbouring?'

'Such as?'

'Well, for one thing, Callum was not, as you so colourfully put it, "mixed up with the likes of me". Not in the sense you imply at any rate. In fact, we had no business dealings whatsoever as I recall. Our relationship, if you must know, was far more prosaic than that.'

'Explain.'

'He was my squash partner.'

'Your what?' This, it would be fair to say, was not what he had been expecting to hear.

'Well . . . squash *coach* might be a more accurate description. I joined the league at the Arun Leisure Centre eighteen months ago, a little fiftieth birthday present to myself.'

Phil smiled at this.

'Callum was coaching you? You expect me to believe that?'

Cunningham returned the smile.

'Probably not, no. Your scepticism is entirely understandable, as it happens. I'm not sure I'd react any differently, were our roles reversed. Even so, it happens to be the truth. But in all honesty it doesn't matter to me whether you believe it or not. I imagine it would be relatively easy to substantiate it if the need were to arise. We booked the same slot most Thursday evenings: six forty to seven twenty. The leisure centre must keep records of bookings, I'd have thought.'

He gently picked at the fish, his movements precise and unhurried. Affected, almost.

'I used to play a lot when I was younger and was quite good, even though I say so myself. So I thought I'd get back into it fairly easily, but I'm afraid the passing years and vanity make fools of us all. One of the first matches I had to play was in a handicap tournament – you know the sort of thing. I had the misfortune, or good fortune, as it turned out in the long run, to be drawn against your boy in the first round and he wiped the floor with me, even though he was giving me God knows how many points. A bit of a wake-up call, I'm afraid.'

He took a sip from his glass and waggled it as if to check whether Phil had changed his mind about the drink. He shook his head and waited for Cunningham to continue.

'Anyway, most of the players in Premier – they hate playing people like me. Waste of their time, you see. They see us off without even raising a sweat. Can't wait to get off the court. Your boy though – he was different. Considerate, I suppose you'd say. I knew he was prolonging rallies to give himself a better workout but he didn't do it in any condescending way. And when he complimented me on any good shots I played, there was nothing patronising about it. He seemed to take pleasure in encouraging me. Then, once the game was over, instead of leaving skid marks in his haste to get off the court, he offered to buy me a drink and we spent half an hour or so talking in the bar. I was . . . I was impressed, I'll admit it. You don't often find such respect in young people today.'

'He was playing you.'

'I'm sorry?'

'I know my son,' said Phil, happy to latch on to an excuse to be hurtful, to prick the balloon of self-satisfied smugness that Cunningham wore like full body armour. 'If Callum was sniffing around you for any length of time, then respect had very little to do with it. You can bet your life he was using you.'

There was a pause while Cunningham made great show of processing this. Then he surprised Phil by chuckling to himself.

'Well, yes. You may be right, of course,' he said. 'What's that phrase they all use these days? The accumulation of marginal gains? I don't suppose Callum was averse to any benefits that might come his way from being associated with me, however loosely. I suppose it's possible – likely even – that he saw me as a means to an end, someone to smooth his way a little by introducing him to a number of useful business acquaintances. He wouldn't have been human if he hadn't kept an eye open for any opportunities that might present themselves.'

'And these useful business acquaintances? Who would they be?'

Cunningham pointed his fork at him.

'Ah, now . . . no disrespect, Mr Green, but much as I'd like to satisfy your curiosity, there are levels of discretion and professional courtesy to consider here. When I enter into any business arrangement, I demand total confidentiality and my colleagues expect no less from me. Not to put too fine a point on it, I'm not sure it's really any of your concern.'

'You don't think so?'

'No. I'm happy to sit and chat with you about your son and fill in a few gaps for you where I can, but there are limits. I'm sure you'll understand.'

Phil folded his arms and leaned back in his chair, lips pursed. Then, having decided on how he wanted to play this and just how far he ought to go, he sat forward again, resting both elbows on the table.

'Understand?' he said, reaching out for the carafe of water and pouring some into a spare wine glass. 'Let me tell you what I understand, OK? I understand that my son was doing quite nicely thank you very much, making a reputation for himself and bringing in more money in a week than I ever earned in a single year back in the day. Then he meets up with you and starts getting daft ideas above his station, mixing with people he should have had enough sense to stay well clear of and within two years he's lying in a field with his head smashed in and you're sitting there with your polite speeches and your refined manners, offering tea and sympathy and inviting me to imagine this is all one big coincidence ... that it has nothing to do with the circles you move in. That's what I understand. And I know all this talk about professional ethics and this cloak of respectability you like to wrap around yourself are just so much window dressing, so let's get real here, shall we? I'll ask you again: who are these business acquaintances you're talking about and, more specifically, which of them might have taken exception to whatever Callum was up to?'

If he'd been hoping that Cunningham might be thrown off balance by the change of tone, the lack of response would have been seriously disappointing. Because, far from being taken aback, he simply dabbed at the corners of his mouth with his napkin, pushed his plate away from him as if tired of playing with its contents, then looked Phil straight in the eye.

'Very well,' he said, clearing his throat and reaching again for his glass. 'I've tried to make allowances for your appalling personal circumstances but that doesn't appear to be getting us anywhere. So let me try a different tack.'

He took another sip, then nodded away to his right.

'You see the lad at the end of the bar who is making a poor fist of emptying the bowl of peanuts without anyone noticing? And the younger one a little further along who is trying, with very little prospect of success, to curry favour with the young lady behind the bar? Well, I'd really rather not put it to the test but I think you'll find that if I so much as raise my voice, they'll be over here like a shot and this conversation will be at an end. You'll be asked very politely to leave.'

Phil promised himself he wouldn't look but couldn't resist it. The peanut grabber was clearly no stranger to the gym. Judging by the way his sleeves seemed to be straining to contain his biceps, he spent a lot of time pressing weights. The would-be Romeo was smaller, wiry, but Phil had seen his sort before. It was easy to underestimate people like him but usually you only made that mistake once.

The younger one chose that moment to nod at Phil as if aware of exactly what they were discussing.

'Now, since civil is apparently off the table and we've decided plain speaking is the order of the day, allow me to tell you this much. I mentioned a while ago that I have no children of my own. If I did, however, I'd like to think that I would know my son a little better than you appear to have known yours, Mr Green. Callum, I'm sorry to say, was an opportunistic chancer always on the lookout for an opening. He was charming, yes. Charismatic? Certainly. Excellent company. Able to adapt effortlessly to any social gathering in which he found himself. A real social animal, you might say. But he was also an unprincipled, self-serving par-venu who dazzled and bewitched people and thought nothing of sucking them dry for as long as it took him to identify the next rung on the ladder. You say he was doing well before he met me but I suspect you don't know the half of it. He had his fingers in so many pies, I doubt even he was able to keep track of everything he was into. If an opportunity arose, he went for it, irrespective of any advice I might choose to give him or any independent risk assessment – because risk is what attracted him to it in the first place. He couldn't help himself. Now –'

He broke off to smile at another diner as he passed, then turned back to face Phil.

'You have suffered a dreadful loss and are at liberty to pick out any version of reality you choose to believe, but whichever one you hug to your chest in search of consolation, I would urge you not to let it blind you to one very important fact. And that is that your son carried around in him more than just the seeds of his own destruction, and needed no help whatsoever from me or any of my business colleagues in sealing his own fate. He was flying too near to the sun, an accident waiting to happen.'

He raised one hand in the air and in true Pavlovian fashion his two minders pushed off from the bar and started to make their way over to him.

'Now,' he continued, eyes still locked onto Phil's, 'I think we've covered just about everything. I'm sorry for your loss and wish I could help but I'm afraid there's nothing I can do. And this conversation is at an end. Mick and TJ will see you out.'

The two minders placed themselves either side of Phil, who made a point of ignoring them. Instead of getting to his feet, he reached across and poured more water into his glass before draining it in one go. Then he placed the empty vessel with exaggerated care next to Cunningham's.

'This conversation may be on hold for now,' he corrected him, 'but I promise you this much – it's far from over. You want to know one thing I picked up in all those years in the life? People like you, you very rarely *do* anything. You're not the sort to get your own hands dirty. But you know how to keep your ear to the ground. It's like you're tuned into this jungle telegraph out there and nothing gets past you because you can't afford to allow that to happen. You always know what's going on. Whatever happened to my boy, whether you were involved or not, you'll know *something*. Don't waste your breath trying to persuade me otherwise. And I'll promise you this much: I'm going to keep turning up at the most awkward moments possible and making a bloody nuisance of myself till you get the message. Any chance I get to embarrass you in public, I'm going to be grabbing it with both hands. Now you need to ask yourself how long you can afford to let something like that persist . . . *Mr* Cunningham.'

He got to his feet and measured himself against the bigger of the two minders.

'And I can see myself out,' he said.

13

NOW: WEDNESDAY, 8ᵀᴴ OCTOBER

OWEN

At least he has his truck now. The older detective, the nicer of the two, thanks him, says they've finished with it. They've managed to get a lot of fingerprints. No big surprise there. He's had it for years and can't remember the last time he gave the inside a good clean; and the previous owner used to ferry casual workers from the collection point in town out to local farms during the fruit-picking season. Must be hundreds of prints by now. They haven't had results back yet but if they come up with a match they'll be sure to let him know.

This Detective Holloway is all right, he thinks. He's never found it easy to relax when the police are around, probably because of his experience all those years ago with Callum's father, but at least this man's heart seems to be in the right place. He's what his mother used to call 'a gentleman'. You get the feeling he's being straight with you. If he asks a question it's because he wants to know the answer. He's not doing it just to have his own suspicions confirmed, unlike the younger one. *He's* different. Much more aggressive. If *he* asks a question it's because he's looking to trip you up. Hasn't smiled once or made any effort to be friendly. Makes it obvious he doesn't believe Owen's version of what happened with 'Julie' and that's a problem – because it just happens to be the truth. And if he can't even recognise the truth when he hears it, he can't be much of a detective, can he?

Owen's glad he has his truck back because Malkie phoned earlier. He'll be on his way through Chichester sometime this morning with a couple of machines for him: an Al-Ko 520BR Premium and an Allett Classic 14L. Malkie's a long-haul HGV driver who delivers gardening supplies to DIY stores all over the country – Europe too, even as far as Poland. He also does a number of deals on the side, picking up mowers that have been thrown out and replaced for no better reason than that they've developed a mechanical problem. Such a waste of money – these two machines would cost around £500 brand new and he knows he can buy them from Malkie for as little as £40 each, then sell them off as reconditioned models for five times that amount on his website. Malkie will moan about how he's being ripped off but it pays for a late breakfast at Arun Valley and an evening meal and a drink on the way back and he'll still have plenty left over. It's not like he's losing out at all. He picks them up for nothing and besides – what else is he going to do with dead lawnmowers?

Malkie says he'll be in the car park of the Arun Valley Shopping Centre around eleven. They usually meet there, mainly because manoeuvring his big lorry around Pagham is a pain. Owen never minds the fifteen-minute drive. It'll be more than worth the effort. If he gets the two machines onto the website as soon as he's home, they'll be gone by the morning. People know what a good job he can do with old mowers.

He's a bit early. No sign of Malkie's lorry just yet, so he takes a parking space near the entrance and gets out of the truck to stretch his legs for a bit. The car park's huge but it's pretty full all the same, more so the closer you get to the main entrance. No wonder the centre of Bognor is on its last legs – everybody's out here. Unless you want Poundland, discount stores, betting shops, amusement arcades and Polish delicatessens, there's no point in going into town anymore. This place has pretty much everything.

It's not just shoppers who come here either. Ahead of him a group of seven or eight young people are sitting around the edge of the large fountain. Some of them have got their shoes off and their feet in the water, even though there's been a bit more of a chill in the air the last couple of days. Most of them are listening to music on headphones or playing games on their mobile phones. They're all wearing dark clothing and he knows they are called Goths. He saw a programme about them once and thinks they're very strange, even if they don't seem to be doing anybody any harm. They appear to be quite happy in a gloomy sort of way.

A couple of members of the security staff make their way across the car park and start talking to them. It looks as if they're being asked to move on, although it all seems light-hearted enough. And then he recognises one of the guards – it's Callum Green's dad. And that shakes him up a bit. He has to look twice to make sure it's actually him. Owen's always pictured him as a policeman because that's what he used to be. Even when he turned up in Abi's garden that time, he still thought of him as

PC Green. He knows he's older now and you can't stay a police-man for ever, but it's never occurred to him to wonder what they do afterwards, when the work gets too dangerous. Now he knows. Typical that he chose to move on to something that means he can still throw his weight around. Telling people what to do seems to be all he's good at. Especially when they're not really doing anything wrong in the first place.

He's so busy watching Callum's dad that he hasn't really looked at his partner. And there's no reason why he should be interested until she turns her head so that she's side-on, and then he notices something familiar about her which makes him look again. He assumes it's just that he's seen her here before but there's a little voice inside nagging away at him, telling him that's not it. He watches as she does some stretching exercises while Callum's dad talks to the Goths. She's resting one foot on the edge of the fountain and straightening her leg before easing into a squat to stretch out the hamstring. Then she does the same with the other leg and he can tell she knows what she's doing. Looks like an athlete.

And the connection is made. Glasses are added. Hair is altered drastically. And now the fizzing inside his head is like the fifth of November: sparks are flying everywhere and his pulse is way above its normal resting rate because he knows her. Knows exactly where he's seen her before.

14

EARLIER: SUNDAY, 21ST SEPTEMBER

PHIL

He was halfway through shaving before he realised that he'd set his alarm in error. He wasn't due in today – one of his days off before the rota threw him back into the twilight world. He thought about going back to bed for a couple of hours but wasn't sure he could square it with his conscience. If he was ever going to pay more than lip service to the notion of getting back into some sort of shape, he needed to meet his reluctance head on and go for a run. There was nothing to stop him other than bone idleness. No injuries. No pressing calls on his time. And it didn't need to be anything too ambitious to begin with. Fifteen minutes today, maybe. Twenty tomorrow. He'd build up gradually as the weeks wore on. Feel the benefit of it later. And it would give Anna something to tease him about next time they were on patrol.

So he bit the bullet, went back into the bedroom and changed into shorts and a sweatshirt, rescuing his trainers from the confines of his kitbag, where they'd been lying unused for too long.

He headed towards the kitchen, then decided to leave breakfast till he got back. The thought of bringing it all back up halfway round the block didn't appeal at all.

It was still dark in the lounge as he walked through. He was just reaching out to open the curtains when he caught sight of the figure sitting in his armchair.

'Jesus!'

His trainers fell from his grasp, bounced off the edge of the settee and onto the floor. At the same time the lounge door slammed shut behind him and the overhead lights were switched on. He swung round, blinking at two other shapes that had materialised out of nowhere, one now barring the door, the other leaning against the shelf above the fireplace, arms folded, legs crossed at the ankles.

'Possibly best if we leave the curtains for now,' said Cunningham, flicking through the TV magazine that he'd picked up from the coffee table. 'A little privacy's always a good thing, don't you think?'

Phil took a deep breath, trying to bring his heart rate back under some sort of control.

'What the hell is this, Cunningham? What are you doing here?'

'Very nice, by the way,' said Cunningham. 'The curtains. Very . . . Laura Ashley. I hear the 1970s are making a comeback.'

'Get the hell out of my house!' Phil barked. 'How did you get in here, anyway?'

Cunningham replaced the magazine carefully, adjusting it so that it sat squarely with the edge of the table.

'Ah yes. Well, the less said about that the better. I had to ask young TJ to bring a bit of his magic to bear on your back door and I'm afraid he had a bit of an off day. It appears he may have damaged the lock itself. But please don't concern yourself – I'll be on the phone to a locksmith as soon as we leave. Any damage will be put right before you know it.'

Phil shifted his stance so that he could keep an eye on the other two as he tried to take stock of the situation. He looked around for something he might use if things turned nasty but realised, even as he did so, that this almost certainly wouldn't be necessary. Whatever the reason for this intrusion, it didn't seem likely that violence would be on the agenda. Unless he was foolish enough to throw his weight around. Cunningham's lads, the same two as the other evening, appeared to be there for show more than anything else. If they were tooled up in any way there was nothing obvious to suggest it, and besides – if this was all about giving him a good kicking as payback for Wednesday evening, he was pretty sure they'd have jumped him as he came through the door or, even better, while he was fast asleep. They wouldn't announce themselves and give up the element of surprise. Cunningham didn't work with amateurs.

But neither was he here for no reason. Phil had never had to deal with him in all his years on the force but the name had always been out there. He'd been very much right-hand man to the Bellamy brothers for some time now and you didn't get close to them without proving your worth. In confronting him the other evening Phil knew he'd thrust his hand into a hornet's nest. It was one thing to do that when your blood was up, another thing altogether to have to deal with the consequences in the cold light of day. He had no idea what Cunningham had in mind and was more than unnerved at the prospect of finding out. But he was also damned if he was going to give him the satisfaction of showing it.

'Taking a bit of a chance, aren't we?' he said, sitting down on the settee with a nonchalance he certainly did not feel and slipping his feet into his trainers. 'Didn't think we'd see you stooping to B&E.'

Cunningham smiled. 'I think you'll find that if it comes down to it – and we both know it won't, incidentally – I started a round of golf about . . . three quarters of an hour ago? Foursomes, so plenty of witnesses there. I'm probably on the fourth green about now. Do hope my putting's showing signs of improvement.'

He got up from the armchair and walked over to the shelf where he picked up the photo of Phil and Sally in Puerto Banus. 'Besides,' he said, 'it's hardly breaking and entering when you yourself invited me over here the other evening. Correct me if I'm wrong but you seemed to be eager enough then to hear any news I might have for you regarding your son. If I've misunderstood, just say the word and we'll be on our way.'

'You didn't seem too interested in helping me out as I recall,' said Phil, tugging the first of the laces tight. 'So what's changed since Wednesday?'

'Well, let's just say I found myself affected by your situation. You're clearly under a great deal of stress at the moment and could probably do with a little TLC.'

'And you don't want a ticking time bomb turning up on your doorstep every five minutes, is that it? Might cramp your style a little?'

'Pretty lady, by the way,' said Cunningham, replacing the photo frame on the shelf. 'Cramp my style? No, I don't think I need to worry about that. Let's just say I've never seen any point in going out of my way to antagonise people. If the choice is there, it makes far more sense to seek some sort of compromise.'

'OK,' said Phil. 'I'm listening.'

And he did just that as Cunningham cleared his throat and took him through what one of his subordinates was supposed to have told him as recently as the previous evening. Much of what he had to say Phil was inclined to dismiss as self-serving nonsense, especially his explanation as to *when* he came by the information. If he knew Ezra Cunningham at all, there was nothing here that he hadn't already known when they talked in the restaurant. He just hadn't seen any advantage in passing it on at the time, and if he was doing so now, it was because he'd had a rethink. He reminded himself that this was Cunningham and that simply taking everything at face value would be a big mistake. There would be agendas hidden in every sentence.

But as things turned out, the tale he told hung together far better than might have been expected, and whatever levels of scepticism he was ready to bring to bear, he found to his surprise that once he stripped away all the flowery language and Cunningham's theatrical delivery, what was left rang true somehow.

The essence was that just under a month ago – Saturday, 23rd August to be precise – Cunningham's chauffeur had been sent to an address in Wick near Littlehampton to pick up an important guest at a dinner party that was being held there. As he arrived at the front door, Callum and an unidentified woman were just leaving. The chauffeur knew Callum from the Thursday night squash sessions and exchanged a few words with him before watching them drive off in a yellow sports car. Almost immediately, according to the chauffeur, a truck came out of a side road and set off in the same direction. He didn't think anything of it at the time, apart from the fact that the driver seemed to be in a hurry.

Five minutes later, having collected his guest, the chauffeur set off for home and was surprised as he passed the Body Shop to see the same truck parked just inside the entrance to the petrol station with its lights turned off, which struck him as dangerous as anyone arriving at speed might not see him there until the last minute before turning into the forecourt. He drove on and a few minutes later the yellow sports car flew past him, followed moments after by the truck which seemed to be going flat out in an effort to keep up.

The chauffeur said it seemed pretty clear that the truck driver was following either Callum or the woman he was with. He toyed with the idea of staying with them to see if anything came of it but he was on a job and his number-one responsibility was to make sure the guest got home safely, so he'd turned off in Felpham and that was the last he saw of them.

He didn't think any more of the incident until he heard, a few days later, that someone had beaten Callum to death in a field somewhere near South Mundham. At first he'd been worried in case it had happened that same evening that he'd picked up his customer in Wick and was relieved when he heard it was actually a couple of days later. Even so, he'd been reluctant to say anything to Cunningham, in the latter's heavily sanitised version of events, because he was worried he might be blamed for not having said something earlier. He'd come forward reluctantly when Cunningham put the word out that he wanted to know of any little whisper that might be doing the rounds.

It could all be nonsense, of course. Cunningham was a master at distorting the real picture and he was quite capable of inventing something as fanciful as this if he wanted to get Phil off his back. But what held Phil's attention more than anything else was the fact that when he asked for a description of the truck, Cunningham shrugged his shoulders and said there wasn't a lot he could tell him. It was just an old truck, the chauffeur had said, with a load of equipment in the back. He was pretty sure there was writing on the side but he hadn't taken it in. Looked like some sort of odd-jobber truck, was how he'd described it to Cunningham.

And *that* got Phil's attention.

Cunningham and his minders left shortly afterwards. As he stepped through the front door, he made it clear that as far as he was concerned he'd now done more than enough to help Phil to move on. And moving on, he stressed, meant precisely that.

'Much as I enjoy these little chats of ours,' he said, 'I don't expect our paths to cross again in the near future. Please don't disappoint me, Mr Green.' And with that he walked off down the path, leaving Phil with thoughts of a red Mitsubishi truck he'd seen parked outside Abi's just recently. And its owner who had made it clear that he didn't like Callum.

And in particular he remembered the flash of temper and the instinctive grab for the heavy spanner.

Time for more phone calls, he thought to himself, stooping to take his trainers off again.

ABI

'Are you OK?'

'Mmm?'

She looked up from the coffee she'd been stirring, startled momentarily. How long had she drifted off for? She tried to remember what Mary had been talking about last time she'd tuned in but the embarrassing truth was she had no idea.

'You seem a bit preoccupied, dear.'

'Sorry,' she said, sitting bolt upright and offering an apologetic smile. 'Miles away. What were you saying?'

Mary laughed. 'Nothing important,' she said. 'Just droning on as usual about the book signing next week. I was just wondering if you'll be able to pop in at some stage and offer moral support. I've got this nightmare vision of me sitting there, hidden behind a great big pile of books and no one turning up.'

Abi patted her hand to reassure her. That was not going to happen. Mary's latest book was flying up the Amazon charts and her loyal army of devoted followers pretty much guaranteed a packed audience any time she appeared in public. No one knew this better than Mary but she was never averse to being reminded of how popular she was.

Abi promised she'd be there and smiled again.

Easing her fork into a cupcake, Mary launched into another anecdote about her agent, who had been making a bit of a mess of negotiations over the sale of foreign translation rights – at least, that was Mary's take on things.

Abi sipped her coffee, eyes locked on to Mary's over the rim of the cup, and tried to focus on what she was saying, but within seconds she found herself sneaking a glance at her watch. Eleven forty-five. She did the maths again in her head. Flight landing around 10.40, an hour or so to reclaim luggage and get back to the car, another hour from Gatwick back to Chichester. He probably wouldn't say anything right away because it was a long flight and Freja would be worn out. Wouldn't be fair to spring something like that on her when she's travelled all this way just to see him. He'd even been making noises about saying nothing till the week was up and it was time for her to go back but she didn't see how that could possibly work. Freja would know something was up. She'd have to.

Not your problem, she reminded herself. She and Adam had been talking this through for a while now and were both quite clear about where the boundaries lay. If he wanted to walk away from his relationship with Freja that didn't mean he was looking to walk straight into another one. And just because she was now on her own and at a low ebb, that didn't mean she was going to throw herself at the first available man. They were friends, had been for a while now. She liked the fact that he was able to listen to her without automatically trying to turn everything round to his own circumstances, and if he offered an opinion it was generally worth listening to. She hoped he appreciated the similar levels of support she was able to offer to him. That's what friends are for, they'd told each other – so often it was practically a mantra. Just because Callum and Freja had been taken out of the equation that was no reason for anything in their own relationship to change.

She had no problem in rationalising it.

But she still found herself checking her watch every few minutes.

'It all sounds a bit off to me,' Mary was saying. 'I mean, if you were in my shoes, you wouldn't stand for it, would you?'

'No,' she said, a shot in the dark.

The smile on Mary's face suggested she had guessed correctly.

PHIL

The Steam Packet was in River Road, just along from the Arun View which he'd always preferred back in the day when he'd been based in Littlehampton. Both pubs were tucked tight against the river, overlooking the harbour, but the Steam Packet had always seemed like the poor relation back in the eighties, dependent on a handful of loyal and committed regulars, while the Arun View attracted diners from a much wider area. About five or six years ago the Packet had actually gone out of business but had recently been taken over by enterprising new owners keen to draw on the history of the building, stretching back as it did to the mid-nineteenth century, when it was a favoured haunt of passengers waiting to take one of the steam-packet ships across the English Channel to Honfleur. As a result of the money and energy that had been poured into renovating and refurbishing it, the balance between the Packet and the Arun View had been redressed to a great extent.

It didn't take Phil long to find Mick Hall. He was sitting on his own at a corner table, looking for all the world like the before photo in a public-health promotion. Phil suspected they were probably more or less the same age but in all honesty Hall looked anything up to twenty years older. His pockmarked face, scarred from what must have been a chronic case of juvenile acne, had the kind of pasty complexion that hasn't seen enough of the sun in recent years. He was unshaven with greasy hair slicked back into a ponytail that rested on the stained collar of his leather jacket. Like its owner, the jacket had clearly seen better days.

He was flicking through a two-day-old copy of the *Little-hampton Gazette* and taking frequent gulps from the pint glass which, he'd made clear earlier, would need constant refilling if he was going to give up his valuable time to answer questions. Over the phone an hour or so ago, Phil had introduced himself as a freelance reporter hired to do background research for an article on the recent murder in South Mundham. He'd decided on this approach because he wanted Hall to be as open as possible and was concerned that identifying himself as Callum's father might put him on his guard.

He needn't have worried. Hall had made a point of turning down Phil's request to begin with, making it sound like a major intrusion into his private life, as if re-opening wounds and exposing painful memories to the light of day might be too much for such a sensitive soul: 'The boys in blue've already had their pound of flesh . . . not sure I can go through it all again.' But Phil had dealt with the Mick Halls of this world for long enough to recognise an opening gambit when he saw one. Hall had been sniffing out the lie of the land, trying to gauge whether there might be easy money in this for him. The moment it became clear that wasn't going to happen, he'd been quick enough to settle for having his bar bill taken care of for a couple of hours. Better than a kick in the teeth.

Phil bought a lager for himself and two pints of some obscure Real Ale for Hall to get things started. As it happened, he was already revved up and ready to go by the time the glasses were placed in front of him. It was difficult to escape the impression that talking about his family and the savage blows life had dealt him were a staple part of his conversational diet. All it took was a glass and a sympathetic ear and he was off. Phil knew that, as with Cunningham, he'd have to be careful not to take everything as gospel. Hall was a serial whinger; everything that had ever gone wrong in his life was down to some malevolent natural force or unseen, shadowy conspirators who naturally had it in for him. Nothing was ever his own fault, so the thumb was pressing too heavily on the scales for him to be a reliable witness.

For the first few minutes Phil was happy to let him talk as randomly as he liked. The looser his tongue became, the more likely he was to wander off script and offer glimpses of what really lay beyond the protective screens his self-esteem threw up . . . or what was left of it. It seemed like an eternity before he got around to talking about Owen. When he did, he made little effort at diplomacy.

'The runt,' he said, breaking off to rinse the bad taste out of his mouth with another swig from his glass. 'Runt of the litter. Couldn't hold a candle to his brother. I know you're not supposed to have favourites when it's your own kids, but it's human nature, isn't it? Can't like everyone. Some kids you take to, some you don't.'

'I didn't know Owen had a brother,' Phil said.

'William. His twin. Proud English name that. The wife kept calling him Willie – used to drive me up the sodding wall. It's not Willie Shakespeare, I used to say to her. It's not Willie Wordsworth. It's *William*. I choose one name, she chooses the other – that's what we agreed. Least she can do is respect my decision and call him by his proper name. How would she like it if I started calling her precious boy O? O-ee?' He chuckled into his glass.

'Not sure *runt*'s the word I'd have used,' said Phil, tearing open a packet of crisps and pushing them into the centre of the table. 'When was the last time you saw him?'

Hall sniffed and helped himself to a handful of crisps since they were on offer. 'Big bugger, isn't he?' he chuckled. 'Bumped into him in town a couple of years ago. Hard to believe it was the same kid. If he gets it from his father, I'm fucked if I know who he is, cos it sure as hell isn't me. But he was the runt back then all right. Came out about fifteen minutes after his brother. Struggling for breath, cord wrapped round his neck or something. Face all blue. Pity they didn't just wrap it round a few more times and have done with it. Could have done us all a favour.'

Phil knew he was expected to react. He'd heard this kind of offhand cruelty many times before and recognised it for what it was. In some people the desire to shock and play up to a carefully cultivated image left them with no room for sensitivity or propriety. Nothing was ever going to hurt or even come close to getting to Mick Hall. And the more he tried to prove as much, the more he gave the lie to it.

'William was your favourite, then?' he asked.

Hall grabbed another handful of crisps from the pack and stuffed them into his mouth. 'Cracking kid. Always laughing – that was the first thing anyone ever noticed about him. Cheeky grin, real sense of mischief, you know? More like me when I was a kid, I suppose. I mean, he used to overstep the mark a bit and you had to slap him down from time to time, just so he knew right from wrong – but it never bothered him, you know? Never sulked about it. Ten minutes later he'd be flying round the room like nothing had happened. You couldn't help but like him.'

'And Owen was different?'

Hall almost choked in mid-gulp. 'Different?' he said, wiping his mouth with the back of his hand. 'Yeah ... that's the word for it. He was different, all right. I always said they knew right from the start, the hospital people. They kept him in for a couple of weeks when he was born – ran all these tests. They said he might have problems with ... fucked if I can remember what. All went straight over my head. Lots of long words. I left that side of things to the missus, to be honest. Not that she needed much persuading to look after him. I told her, it *was* twins she had. There was another kid who could do with a bit of attention as well if she could tear herself away for a couple of minutes. Just as well I was there or William wouldn't have got a look in. She hardly left Owen's side for the first few weeks.'

'So you felt . . . what . . . that she neglected William?'

'I'm not having a pop at her,' said Hall, nodding at one of the other customers who'd just entered the bar. 'She did the best she could. But Owen took up so much of her time. Practically *demanded* it. He was such a needy little prick and she was so worried about what the hospital had said about how he might be a bit on the slow side. She was determined that wasn't going to happen. Not on her watch. You know that thing they do now – where they make sure women and minority groups get jobs they shouldn't necessarily get?'

'Positive discrimination?'

'That's the one. Positive discrimination. She was doing that long before all these do-gooders got hold of the idea. She wasn't going to let Owen fall behind if she could help it. I mean, William was a bright kid, right? Reading before he went to infants' school, you know? Must have been four and he was sitting there working his way through these old *Janet and John* books she'd kept from when she was a girl. So when Owen couldn't do the same she used to spend hours with him, going through the same bloody pages over and over again. Christ, even I knew the books off by heart after a while, so it's no wonder Owen managed to recognise a few words eventually, and when he did . . . fuck me! You'd have thought he'd done one of those Ruby cubes or something.'

'Maybe Owen was just better at other things,' prompted Phil. 'Isn't he good with numbers?'

'Good? He's unbelievable. But it's not like he can take any credit for it. It's not something he's worked at, sorted out for himself. He was born with it, know what I mean? I always said it was something to do with the way he came out. I mean, when that cord was wrapped round his neck and he was being starved of oxygen for however long it was, you're not going to tell me that doesn't bend you out of shape in some way. It's got to make you different, put a bit of a kink in the system somewhere. The poor little sod lost out in so many other ways, there was bound to be a bit of compensation somewhere. Anyway, when the wife found out he'd got this *gift,* I suppose you'd call it, she clung to it like a fucking life raft. Like it made up for everything else. Turned it into some sort of party piece. Used to piss me off no end, to be honest. The moment anyone came round, she'd go, "What's twenty-seven times twenty-four, Owen?" And he'd be like, "One thousand and whatever," before you'd even worked out what the question was. And then, of course, because it all had to be balanced out properly, William would have to read something and who the fuck wants to sit there and listen to a four-year-old telling you about some cat sat on a fucking mat? You could see whoever it was rolling their eyes the moment she wasn't looking cos she did it every sodding time. No wonder people stopped calling after a while. I mean, you want to see a performing seal, you go to the zoo, right?'

He drained the second of the glasses and waggled it in front of Phil's nose. Phil got up and ordered a refill from the bar. Just the one. There was still a detail he wanted to pick up on.

'So what happened to William?' he asked, as soon as he'd returned to the table.

Hall said nothing for a moment. A group of half a dozen or so people had arrived to take up their reservation and order drinks from the bar. An old golden retriever hauled itself to its feet, turned a couple of circles and then collapsed again in a heap alongside an elderly man who reached down absent-mindedly and scratched the dog's ear without looking up from his *Mail on Sunday*.

'His brother happened to him.'

'His brother? How d'you mean?'

'Six years old, they were. Way too young but they'd both been on at me for months about how they wanted a tree house in the garden. Tree house, my arse. We hadn't even got a fucking tree. But they'd been to this kid's birthday party and the complete dickhead of a father had put up this platform on stilts and then built a playhouse on it. You know the sort, with steps going up one side and a slide and ropes coming down the other? Never saw it myself, just went by what the wife told me. Anyway, the moment they got home it was, "Can you make us one, Dad? Please, Dad. Robin's dad made *him* one." Like I've got all the time in the world and no way am I a proper father unless I do this. I kept fobbing them off, hoping they'd forget about it and get into football or something but they kept on and on and the wife was just as bad, so in the end I gave in just to shut them up. Paid this mate of mine to come round and do most of it cos I'm useless with my hands – always have been. Useless at most things.'

He paused for a moment and used a finger to trace circles in the beer that had leaked onto the table. For just a moment it was possible to catch in his distracted stare a glimpse of the family man underneath all the bravado.

'Anyway,' he continued, 'they came home from school one day and saw this bloody great thing in the garden and you'd have thought all their Christmases had come at once. All of a sudden I was the best dad ever and they wanted to sleep out in it that first night, so guess who had to kip out in a sleeping bag on the lawn to keep an eye on them? Right in the middle of an ants' nest too. Woke up, I'd got bites all down one arm.' He chuckled at the memory, but it didn't stay around long enough to lighten the mood.

'Then one day I was at work and the boss called me in. Said I'd better phone home cos the missus was screaming the place down and when I did it was one of the neighbours who answered and told me she'd just left. She was following the ambulance to the hospital and wanted me to meet her there, and I'm like, "What fucking ambulance?" and that's when I found out William had fallen out of the tree house and landed on his head. The first-aid guys had taken ages to move him cos they were worried about his neck, maybe even a fractured skull. Anyway, the boss took my keys off me and drove me there himself. Said I wasn't in a fit state. And by the time I got to the hospital they'd got the wife and Owen in a side room and she was in tears and you know the first thing she said to me when I came in? Before I'd even had a chance to ask what happened. "Owen was with me in the kitchen, practising his reading." That's what she said. And I thought, *OK* . . . bit weird, but then again maybe she's in shock. Only she must have said the same thing half a dozen times while we were waiting there for someone to come in and explain what was going on cos I remember thinking yeah, well, maybe if she'd been keeping an eye on William instead, this wouldn't have happened.'

He held out a couple of crisps to try to entice the retriever to get up and claim them but the dog had already stirred once in the past few minutes and showed no interest in doing so again for such feeble pickings.

'Anyway,' he continued, 'this surgeon comes in when he's good and ready. Looks about twelve, all pleased with himself, like he's just hit puberty. Starts using long words and I'm just about to ask him if someone shoved a dictionary up his arse when he was a kid and can't he speak English so we've got some vague idea what the fuck he's talking about when this nurse pokes her head round the door and says he's needed in theatre urgently. And we can hear all this commotion going on next door, machines bleeping, alarms going off, people hurrying here, there and everywhere – you know the sort of thing. Only no one's telling us a fucking thing. We must have been in there for half an hour on our own, wondering what the fuck was going on before he came back with a face like a slapped arse and told us he was sorry – there'd been a massive bleed on the brain or something and they hadn't been able to do anything to save him. Gone. Just like that. Like flicking a switch. And I'm holding onto the missus for dear life cos I swear she'd have hit the floor otherwise and all I can hear is Owen, sitting there in the corner, playing with this toy Bugatti we bought him and singing some bloody stupid song to himself, over and over, like nothing had even happened. And I know he was only six, but even so ... Jesus Christ! There should've been something there, you know? Should've been something.'

He shook his head and made deep inroads into the next pint. At this rate, Phil calculated, he'd get through five or six in an hour. He wondered whether this was a regular routine or maybe he was taking advantage of the opportunity Phil's interview had afforded him. Probably a bit of both, he decided.

'I'm sorry,' he said, meaning it. He was trying hard not to recall the moment, less than four weeks earlier, when he'd learned of the death of his own son. Whatever his opinion of Hall as a person, they had at least that much in common.

'Yeah, well . . .' Mask of indifference firmly back in place. Nothing gets to Mick Hall. 'Anyway, the next few weeks I figured I needed to see if there was some way I could build some sort of relationship with Owen. I mean, I knew it wasn't going to be easy. As far as I was concerned, the good sperm had been taken from us and we were left with the bit that should have run off down the wife's leg, but she was a real mess herself so I thought what the hell. I took him to the cinema, brought him little treats that I'd picked up on the way home from work – you know, nothing much. Just sweets or chocolate. He had this thing about Jelly Tots – you remember them? Ate the things by the bucketload. But it didn't matter what I tried; he just didn't seem comfortable with me. Kept fretting all the time if we were out together: "When are we going home?" And the moment we got back he'd go rushing up to her and cling on as if they hadn't seen each other for a year or something. I guess you can't fool kids, can you? They always know.'

Callum was the same, Phil remembered. Always more comfortable in Sally's company. Always sensing he'd get a better deal out of her than he would out of his father. Go for the instinctive sympathy every time. He felt he understood the sense of rejection Hall was trying to articulate, even though he hoped to God he hadn't anything like as much with which to reproach himself.

'So about two or three months go past and the wife and I, we're still struggling to get our heads round what happened. Part of the problem for me was I just couldn't make any sense of it. William was such a confident little kid, used to shin up and down that ladder to the tree house like something out of *Jungle Book*. I didn't understand how he could have fallen like that. And I mentioned it to her a couple of times and straightaway she's slipping in comments like she didn't know, she wasn't there, she was in the kitchen with Owen. And I'm like, "For fuck's sake, will you shut up about Owen for five seconds? Why do you keep going on about where Owen was?" And I think it just sort of started from there, you know?'

Phil looked closely at him.

'You think Owen had something to do with his fall?' he asked.

'I don't know, do I? I wasn't there either. But the thought just sort of crept up on me over a period of time and I must have done a bad job of keeping it to myself cos one day she lost it completely and started having a go big time. Said she knew what I was hinting at. What sort of a father was I? How could I think for one minute my own son could do something like that? And the best joke was it wouldn't even have occurred to me if she hadn't kept banging on about it. And then, final straw, I heard him in his room one evening, shouting at William. I mean, he used to talk to him all the time as if he'd never gone away and Jesus, that was tough. But this time, must have been about three or four months after the accident, he was yelling at him, saying it was his fault. Something to do with this Bugatti car he had, how it was his not William's and how many times did he have to tell him he wasn't allowed to play with it unless he asked.

"Your fault", he kept saying. "Your fault." And, I mean . . . you hear something like that, you can't help asking yourself what he's talking about, right? What exactly was *William's fault*?' He sketched the speech marks in the air.

'So,' he continued with a shrug, 'that was just about it for me. I left soon after, and never went back – which, OK, it doesn't exactly make me father of the year, but you know that thing they say about walking a mile in someone's shoes before you judge them? Maybe when you've kissed your own kid goodbye and set off for work, not knowing that's the last time you're ever going to see him – maybe when that happens to you, you can come back and point the finger, yeah?'

Phil bit his tongue, held his breath, worked his way through every cliché known to him. Said nothing. Instead, he got up and thanked Hall for his time.

'You're not going yet, are you?' Hall replied, dismayed that his meal ticket was suddenly on its way out of the door. 'There's plenty more I can tell you.'

Phil thought about throwing a fiver on the table, then thought again.

He felt he'd heard enough.

ANNA

By nine o'clock she'd considered the alternatives and reached the depressing conclusion that bed was as good an option as any. She'd worked her way through a mental checklist, crossing items off one by one:

TV? Crap. Mental candy floss.

Go for a run? Seriously? Again? How many times could she do that in one day without asking herself a few pointed questions?

Read a book? Not in the mood.

Call a friend? Sure. Nine o'clock on a Sunday evening. Not like that would set alarm bells ringing or anything. Her friends thought she was desperate enough as it was – the last thing they needed was more ammunition.

Give in, grab a bottle and go join the party downstairs? No way. She knew she'd only been invited as an afterthought, a courtesy gesture designed to ensure she was inside the tent pissing out, rather than the other way round. The last thing they wanted was for her to start complaining about the noise. And that was the generous interpretation; a more plausible one was that there was a serious shortage of women on tap and someone had come up with the bright idea of drafting in what's-her-name from upstairs. Better than nothing. Well, sorry, but she wasn't about to be the token *anything*.

People had been arriving for the past half hour or so and her flat had been resounding to doors crashing, footsteps on the stairs, voices getting louder by the minute. The hilarity of it all. No way. Bed was starting to look appealing. She knew there was a danger she might end up lying there for hours staring at the ceiling and straining to piece together fragments of conversation from the balcony below but she might get lucky and drift off to sleep before the pubs emptied and the mayhem really kicked in. Worth a try at any rate – in the absence of anything better.

She was so caught up in feeling sorry for herself that she almost missed the phone call, picking up on the vibration only at the last minute. She snatched her mobile from the coffee table and checked the caller ID.

'Hey,' she said, throwing herself onto the settee and striving for a cheery nonchalance to disguise the sheer relief she felt.

'Anna?'

'Phil?'

'Is this OK?'

'Is what OK?'

'Ringing you like this.'

'Of course. Why wouldn't it be?'

'I was worried it might be a bit late.'

She looked at her watch. 'It's only just gone nine,' she said, laughing at the irony of it all. 'My social life may not be sizzling right now but even I draw the line at going to bed *this* early.'

'If you're sure . . . Only it can wait till morning.'

'No need. Now's fine.'

'I don't know why I rang, really. I mean, we could talk about it while we're on patrol, if you'd prefer.'

'It's the duck joke, right?'

'The what?'

'You didn't get it and were too embarrassed to say so.'

'Very funny,' he said. 'No, it's not that. It's something you said earlier this week. About how I ought to be doing a bit of digging around to see if I can come up with something that will . . . you know.'

'The private-eye thing?' she said, swinging her legs down onto the floor. 'Tell me you're going to give it a go.'

'Well, I was thinking maybe –'

'You'll need a glamorous assistant. All the best private eyes have one. Someone who works as receptionist and keeps his life in some sort of order and listens while he bounces ideas off her, and he sort of takes her for granted at first, like she's only there to answer the phone and make coffee, only eventually he gets to realise how clever she is and she's the one who spots the tiny detail that he's been overlooking which means he can make that crucial breakthrough. I could do that. I could be a sort of Lois Lane to your . . . whoever it was?'

'Superman?'

'Superman wasn't a private eye, dummy.'

'Whereas Lois Lane *was* a receptionist, right?'

'I think you might be missing the point.'

'Anyway, we're getting a bit ahead of ourselves here,' he said. 'I was thinking more of an informal sort of thing. What you said the other day, it got me thinking, and tonight I finally got off my backside and did something about it.'

'Did what exactly?'

'I went to see Owen Hall's father.'

Without me? was the thought that leaped unbidden into her head. *Why didn't you think to ask me?*

'And? What did he have to say?'

'I'll fill you in tomorrow. But it was really interesting and it's given me an idea as to where I might go from here, only . . . I don't think I can do it on my own. I'd need help with it.'

There was something in his tone of voice, a strange sort of hesitancy that hinted at the need for caution.

'Is it legal?' she asked.

'Yes,' he said. 'I think so.'

'Is it dangerous?'

'No, not really.'

'You think so and not really? Wow, you really know how to sell an idea. I'll need to think about all this.'

'Really?'

'Thought about it. I'm in.'

'You had me worried there for a minute,' he laughed. 'But you don't know what I'm going to suggest yet.'

'I know,' she said, leaping up from the settee and hunting down her Converse trainers just in case. 'You fancy meeting me for a drink so you can tell me more?'

'What? Now?'

'Sure. Why not? You got something better to do?'

'Ah, no. Not really.'

'You know Spoons in the Queensway?'

'Spoons?'

'Wetherspoons.'

'You mean the Hatter's Inn?'

'I can be there in ten if that's any use.'

'You sure that's OK?'

'Well, it means I'll have to put off cutting my toenails till tomorrow but I can live with that if you can.'

There was a pause and for a moment she wondered if he was trying to come up with an excuse. Then his voice came through, loud and clear.

'OK. Ten minutes. See you there.'

'And that,' she said as she closed her mobile, 'is what you call a date. Sorry, boys – this token lady's otherwise engaged.'

15

NOW: WEDNESDAY, 8TH OCTOBER

PHIL

'Get in!'

It wasn't difficult to pick out Holloway, even though the car park was still heaving. He'd driven right up to the front of the complex and parked across one of the loading bays where he stuck out like a sore thumb. He was standing with one leg outside the car, head peering over the driver's door. And he looked less than pleased to be there.

Phil, who had half an idea what might be happening here, suggested to Anna that she might like to walk on without him for a while and made his way over to the car. Holloway had missed nothing, his eyes fixed on her as she stepped back inside the foyer.

'That would be the elusive Julie, I suppose?'

Ah!

Phil waited until Holloway had clambered back into the car, then followed suit. Before he'd even closed the passenger door, the engine roared into life and they shot forward, weaving their way in and out of the rows of vehicles until they came to an area at the far side of the complex where the local buses picked up and deposited passengers from Bognor and Chichester every fifteen minutes. Holloway swung two wheels up onto the grass verge and parked there, far enough removed from the hubbub of daily life at Arun Valley to be confident that they wouldn't be overheard. He left the keys in the ignition but flicked a switch to open the window and unfastened his seat belt. Then he leaned back in his seat, tugging furiously at his tie and undoing the top button of his shirt.

'You bloody idiot,' he sighed.

'I'm not apologising.'

'Did I ask you for an apology?'

'And if you're looking to have a pop at someone over this, then leave her out of it. It's my fault, OK? My idea not hers.'

'Jesus.'

They sat there in silence for a moment or two, Holloway staring off into the distance while Phil fiddled subconsciously with his radio mic, making sure it was turned off. He suspected they were probably out of range of the Control Room by now but he didn't want to take any chances.

'So how did you find out?' he asked eventually.

'Owen Hall called us.'

Phil waited for elaboration, which didn't appear to be forthcoming.

'OK. How did *he* find out?'

Holloway dragged his thoughts back into the car and turned to face him.

'He saw her. Here. With you. How d'you think?'

Phil nodded. There had always been a risk that might happen. Most people in the area came to Arun Valley at some time or other and he and Anna weren't exactly low profile. Even so, a bit unlucky, he thought.

'You want to tell me what you thought you were doing?' asked Holloway. 'Apart from wasting valuable man hours, that is. I've spent the last hour or so playing the sympathy card with my boss, telling her you're not yourself after what happened to your boy and that all those years on the job ought to entitle you to a little bit of slack. Trust me, she needed some persuading. What in God's name were you thinking?'

Phil wasn't sure how to respond. He didn't imagine for one minute that anything he had to say was going to cut much ice with Andy Holloway at the moment.

'Quite apart from the damage you may have done – and trust me, we'll get to that in a minute – what on earth gives you the right to put that girl's safety at risk like that?'

'She wasn't at risk.'

'No, of course she wasn't. Keep telling yourself that. You can't have it both ways, for Christ's sake. You're so sure Owen Hall represents a danger to society, yet you're happy to mess around with his head and then send her off with him in his pickup? How does that work?'

'She was never in any danger. They were never out of my sight. I was right behind them all the way.'

'Oh right. No chance of anything going wrong there, then.'

'And she does MMA. She can look after herself if she has to.'

'And your boy was handy enough, if I remember rightly, and had a baseball bat for extra protection.'

'Yeah, well, thanks for the reminder, Andy. I guess that'd slipped my mind.'

Holloway held up his hand to apologise for his clumsiness and Phil was reminded instantly of what a decent bloke he was. A genuinely good man. Holloway's opinion of him mattered for some reason. He didn't want to be thought of as some hapless amateur stumbling around in the dark and trampling everything he came across into the dirt. He wanted him to understand.

'I had to try something,' he said eventually. 'I tried talking to you about it but didn't feel like I was getting anywhere. And you weren't looking in the right direction.'

'Oh really? And that would be your considered opinion – based on all the evidence and all your years in Major Crimes, I suppose?'

'It's Hall, Andy. Forget all the other crap about jealous ex-husbands and the Bellamy brothers and people who've been ripped off in dodgy financial deals. They're just a sideshow. It's Hall who killed Callum and I had to find some way to get you to take him seriously.'

'I repeat. Evidence.'

'The guy's not right in the head, for God's sake. He's an accident waiting to happen. I'm not denying he had a tough time of it as a kid, but the guy needs help. He shouldn't be out among the general public. You've only got to talk to him for five minutes to see that. He was following Callum just two nights before he was killed. What more do you want? And the temper on him – it's something else. He nearly came after me with a spanner the other day for no reason. Out of nowhere. There was just this . . . this *explosion* of anger. If you'd been there –'

'And yet you still felt comfortable about putting her in the truck with him?'

He tossed his head in irritation.

'And that's it?' continued Holloway. 'That's your evidence?'

'It's enough for me.' He sighed, took a deep breath. 'Look, Andy – I'm not stupid. I know you need more than that. I just thought maybe if we put him under a bit of pressure he might start to panic a bit, make a mistake. There's got to be some way of tying him into all this. He can't have thought of everything. He'll have slipped up somewhere.'

'It's not how we work, OK? I don't need to tell you that, for God's sake. We don't just pick our square peg and then try to find some hole we can ram him into. It's the other way round. We go where the evidence takes us because eventually that's how we're going to prove who did it.'

'But that's the point,' snapped Phil, his frustration coming to the boil. 'How are you going to find the evidence? Why aren't you searching his truck? Have you been through his house? Have you tried taking him in and sweating him for a few hours? I just don't get why you aren't doing more to spook him. Have you talked to his father? I went to see him and even *he* hasn't got a good word to say about him. Did he tell you about the other boy? His twin brother, and what happened to him? And what about the photos I put in his truck? I bet he didn't tell you about those, did he?'

'He did, as a matter of fact.'

'Straightaway? Or after he'd had a chance to work out you might have seen them on CCTV?'

Holloway opened his mouth to reply, then closed it again. He drummed with his fingers on the dashboard while he worked out the best way to respond. Then he shook his head and sighed, as if the effort to keep things on an even keel was taking its toll.

'Phil,' he said. 'All those years on the job, you still haven't got a clue how we operate. The absolute tonnage of what you don't know would sink a freighter, I swear to God. You remember the first thing I said to you? How you needed to stay out of this and leave us to do our jobs? How I wouldn't be able to tell you what was going on for solid operational reasons but you just had to trust us? You don't have a bloody clue what we're doing on a day-to-day basis and you make that obvious every time you open your mouth, yet you think it's OK not just to formulate half-baked theories but to pursue them with no regard to the havoc you're wreaking.'

'Great, you tell me nothing and then it's my fault somehow for not being in the picture –'

'Wrong. I don't blame you for knowing nothing. I blame you for acting as if you know *everything*. You're so convinced it's Owen Hall that you've shut your mind off to all other possibilities.'

'What other possibilities?'

'No – we're not doing this. I'm not feeding you a list of suspects so you can go off and harass them the way you did Owen Hall. *And* Ezra Cunningham, for God's sake. Have you got a death wish or something? You're going to stay out of it, you understand?'

'Dream on.'

'I mean it, Phil.'

'Yeah, well, so do I.'

They sat there in silence for a moment, each aware that nothing was going to be achieved by gradually cranking up the volume. Holloway snapped the sun visor into place to shield his eyes from the glare that was reflecting off the windscreen.

Phil, for his part, opened the passenger door to allow a stiff breeze to circulate throughout the car.

Holloway picked up where they'd left off. 'Look,' he said, pressing his neck against the headrest as if trying to drill a hole through it, 'I can only imagine what you're going through and how frustrating it must be, but I can't have you thinking we're sitting on our thumbs and doing sod all. You think we're not looking at Owen Hall? You're wrong. I'll tell you this much in the strictest confidence, OK? If it gets out, I'll come after you with a baseball bat myself because this is just between you and me, right? For old times' sake.'

'OK.'

'You're wrong. You're so wrong on so many levels I can't even begin to tell you. We haven't ruled him out by any stretch of the imagination. We just haven't managed to come up with anything so far that ties him in directly. Everything's circumstantial. Motive? Yeah, he's angry about the way he was bullied at school and blames your boy for it. Big time. But it would be nice to have something a bit more substantial than that. Lots of kids get bullied. They don't necessarily go after the chief culprit with a baseball bat – and certainly not twelve years later. Opportunity? Maybe – just about. But it would be the tightest of fits because we know he was picking up his ticket from Cineworld at eight forty-two. We've got a definite time for that and CCTV footage of him in the car park. It was him all right. And unless your daughter-in-law is going to come up with yet another version of exactly when she left his place that makes it really, really tight. So what we've got here is a real Catch-22 situation. We need to come up with something that ties him to the scene in Honer Lane and right now we haven't got a single shred of physical evidence to suggest he was anywhere near there. Nothing. Zilch. And in order to get it we'd probably need to search his house and do a more comprehensive forensic job on his truck but we can't do that without a warrant and to get that we need something that ties him to the scene. Like I said, Catch-22. And unlike you we can't just go flinging accusations around based on personal dislike and prejudice. We need evidence. So we'll keep looking, keep chipping away, until we find out who did it, which we will do eventually. Put your house on it. We'll get there in the end. And when we do, I'll tell you what . . . you'd better hope it wasn't Owen Hall who killed your boy because, if it was, our chances of gaining a conviction have just been made a damned sight more remote than they were before you started pissing on them from a great height.'

'What d'you mean?'

'What I mean is that you've opened such a bloody great hole that any defence solicitor worthy of the name is going to be able to drive a bus through our case it if it ever makes it to trial. Whether you accept it or not, we're dealing with a vulnerable adult here and it's not going to take Perry Mason to come up with grounds for dismissal. It's not like the old days. They scream entrapment at the drop of a hat nowadays and this is like a textbook definition of the word. You couldn't have done a better job of protecting him if you'd tried.'

'So because he's vulnerable that means he can't be touched? Is that what you're telling me?'

'No. What I'm saying is because he's vulnerable, we need to play it by the book and have everything tied up neatly. No short cuts. No loopholes. And no bloody sideshows the defence team can seize on to blow smoke in the jury's eyes. And I understand it's a long, drawn-out process but if it's too slow for you and you feel left out of things, just grow up for Christ's sake! This isn't about your need to prove something to yourself or whatever it is that's driving you on here. It's about you keeping out of the way and letting the professionals do their job, and if you can't do that –'

He broke off, leaving the rest of the threat unspecified. Phil was still smarting over the crack about wanting to prove something to himself, more so because he recognised more than a grain of truth in what Holloway had said.

'So just how much trouble am I in at the moment?' he asked.

'Not as much as you ought to be,' came the reply. 'This is your official reprimand. Warning as to future conduct. I've told them you're a reasonable bloke under unimaginable pressure and that once you get your head out of your backside they can trust you to do the right thing. I've called in a few favours but from hereon in you've got to be squeaky clean. I can't have you flying off on kamikaze missions like the last one, Phil. You need to stay out of it.'

Phil took a handkerchief out of his pocket and blew his nose. 'I'm sorry,' he said.

'I thought you said you weren't going to apologise.'

He shook his head. 'Not what I meant. I'm not sorry for what I've done. I'm apologising because I know I can't just stay out of it.' He shrugged his shoulders. 'I'm sorry. I can't.'

'Then they're going to throw the book at you.'

'So let them. He's guilty, Andy. I know we don't have any evidence yet. But he did it. And I'm not going to stand back and watch him get away with it. You tell me your hands are tied. OK. I understand. But mine aren't, and if there's a way of finding something that ties him to the scene, I'm going to find it. One way or another. I'll find it.'

There was a brief silence, then Holloway snatched the keys from the ignition and got out of the car. He shut the door behind him and walked over to one of the picnic tables dotted around the rear of the complex, rolling his head to stretch his neck muscles as he did so. Phil watched as he took off his jacket and laid it on one of the wooden benches before taking a seat there. He gave it a minute or two, then followed him, sitting on a bench alongside. A small plane trailing an advertising banner made a coughing sound, causing them both to look up in momentary concern before the engine picked up again. They watched as it flew off across the open countryside, heading towards the Sussex Downs in the distance.

'I remember I had a good chat with your wife once,' Holloway said eventually. 'Sally, right?'

'Right.'

'You invited the Littlehampton boys to a house-warming party. Years ago, this. Barbecue, I seem to remember. And your kid must have been two or three at the time. I remember he had this double-decker bus thing – you remember? You sit astride them and scoot your way round the place? And he was flying round your back yard on it all evening. Kept crashing into people's ankles.'

'Yeah, that'd be about right,' said Phil, chuckling at the memory although it hadn't seemed quite so amusing at the time. Every door, in fact just about every item of furniture at ground level, had dents and scuff marks where Callum had driven full-tilt into it. They'd tried taking the bus away from him one evening and he'd screamed the place down until they relented and gave it back. Was that the start of the slippery slope, the point where they should have stood their ground? No means no?

'I'd just moved over to CID and I'd been bending your ear for months about doing the same. Surely you weren't going to stay in uniform for the rest of your career. I remember telling Sally you were the most stubborn person I'd ever met.'

'She wouldn't have needed telling.'

'No, you're right. She didn't. But she insisted it wasn't just a case of sheer bloody-mindedness. According to her, you only dug your heels in when it mattered. Most of the time, she said, you were a soft touch and she had to be careful not to take advantage of you because you were so generous about things. But when the chips were down, when it really mattered, she said you had the turning circle of the *QE2*. Once you'd picked your course and set sail, there was no way anyone was ever going to get you to turn round. *QE2*,' he added, sketching a straight line out ahead of him with the vertical palm of one hand.

'And you've just remembered that?'

'Yeah,' said Holloway, rolling up his shirt sleeves. 'Funny that.'

A woman and two teenagers came into the picnic area, carrying afternoon snacks on trays they'd picked up in one of the takeaway franchises on the ground floor. She smiled as she walked past, heading for the most distant table available.

'I need your help here, Phil,' Holloway said.

'With what?'

'If I'm not going to be able to turn the *QE2*, the very least I need to know is what sort of waters she's sailing in. If I know there are icebergs coming up, maybe I can find a way to steer the ship past them.'

'You want to try that in English?'

'Next time you get some bee in your bonnet and want to go off on one – and we both know it's a question of when rather than if, right? – I want you to ring me. Right away. Before you go ahead and do something we'll both end up regretting.'

'Why? So you can talk me out of it?'

'Yes. Absolutely. If I can. But even if I can't, it may be that I can give you a bit of context. If there are things I can tell you that might stop you from making a complete arse of yourself, I'd like the chance to do that.'

'I don't want you to do anything that's going to put your own job at risk,' said Phil, trying to work through the implications.

'Not going to happen,' said Holloway, with a wry smile. 'I'm too close to getting out to allow something like that to happen. But if you're adamant you're not just going to walk away from this –'

'I am.'

'Then it's the best way I can think of to limit the damage. Someone's got to keep an eye on you – protect you from yourself. But I'll need you to be straight with me. I'm going out on a limb here.'

'OK,' said Phil, looking at his watch and realising he'd need to be getting back to work before long or Langford and his cronies would be setting out to track him down. 'I appreciate it. And I promise I won't try anything without clearing it with you first.'

Holloway patted him on the shoulder as he got up and headed for the car. Phil followed but made no effort to get in, deciding the walk back would do him some good. Sitting hunched over, first in the car and then on the wooden bench, had left him feeling stiff and awkward in his movements. He'd need the rest of the afternoon just to loosen up again.

'Don't want to push my luck,' he said, resting his arm on the roof of the car and leaning in through the passenger window, 'but is there anything more you can tell me?'

'Like what?'

'Dunno. Just wondered whether you wanted to nudge me in any particular direction. Easier to turn me round if I haven't set sail on the wrong course in the first place.'

'Cheeky bugger.' Holloway fastened his seat belt and switched on the ignition. 'You be careful,' he said as he pulled away. Phil watched as he headed for the exit. Then, as if acting on some last-minute impulse, the car swung round in a wide arc and came back towards him.

'We need the bat,' Holloway said.

'The baseball bat?'

'Until yesterday we didn't even know for sure it existed. Now we need to find it.'

'What d'you mean you didn't know? It was Callum's. He kept it in the boot of his car.'

'You ever see it?'

Phil thought for a moment.

'Well . . . no.'

'Callum ever mention it to you?'

'No, but –'

'We've asked everyone about it and so far no one other than Abi knew he had one. At least no one's admitting it. Struck us as a bit odd, given the sort of character your Callum was. Bit of a lad. Liked to show off a bit. I'd have thought he'd be the sort to take it out now and again in front of his mates. Let them know he was tooled up.'

'But like you say, Abi knew he had it,' he said.

'Yes. She did, didn't she? If she hadn't told us about it, we might have been looking for a different weapon altogether. I mean, the lab techs aren't saying it was definitely a baseball bat but they agree it could have been and given that he had one and it's now disappeared, we've been assuming all along that's what it was.'

'Well, there you go then.'

'But if she was lying about the bat for some reason –'

'Oh, for Christ's sake!' said Phil, as he realised where this was going.

'You know we have to go there. First thing you always do in a case like this is look at the family. Rule them out before you start rooting around elsewhere for evidence. And she *did* lie about where she was and got Owen Hall to cover for her. Who's to say she wasn't involved in it with this Adam Kitchener she's supposed to have met afterwards? We checked that out and the pub was packed that night. No one remembers seeing either of them there.'

'You're not seriously trying to tell me you think Abi had anything to do with it?'

'No, not really,' said Holloway, breaking into a broad grin. 'Just showing you the dangers of picking your suspect and then making the evidence fit. Anyway, she *was* telling the truth about the bat. We've been checking his emails. There's one from this time last year – an order for a baseball bat from Amazon, and an invoice for it on one of his accounts. He bought it all right. We find it and we'll get a warrant for just about anything.'

'That's not going to happen though, is it?' frowned Phil. 'He'll have got rid of it, surely. No one would be stupid enough to keep it.'

'That's pretty much what we thought,' said Holloway. 'Until we saw a picture of it.' He took his mobile from his pocket and scrolled through his photos. Having called up a picture, he used his thumb to stretch it until it filled the screen. Then he passed the phone through the window for Phil to take a look.

'Don't know about you,' he said, 'but if it *is* Owen Hall who took this bat to your boy, I reckon there's a fair chance he kept it somewhere. You think he could take it away and burn it?'

16

THE DAY OF THE MURDER:
MONDAY, 25TH AUGUST

OWEN

She likes the designs. More than that – she *really* likes them. He's been anxious about this all day. His fingers were actually trembling just now as he switched on the laptop and called the plans up onto the screen to show her. Four of them. Took him eight hours yesterday to put them together and another six today, not to mention the hours he lay awake on Saturday evening, just planning, planning, planning until he'd got it right in his head. Four designs, each with a different budget. Money shouldn't be a problem for her but he doesn't want her to be able to use it as an excuse for saying no, so he's kept his own profit margins as low as possible. And if he really hopes she'll go for the most expensive of the four, it's not because of the money. It's because it will take longer to get the work done and that means he'll be there for two or three months at least, and if she's pleased with what he's done, she may want to keep him on as her gardener. This could turn out to be a long-term thing.

It'll be like the old days. She was always his first port of call when he arrived at school. He used to seek her out in the playground, follow her around, sit with her and her friends at one of the picnic tables until the bell sent them off to lessons. She was part of his daily routine back then and routine mattered so much.

Abi Jessop (he still couldn't bring himself to call her Abi Green, even now).

Abi: total = 12, multiple of 3. Owen: total = 57, multiple of 3.

Safe. Happy.

Abi Hall: total = 45, multiple of 3 and 5. Owen Hall: total = 90, multiple of 3 and 5.

Safe. Happy.

When he was taken out of school for good, his one big regret was that he would inevitably lose contact with her. Given that her family lived in one of the villages nestled in a cluster somewhere north-west of Chichester, there was no way of staying in touch and sure enough they'd drifted apart. He'd even heard she'd moved to France, yet although he hadn't seen her since their time together at school, he'd never actually stopped thinking about her. Not completely. She was always hovering at the edge of his thoughts, just out of reach. And then, that phone call right out of the blue. She hadn't forgotten him either. Now she's taken the plans with her and promised to call in the morning to let him know which one she's going to choose. And things will be back the way they were. Back to normal. Everything in its place.

The grandmother clock in the hall is the first to start chiming, closely followed by the old mahogany clock on the mantelpiece above the fireplace, which seems to lose a minute or so every day and comes a more distant second as the day progresses. Two deep chimes from the first, two tinny pings from the second.

Seven-thirty.

He hasn't had supper yet and even though the programme doesn't start till 8.45, which means the film won't be under way until nine at the earliest, he decides on the spur of the moment to leave now. There's a KFC at Chichester Gate and he fancies something a bit more filling than the soup he was planning to have. If he leaves in the next couple of minutes, that should leave him with plenty of time.

He touches the spot on his cheek where she went up on tiptoe and kissed him just now.

It's going to be a good evening. The perfect end to a perfect day.

He takes the back road to Chichester, through Lagness and North Mundham. It's more direct, and even though it can be frustrating to get stuck behind farm vehicles coming in and out of Barfoots or one of the many nurseries that line the road, it's a much more pleasant drive through open countryside than it is battling the heavier traffic on the main road. This way won't bring him out onto the A27 until the Whyke roundabout. He'll be practically at Chichester Gate by then.

He's looking forward to the film. There aren't many things he and his mother used to do together that he's kept going since she died but this is one. They used to have a family membership pass, went to Cineworld at least once a week, sometimes more. The films weren't always that good. 'They don't make them like they used to.' She used to say that nearly every time. 'Give me Paul Newman or Steve McQueen any day.' Never really mattered to him though.

A trip to the cinema was always an adventure: big screen, surround sound, big bag of popcorn and a huge cup of Diet Coke which he could slot into the holder next to his seat. He doesn't have a season ticket anymore. Can't afford it, so he has to be more selective about the films he watches, but he still probably goes at least once a month. Something to look forward to in the evening.

North Mundham Primary School coming up on the right. Light at the pedestrian crossing immediately out front is red even though there are no children around now. An old man is hobbling across the road, swinging his legs in an unnaturally wide arc to take the pressure off his protesting hips. At the front of the queue of traffic coming from the other direction is a pony and trap – two lads up front looking very pleased with themselves. He's never liked horses. Feels uneasy around them. Remembers when his mother handed him an apple to give to an old shire horse at a children's farm years and years ago. Something about the way it slurped the apple out of his hand and swallowed it in one go, leaving saliva trails on his fingers and the sleeve of his coat. Never been near one since.

The lights change and he pulls slowly forward. Eases past the queue on the other side of the road, which stretches around the next bend. One of the cars is a flashy-looking sports job. The driver's hunched over, trying to get something from the glove compartment and he just has time to decide there's something familiar about him before it dawns on him. He's now two or three cars further down the road but looking back in the rear-view mirror he can see the driver's sitting upright again. Even from behind he knows it's Callum. Instantly. Not likely to mistake him for anyone else.

And he's a hundred metres or so along the road before he asks himself what he's doing over this way. It must be at least twenty minutes since he rang Abi to say he was on his way to Bournemouth. He should be the other side of Portsmouth by now. Instead, he's not that far from Honer Lane and that cottage, the one in South Mundham where he went with that woman on Saturday evening. Is it a coincidence? Has he got a good reason for being here or is he lying to Abi again?

He knows he's going to have to find out. Can't just leave it. So he drives on to the next roundabout. Left to Selsey, right to Chichester. Ignores both and doubles back on himself, returning to where he last saw Callum's car. It's nowhere in sight now but that doesn't matter. He's got a pretty good idea where he'll find it. It's not like he wants to catch him up – he just needs to know for sure.

He turns right at the roundabout opposite the Walnut Tree, drives down Mill Lane. Passes two cars coming the other way, both of them multiples of three. Hasn't seen a prime number since he set out, which tells him he's on the right track. Wonders what to do next. This would be so much easier if Abi was here in the truck next to him so she could see for herself what Callum's up to. Telling her won't be enough. She won't believe him. May even decide she doesn't want anything more to do with their plans for her garden – no one likes telltales is what Willie says. What he needs is evidence. If he can get a photo of Callum's car outside the cottage with a date and time stamp, he can store it away somewhere, carry on collecting snippets like this for the next few weeks. Then, when he's got enough in the file, he can present all the evidence to Abi in one go. Not even Callum will be able to talk his way out of that one. And Abi will thank him eventually. She'll realise his heart was in the right place.

He's in Punches Lane now, turning into Honer Lane and heading towards Pagham Harbour. Driving more carefully. The farmhouse cottage where they went the other night is about a mile along on the left, just before the road peters out. Callum should be there by now, has probably gone inside. But what if he hasn't? What if he's just there to pick her up? The last thing he wants is to find Callum coming back towards him on this single-track road. How's he going to explain what he's doing all the way out here if that happens? Whatever he says, Callum's not going to believe it. He'll know he's being followed. Maybe it would be better just to turn round and go back. Forget about the whole thing. But he doesn't want to give up on the idea if it means he has nothing to show Abi. He needs to think about this. So he drives through an open entrance to one of the fields and parks the truck where it won't be seen from the road. Gives himself time to think through the possibilities.

The best thing to do, it seems to him, would be to leave the truck here and go the rest of the way on foot but that might leave him a bit exposed. If it was just a couple of hours later, he'd feel happier about things but although there are heavy, dark clouds overhead and the light's fading fast he reckons it'll be another hour at least before he has enough cover and he can't possibly wait here that long. This whole Bournemouth trip might be just one more lie but, if it's not, then Callum may only be calling in for a few minutes. Could be coming back down the road any time. Bye bye photo. He can't take the chance. If he's going to do something, it has to be now.

So he leaves the pickup where it is, tucked away out of sight, and jogs round a couple of bends in the road, his ears straining for any sound resembling an approaching vehicle, making a note of where all the entrances are in case he needs to get off the road as a last resort. Another bend. Fifty more metres of road ahead. And another bend. He's starting to wonder whether he might have underestimated just how long this would take on foot. Then he turns one more corner and there's the cottage, no more than thirty metres away from where he's standing. And there's a car in the drive, only he can see straightaway it's not Callum's. It's a yellow one, the same one the woman was driving when she picked Callum up in the car park on Saturday evening. The one Callum was driving just now was black, only he can't see any sign of it. There's a garage tucked up against the cottage but her car's blocking the entrance – his can't be inside unless she moved hers to let him get past and why would she do that?

He wonders whether he might have got it wrong. Maybe Callum wasn't planning to visit her after all. What if he was on his way somewhere else when Owen passed him? The fact that he was near South Mundham might be just a coincidence. And if he's not coming here at all, there's not going to be any photo.

But even as he's coming to terms with his disappointment, another possibility occurs to him – one that's far more alarming. What if he *is* coming but went somewhere else first? If that's what's happened, he could turn up any minute and there's only one road back out of here, all the way down to Manor Lane. He needs to get out of here. Now.

He turns and runs back down the road towards his truck. His breathing's becoming more and more laboured by the minute. He's not an athlete. He's strong but not built for running and it's only a growing sense of desperation that drives him on. He reaches the truck and doubles over for a few seconds to get his breath back. Then he gets in, turns the key in the ignition. Nothing. He tries again – it splutters, then dies. And again. He slams his hand down on the dashboard, curses himself for having got into this mess. Takes a deep breath and tries again. This time the engine roars into life and he gives a sigh of relief. It might be his day after all.

He releases the handbrake and pulls out of the entrance to the field. Revs a little too hard, causing the wheels to struggle for purchase as he swings out onto the single-track road and heads back towards North Mundham.

And as he checks out the first bend, no more than fifty metres away, Callum's car comes cruising into view.

They both come to a halt, facing each other. Callum gets out of his car first and stands there for a moment, one hand resting on the door. Owen isn't sure what he's doing. He can't be checking to see if there's any way he can squeeze past. It must be obvious even from inside the car that one of them is going to have to back up. He'll have worked out whose pickup it is and it looks to Owen as if he's trying to decide whether there's any way this could be a coincidence. He thinks about getting out of the truck as well but can't move. His body won't respond. He's desperately trying to come up with an explanation as to why he's here, on a road leading nowhere, at exactly the same time as Callum. And he's coming up empty. There's nothing there.

After a few seconds, Callum pushes himself away from the car and walks over to the driver's side of the truck. The window's open. Owen wishes it wasn't, but shutting it now would only make things worse. He's painfully aware that Callum could reach in if he wanted to and grab him by the scruff of the neck the way he always used to. One of his favourite tricks was to take hold of Owen's tie and pull it so tight that he could hardly catch his breath. Then he used to grab hold of the end of it, turn his back and hold the tie over his shoulder, frogmarching him round the playground and asking everyone if they'd seen his pet mong, which Owen always used to think was a breed of dog until his mother put him straight and stormed up to the school to complain. Again. Owen isn't wearing a tie now but the pungent mix of fear and shame is as clear and present as it was all those years ago – sharp enough to block out the fact that he's now several inches taller and at least three stone heavier than his tormentor. He really wishes he hadn't decided to follow Callum. If he could only turn the clock back fifteen minutes or so, he could be ordering his KFC right now.

'Like to explain what you're doing all the way out here?' Callum asks, his head cocked to one side as he peers into the truck, forearms resting on the door panel.

Owen blinks. Swallows. Blinks again. Surely there must be an answer somewhere.

'I asked you a question,' Callum says again. He's not shouting and doesn't look particularly angry. Seems more puzzled than anything else, but Owen knows from bitter experience it won't take much to tip him over the edge. He can snap just like that. 'Are you following me or something?'

Owen shakes his head. An excellent answer occurs to him: how can he be following Callum if they're going in opposite directions? But the words can't find their shape somehow. Nothing is getting through.

'I th-thought you were g-going to B-B-Bournemouth,' he says eventually, aware that it's no sort of answer. And it certainly isn't going to satisfy Callum who looks up the road briefly, as if he can see round bends and seek out the cottage in his mind's eye. Then he turns back to face Owen, his face screwed into a frown.

'I am,' he says after a moment's reflection. 'I've just got these papers to drop off at a client's place first ... not that it's any business of yours. And you still haven't told me what you're doing here.'

At last a thought creeps into Owen's head and he's so relieved to find evidence of activity there that he blurts it out without thinking it through.

'I was just c-calling in on Mr and Mrs B-Brady,' he says. 'I d-do their garden for them.'

Callum considers this for a moment.

'Mr and Mrs Brady, eh? So where do they live?'

Owen is about to point behind him when it occurs to him there are only three houses in that direction before Honer Lane comes to a dead end and one of them belongs to Callum's girlfriend. How difficult would it be for him to check with her and find out who the other places belong to? So he tells the truth.

'They live down there,' he says, pointing ahead to where Callum has just come from. 'In Manor Lane.'

'So what are you doing up here then?' asks Callum.

'I was ... I was w-wondering if there's another w-way out up here. If m-maybe there's a road that j-joins up with the P-Pagham road. I've never b-been up this way before.'

Apart from Saturday night. He dismisses the thought imme-diately, anxious not to give anything away. Callum has always known which buttons to press, seems instinctively to know what he's thinking. To his dismay he can feel the blood beginning to rush to his cheeks and doesn't need the quick glance in the mir-ror to know he's blushing.

'Bullshit!'

Callum steps away from the truck, looks back at his car for a moment.

'No,' Owen says, scrambling now. 'I –'

'You think you can lie to me, you fucking idiot? I can read you like a book. Always have done. Jesus wept, you were following me.'

Owen shakes his head but doesn't trust himself to say anything.

'Yes, you were. I don't know how you knew where I was going but you were following me. Why? Have you done this before?'

'N-n-no. I p-p-promise I w-wasn't f-following you. I was –'

'Yeah, I know – you w-were j-j-j-just c-c-calling in to s-s-see your g-g-good f-f-friends Mr and Mrs B-B-Brady.' Callum shakes his head in disgust, looks at his car again. He stands there, deep in thought. Owen has no idea what he's thinking but he's pretty sure he won't like it. They're in the playground again, the lunch hour is stretching away into the never-ending distance and Callum's looking for a bit of fun to pass the time.

'Fuck it,' he says eventually. He turns and walks over to his car. Owen is hoping the moment's over, that he'll get in and wait patiently for him to reverse into a passing space, which he'll be more than happy to do. No harm done. But instead, he goes round to the back of the car and opens the boot. He takes something out and slams the lid shut. Then he comes to the front of the car again and Owen can see now that he's carrying what looks at first like a large club but turns out to be a baseball bat. Callum looks over towards him, still sitting hunched up in the pickup, not daring to move. He pauses for a moment as if thinking things through. Then he grins, pats the bonnet of his sports car and says, 'Sorry about this, lovely,' before drawing back the bat and taking a swing at the offside headlamp. There's a loud bang as the glass shatters and he stoops to inspect the damage. Then he walks over to the driver's side and takes aim at the other one.

At some stage during these bizarre events, Owen must have got out of the truck without thinking because he's aware all of a sudden that he's walking over towards Callum. He hasn't made a conscious decision to interfere but he doesn't understand what's going on and can't just sit there and watch Callum trash an expensive car for no good reason.

He's trying to make sense of it but nothing computes. What's unfolding in front of him is so beyond his experience that he's genuinely unnerved by it. He snaps out of his trance and takes a step back as Callum turns and starts towards him. Then another two steps. Callum stops, holds up his free hand.

'Whoa,' he says, chuckling to convey his amusement. 'Take it easy, OK? Where d'you think you're going?'

'I want to g-go now,' Owen says, still edging closer to the pickup.

'And how exactly d'you think you're going to do that with my car blocking the road? Relax, will you? What's the matter? Is it this? Is this what's worrying you?' He holds up the bat and looks at it as if surprised to find it still there in his hand. 'Here . . . I'll put it down, OK? Look – on the floor, right?' He lets the bat fall at his feet and shows his free hands to Owen, as if this ought to reassure him in some way. It doesn't.

'OK,' he continues. 'You say you want to go. Fine by me. Only I need you to do me a favour first.'

'I've got to go to the cinema.'

'Yeah, I get that,' he snaps, irritated. 'Thirty seconds from now I can be backing up into that field over there and you'll be able to get past with your truck. Then you can go and watch all the films you like. Only first there's something I want you to do for me.'

Owen thinks about it.

'You want me to give you a lift?' he asks.

Callum stares at him for a moment, then bursts out laughing, his eyes watering with amusement.

'Jesus, it's like talking to a fridge. No, Owen – I don't want you to give me a lift.'

'So what do you want?'

'I want you to hit me.' He pauses as he sees Owen eyeing the bat on the ground. 'Not with that thing – you fucking kidding me? I want to be able to walk away from here, not spend two weeks in intensive care.'

Owen looks at him, waiting for him to start laughing again because obviously this is a joke. He's never been very good with jokes. Never really understood them. Only Callum isn't laughing. He looks serious.

'You want me to hit you?'

'Yes.'

'But why?'

'What's with all the questions? Never mind why. I want you to hit me – just the once. Not too hard, mind. Just enough to mark me up a bit.'

'I don't understand.'

'There's nothing to understand. Just do it. Go on – one free shot. About here would be best,' he says, pointing to an area near his left eyebrow. 'Come on, big boy. Think of all those times I picked on you at school. You must have dreamed of doing this some day. So here's your chance. Grow a pair, for fuck's sake. Have a go. Just the one.'

Owen shakes his head. 'No.'

'What d'you mean, no?'

'No. I don't want to.'

He can hardly believe he's saying this because Callum's right. There were many times when he'd entertained fantasies as a tormented teenager, most involving Callum falling under the wheels of a bus or coming to a sticky end because he'd picked on the wrong person for once. If he'd been offered the same chance back then, he'd still have turned it down, but it would have been because he knew there would be repercussions and Callum would turn it back on him somehow. There would be a catch – there always was. If he's equally hesitant now, it has nothing to do with fear . . . at least, he doesn't think so. He's bigger now than he was back then. He doesn't like violence – has never been involved in a fight in his life – but he imagines that if he ever had to defend himself he's big and strong enough to do it. No, his reticence now is more to do with uncertainty. He doesn't know what he's dealing with here. It's such a ridiculous request. What Callum did just now to his car is bad enough, but no one in his right mind would follow that up by asking someone to punch him. It doesn't make sense. He's sure there has to be a trick in there somewhere.

Callum looks angry for a moment, is about to protest. Then he heaves a sigh and stoops to pick up the bat.

'Should've known,' he says. 'Fucking pussy. What's that they say? You want a job done properly, do it yourself.'

So saying, he holds the bat vertically out in front of him, both hands gripping the handle. He closes his eyes for a second or two, takes a couple of deep breaths, blowing the air out in long, steady streams. Then he jerks the bat towards himself, stopping it at the last moment. He bursts out laughing and asks Owen if he's sure he doesn't want to help. Then, in the absence of any reply, he assumes the position again and this time goes through with it, hard enough for it to cause him to stagger sideways although it looks to Owen as if he held back a little at the last moment. It would probably hurt and there may be a slight swelling but that's all.

Callum staggers slightly on his way over to his car and peers in the wing mirror before slipping inside to check the rear-view one for a better look. 'Shit,' he says, as he presumably comes to the same conclusion as Owen. Nothing there to speak of.

He slides back out of the car and leans against the bonnet. Lines up the shot for a second time. Owen can't help himself – he asks him not to do it. Callum asks if he's changed his mind and he shakes his head.

'Well, then,' says Callum. And this time he manages to go through with it with a little more conviction. He slumps sideways, clearly dazed for a moment or two, then runs a finger over his eyebrow which has been split open, releasing a trickle of blood down the side of his face. He curses, throws the bat to the ground, tries to take a few steps forward but his balance is off and he veers away to one side. Owen reaches out and catches hold of him. Eases him gently to the floor where he sits with his head in his hands. As he slides down, the blood from above his eye smears across Owen's shirt front, making a mess of it. Callum shakes his head as if trying to clear it, then he gives a loud whoop which, if anything, seems even crazier than anything that's gone before. It's almost as if he's celebrating.

'Are you OK?' Owen asks.

Callum looks up and blinks at him.

'Is my eye closing? I think it's closing,' he mutters. And sure enough there's a large swelling above the eyelid which is rapidly forcing the left eye shut.

'You need to go to the hospital,' Owen insists. 'You'll need stitches in that.'

Callum laughs, shapes as if to get to his feet, then decides that may be a little over-ambitious right now. He needs another minute or so.

'Later,' he says.

'I don't understand,' says Owen, as if repeating it might bring some sort of enlightenment.

'No, of course you don't. I was using words. Life's one big mystery to you, isn't it, big boy?'

Owen leaves him there for a moment and goes back to his truck. On the front seat there's a bottle of Evian which he tucks under one arm while he rummages around in search of a cloth he can use. He rejects two before finding one that's relatively clean. Then he carries the bottle and the rag back to where Callum is checking his mobile, before snapping it shut with a groan of frustration.

'Shit. No reception. Would you believe it?'

He takes the bottle from Owen, unscrews the top and takes two or three deep swigs from it, then uses the rest of the contents to dampen the cloth. When it's wet enough, he dabs tentatively at his eye, wincing as he wipes the blood away. It forms a messy patch again almost instantly.

'Who are you trying to phone?' Owen asks. 'Do you want an ambulance?' He feels he should be doing something more than standing around, watching helplessly. Maybe they ought to go to the woman's cottage. They can phone from there. That would just about set the seal on a crazy evening. Doesn't get much weirder than that. Plenty of chances to take a photo there.

'OK,' says Callum, as if reading his thoughts. 'You really want to know? I was going to phone the police.'

'Why?'

'Why,' he repeats to himself, not as a question, more as a problem that needs to be addressed. 'Well, let's see how this sounds, shall we? I was meant to be on my way to Bournemouth, Officer, only I realised at the last minute that I'd forgotten to get these important papers signed by one of my clients, so I drove over here first. I got this far and then this truck was coming the other way and I knew who it was cos it's this guy who does gardening jobs for us . . . nothing much, you know? He's a bit on the simple side, to be honest, but we give him a bit of work every now and again, just to help him keep his head above water. Just doing our bit for care in the community, right?'

He throws his head back and cackles. Owen can see that his eye is now little more than a slit. It's also changing colour, yellows and purples seeping into the picture.

'Care in the community,' he chuckles. 'Like it. I'll have to remember that. Anyway, Officer, I get out of the car to ask him if he'll back up and unfortunately he's in one of those moods of his. Don't happen often but when they do the best thing is to stand well clear cos he can be a total lunatic when the red mist comes down. And he starts shouting at me and I'm trying to calm him down but he's not listening and next thing I know he's pushed me out of the way and kicked in one of my headlights with those bloody great boots of his. So I yell at him and try to stop him doing the same to the other one, only he swings round and smashes me right in the eye and I must have blacked out for a second or two cos next thing I know I'm on the floor and he's stomping over to his truck. And I'm worried he's going to start it up and just plough straight through my car and ram it into the ditch or something so he's got enough room to get past. So I go to the boot of my car – and I know this is stupid but I was dazed I guess. Wasn't really thinking straight. Anyway, I get this baseball bat out of the boot, just for self-protection, you know? And . . . no. Maybe not,' he says, breaking off from his story. 'Maybe it'd be better without the baseball bat. I'm the victim in this, right? Don't want to introduce anything that might confuse things.'

He's mumbling more to himself now than to Owen, thinking things through as he goes along. Owen is still standing there, stunned by what he's hearing.

'But . . . that's n-not true,' he says. 'Any of it.'

Callum laughs.

'Shit, nothing gets past you, does it?'

'I don't understand. Why would you make up something like that?'

'Ah well,' gasps Callum, bending over and reaching for the next breath. 'That's the best bit. You see, I've got two major problems in my life right now. Actually that's a lie. I've got plenty, but only two you can help me with. One is that I still can't quite make up my mind whether you were following me or not just now. If you were, I don't know how much you know or suspect and I'd like to believe it's all a big coincidence, us meeting up here like this, but I don't think I can afford to take the chance. In fact, let's be honest. I think you're full of shit. Don't believe you. So I need to sort that out for one, make sure no one's going to believe a word you say.

'And the second problem is, I had to put up with three years at school with you slobbering all over Abi, acting like you were something special in her life when the plain and simple truth is she just feels sorry for you, mate. She doesn't want to hurt your feelings. Me, I don't give a shit, so I don't have any problem telling you what I think. You're an embarrassment. You shouldn't be allowed to mix with normal people. They don't want to look up in the middle of their lunch and see you spreading yours all over your face. They don't want to sit there for half an hour waiting for you to get your tongue round a simple sentence. F-f-f-f-fuck that! And I for one don't want to find you leeching off Abi's good nature. I thought you'd have got the message when I used to kick you around the playground but I keep forgetting what a slow learner you are, so let me spell it out nice and simple for you. I don't know how the fuck you wormed your way back into our lives but you can just worm your way back out again. If you imagine for one minute I'm going to put up with you hanging around like some fucking ghoul, you obviously don't know me very well.'

He leans back and rests the back of his head on the bonnet for a moment. Owen meanwhile is shell shocked. He stands there open-mouthed, trying to take it all in. He's wondering what to do next but all he can think of is Abi. What's she going to think?

'You can't do this,' he protests. 'I'll t-tell the police what really happened.'

'Yeah, well g-g-good l-luck with that,' Callum mimics. 'He's lying, Officer. I didn't hit him. He smashed his own car up and then he hit himself in the face with a b-baseball b-bat. I just stood there and watched. Fuck, that hurts,' he adds, dabbing gently at his eye once more.

'It's the truth,' says Owen, and he can feel the exasperation building inside him. No way can Callum be allowed to get away with this unchallenged.

'Says who? It's all going to come down to my word against yours. Which of us is going to sound more convincing, d'you think? A successful, articulate entrepreneur – fuck me, there's a word for you. How long would it take you to say that? A successful businessman with no reason to lie or a bumbling idiot who can't string three words together without st-st-st-stuttering? You want my advice, you'd do well to start getting the kinks in your version ironed out. You reckon anyone's going to believe your explanation for being here? If we knock on Mr and Mrs Dooberry's door or whatever their name is and ask if you've called in to see them this evening, are they going to back you up on that? I don't think so. Far as I can see, the only reason you could possibly be way out here is to set up an opportunity to beat the shit out of me. You think anyone's going to think differently by the time I've finished, you've got another think coming.

Oh, Jesus,' he groans, turning his head away in disgust. 'You're not going to start crying, are you?'

And he is. He can feel the tears pricking at the corners of his eyes. It's all too much for him to take in. He knows Callum's right. He's never been very good at explaining himself. No one will believe him. He feels helpless and can feel the rocking on its way. Any minute now he'll start swaying to and fro. Another excuse for Callum to laugh at him.

So what are you going to do about it? asks Willie, who's appeared out of nowhere. Willie, who always seems to leave him to go through all the painful preliminaries and then steps in at the last minute to take all the credit.

'I don't know.'

Yes, you do.

He's looking at the bat which is still on the ground next to Callum.

'I can't do that,' says Owen.

'Who the fuck are you talking to?' asks Callum, struggling to stand up.

Yes, you can. He asked you to hit him, remember? It was his idea.

Owen watches as Callum reaches down to pick up the bat. He knows he can't let him do that. Steps in and slams his foot down on it, trapping Callum's fingers underneath, causing him to yelp. It's an odd sound, high-pitched. Almost girlish.

So, says Willie. *You heard the man.*

Next thing he knows, it's starting to rain. It's not heavy just yet, but the first fat drops are starting to fall on his upturned face and he can sense much more is on the way. He listened to the weather forecast this morning and they said there would be heavy rain later, maybe even a storm or two.

Willie's starting to get anxious.

What if someone down there decides to go for a walk to Pagham Harbour?

'It's raining, Willie.'

People don't walk in the rain? What if someone in one of those three houses is planning to go into Chichester for the evening? Anyone comes along here before you've cleared up, what are you going to do? Whack them too?

He's made a list of things Owen needs to do. And quickly. Willie's good with lists – nothing written down but he never seems to forget anything.

Number 1: get him off the road and into his car.

Easy. He drags Callum round to the passenger side, opens the back door and throws him onto the seat. There's a crack as his head hits the door going in and one arm flops down to the floor in what looks like a reflex motion but Owen's not concerned. He knows he doesn't need to worry about Callum ever again. One look at his face and you can tell. He's gone. He slams the door shut and it springs back open because his foot's in the way. He reaches in and bends Callum's knee so that there's room for his leg inside, then slams the door again.

Number 2: get the car off the road and put it where it can't be seen.

Owen remembers the field where he hid the pickup. That would do nicely but his truck is in the way. So instead he climbs into the driver's seat of Callum's sports car, turns the key which is still in the ignition, and promptly stalls it the moment he tries to reverse. The clutch is fierce, very different from his pickup's.

He tries again and backs up the road as quickly as he can, the car leaping in fits and starts as if suffering from a mechanical equivalent of Tourette's. He's careful not to misjudge things and slide off into a ditch. That *would* be a problem. He's aware of the risk of some other vehicle coming this way but there's no panic there. Instead there's an odd sense of purpose, an inner calm he doesn't remember feeling before. No point in fretting over things that lie beyond his control. And anyway, Willie knows what he's doing.

Eventually, he finds a field that is just about perfect. Open entrance, high hedges and a section that's almost cordoned off by bales of hay and odd bits of machinery. He drives the car in and makes a token effort at obscuring it with a few branches that are lying around, although he knows he doesn't have long enough to do a decent job. He needs to see to the next item on the list.

Number 3: get out of those clothes.

He's not sure about this but feels he has to trust Willie's instincts. There's this smear of blood down the front of his T-shirt where he'd tried to ease Callum's fall. He can't afford to have anyone see him looking like that. His work overalls are in the truck. He quickly unlaces his boots and takes them off so that he can slip out of his jeans. Then he takes off the T-shirt as well and steps into the overalls. Willie's insisting he hide the clothes for now. *One of the compost bags in the back.* He clambers up and pours some of the contents out of one of the bags. Then he puts the jeans and the T-shirt in and scoops enough compost back in to hide them. He feels more than a little miffed about this. He doesn't mind so much about the jeans but the T-shirt is one of his favourites. It has a picture of Bognor Pier on the front and on the back it says: *My mum went on holiday to Bognor and all I got was this lousy T-shirt.* He bought it a couple of years ago at a car-boot sale at Fontwell. It's a joke – still makes him smile even now every time he puts it on. But Willie insists, so into the bag it goes. Then he opens another one and does the same with the baseball bat. Can't leave that lying around. Later, Willie explains, he can get rid of the bat and the clothes. Make a bonfire out of them. Now all that matters is the next item.

Number 4: get out of here.

His watch tells him that it's still only 8.32. Hard to believe so much can have happened in such a short space of time but it has and he's been lucky so far. No one has gone for a walk. No one has decided to go out for the evening. But all the good work of the past few minutes will count for nothing if he does anything to draw attention to himself. The light's fading all the time, especially now the rain clouds are directly overhead. He wouldn't normally put his sidelights on just yet, but he does now, just in case some passing police car might take exception. He drives at five miles an hour below the speed limit, anxious not to give any of the locals a reason to take note of his vehicle. He couldn't drive more carefully if he tried. And when the road broadens out into a two-way street at last, he turns to Willie and smiles. They should be safe now. Still plenty to do but they should be OK.

Number 5: drive to Cineworld.

He needs to pick up his ticket and watch the film. Willie doesn't see why anyone should ask him where he was this evening, but there's no harm in providing himself with a nice alibi just in case. It's too late for the KFC now but he'll make up for it with the popcorn. Go large instead of the usual medium. He feels a little self-conscious in his overalls, wonders if it might look a bit odd. But all he needs to do is get his ticket from the machine and he'll be inside in the dark in no time. No one will be able to see him there.

He decides he's going to enjoy the film. He could do with something to take his mind off things.

It's a late finish and despite the popcorn he's ready for a proper meal by the time he comes out into an absolute downpour. KFC shut a few minutes ago so he picks up a takeaway from Masala Gate and heads for home, windscreen wipers barely making an impression on the wall of water sliding down his screen. He makes a detour to the Southern Cross industrial estate and burns the clothes in a large oil drum at the back of a garage, using petrol to encourage it along a little as the rain sluices down. He waits till he's sure the job is done, then leaves the final bits of rag to burn themselves out.

At home, he warms the meal through in the microwave, munching on a complimentary poppadom as he does so. Then he takes the food into the conservatory and eats it on a tray on his lap, thinking about two minor acts of rebellion that he's committed this evening. Ones that he's secretly quite pleased about but which have not pleased Willie one bit. He's moaned about them all the way home. Says Owen's an idiot for even thinking about it but then again Willie doesn't know everything. He was really helpful this evening, so much so that Owen doesn't know what he'd have done without him. But even though he's always been a quick thinker, he's not as clever as he believes he is. Not by a long chalk.

Owen's given way on most things, including burning his favourite T-shirt but he's drawn the line at the other two. Willie can whinge as much as he likes about how dangerous it is to keep them but he's not going to change his mind on this. He's keeping them.

The bat will need attention. He'll have to scrub it clean, maybe even plane it down a little to make sure there are no traces anywhere on it. There are a few indentations here and there but there would be – it's a baseball bat. It's bound to have taken a few knocks over the years. But he'll get to work on it, clean it, smooth it out, rub it over and over again with linseed oil until it's guaranteed one hundred per cent safe. And even then he'll find somewhere to keep it, somewhere that can't rebound on him. Because you never know. You hear such amazing things about what they can do with forensics nowadays. He'll find a way to make sure they can't possibly tie it to him.

But what he's *not* going to do is burn it. He's known that from the moment he caught a glimpse of the logo, stencilled in blue just below the handle. There's a large capital K with a smaller capital C looped onto its downstroke. And under that is the number 69. KC 69. He's googled it and discovered the KC stands for Kansas City. It's a Major League baseball team and the number refers to the year they were formed and allowed to join the American League.

Six, nine, sixty-nine: all multiples of three. Safe.

How can Willie think he's going to burn that?

Not going to happen.

And then there's the package he found on the front seat of Callum's car when he was ditching it. Willie's *really* unhappy about this. Says it's going to come back to bite him sometime but that's just panic on his part. He always gets like that if he feels his position with Owen is threatened in any way. But the moment he opened it and saw the necklace inside, he knew what to do with it. He just knew.

There was a capital H and a small x written on the wrapping paper and, even though he doesn't know what her name is, Owen is sure he knows who it was meant for. But that's not going to happen. She's not going to get her hands on it. Callum was married. If he was going to buy expensive presents for anyone, it should have been Abi, not this other woman. And it's Abi who's going to get it. Her birthday's coming up soon, just over a fortnight away. He'll make it a present from him to her, something that will show her how important she is to him. How pleased he is they're back together after all these years.

He wasn't the one who bought it of course, which makes it a bit of a lie, but he won't let that worry him. He remembers how difficult he used to find it to tell lies when he was young but he's learned over the years that sometimes it's OK. Sometimes it's the right thing to do. That day all those years ago taught him as much. He remembers his mother holding on tight to him, whispering to him over and over again: '*You weren't in the tree house. You were in the kitchen with me. We were practising your reading. Where were you?*' All the time while they were waiting for the ambulance to arrive. Then all the way to the hospital. She made him say it till he was word perfect.

So he knows it's OK to lie sometimes. Even to Abi.

And he might as well get used to it.

He's going to have to do it a lot more before this blows over.

PART THREE

17

FRIDAY, 5ᵀᴴ DECEMBER

DANNY

This fatherhood malarkey is like one long party, he thought to himself as he rearranged a few items on the shelves while Yvonne opened up. He didn't remember it being quite like this when Kayla was born. He certainly didn't have people whooping as he came in through the door and pressing small presents for the baby on him before he'd even removed his anorak and cycle helmet. Then again, he reminded himself, he'd been relatively new to the shop back then. They all knew him better now, viewed him as a friend almost. And he decided he liked it – this sense of mutual support, corporate wellbeing.

It was funny the way things turned out sometimes. He'd always seen himself as one of the worker ants: do the job nine to five and do it well by all means, but it was very much an 'us-and-them' situation as far as he was concerned. Once you pulled your cycle helmet on and headed off home you left the place well and truly behind you. Never thought about responsibility. Never wanted it.

Lately though, and especially since the arrival of Jamie Carragher Locke just a few days earlier, he'd caught himself feeling differently about things once or twice. Nothing major – just taking an interest in the way Yvonne operated, watching closely to see how she managed to chivvy people along and get them to do things without ever getting their backs up. He'd started to wonder whether he might be able to do something along those lines, and put himself up for promotion one day. The staff liked and respected him, and he was good with customers. Was it that ridiculous an idea?

He'd mentioned it to Evie and she was all for it, suggesting he ought to have a word with Yvonne about management courses. Not so long ago he'd have laughed at her but last night he'd lain awake for ages, looking at it from all angles and thinking she might be right. Maybe he *was* ready for something like this. And the money would certainly come in handy. He decided he'd try to grab a word with Yvonne when no one else was listening. He didn't see what harm it could do.

There was no chance early on in the day. The first customers came in a bit of a rush as usual – a handful of individuals there for a specific reason rather than the casual browsers who replaced them after the first few frantic minutes. Then, just as the initial onslaught was starting to die down a little, they were joined by a small, dapper man who strode into the shop and then looked around uncertainly as if searching for someone in particular. Filled with this new sense of purpose, Danny walked over and asked if he could be of assistance.

'I'm sure you can,' said the customer. 'I was hoping to speak to the manager.'

'I'm afraid she's serving at the moment, sir,' he said, nodding in Yvonne's direction. 'Can I help at all?'

'Oliver Dodd,' said the man, resting his briefcase on one of the display cabinets and taking a card from his jacket pocket. 'I'm here to carry out the audit.'

ABI

Nearly four months on and still the calls for Callum kept coming.

Just before five o'clock, Abi was in the kitchen, getting ready to lift the sugar paste to cover the cake drum, which was a delicate operation at the best of times. When the home phone rang in the lounge, she did her best to ignore it. She told herself she could always check the missed call later at a more convenient moment, but this next stage would need all her concentration and she didn't want the distraction of wondering who had been trying to get in touch. So with a sigh she stepped back from the work surface and walked through to the lounge. It was an unfamiliar number, another cold caller more likely than not.

'Hello?' she said, doing her best to keep the irritation out of her voice.

'Oh, good afternoon. I'm sorry to trouble you. Would that be Mrs Green?' A woman's voice. Polite. Professional.

'Speaking.'

'My name is Yvonne Wood. I'm calling from Estelle Roberts.'

'From where?' She went back into the kitchen and tucked the handset under her ear as she rummaged around in one of the unit drawers.

'Estelle Roberts. In Arun Valley. We're conducting a customer-satisfaction survey and wondered if you could just help us out. Is this a convenient time?'

'Not really,' said Abi, stepping back over to the work surface to check the sugar paste once more.

'I promise it will be very quick. It's just that as a company we're re-evaluating our refund policy and we'd really appreciate feedback from our customers. It was actually *Mr* Green I wanted to speak with. I don't suppose he's there at the moment, is he?'

'No. I'm afraid he's not.'

'Only he bought a necklace from us a few months ago and –'

'My husband is dead.'

'I'm sorry?'

'He died back in August.'

'Oh . . . Mrs Green.'

'So if you'll excuse me –'

'Of course. I quite understand. I had no idea.'

'I'm in the middle of making a cake and haven't even started thinking about dinner.'

'Absolutely. I'm so sorry to have troubled you –'

Abi didn't hear the rest. She ended the call and returned the handset to the coffee table in the lounge, determined not to answer if it rang again. Anyone else trying to get in touch with her could wait until she'd finished working on the cake.

Out of sight, out of mind.

When she came to look back on it later, she was never quite able to pin down just what it was that made her think again. A touch of guilt maybe at having been so brusque? And somewhere deep in her subconscious, her thought processes must have been hard at work, teasing here, linking there, *knit one, purl one* until a pattern emerged almost before she'd realised what was happening. She couldn't identify any single stitch though and swear, hand on heart, that this was her Eureka moment, her blinding epiphany. But synapses must have started crackling or whatever it was synapses did and some remote corner of her brain started juggling with a few random pieces and tossed them around until somehow, magically, they all fell into place because it couldn't have been more than ten minutes later that she found herself picking out the number from the call log and ringing the woman from Estelle Roberts.

18

MONDAY, 8ᵀᴴ DECEMBER

OWEN

He grabs hold of the large sack with two hands and tries to lift it. No chance. If he's not careful he'll do himself some damage. Instead, he drags it over to the door of the shed, manoeuvres it over the raised threshold, down two steps and onto the lawn where he leaves it next to a number of packing crates that he'd hauled there and emptied earlier.

He tips the contents of the sack out onto the grass and works his way through them, item by item, adding them to the three existing piles. One will go straight to the tip or to a bonfire, another will go back into the shed once he's finished. The third pile – the items about which he's undecided – will go into a corner of the garage and stay there until the Aldertons get back from their winter break in Lanzarote. They have a holiday home there, use it as their base every year from early October until just before Easter. They like to pop back for a week or so over Christmas so that they can see their children and grandchildren over the festive period, but otherwise they won't be around for six months.

For the past three winters they've left him a key to the garden shed and paid him a retainer to keep the garden tidy and do a number of odd jobs around the outside of the property while they're away – the occasional tree that needs to come down or bush that needs to be taken out. Suits him just fine. He's his own boss, can decide when he wants to go round there, making it dovetail with all the other jobs he has at any one time.

These, as it happens, are few and far between at the moment. Wrong time of year. Not a lot of money around at the moment for some of his customers. And others still seem a bit wary after the interest the police showed in him during the autumn. Things would be easier from the financial point of view if the project at Abi's had amounted to anything but the less said about that the better. So he's glad of the work, happy to deal with the relatively unchallenging and mindless task of clearing the shed to create more space for the summer.

One of the first items he takes out of the sack is the baseball bat. The shed has been the perfect hiding place; somewhere no one would think of looking. Every time he comes here he can't resist taking it out and having a look at it – does so now, holding it up to the grey morning light. There's not a mark on it, which is hardly surprising; he's scrubbed it so many times, smoothed over a few rough edges, working particularly hard on the bottom half of the bat where telltale signs might have lingered and then swamped it in oil so he's pretty sure nothing can be picked up by forensics. Better safe than sorry.

Willie has been on at him ever since they got back that night. He keeps whining about how the KC ought to count as well. *Throw that into the mix and you get eighty-three which any fool will tell you is a prime number.* Owen doesn't listen though. He's the expert when it comes to this sort of thing. It's not a number plate – the letters don't count.

He's been keeping it in the sack along with any number of items the Aldertons have accumulated over the years: a collection of utensils for the barbecue, a multi-coloured boules set, a couple of footballs and a miniature cricket bat for when the grandchildren come to visit, several tent pegs and a mallet (though he hasn't come across any sign of a tent so far). The baseball bat doesn't look remotely out of place in there and the beauty of it is that unless they decide to pop back for Christmas he won't need to find somewhere else to keep it for four months. Plenty of time to decide what to do with it then.

Gripping the bat tightly, he stands with feet wide apart and takes a few practice swings. It stirs fragments of memory into life, more instinctive than visual. There's an awareness rather than an actual picture. He feels as if he's been liberated or vindicated somehow as he swipes at fresh air, the momentum almost hurling him off his feet. He has no real recollection of those few moments in Honer Lane – there's just the before and the after and he doesn't really trust what he thinks he remembers in between. Impossible to separate what actually happened from what has been stitched together by a febrile imagination. But he knows how good this bat makes him feel and that's all that matters. It's a lucky omen. How could it be anything else?

His mobile pings in his pocket to tell him he has a message. He doesn't want to be sidetracked because the forecast is for heavy rain around midday and if it comes a little earlier he could find himself with all the shed contents still out in the open. So he ignores the text for now, wipes his prints off the bat handle and buries it deep in the sack before continuing to sift through the other contents, sorting them into the appropriate piles.

Five minutes later he's interrupted again by his mobile – a call this time. He takes it out of his pocket to check who's ringing and his heart gives a little leap when he sees the name before he comes to his senses. Funny how these things work. He can tell himself as often as he likes that she let him down and that he doesn't want anything more to do with her, but his instincts betray him every time. He has no idea why she's ringing now – doesn't *want* to know. After all she's put him through recently, Abi Green – she still calls herself that even now, after everything she's found out about Callum – Abi Green can wait.

As if.

Two minutes later he picks her number from his list of favourites and rings it. She answers almost immediately. Thanks him for calling her back, says she wasn't sure he would. *Dead right,* he thinks. She doesn't know how close he came to ignoring her.

He listens as she explains. Says she wouldn't blame him if he refused to have anything to do with her after the way she behaved before but she really needs to talk with him about something. If he'll just give her a chance to explain . . .

Two minutes ago there was nothing she could have said that would have made him want to give her the time of day. He hasn't forgiven her and won't. He's not about to forget the way she reacted to finding out he'd been in her bedroom. The way she treated him the following morning was unforgivable. He turned up for work as usual, ready to apologise because, OK, he knew he'd overstepped the mark. He could accept that much. Knew women could be funny about their rooms, about what they saw as an invasion of their privacy. Wouldn't have bothered him one bit if the shoe had been on the other foot but he'd brought it on himself so he was ready to say sorry and move on.

Instead, she pulled the rug out from under him. Called him into the kitchen and made him sit at the table like a naughty schoolboy. She was cold as ice – told him she'd spent a lot of time the previous evening thinking through what he'd done, and she didn't feel she could trust him anymore. She was worried about the way he'd been behaving recently: first the expensive necklace, now the intrusion into her privacy. She felt he was misjudging the nature of their friendship and making assumptions with which she wasn't entirely comfortable. She'd talked about it with Callum's father of all people, as if it was any of his business, and come to the conclusion it would be better if they shelved the garden project for the foreseeable future. She might feel differently a few months on but she didn't feel comfortable having him there right now. She needed time on her own to come to terms with everything that had happened in the past couple of weeks.

It had taken him a few moments to realise what she was saying. That all those hours he'd spent, drawing up different plans to make sure there was at least one that would meet her needs, were all for nothing. That what she was actually telling him was that he wasn't going to be working on her garden at all. When the message got through, he'd gone from upset to desperate and then angry in a matter of minutes. He knows he said one or two things he probably shouldn't have, including a snippy remark about whether her new boyfriend was going to be asked to stay away as well so she could have this space she needed, but it's not like that influenced her decision in any way. She'd already made up her mind – so much so that when he rang later that evening and again the following day to beg her to reconsider and promise that he wouldn't ever go into her room again, she'd put the phone down on him.

It's been almost three months now and he's had a long time to make up his mind as to how he feels about the whole business. And if anyone had told him, when he answered the phone just now, that he would allow her to talk him round, he'd have insisted they were wrong. But even though he's using all the right words and saying he doesn't think there's anything she can say that he wants to hear, he's aware that his heart is thudding violently, insisting on the right to be heard. And even as he tells her he's busy now and ends the call suddenly, as if desperate to quit while he's still ahead, there's a substantial part of him that's yelling at him to take it back. Call her. Tell her he's sorry for being so unkind. He didn't mean it. You can't wipe out all those years just like that. Somehow the past just won't let go.

So when a text comes through a few minutes later – 'Sorry. Understand and don't blame you. Deserve nothing less. Your friend, Abi' – he rings back almost immediately, fingers struggling to hit the right keys. And he tries to conjure some sort of moral victory from the fact that he's told her he's busy right now and won't be able to see her till this evening at the earliest, but he's not fooling himself for one minute. He just hopes he's fooling her.

So, 6.30 at the Lion in Pagham.

He wonders what that's all about.

PHIL

Decorations, he told himself. Seventeen days to Christmas and he still hadn't fetched the boxes out of the attic: one long, thin one containing the artificial tree, two more compact ones containing various baubles and lights and traditional decorations that he and Sally accumulated over the years.

He knew exactly where they were – just off to the right, tucked away in a recess formed by the lagged pipes and the support beams, out of harm's way. Decorating the lounge each year used to be something of a family tradition. Sally used to prepare mulled wine and mince pies; he and Callum, when he was still young and enthusiastic about such things, used to fetch everything down from the attic and get the tree set up. Then they decorated it as a family, he and Sally smiling complicitly as they pretended not to notice each time Callum sneaked one of the chocolate figures away from view.

That first Christmas after Sally died – 2012 – he decided not to get the boxes down from the attic. They stayed where they were all through the festive period. Maybe if Callum had come to visit more often and shown some sort of enthusiasm for keeping the tradition going it might have been different, but Callum was Callum. So Phil had sat there in an undecorated lounge, thinking he would be better off in an ascetic, joyless room than one awash with colour and lights. He hadn't made the same mistake last year and wouldn't again, irrespective of what had happened so recently. He would definitely be decorating the room this year . . . as soon as he felt up to it.

He heard his mobile ringing and almost didn't bother to answer it. At the last minute he checked to see who it was and changed his mind.

'Hello, you.'

'Hi,' said Anna. 'How's the invalid?'

'Not great, but thanks for asking.'

'You don't sound so bad.'

'So how bad should I sound?'

'Dunno. I was expecting a cough. Blocked nose, maybe.'

'Sorry to disappoint you,' he said, his voice sounding an octave lower than usual. 'But last night my temperature was 101 if that makes you feel any better, and my throat feels like someone's taken a sheet of sandpaper to it.'

'Hmm . . . ironic really. Is that the word I mean?' she asked. 'Only I seem to remember this great big security officer on patrol just a few days ago, looking down his unblocked nose at all those lesser mortals who'd gone down with the flu bug and grumbling about how in the old days it was regarded as some sort of stain on your character if you ever missed a day's work through illness. Something about how half the people who hadn't turned up that week were probably in Chichester doing their Christmas shopping. How crowded was it, by the way? You get everything you need?'

'I'll have you know I slept in all morning,' he said, reaching for a tissue and dabbing at the corner of his eye which had developed an irritating leak in the past hour or so. 'Forced myself to come down and have a bowl of soup for lunch, then promptly dozed off again in front of the fire. Would probably have slept through till tonight if Andy Holloway hadn't rung.'

'What did *he* want?' she asked, sounding a little more serious now.

'Nothing urgent. Just a quick update.'

'He's not pulling the plug, then?'

'Nope.'

'So it's still on?'

'Yep.'

'So what does that mean exactly? Is it all official?'

'Dunno. Didn't ask. I promised I'd keep him in the picture and that's what I've done. The rest is for him to sort out.'

'But he didn't warn you off?'

'No.'

'OK. That's good.'

'So how's *your* day going?' he asked, keen to keep the conversation going.

'Hang on,' she said, and he heard footsteps echoing off a hard surface. 'Just making sure Big Ears can't hear me,' she explained. 'My day? Yeah, well yours sounds pretty good from where I'm standing. I'm more than ready to swap, I tell you. You know who they've paired me with?'

'Not Gonzo?'

'Who else? You've heard the latest, I suppose? About you and I?'

'You and me.'

'What I said. Apparently the Keystone Cops upstairs have decided you and me are in a relationship.'

'You mean we're not?'

'Screwing like rabbits, it seems. Have been for months. Gonzo decided it was up to him to do the decent thing and let me know.'

'So you're not a lesbian anymore, then?'

'Apparently not.'

'Wonder what they think is worse, you being gay or throwing yourself at someone old enough to be your father.'

'I know. You'd have to be one of those people in the war to work out what goes on in their heads.'

'Soldiers?'

'No. The ones who had to break all the codes and things. You know.'

'The Bletchley Circle.'

'Ha ha. Very good. You think I don't know that's a Tube station? Codebreakers. That's the word. Different planet. Anyway, you make damned sure you're back tomorrow whatever you do cos if I have to spend another day patrolling with him, one of us isn't going to make it through to the end of the shift.'

'I'll do what I can.'

'Dose yourself up. Loads of Lemsips and paracetamol and stuff.'

'Lemsip *is* paracetamol.'

'I know that. But after a couple of Lemsips I can't stand the taste anymore.' She paused. 'Anything you want me to bring round to you? Soothers? Olbas oil? Some sort of cough medicine? I could drop it off on the way home.'

He laughed.

'How is Rose Green on the way home exactly?'

'It is if I go via your place. You want any or not?'

He thanked her but assured her he was well stocked up with everything he needed.

'So was that why you rang?' he asked. 'To make sure I was OK?'

'Pretty much. Got another bit of news for you though. If you're interested.'

'Go on.'

'Nearly forgot, what with all your whinging. You remember my first MMA fight that got cancelled?'

'Sittingbourne.'

'Right. Well, they've rearranged it. Only this time it's going to be here. Heard this afternoon. Our guys've already booked the Jenese Arts Centre in Linden Road, just up from where I live. You know it?'

He did. Baz had booked the same place for a couple of boxing promotions before now. Compact space, good atmosphere. Not much room for a big audience but he wasn't sure how big a crowd an MMA promotion would draw anyway. The acoustics were good though – those who did turn up would be sure to make plenty of noise.

'So when is it?'

'Sunday afternoon. Two till five.'

'You know who you're fighting?'

'No. Why? Are you thinking of coming along?'

'Might do.'

'You want to see me get my nose rearranged, right?'

'Actually,' he said, seizing the opening before his safety valve had a chance to kick in, 'I was wondering if you'd fancy a meal afterwards?'

'A meal?' The pause was just long enough for him to wonder if there was a way of taking it back. 'You mean . . . as in a *meal* meal? In a restaurant?'

'If you think you'll be up to it. I'll bring some plasters and a sling with me.'

He found himself wrapping the tassels on the blanket around his fingers while he waited for her reply.

'Yeah, I'll be up to it.'

'Good,' he said. 'It's a date, then.'

And again, even as he said it, he wished he could claw the word back out of the air.

Date, for God's sake.

OWEN

She's there waiting for him when he arrives. Bit of a surprise, that. His mother always used to say it's a woman's prerogative to be late but he's started to realise that a lot of things his mother used to say aren't very reliable. Probably applied more to her than women in general. He's having to make up his own mind about things more and more lately.

She looks different ... something she's done to her hair. It's shorter, follows the shape of her face more than it used to. Suits her, although he doesn't think telling her that would be a good start to the evening. She needs to know that just because he's agreed to meet her and hear what she has to say, that doesn't mean she's forgiven. She needn't think it's going to be as easy as that.

She already has a glass of red wine in front of her so he asks for a glass of water from the bar. The woman serving wonders if he wants sparkling or something else he doesn't recognise. He says he just wants water from the tap and she brings him a glass without charging him. He takes it back to the table in the corner of the lounge bar where Abi is waiting for him.

She starts off by apologising again. Says she doesn't know what was wrong with her back then. Can only assume it was some sort of delayed shock because she's been the same with everyone – he mustn't assume it's just him. Maybe it was finding out that Callum had been seeing someone else. 'Trust issues', she kept slipping into the conversation. She had trust issues, lost confidence in herself and everyone around her. *Like that excused anything.* Says she needed to shut herself away and start rebuilding her life by taking a good look at it and deciding what was worth holding onto. She's done all that and come out the other side. Thinks she's got her head straight now.

He's listening to this with a straight face, determined to give nothing away. He'd like to believe what she's saying but that's precisely why he needs to be on his guard. He knows what he's like, especially when it comes to Abi. He can zip everything up tight and build a protective wall around himself and she'll still find a way through if he's not careful. It's taken him three months to get over what happened. He doesn't need Willie chirping in his ear to recognise that. Knows how important it will be to keep his defences up.

She asks him how he's been and he's not sure what to say. On the way here he was all for embellishing things a little, inventing big projects that would make her think he hasn't been bent out of shape because of the way she treated him. Now he finds himself going in the opposite direction: not much work around, struggling to fill the gap she created in his schedule. And there's enough self-knowledge there for him to realise what he's doing. He wants her to feel guilty. Wants her to understand exactly what she did to him by shutting him out like that, so soon after they'd got back together. So when he talks about his social life, he's keen for her to see that he doesn't really have one. Goes to the cinema occasionally – and always on his own. Otherwise he spends his evenings at home. He's screaming *look at what you've done* without actually saying it, and it's working because he can see she understands. It's written all over her face. And it feels good.

He asks her if she's only brought him here to apologise and she says no. He can tell she's been working up to something and now she comes out with it. Says she doesn't know how to ask because she feels she's sacrificed the right to any favours with the way she's behaved, but she wonders if he'd be prepared to come back and work on her garden after all, just as they'd planned back in September. The whole area's a mess and she's found herself looking at the plans again in the past couple of days, kicking herself for not going ahead with them when she had the chance. They're so good and she'd really like him to pick up where he left off, perhaps sometime in the spring, because she's been told all of the investigations into Callum's finances should have been settled by then. She knows she could simply show the plans to another landscape gardener and ask him to do the work but that would feel like another betrayal and besides ... she wants *him* to do it. Does he think he might be prepared to give it some thought at least?

He doesn't need to. He's already doing the calculations. But he's not going to let her know that. There are things he wants to know first – reassurances he'll need if he's going to be convinced her apologies are genuine and heartfelt, not just some passing whim that's come over her. So he asks her about Callum's dad.

'What about him?' she says.

'I thought he was dead against me doing the g-garden project.'

'Yes, well ... it's not up to him, is it?' And there's something in the way she says this – a note of bitterness creeping into her voice – that makes him sit up and take notice.

'He's never l-liked me,' he says, trying to draw her out a little more.

'I know,' she says. 'I didn't realise back then, but I do now.' There's a long pause, during which he forces himself not to ask any questions. Let her get to it in her own way instead. And sure enough she starts to talk to fill the empty space. Tells him about the way Callum's dad has been behaving in the past few weeks, more or less avoiding her. She'd always thought he was a nice man, a friend even, while Callum was alive but now it's pretty clear how central his son was to all that. Take him out of the picture and there's not enough there to keep him interested.

And worse than that, they've had an argument. She'd picked up on a bit of an atmosphere every time she mentioned this friend of hers . . . Adam. He obviously didn't like the relationship. Felt it was inappropriate, given that Callum had been gone for such a short time. And even though she kept insisting it was no more than friendship he seemed to take exception to the fact that it had all started while his son was still alive. Couldn't get his head around the fact that she'd been with this Adam while Callum was being killed. So they'd had a few sharp words about it one evening and since then they'd seen very little of each other.

'It's a bit ironic really,' she says, draining her glass. 'I'm not seeing Adam now either. Not away from work, anyway.'

And this is something he really wants to hear about but she won't be drawn on it. Says, 'That's for some other time.' She doesn't want to bore him with her problems this evening. And he wants to tell her he won't be bored but doesn't know how to do it without giving away just how anxious he is to hear all the details. So he tries to come up with a way of bringing her back to it, but she says she has to go. She wants to thank him for listening. She won't press him for an answer just yet about the garden project but even if he decides he doesn't want to do it she'd still really like to stay in touch if that's OK with him. She's been thinking ahead to Christmas and feeling sorry for herself. Now that there was no Callum, she'd been assuming she'd cook lunch for his dad at least on Christmas Day, given that he was on his own too, and that had given her something to focus on. But that didn't seem likely now. And Adam . . . she gives a sad smile which lifts his spirits even further. Something's not right there. He knew it. Could have told her if he'd thought she'd listen.

She gets up, pats his arm as she says goodbye. No kiss on the cheek this time but she does say that she'll buy him dinner later in the week if he decides he's willing to turn the clock back and go along with their original plans for the garden. He says he'll think about it and watches her leave before going off to the bar to buy himself a packet of crisps to celebrate.

He thinks he's handled that very well.

Willie, needless to say, doesn't agree.

Stupid, he says, as soon as she's gone. *Stupid, stupid, stupid.*

'Why stupid?'

You are *kidding me, right? You seriously have to ask? For Christ's sake, wake up, will you? You're putting everything you've done in the last three months at risk. You've only just started to get your act together and now, after everything she's put you through, all she has to do is crook her finger and you come running like some lovesick school kid. Before you know it you'll be right back at square one.*

'No, I won't.'

You will too. It's like watching a train wreck in slow motion, it's so bloody obvious what's going to happen.

'You're wrong,' he protests. 'She's not like that. You make her sound mean. And anyway, it's different this time.'

Different how exactly?

'Because this time she was in the wrong and she knows it. And I didn't just give in like you're making out. I was really firm with her.'

Sure you were. Keep telling yourself that. Listen, this special relationship *you want with her. Friendship. Whatever you want to call it. Not gonna happen, OK? She's not interested. What else has she got to do before you get the message? She can't make it any clearer. It's how women are, right? They want different things from different people. You've always been her friend but for some reason that's not enough for you. You don't want to share her.*

Owen shakes his head. 'Not true.'

Is too. First it's Callum, then it's this new guy and you know what? If he gets nudged out of the picture there'll be someone else lurking around the corner and then someone else after him too. There'll always be someone else cos women need someone like that in their lives. But if you think it'll ever be you, you're fooling yourself.

'I'm not listening.'

Yeah, well, that'd be a first.

'You don't know everything.'

I know this much. If you let her buy you dinner, that's not the start of a slippery slope. That's you taking a run at it and flinging yourself over the edge head first. You need to think hard about what I've said. It's your only chance.

He's gone now. Had his say. He thinks that'll be enough because it always has been till now. But not this time. This time Owen knows better. And he *will* meet Abi for dinner because that's what he chooses to do. He's not the soft touch Willie thinks he is. That *everybody* thinks he is. He can meet her for dinner and decide for himself how things stand. He's not an idiot.

And besides, he wants to hear what she has to say. He's curious.

And it's only dinner anyway.

Where's the problem?

19

THURSDAY, 11TH DECEMBER

OWEN

She's wearing the necklace.

It's the first thing he sees as she enters Prezzo's and his first thought is *told you so* as she walks over towards him. She takes off her coat and drapes it across the back of the chair, tutting and shaking her head as she apologises for being late. Accident on the A27 which meant all the traffic dropped down onto the Fishbourne Road. Queues everywhere.

'Last thing I needed,' she says, taking her seat and picking up a menu. 'Have you been waiting long?'

He tells her no, only ten minutes or so. He's still looking at the necklace. She realises what he's doing and smiles sheepishly.

'You don't mind, do you?' she asks. 'I was looking through my winter jumpers and came across it by chance. I'd forgotten it was there to be honest. Does that sound awful?'

He shakes his head, although he feels instinctively the answer ought to be *yes*.

'When I saw the box I couldn't help having a look and once I did that, of course, I had to try it on. It looks so lovely. And then I thought, *why not wear it tonight?* Maybe that was a bit insensitive of me. I'd understand if you'd rather I took it off.'

She raises both hands behind her neck as if just waiting for him to give the word. He shakes his head – no, he'd like her to keep it on. Then he remembers he's meant to be keeping his distance.

'I thought you'd got rid of it,' he says. 'You said you were going to sell it or give it away to a charity shop if I didn't take it back.'

She purses her lips, looks apologetic.

'I said a lot of stupid things back then, Owen. I wasn't in a very good place. And I really did want you to take it back because I felt so bad about how much it must have cost you, so when you kept refusing I just . . . I don't know. Anyway, I'm glad I didn't.'

He wonders what she'd say if he asked her to give it back to him now. The thought just pops into his head from nowhere. He's not trying to be cruel but it does feel as if there's been something of a shift in the balance of power and it's tempting to see how far he can push it. In the end, it's only the knowledge that Willie would like nothing better – has been urging him to do it for ages – that stops him.

'Have you ordered?' she asks. He shakes his head, says he thought he'd wait for her. As it happens, he's not really sure what to choose. Doesn't know whether Abi will want a starter as well as a main meal and since she's insisted this is her treat he doesn't want to presume too much. So he's decided he'd rather wait and then go for the same as her. And a glass of water.

It's his first time in Prezzo's. He's not been to many Italian restaurants before but he didn't really feel he could argue since she's the one paying. He likes this place though. There's a group of people who look as if they could be students in the far corner, all sitting round three tables that have been pushed together. He's counted and there are nine of them. Three tables. Nine people. And over to the left there's a table with two couples and two young children waiting to have their orders taken. Table for six. This is a good place. He feels comfortable here.

A waitress takes their order. She has a strong accent which he finds difficult to understand but Abi helps out. Doesn't sound Italian. Eastern European more like. She smiles a lot though and brings him not just a frosted glass but a whole carafe of ice-cold water. He likes her too.

As a starter Abi goes for baked mushrooms stuffed with Grana Padano and mozzarella cheese, garlic, onions and breadcrumbs. He has no idea what half of this means but he likes mushrooms and cheese. Whatever Grana Padano is, he'll eat it. For the main course, she's chosen something called an arrosto. He doubts very much whether he's eaten as many as 20 per cent of the items listed here at any stage in his life and the idea of trying to pronounce them or, even worse, having to point to one of them and say *that one,* is too humiliating for words. So he nods again – *same for me, please*. Resists the temptation to play safe with a side order of chips. Thinks to himself maybe this is the sort of thing he ought to know about. Time he branched out a little.

While they wait for the starters to arrive she hands her mobile to one of the waitresses and asks her to take a photo of the two of them together. He's not altogether comfortable with this. Never likes having his photo taken. Always feels when he sees the finished product that he looks misshapen somehow, out of proportion. He thinks he can look quite good in a mirror but somehow the transfer from reality to print never fails to disappoint. He feels he ought to make the effort though. Abi is in such a happy mood and he doesn't want to do anything to dampen it.

She thanks him for agreeing to pick up where he left off so abruptly with the garden. Tells him she'd still like to go ahead with the most expensive of the plans. When she says this he takes a long sip of water from the frosted glass to hide the smile that's threatening to break out across his face. That will take something like three months for him to complete and even then there will be scope for him to extend it into other areas if she decides she likes what she's seen so far. The money's an obvious plus because it's been a tough few months but that's not the reason he's smiling.

The only possible snag is she can't say yes for definite just yet. Callum's fault as usual. The authorities are still examining several of his accounts where there are suspicious transactions so she doesn't know yet which money she'll be able to use and which will still be frozen. A lot of it goes straight over his head but if there's one thing he does understand it's that everyone else is beginning to understand that Callum wasn't someone you could trust. Maybe if the police are now saying the same thing she'll realise what he was like all along.

And the good news just keeps on coming because Abi seems even more upset now with Callum's dad. It seems he rang last night to say he's decided to spend Christmas morning with a group of friends from the boxing club instead of her. No apology – just a message on her voicemail. She's really angry about this, thinks it's just plain rude. And Owen wonders whether maybe, when she's calmed down and had a few days to think it through, it will dawn on her that *he* spent last Christmas morning on his own as well and hasn't got any plans for this year either. Is there some way he might slip it into the conversation or would it be better to let her find her way there in her own time? Maybe the latter, he tells himself. Better coming from her.

He's still waiting for some sort of news about the state of her friendship with this Adam person but she seems to keep swerving away from the subject every time they come anywhere near to it. She was the one who raised it after all – and she did say, 'That's for some other time'. Well, this is some other time. He doesn't want to rush things but it's starting to look as if she'll never get round to it so in the end he just asks her outright. And her face darkens as she looks down at the table, folding her napkin into squares that get smaller and smaller each time.

'I'm afraid I . . . misjudged him,' she says.

'What d'you mean?'

She shakes her head.

'I don't want to spoil this evening.'

'Has he done something to upset you?'

She unfolds the napkin again and puts it on the table next to her drink.

'It's probably my fault. I . . .' She's rearranging the cutlery in straight lines, anything to keep her hands busy. 'I made the mistake of thinking we could be just friends. Like you and me, you know? I mean, he was such a good laugh at work, always joking around, happy-go-lucky. And he really seemed to be interested in me . . . me as a person. I mean, with Callum I'd got used to being some sort of trophy he fetched out of the cupboard and dusted down whenever he needed to impress other people.'

She takes a sip of red wine and looks at the glass as if nodding her approval.

'Adam though,' she goes on, 'he really knew how to listen. I mean, he had this way of making me talk about myself, even though I didn't realise what I was doing. I used to tell him so many things I'd never even told Callum. And he seemed to hang on to every word I said. Not many men are like that.'

I'm like that, he wants to scream. *I can be like that. Look at me now – I'm listening to every word you say, just like I always have done.* But he says nothing. And he's noticed that she's talking now in the past tense whenever she refers to Adam.

'Anyway,' she says. 'We started meeting outside work. Nothing serious, you know? Just friends. . . or at least that's how I saw it. I mean, it's not like either of us was free to start up anything else. I was married to Callum and Adam had this girlfriend who was out of the country but who he was obviously close to, so there was never going to be anything between us. At least that's what I thought. Only things started to change – ever so slowly but enough for me to get wind of what was going on.'

'How did they change?' he asks. He knows asking questions is something he's expected to do. It shows he's really listening.

'Well, first he dumped his girlfriend. She flew in from Africa for a week just to see him and he waited till the last day then told her he wanted to finish it. Just like that. And I thought that was a bit harsh but it wasn't really any of my business, so . . . Anyway, then he started trying to engineer ways of seeing more of me. And if I wasn't available for some reason he'd want to know what I was doing instead that was so important and it all started to feel a bit . . . you know. Uncomfortable. I felt he was pushing me into a corner and I'm not ready for anything like that. Despite what Phil seems to think.'

She breaks off as she sees the waitress approaching with their starters. He's frustrated by the poor timing but he needn't worry – she's in the mood now and as soon as the waitress has gone, she picks up again where she left off.

'Anyway, last weekend – Sunday it was – he invited me round to his flat. Said he'd cook dinner for me to say thank you in advance for feeding his cat. He's away in Leeds this week, staying with friends from university so I agreed I'd pop round there every morning and put food out for her. Thing was, I'd been feeling a bit under the weather for a couple of days, a touch of this flu that's going around. By about four or five in the afternoon, I was really struggling and had to ring up and cry off. And he went mad.'

She pops a mushroom into her mouth and pauses to savour it.

'I mean, absolutely ballistic. Started griping about all the money he'd spent on the food and how he'd already started preparing it. Surely I could give it a go. And when I said I really didn't think so, he slammed the phone down, and when I tried to ring him back he wouldn't answer. Just kept going to voicemail. I was so shocked. I mean, I hadn't seen it coming.'

Owen has almost cleared his plate already. Wonders if it might have been more polite to take his time and keep pace with Abi but she's doing all the talking here and the starter's practically disappeared before he knows it.

'That's stupid,' he says, feeling strongly that he should be saying something profound here to demonstrate his support. 'He can't expect you to go round if you're ill.'

'That's only half of it,' she continues. 'Later that evening I was lying on the settee in my dressing gown and there's this banging on the window. Scared the life out of me. So I jumped off the settee and peered round the edge of the curtain and he's standing there, asking me to open the door. Says he needs to talk to me. And he's yelling so loud I think I'm going to have to let him in or the neighbours will all be wondering what on earth's going on. So I open the door and he comes marching into the front room. And I've hardly had a chance to shut the front door before he starts up with the accusations: what's going on? He knows I'm seeing someone else – who is he? And I mean, he can see I'm telling the truth about feeling ill cos I look like death warmed up and the lounge is like a pharmacy for God's sake, but he's still harping on. And it's only when I burst into tears and he can see he's scaring me that he snaps out of it and starts to calm down a bit. Next thing I know, he's trying to hug me and apologising over and over again and it's the last thing I want so I end up pushing him away and telling him to get out. And next day he disappears off to Leeds and Muggins here is stupid enough to go round and feed his cat for him all week. Well, not the cat's fault, is it? Don't want it to starve.'

She empties her wine glass and signals to a passing waitress that she'd like another.

'So I guess you could say I'm not doing very well in my choice of men,' she says with a rueful smile. 'I seem to have a gift for picking the wrong ones. One bad decision after another. I spent all Sunday night thinking it through and I think that's what made me realise how unfair I'd been on you. I mean, you know you shouldn't have done what you did but it's not like it's the greatest crime in the world, is it? And I thought maybe I shouldn't have listened to Phil when he told me trusting you was iffy. But it was a bad time and I wasn't thinking straight, even though that doesn't really excuse the way I reacted. You've always been a good friend. You certainly wouldn't yell at me and scare me the way Adam did.'

'You want me to go round and see him when he gets back?' he asks.

She looks shocked.

'No, Owen. God, no. That's not why I told you.'

'I could warn him not to bother you again.'

'No – honestly. I don't want you to do anything like that. In fact, I'll be cross if you do. Besides, there's no need. First chance I get, I'm going to meet him somewhere where he can't make a scene and tell him I don't want to see him anymore. I'll sort it myself. I don't want you to get involved, OK?'

He nods. OK.

'Promise?'

Nods again. It's just a nod. Doesn't mean anything.

She reaches across the table and pats his hand. Thanks him for the offer. It's nice to feel protected. He tries to pat hers as well but she's already withdrawn it and he picks up his glass of water instead.

Throughout the rest of the meal, she asks him about what he's been doing but there are more silences than earlier and he gets the impression her thoughts are drifting elsewhere. It's almost as if she's building up to something but isn't sure how to bring it into the conversation. He wonders if it's Christmas Day that's bothering her, whether it's occurred to her that he might be the perfect person for her to invite round for lunch so that she doesn't have to spend the day on her own. Maybe she's thought about asking him but is afraid he'll say no.

So he tries his best to work the conversation round to the right subject by talking about putting up decorations, thinking about what presents to buy. He even makes a joke of sorts about how she needn't worry – he won't buy her another necklace. And she smiles but it's clear she's not really with it. Maybe she's still a bit under the weather and the evening is gradually knocking the stuffing out of her.

Then, just as he's starting to run out of ideas, she takes a sizable drink from her wine glass and tells him there's something she'd like his opinion on.

'Would you mind? You'll probably think it's just me being stupid but it's been bothering me and if I don't tell someone soon, I'll go mad.'

His first thought is, *at last*. He hasn't got a clue what it is she wants to ask him, doesn't care how stupid it is. What matters is, she wants an honest opinion from someone she trusts. And she's asking *him*. He nods to tell her to go ahead. Puts on his listening face.

And what she has to say *is* nonsense. If there's one person in the whole world who can say with absolute authority that she's got the wrong end of the stick altogether, it's him – because no one knows better than he does what happened to Callum that night in August. Even so, Abi's been doing a bit of thinking, putting two and two together and she's come up with an answer that's so wide of the mark it's almost embarrassing. But the more he listens, the more he likes what he's hearing. And the more the wheels start to turn.

What's bothering her is the fact that on the night Callum was killed, when she left Owen's place, she went off to meet Adam for a drink, just like she'd told the police. The thing is though, Adam turned up late. Made some excuse – she can't remember what it was now, but she knows she was definitely sitting there on her own for quite a while before he finally showed up. And when the police asked Adam what time they were at the pub, he said it was about 8.15 and she didn't think to question it back then because why would she? But now she's given it a bit of thought, she's pretty sure she can't have got to the pub much before 8.15 herself and she knows she waited a good twenty minutes or so before he finally showed up.

And what she wants to know now is: should she go and tell the police she was wrong about that time too?

'I've already changed my statement once,' she says, pulling a face. 'If I do it a second time, they're going to go mad. They weren't happy with me the first time it happened. But I don't know what to do. Do you think I ought to tell them anyway and leave them to make up their own minds?'

And though the answer's blindingly obvious from his point of view, nevertheless he takes his time over it. He wants her to see that he's been listening carefully, but there's only one answer he's ever going to give her – he'd be mad not to take advantage of an opportunity as good as this. So after what he considers to be a decent interval he tells her she needs to go back to the police and tell them what she knows. The timings in things like this might be crucial. She has to tell them. And an excellent evening is getting better by the minute.

He was right about the necklace. He knew she'd like it. Knew she'd have to wear it in the end. And it looks as if it was made for her. It's perfect.

And he's right about the baseball bat too.

It's going to come in handy after all.

It's just a question of working out how.

20

SATURDAY, 13TH DECEMBER

OWEN

Saturday is his favourite day of the week. Not by a lot – the others have all got something to be said for them too. Monday to Friday he gets to work in the fresh air for the most part, physical labour which has enough variety to keep him interested and wears him out so that he's guaranteed a good night's sleep. Sunday mornings he sets aside for maintaining the website, designing plans for customers and keeping his accounts up to date. In the afternoon he allows himself three or four uninterrupted hours of tinkering in the garage, restoring old mowers to their former glory.

But Saturdays have the edge over the other days because from the moment he gets up it's all about him. He likes to start with a lie-in, maybe until as late as eight o'clock if the mood takes him. Leisurely breakfast while he listens to Radio 2 – cereal always and a fry-up if it doesn't feel like too much trouble. Then he clambers into the truck and drives off to a car-boot sale somewhere. Hunter's Lodge is his favourite but it's not there all year round. He's tried most in the area and can usually find one that will fit the bill.

And in the afternoon he likes to check the listings for Cineworld in the hope that there might be a film worth seeing. If there is, he usually tries for a showing around late afternoon/early evening and picks up fish and chips on the way home. If not, he might work out on the weights in the spare bedroom or try to find something worth watching on TV. He's generally in bed by nine o'clock but sees that as a positive. Apart from anything else, the later he stays up, the more likely it is he'll have Willie in his ear, moaning about something else he's done wrong. An early night can seem like a blessing.

So he's feeling good about things this morning, pouring cereal into his bowl and checking the sell-by date on the milk carton he's just taken out of the fridge, when the phone rings. He doesn't get a lot of phone calls apart from pre-recorded messages from insurance companies and requests for help with a survey from people with such heavy accents he can barely understand what they're saying. They don't normally ring this early. If he gets a call before nine, especially at the weekend, it's usually Malkie, ringing to let him know there's another mower he's looking to pass on to him.

But this time it's Abi. Her voice sounds weary – a bit strained, as if maybe she's had a bad night. And she wants to know if he's busy. Could he do her a favour? He supposes he could tell her about the car-boot sale but, if he does, she might decide not to bother him next time and ask someone else instead. He can't expect to become the person she automatically turns to and then turn her away the first time she needs help with something. So he tells her no – he hasn't got anything planned.

She asks in that case whether she could borrow him for an hour or so. She'll go over it with him later rather than explain over the phone if that's OK with him. She'll come and pick him up to save him the trip out to Bosham.

'This is so sweet of you,' she says. 'I really appreciate it. Will ten be OK?'

He says ten o'clock will be fine.

'Where are we going?'

'To the allotments,' she says.

And she's gone before he can ask what on earth they might be doing, visiting the allotments. But maybe that's what life is like when you have a close relationship with someone. Maybe life is full of surprises and strange requests just like this. He wonders how people manage to create any sort of routine for themselves.

He goes back to his breakfast and takes his time over it, flicking back through the pages of the conversation they had just now for clues. It doesn't matter what she wants him for. It's enough that she does. That she's rung *him* rather than anyone else. But she's never said anything about renting a plot at the allotments before and he's pretty sure Callum wouldn't have gone near anything that involved manual work. He wonders if maybe he misheard her, then tells himself he'll know soon enough anyway, when she comes to pick him up. To pick *him* up.

He finishes his breakfast and goes upstairs to change out of his old sweater with holes in the sleeves and into a more presentable one. Doesn't want to run the risk of showing her up.

Ten o'clock takes forever to arrive. She's actually five minutes early which is just as well. He'd have worn a hole in the carpet otherwise. He's outside before she's had a chance to get out of the car. Panics for a moment as he slams the door until he feels his house keys safely tucked away in his pocket. He hasn't thought to bring any money with him and checks with her whether this will be a problem. She shakes her head and drives off as soon as he's in the car.

Sports car. Brings back unpleasant reminders of the panic he went through, trying to reverse Callum's BMW along Honer Lane. Apart from those few moments the only vehicles he's ever driven are his Mitsubishi pickup truck and a twenty-year-old Marina his mother always used for trips to town. Engine used to scream in protest if he tried to tease it out of third gear. This car's different all right. A bit unnerving at first – that sudden surge which pushes him back in his seat – but he decides he could get used to it. He imagines it in the summer months with the roof down. Maybe he and Abi might go for a drive in the countryside one Sunday when the weather's warm enough. It's what friends do. He's seen it often enough in old films from the fifties. Cary Grant. Audrey Hepburn. They could take a picnic somewhere in the Sussex Downs.

He asks her where they're going now and when she turns to face him it's the first chance he's had to look at her closely. He can see now that her eyes are red and puffy, as if she either has a cold or maybe hasn't slept much. He asks her if she's OK and there's a bit of a catch in her throat when she answers.

He listens while she explains why she needs his help. It's Adam causing problems again. He arrived back from Leeds last night and rang to thank her for looking after the cat and to apologise for his behaviour the previous weekend. Seemed to think all he had to do was say sorry and all would be forgotten. Abi says she accepted his apology, which is a bit much really,

Owen thinks; she wasn't that understanding with *him* when *he* stepped out of line and all he'd done was have a look in her bedroom. He hadn't shouted at her or anything like that and yet it had taken her nearly three months to forgive him, not just a measly phone call.

But Adam clearly doesn't know when to stop pushing his luck because the next thing he did was to ask if she fancied meeting up with him sometime over the weekend. They could go for dinner – his treat.

'Obviously I said no,' she explains now. 'I don't really want to be on my own with him. I don't feel comfortable. Not now I've seen another side to his character. I didn't put it in quite those terms but he's not stupid. He knew what I was really trying to say and that just set him off again. He started to get angry.'

He's not the only one. Owen's fidgeting in his seat. This Adam Kitchener needs to know he can't go around upsetting Abi like that. And there must be something in his posture that gives away his agitation because Abi puts a hand on his knee. Tells him it's all right.

'Angry's probably the wrong word,' she reassures him. 'Sulky's more like it. He went all cold and distant, just like before. Said he'd be round first thing to collect his spare keys from me. Anyway, I didn't want him coming round to my place this morning. Not after his last visit. So I said I'd drop them off instead. He'll be at the allotments in Sandringham Way all morning. And that's better than going round to his place because I'm guessing there will be other people around and he'll have to behave himself. But just in case, I thought maybe I could ask you to come with me. I'd feel better if I had you there too. Safer.'

And he likes this. Likes it very much. The idea of acting as Abi's protector is an appealing one that's been carrying him through his weights sessions of late. Now he knows all that hard work hasn't been for nothing. Abi will feel *safer* with him around. That's the word she used. *Safer*.

She stresses again that all she wants him to do is be there. He mustn't get involved.

'Even if Adam loses his temper and starts to say things you think are hurtful, I want you to stay out of it. You have to promise, Owen.'

'OK.'

'Seriously. I mean it. I've got to know I can trust you on this. If I can't, tell me now.'

So he promises again. He's not going to do anything if that's what she wants. He'll just stand there and watch. Be there for her. He can do that.

She turns into Hawthorn Road, ignoring the twenty-miles-per-hour signs and following the directions coming from her mobile. When they reach the Wheatsheaf, it tells her to turn left into Sandringham Way, a narrow road with terraced houses down one side and the allotments on the left, protected by wire mesh fencing about six-foot high. In front of the houses there's a parking bay in which cars are jutting out at an angle to make more room. Abi picks a gap and swings into it, leaving just enough space for Owen to get the door open and squeeze through.

They cross the road to a padlocked gate. There's a plastic-covered notice, one corner unattached and flopping forward, which says: *Please be reminded that the gate must remain locked at all times by order of the town clerk.* Even so, as Abi nudges it with her foot it swings open.

There's a network of green pathways ahead of them, threading their way through the separate plots of land. Some areas are neatly maintained, covered in black plastic ground sheeting to protect the soil. Others look as if they haven't been tended for quite some time, with bits of wood left lying around among the weeds. They walk past a white plastic chair lying on its side and a wheelbarrow that's been left upright and is now rusted through from all the rain that's gathered in it over the years. Such a waste. Some of the panes have been smashed in the greenhouse that's nearest to the road – an easy target for local kids with nothing better to do with their evenings.

There are half a dozen or so people dotted around as far as Owen can see. No surprise the areas they're all working on look cared for. One person looks a lot younger than the others. He's sitting on a stool, putting the finishing touches to the shed he's been staining a dark green colour. Seems like an odd time of year to be doing that but he's not making a bad job of it. Owen thinks he might have found a kindred spirit for a moment until he realises that this is where Abi is heading as she picks her way carefully through the damp grass.

Kitchener looks up, sees who's approaching and goes back to his work. Abi waits until they're about ten yards away, then turns and whispers to Owen to wait here. She'll call if she needs him. He knows it can't be because she wants to talk in private because, unless they're going to whisper or go inside the shed, he's close enough anyway to hear whatever they have to say to each other. He assumes she still doesn't quite trust him enough to keep his word – is worried he might get angry and lash out suddenly. He reminds himself that he's promised her – she can trust him. Whatever happens, he'll stay out of it or next time she'll ring someone else.

Kitchener doesn't make any attempt to acknowledge their presence. Just carries on staining the wood. Owen wishes he'd had a chance to see him before now because it would have saved him a lot of unnecessary worry. There's no way he would have seen him as serious competition if he'd had a chance to size him up. He's no more than medium height – taller than Abi, for sure, but nowhere near six foot. Five eight, five nine at most. Owen would tower over him if they stood back to back. Could probably carry him under one arm.

And he's not even good-looking. He's got a long, thin nose which gives him a ferrety look and he's trying for some sort of designer stubble which just comes across as wispy and scruffy, as though he couldn't be bothered to shave for the past few days. Much as he used to hate Callum, Owen has to admit there was something about him. He was good-looking enough to have all the girls in school chasing after him and confident enough to have most of the boys wanting to be his friend. This weed though? Different kettle of fish altogether. He must have got it wrong all this time. There's no way Abi would ever have chosen him as her partner.

A weed in the allotments, he thinks to himself. And he's quite pleased with that.

Abi's standing right next to Kitchener now so that he can't ignore her.

'I've brought your keys,' she says, putting her hand in her coat pocket and offering them to him. He looks at them for a moment, then holds out his hand so that she can drop them into it. She misses and they fall to the ground, almost landing in the paint pot. He shakes his head, retrieves them and puts them in his pocket. Then he gets to his feet. *Definitely,* thinks Owen. *Five-nine at most.* And now that he can see more of him he realises that there's almost nothing to him. Obviously doesn't look after himself. Looks as if he's never done a day's manual labour in his life. Works in a bookshop? Big surprise.

Kitchener still hasn't said anything. Walks over to several piles of empty flower pots that are stacked inside each other. Chooses a pile, takes out the first two pots, reaches inside the third one and retrieves something which, from where Owen's standing, looks like another key. Then he goes to the shed door and unlocks it. Owen's not sure why they're standing around waiting but he can't catch Abi's attention without speaking and he's promised he'll stay out of it. He can wait. Five minutes from now they'll be back in the car and it will all be over.

Kitchener comes back out of the shed, holding a plastic bag with 'Monsoon' printed on it. He locks up and returns the key to the same place – third pot in the stack. Then he hands the bag to Abi who looks surprised to receive it.

'It's a jumper,' he says, sitting back down on the stool and picking up the brush again. 'Bought it in Leeds. Thought it'd look good on you.'

Abi doesn't even open the bag to look inside.

'Adam . . . I can't take this.'

'Early Christmas present,' he says, shrugging his shoulders. 'Keep it. It's not like there's anyone else I can give it to. And it's a helluva long way to go for a refund.'

'I can't,' she says. And Owen thinks, *poor Abi*. People always queuing up to give her presents which she can't keep. At least she knows now she can wear his necklace any time she likes. He doesn't think somehow that she'll be doing the same with some cheap jumper two months from now. No comparison.

'Sorry about the bag,' he says. 'Was going to wrap it but then I thought why bother? Not as if I give a shit.'

Abi takes half a step back as if she's been physically manhandled but says nothing. Kitchener meanwhile seems to take an interest in Owen for the first time.

'Who's he?' he asks, nodding his head in his direction.

'A friend of mine.'

'Oh. A friend.' There's a sarcastic chuckle along with this but Owen knows his job is to ignore it. 'Where'd you find him? Rent-a-Shrek?'

Abi says nothing, just stares at him for a moment before throwing the bag at him. He instinctively puts an arm up to block it, realising too late that it's the one holding the brush, which slides down the outside of the bag, leaving a green smear on it. He swears and snatches up the bag to check that the jumper inside is undamaged. Abi meanwhile turns on her heel and walks away.

But Kitchener hasn't quite finished yet.

'Hey, big boy,' he calls out as they head back towards the gate. 'You want a piece of advice?'

Owen stops and half-turns but Abi puts her hand on his arm to encourage him to keep walking.

'Where you are now, mate? Been there.' Kitchener's voice rings out, causing one or two other gardeners to look up from what they're doing. 'Been there and got the T-shirt. Not the first either. Well-worn path you're treading, I tell you.'

'Ignore him,' Abi whispers, taking his arm and steering him away from there. 'Don't listen.'

'Don't know what she's told you, pal, but if you think she's latched onto you because of your looks, get yourself a bathroom mirror. She's after something. Bet your arse, she's using you somehow.'

And Owen can still hear his mocking laughter long after they've got back into Abi's car and driven off.

Later that evening, he's feeling pleased with himself. He's had an idea. It's a good one, which means Willie doesn't like it. In fact, it's a *very* good idea, which is why Willie is alternating between whining and sneering, with lots of references to necklaces, baseball bats, wasted breath and deaf ears. But he can whinge as much as he likes, he's not fooling anyone. They both know it's the right thing to do. The only thing wrong with it is that Willie's not the one who thought of it. He's got used to seeing himself as the ideas man. Thinks if it doesn't come from him it can't be any use.

Well, now they both know that's not true.

Funny how today's turned out. Last thing he'd expected this morning was that he'd be spending his evening scribbling ideas onto a sheet of paper and making sure everything fits. But the plan's more or less there. He knows what he has to do next. It's just the final piece that won't slot into place, the bit where the police know where to look. He's had a few thoughts but none that will guarantee he's in the clear. Not one hundred per cent. And this can't come back to bite him, whatever happens. He won't go through with it unless he's quite sure. It's just that everything he's come up with so far has had a flaw in it somewhere and Willie's been quick to pounce on it. Says it's what happens if you go off half-cocked at things. *Haven't thought it through, have you?*

But that's just what he *is* doing and he'll get there eventually. Just because there are still a few details to iron out doesn't mean he can't at least set it all up. The most important thing right now is moving the bat from the Aldertons' shed. It's got to come out sometime soon anyway in case they decide to come back for a few days over the Christmas period, so why not move it to where it can cause the most damage? Where it belongs. The rest will take care of itself one way or another.

Willie's still bleating on about the risks involved which just goes to show how things are changing around here at last. Not that long ago it was Willie urging him to pick the bat up off the ground and get rid of Callum once and for all. If it's risks he wants to talk about, they could always start there. He didn't seem to have any problem with putting everything on the line then, did he? But now, because he can see he's not the one taking the lead all the time, it's all *Wait. Think. Don't rush into anything*. Like he's the only one capable of taking the big decisions.

And he's rabbiting on now about using the probability test to make sure and Owen thinks maybe that's not such a bad idea. If nothing else it'll shut him up for a while because he has no doubt whatsoever the die will fall in his favour. Everything else has done. The necklace. The bat with the special numbers. When the right number comes up on the die, not even Willie will be able to argue against it. Then maybe he'll get some peace and quiet at last.

So he goes to the chest of drawers in the lounge, opens the middle one and fetches out the Trivial Pursuit which his mother used to play with him. He takes a die from the box, then sits on the floor in the kitchen where the lino will guarantee a free, unimpeded roll – he doesn't want there to be any ambiguity about the outcome here. He holds the die up to his mouth, whispering words of encouragement, even though he's sure there's no need, shakes his hand and opens it, letting the die scud across the floor where it cannons into the base of the sink unit and rebounds out into the open. He shuffles along on his backside and picks it up.

It's a one.

One? What does that mean? It's a nothing number. Neither fish nor fowl, as his mother used to say. If it was a three or a six, that would be as clear a green light as you can get. Two or five, he'd know to back away. But a one . . . that doesn't tell him anything. So he throws again . . . and of course, that's not good enough for Willie who seems to want to make up new rules as he goes along, because he's insisting this means the plan is no good. If it had anything going for it, a three or a six would have come up. Throwing again is bucking a system they've always relied on in the past. But he doesn't get to decide. Owen does.

He throws again.

It's another one.

This time he doesn't even hesitate which means there's no time for any objections. He grabs the die and throws again. He'll keep going till he gets a clear message.

This time it's a four, and another argument is looming. Willie says he's had three attempts. Three is the lucky number and yet the die still hasn't managed to come up with a three or a six. That ought to be a clear enough warning for anyone. But Owen's not listening. He's marshalling his own troops instead.

For one thing: one plus one plus four makes . . . six. Multiple of three. And if you take the numbers as a whole instead of separately, that gives you 114 and, as any fool knows, that's a multiple of three as well. You can't get a clearer green light than that. But Willie's not having it. He's howling with derision, accusing Owen of cheating, of bending the results to fit the overall pattern he wants to see instead of letting the die decide as they've always done in the past.

But his outrage is just so much hot air.

It's good enough for Owen.

And he knows what to do next.

It's nearly midnight when he steps out into the cold night air. Frost is already starting to form on the windscreen, a stiff breeze singing in his ears. He's usually in bed by nine so this is very late for him. Adrenaline keeping him awake. Heart pumping.

The bat's lying on the passenger seat next to him. He reaches down from time to time to check it's still there. He collected it earlier this afternoon from the Aldertons' shed. Nothing suspicious about that – neighbours are used to him being there at different times of the day. He was anxious driving back home as he is now, sticking religiously to the speed limit, taking care not to do anything to draw attention to himself. If the worst comes to the worst and he's stopped by the police, he has a cover story ready. He found the bat in his shed, knows the police have been looking for it. He assumes someone is trying to incriminate him and he is on his way to hand it in to the authorities.

Except he isn't, of course.

Just as he did earlier, he's keeping a close eye on any cars behind him in case he's being followed. It's much easier at this time of night. There's very little traffic on the road and he's seen no suspicious lights in the rear-view mirror. He takes a far from direct route, using a handful of narrow back streets, doubling back on himself, stopping occasionally . . . just to make sure.

When he's quite certain it's safe to do so, he turns into Sandringham Way and pulls into a space just a short distance from where Abi and he were parked earlier. He turns off the engine and the lights. Sits in darkness for a few seconds, looking around and making quite sure he's on his own. No lights come on in any of the houses, no curtains twitch, no one chooses that moment to open the front door and leave empty milk bottles on the front step or call for the cat to come in. He gets out of the pickup and closes the door as quietly as he can, checking further along the road. Even this late at night, people might still be about and he needs to make sure no one sees him for the next few minutes. He waits a few seconds longer, then opens the passenger door and picks up the bat, stroking it gently with his gloved hands. He'll miss it, that's for sure. He's wondered about looking online for an exact replacement, something he can order and then keep as a souvenir. But that means leaving a trace and he knows he can't afford to do that. It will have to go. But at least it's going to be put to the best possible use.

Checking carefully one last time, he crosses the road and nudges the gate to the allotments with his foot. It's locked this time but that's no problem for someone of his height. He throws the bat over the fence, then grabs the top of the gate with both hands and pulls himself up, swinging a long leg out, using it as a lever to haul himself over before dropping as soundlessly as possible on the other side.

It's pitch black. There are no street lights to help him and he can barely see more than a few yards in front of his face. He picks his way carefully along the pathways, remembering the route he and Abi took earlier. A dog barks somewhere in the distance, too far away to represent any threat. There's the occasional sound of a car driving down Hawthorn Road, otherwise the silence is as deep as the all-enveloping darkness. Just the crunch, crunch, crunch of his feet as he trudges forward. Nothing else.

His eyes are gradually starting to adjust and he can now make out dark shapes looming up around him. He remembers the white plastic chair that's still there, lying on its side. And here's the wheelbarrow – he can't see the hole in it from here but this is definitely the right path. If he just branches off left sometime soon, he ought to find . . .

And here it is. There are a number of sheds dotted around here but he made a note at the time. The one he wants is the fourth along. He stops in front of it and wonders whether to take off a glove and prod it to see if it's still sticky from earlier but stops himself in time. No prints. He can hardly claim he left them earlier – he never came within yards of the shed. *Play safe. Keep thinking.*

He steps to the side of the shed where the rows of empty flower pots were. He hasn't brought a torch with him because he doesn't want to run the risk of someone spotting the beam of light and calling the police but he decides it won't do any harm to use the light from his mobile just for a few seconds – there are so many pots lying around and he wants to make sure he's got the right stack.

He thought he was watching carefully earlier and taking everything in but his memory seems to be playing tricks on him. Finding the right stack isn't as straightforward as he's imagined. He wonders whether Kitchener moved them around after they left or maybe even took the key home with him because the first few stacks are all empty. He tries every pot in each stack, not just the third one down, just in case he got it wrong earlier. No luck. And he's starting to get very angry about the whole thing because it's not going to be the same if he has to break in. He doesn't want to leave behind clear evidence of a forced entry. That won't fit the overall plan. Then, at something like the sixth or seventh attempt, he takes out the top two pots and slips his fingers inside and there it is. He tips the key out into the palm of his hand and closes his fist round it, taking deep breaths to compose himself. He realises he's sweating a lot despite the cold. But he has everything he needs now.

It's on.

21

SUNDAY, 14TH DECEMBER

ANNA

'Hi', she said, fumbling for her alarm clock and squinting to make out the time.

'Hello you. You awake?'

'No. I've got this habit of talking a lot in my sleep.'

'Sorry. Thought you'd have been up ages ago. It's gone eight.'

She yawned, scratched her head with the mobile.

'I just love the way you say the two things like they're related somehow. Who in their right mind is going to be up before eight on a Sunday?'

'Thought you'd be getting ready, you know? Psyching yourself up? Big day and all that. Thought I'd phone, see if I could help in any way.'

'Help?'

'You know, in case you wanted the benefit of my experience.'

'You always give advice to girls before a first date?'

'I'm talking about the fight.'

'I know. Yanking your chain, Mr Green. Bit too early in the morning for you, is that it?'

He sighed. 'No. I'm wide awake. You're just too quick for me.'

'See,' she said, curling herself into a ball and snuggling up under the quilt, 'we agree on so many things. Is that it, then? I thought you might be ringing with more news.'

'About?'

'Your friend, DI Holloway. Heard anything yet?'

She'd nearly rung him the previous evening but had decided against it even as she called his name up in her contacts. Maybe a bit too transparent? She didn't want to give the wrong impression.

'Not yet, no. Probably looking at a couple of days,' he said. 'If it works –'

'Of course it'll work. I'm serious about this, you know. I told you before. I think we could be dead good at this sort of thing – you with all your experience and contacts and me with my imagination. We're in the wrong job.'

He laughed. 'You think so?'

'I know so. You know how many private investigators there are in Pagham?'

'None?'

'None. I Googled it. Now there's a sign if ever there was one. What's that if it's not a gap in the market?'

'You don't think maybe that's because there's no call for a PI in Pagham?'

'Why? What's wrong with Pagham? You telling me there's no crime there or something? They don't have affairs? They've all got ice in their veins? Your problem is you walk around with your eyes shut half the time. I'll bet there's all sorts of things going on, but you just haven't picked up on them. If you had me there to keep your wits about you, you could get yourself set up: Phil Green, the Pagham Private Investigator. Once you're established, you'll have to beat them off with a stick.'

'Don't want to sound picky,' he said, 'but doesn't that spell PPI? You sure you've thought this through?'

'Yeah, go on. Laugh if you like. Just remember, they laughed at that guy when he said the world was round.'

'Oh yeah. That guy.'

'I know his name, OK? It's just too early in the morning, like I told you. Point is, you'll see. Some day, when we're raking it in, you'll look back on this moment and thank me for changing your life. We'll see who's laughing then.'

'I'm sure it'll be you,' he said. 'Usually is. Anyway, got to go. Just wanted to wish you good luck, that was all.'

'Shan't need it, but thanks anyway. Were you serious by the way?'

'About what?'

'About ringing to offer me advice?'

'Of course. Why? You think you need it?'

'Like you said, you're the one with all the experience. If you've got any tips you'd like to pass on –'

'So what is it? You nervous or something?'

'A bit.'

'Well, don't be.'

She laughed. 'Great. Is that it?'

'No,' he said, and she could tell even over the phone how pleased he was that she wanted his help. 'You want some quality advice?'

'Please.'

'OK. Golden rule?'

'Yes?'

He paused.

'Make sure you bring your purse with you. Never assume the other guy's paying for your meal too.'

'Oh, for God's sake.'

OWEN

His immediate thought as he opens the front door is, *surely not!* Surprise first and foremost, with maybe a touch of dismay thrown in for good measure. He thought he was more or less shot of them. *What is it now?*

This is turning out to be anything but a typical weekend. Yesterday was all over the place. Routine shot to pieces. No gentle stroll around a car-boot sale, no film worth watching at the cinema, not even a weights session in the room upstairs, which would have been his normal response to a free afternoon. And no early night either – it was gone one o'clock before he pulled the sheets up around his ears and pressed his feet either side of the hot-water bottle to try to ward off some of the chill he'd brought back from his nocturnal adventures. Couldn't remember the last time he'd been to bed that late.

And now, having slept in for a couple of hours to compensate, he's barely switched on the laptop to start work on his accounts and there goes the doorbell – that silly little chime his mother chose because she liked to sing along to it. And when he opens the door, they're the last people he's expecting to see.

The older one, Holloway, is on the doorstep itself, finger poised to ring the bell again. His partner – the one who never smiles and is always watching, watching, trying to find fault – he's standing a bit further back, leaving the talking to his boss for now. They've got it wrong, he feels like telling them. He's watched enough films to know how this is supposed to work. It's the bad guy who goes in first. It's his job to unsettle the suspect with threats and intimidation, maybe even violence (although that may be just in America, he supposes), then the nice guy comes in with something to drink and maybe a small snack.

All friendly. Tries to persuade the poor unsuspecting victim there's at least one person in the building who's on his side.

Holloway goes ahead and presses the bell for a second time, even though the door's already open. Smiles and bobs his head back and forth in time with the music as the tune tinkles away inside the house.

'Takes me back a bit,' he says, and at least you can believe in his smile. It looks natural, not just for show. 'You're too young to remember but all the ice-cream vans used to play that. Haven't heard it since I was a kid.'

Owen stands there and waits. Doesn't ask why they're here. Won't give them the satisfaction. They can stand there all day as far as he's concerned. He's given up worrying about what the neighbours might be thinking. Those who've known him long enough and were friendly with his mother, like Mr Mitchell and his wife, they're on his side anyway. They all think it's a disgrace that he can't just be left in peace. Some of the others, especially those who've never shown any interest in talking to him even before all this business, probably see it as confirmation that they were right all along. He's not going to worry about them. They don't know him so who are they to judge?

'You busy?' Holloway asks eventually.

'Yes.' Firm. Nice and clear.

'Well, you think you can spare us an hour or so of your time?'

'For what?'

'We were wondering if you'd like to come with us – not far. Shouldn't take long.'

'Why? I'm not going anywhere without Mr M-Mitchell.' Might as well get that straight from the outset. If they think he's coming back into the station for another of their friendly chats, they can think again. He doesn't have to do anything or go anywhere unless he wants to – not without an appropriate adult to offer support. All the same, he'd like some sort of idea as to why they've turned up out of the blue like this. He was hoping he'd seen the last of them.

Holloway casts a look over his shoulder at his partner but he doesn't notice. He's still looking at the floor, almost as if he's sulking.

'You're more than welcome to invite Mr Mitchell along if you like but you won't need him. We're not going to the station.'

'So what do you want with me?'

'Well, let's just say we're aware we've been a bit of a nuisance, Owen. We know you've resented the attention you've been receiving and, well, we can understand how you'd feel that way. But we thought you'd like to know that's all in the past now as far as we're concerned. We *think* we're just about to put the whole Callum Green case to bed and we were just wondering if maybe you'd like to be in on the final act.'

Owen's heart skips a beat. He's not sure what's going on here but his defences are up. Instantly. What does *put the whole Callum Green case to bed* actually mean? Is he saying he thinks they know who killed Callum? If so, how? It can't be the bat, can it? Surely they haven't found it already. He can't quite get his head round it and feels he needs to ask a few questions to make sure he knows what's going on, but what's the best way to do that without arousing suspicion? What would someone who was totally innocent be asking right now?

'I don't understand,' he says eventually, opting to play as dumb as possible. 'Why would you want me to b-be there?'

Holloway nods to acknowledge that this is a perfectly valid question under the circumstances. Then he steps to one side and turns to face his partner, who looks up for the first time and, after a brief pause, takes half a step forward as if invisible hands are pushing him against his will.

'We think we may owe you one, Mr Hall.'

'Owe me one?'

'An apology.' His voice is a lot softer than it was when he was barking questions across the table at him not so long ago. It doesn't sound much like a genuine apology though; more like something he's being forced to go through with. But it's not like Owen cares. If he's having to say he's sorry, that can only be good news, can't it?

'Not for bringing you in for questioning or calling round as often as we did,' he's quick to continue. 'We had a job to do and we had to look at everyone, not just you. There was nothing personal in it. But there was a lot of pressure on us to get a result and maybe we weren't as careful as we might have been.'

He risks a sideways glance at his boss, clears his throat and continues.

'There's a chance, in coming after you like we did, we maybe didn't give enough thought to the problems it might be causing for you . . . you know, your business and everything. We could probably have handled it with a little more sensitivity and we wondered if maybe it would go some way to making it up to you if you could be there when we arrest the person who's actually to blame for all this.' He pauses. 'If you want to, that is. It's your choice.'

He holds out his hand and it takes Owen a few moments to realise he's supposed to shake it. He's thinking rapidly now. He's pretty sure he can see what's going on here. It's Misery Guts who's doing the apologising because he's been put on the spot. He's been given no choice. If he had to guess, he'd say the two of them have been arguing for some time over whether or not he's the one who killed Callum. The knowledge that it's the one who was right all along who has to do all the apologising is too delicious for words. Owen takes his hand and shakes it, making sure he grips it good and tight before letting go. Hopes he'll carry some muscle memory of the moment around with him for a day or two.

He turns to Holloway and asks who they're going to arrest and is told they can't say just yet. Operational reasons. Strictly speaking, they shouldn't be extending him this opportunity. They could get into trouble with their bosses if they ever found out. If he does come with them, he'll have to stay in the background and just watch as things unfold. If he's happy to do that, they're OK with him being there. They feel they owe him that.

They're in trouble with their superiors, he tells himself. They've gone too far. They're worried that when this is all done and dusted, there might be an official complaint about the problems they've caused for him on a professional level. Mr Mitchell has already been kicking up a fuss over loss of earnings while his truck was taken from him. There's going to be hell to pay if there's any suggestion that the police might be liable for compensation. They're the ones who have to be careful now. And it's nice to have the boot on the other foot for once.

So he thinks he might go along after all. He smiles to himself and reaches inside the front door for his jacket.

'So where are we going?' he asks.

Holloway taps his nose as if they are fellow conspirators.

'An allotment,' he says, in a theatrical whisper.

And this is good, Owen thinks to himself.

This is very, very good.

*

It's about a ten-minute drive from his house to Sandringham Way. He's sitting in the rear of the car, staring at the backs of their heads and wondering whether he ought to be asking questions right now. He doesn't want to come across as too desperate for details but at the same time doesn't it look a bit suspicious if he shows no curiosity at all and just sits there like a lemon? If he was innocent, surely there are things he'd be expected to ask?

Not so much the *who* – that's straightforward. The moment they told him where they were heading, it was obvious who they were going after. But it's the *how* that's exercising his thoughts. Like, how did they know where to look? Had they already decided Kitchener was a suspect? Had they been following him? If so, it occurs to him, they'll know all about yesterday when Abi took the keys back. Should he mention that now? As soon as they referred to the allotments he'd be bound to say something, wouldn't he? *The allotments? I was there with Abi just yesterday.* Would look a bit odd if he didn't.

In the end, the decision is taken away from him. Misery guts, who's clearly trying to do a bit of damage limitation, has started talking again, asking how Mr Mitchell is, as if he's remotely interested. It's a joke really. He's asking questions about Owen's work now. Wants to know how he first got into repairing mowers and the whole landscape-gardening thing in the first place, as if he's always been dying to ask. *All friends together here.* They must think he's stupid.

When they turn into Sandringham Way, the same parking space he took just a matter of hours earlier is still available but they drive past it and park further along, tucked just inside a side road. Holloway turns off the engine and explains they need to stay out of sight for a moment. They just need to wait a few minutes. He asks what they're waiting for and Holloway puts one finger to his lips. Shhhh. Won't be long now.

It's all very mysterious.

Then, about five minutes later, there's a crackling voice over the radio and both policemen unbuckle their belts and get out of the car. He starts to do the same but Holloway pokes his head back in and asks him if he'd mind staying where he is.

'We need to go on ahead,' he explains. 'You're not here, remember?'

He does, but he's been banking on the fact that he'll be able to persuade them to let him tag along. There doesn't seem much point in coming here if he's just going to sit in the car. There's nothing for him to see or do here. He says so and the two policemen talk about it before Holloway points to the jacket he's wearing. Tells him to put the hood up, give them two minutes, then walk over to the fence. He'll be able to see everything from there. But he mustn't get too close. It's really important that no one sees him. And above all else, he mustn't come over to join them or get involved in any way or it will put the whole operation at risk. Does he understand?

Well, no – he doesn't. And says so. They're patient with him, remind him he's only here as a favour. He needs to stay out of it unless they specifically ask him to get involved. Can they trust him to do that? If not, says Holloway, he should say so now and one of them will take him home.

So he backs down. He doesn't want to miss this. They've obviously been waiting for someone to arrive. Presumably this someone is Adam Kitchener, the same person who was sitting there on his stool only twenty-four hours earlier, waving his brush about and sprinkling insults around like confetti. If he's going to get his comeuppance now, Owen wants to be there to see it. He wants to see that sneer wiped off his face, revel in the moment when Kitchener realises he's about to be arrested for something he didn't even do. And yes, it would be nice to be right there in his eyeline when it dawns on him what's going on but he'll settle for watching from a distance if that's all that's on offer.

He'll take his victories however they might come.

He tells them he understands. They can trust him. He'll watch from the fence and make sure no one can see him.

Holloway reminds him: 'Two minutes, OK?'

He nods and watches as the two of them walk off round the corner, heading back towards the gate.

He starts counting off the seconds. Says the multiples of three out loud as he comes to each in turn. Shouts the multiples of three and five combined. Whispers the primes and crosses his fingers. He almost leaps out of his skin as the radio crackles suddenly and another garbled message fills the car. He decides he'd make a useless policeman. Taxi driver too. There's no way he'd ever understand these messages. Gets about one word in ten. He wonders if it's the same for everyone when they first start out. Maybe it gets easier if you stick at it long enough. He'll ask when they get back if he remembers.

The message has interrupted his counting but he thinks it must be getting on for two minutes now. Tells himself it doesn't matter if he's a few seconds out either way. He doesn't think they meant two minutes exactly. He gets out of the car and puts his hood up. There's a fairly stiff breeze sweeping across the allotments and, because he's walking into it, the hood is blown back down onto his shoulders again before he's walked five paces. He has to hold it in place with one hand flat on top of his head.

He walks over to the fence and looks back along the road to see where Holloway and his partner went. Because he's looking at the gate, he doesn't see them straightaway but they're actually bending over the open door of another police car which has pulled into the parking space they ignored just now. Two men get out of the car, followed by a third figure emerging from the back.

It's Kitchener.

Owen can't see his features very clearly from here, especially as the wind is making him blink rapidly to keep the tears at bay, but the atmosphere seems pretty relaxed. He hears a peal of laughter and one of the policemen pats Kitchener on the shoulder. Then they lock the car and head over to the gate. Kitchener rummages in his pocket and after a few seconds they all pass through with him leading the way.

They haven't actually found the bat yet, he thinks to himself. If they had, there wouldn't be any point in all this and Kitchener certainly wouldn't appear so relaxed. They're fishing. He assumes they've only just found out about the shed somehow and are hoping they'll find something in there. And they will. Kitchener's leading them to it without a care in the world. Owen remembers a sleepy, sunny afternoon, when he and Willie were both sitting in the garden, watching a pigeon pecking away at grass seeds their dad had sown earlier that morning. It was working its way in a straight line across from one side of the lawn to the other, totally unaware that the neighbour's cat was crouching in the bushes, no more than ten feet away. Nine. Eight. Seven. Lost in its own little world although the two boys could see it all unfolding in glorious slow motion right in front of them.

This was just like that. The same sense of inevitability. The same pounding in his temples. Willie had clapped his hands just as the cat was ready to pounce and the pigeon had flown off, leaving the cat clawing at thin air. No one's going to be doing the same for Kitchener.

Owen walks briskly alongside the fence until he's a little closer to the action, hidden from view by a tall hedge from behind which he can peep occasionally and keep track of what's happening. From where he's now standing he can see quite clearly the shed which Kitchener was staining just yesterday morning. He's expecting them to come into view at any minute so he steps out for a moment to identify exactly where they are. And for some reason he can't actually see them. There's the white plastic chair and the wheelbarrow and the greenhouse with the broken panes of glass. He tracks back from there, follows the path with his eyes all the way back to the gate but there's no one walking along it as far as he can tell. Quickly, he scoots back to the other side of the hedge in case the different angle offers a better view but it doesn't seem to make any difference. Somehow they've managed to vanish into thin air and there's a momentary feeling of panic that is only partly offset when he finally picks out a group of people over the far side of the allotment, gathered round another shed which seems to have been painted the same colour. Someone, presumably Kitchener although it's hard to be sure from this distance, has stepped forward and is fiddling with the door. It looks like he's unlocking it while the others stand back and watch.

Wrong door.

Wrong shed.

They're not even in the right part of the allotment.

Stupid!

His first instinct is to call out and tell them. He has no idea how Kitchener has managed to get a key to a different shed altogether but it's pretty clear what he's up to. He's trying to mislead them, keep them away from the one where the bat is tucked away, waiting to be found. And there's something about that which strikes him as odd but it's gone almost before it's occurred to him because there are more important things to worry about here. Someone needs to let them know what he's up to.

But he can't yell out to them. They couldn't have been any clearer – he's not meant to be here. He can stand there and watch but he's not allowed to interfere in any way. Apart from anything else, this could all be part of the trap they've set for Kitchener. Maybe they know which shed is the right one and the fact that he has led them to the wrong one is playing right into their hands. If he blunders in, he might wreck everything. Maybe it's best if he does as they've asked for now and stays out of it. As far as he can tell, waiting a few minutes isn't going to make a lot of difference.

So he stays where he is and watches as Kitchener steps back and two of the figures go inside the shed. There's a wait of about three to four minutes, during which Kitchener saunters casually up and down, smoking a cigarette as if he hasn't a care in the world. Then they come back out again. Empty-handed. *Well there's a surprise.* There's a brief discussion, then all of a sudden everyone's shaking hands and they start to make their way back towards the gate. Owen decides it's time he returned to the car because it won't be long before they're on the street again and he can't afford to be seen.

When he gets back to the car he clambers into the rear seat and waits for them, tapping his foot impatiently. It's just as well he did decide to come in the end. If he hadn't, he'd have missed all this and Kitchener would have got away with it. As it is they're going to look pretty stupid when he tells them where they should really be looking. He thinks he might just enjoy the next few minutes.

Two minutes later he sees them come round the corner, walking slowly, deep in discussion. Neither of them looks very pleased with the way things have turned out. They're not arguing as such but Holloway certainly isn't smiling now and it looks as if he might be taking his frustration out on his partner, who looks more miserable than ever. Owen says nothing as they get into the car. Instead he watches and waits as they decide how best to break the news to him.

It's Holloway who eventually speaks first.

'We have . . . a bit of a situation,' he says.

'What sort of a situation?'

They both look at each other, then Holloway sighs.

'I'm afraid we've brought you out here for nothing,' he says. 'We didn't find what we were expecting. It was worth a go but –'

'Maybe you ought to try looking in his shed,' says Owen.

'I'm sorry?'

'I said, you should look in his shed.'

Misery Guts shakes his head and tuts as if to suggest that he doesn't like being told how to do his job. His apology seems to have had a very short shelf-life.

'I thought you were watching. That's what we've been doing for the past ten minutes.'

Owen wishes he would turn round to face him so that he can look him in the eye. *But you can't have everything*, he thinks to himself.

'That's not his shed,' he says.

There's a sigh from Holloway and a snort from his partner.

'With all due respect –'

'It's not his shed,' he insists. 'Either that or he's got more than one. His is on a different path. You weren't even in the right part of the allotment.'

And this gets their attention all right. They're cautious at first, handling this new piece of information like an unopened Christmas present that they're sure is going to disappoint. They still think he doesn't know what he's talking about. Want to know how he can be so sure. So he tells them about how he and Abi came here yesterday morning to return Kitchener's house keys. He knows exactly which shed it was. He can take them to it and they'll be able to see for themselves that it's been freshly painted. Still probably a bit sticky to the touch even now.

And that changes things. Now they think they might be onto something, everything's happening at a hundred miles an hour. Holloway swears and grabs his mobile. He's talking to someone in the other car, asking where they are now and when he gets his reply he tells them to drive around for a few minutes and then bring Kitchener back.

'If he wants to know why, tell him there's something else we need to check with him. In fact, tell him what you like – just bring him back and make sure you keep him in the car until you hear from me. Is that clear?'

While Holloway's barking out the orders, his partner gets out of the car and signals to Owen to do the same. They wait till he's ended the call, then the three of them head off towards the gate again. It's locked but Owen swings himself up and over in one easy movement as he did just last night. Holloway mutters to himself and needs a helping hand from his partner but some-how they scramble over and Owen takes the lead, striding out ahead along the path in the opposite direction from the one he'd watched them take a few minutes earlier. He looks back from time to time and waves them on. Before long the left-hand turn brings them to a row of sheds with the freshly painted green one standing out from the others.

Owen comes to a halt in front of it.

'This is his,' he says.

'You sure?'

'Yes.' He presses his finger against the door and there's no residue which comes away, but it's still vaguely sticky and besides – any fool can see it's just been painted. He invites them both to check for themselves, then stands back as Hol-loway tries the door. It's locked as well.

'You need to be sure about this,' he says. 'If you're wrong –'

'I'm not wrong. This is the shed he was painting yesterday.'

Holloway thinks for a moment, then turns to his partner.

'Get him over here,' he says. 'We need the key.'

'No need,' says Owen. He's enjoying himself now, taking the lead and practically doing all their work for them. He steps across to the empty flowerpots and manages to pick out the right pile first time. Removes the top two, tips up the third and the key drops to the ground. He stoops to pick it up and hands it to Holloway who looks amazed.

'How did you know it was there?' he asks.

'He unlocked it yesterday while we were here,' he says and they both nod to each other, pulling on gloves as they step inside. Holloway asks him to wait outside while they search and that's fine by him. He doesn't need to be in there to know what will happen next. He's happy to wait patiently while they rummage around and it's not long anyway before they finally emerge. They're both wearing gloves and Misery Guts looks almost happy for once. He's the one holding the baseball bat as carefully as possible in case there are any prints or traces that need to be protected. Which there won't be. Not after all the treatments he's given it.

'What's that?' he says, because he thinks it's a perfectly natural thing to be asking under the circumstances. They don't reply immediately because they're concentrating on what they're doing. Holloway removes a long, thin protective sleeve from his coat pocket and they slip the bat inside it. It's exactly the right size which is not so surprising – they knew going in what they were hoping to find.

'We're rather hoping it might be the murder weapon,' says Holloway, looking closely at the bat through its protective sheath. Misery Guts stoops to take a better look.

'Not sure we're going to get anything off this,' he says. 'Looks like someone's done a real number on it. Practically rebuilt the thing by the looks of it. And there's enough oil on it for a stir-fry.'

'It's where we've found it that matters,' says Holloway. 'Anything else is just a bonus.'

He hands the bat to his partner again and takes his mobile out of his pocket. Gives directions to whoever's on the other end of the line and says they can bring Kitchener in now. They're ready for him. Owen wants to play as active a role as possible in proceedings so he asks if they want him to go back to the gate to show them the way but Holloway says no – best if he stays here. Then he stands with his arms folded, thumb and forefinger stroking his chin, deep in thought. His partner is still looking closely at the bat so there's no conversation for a minute or so while they wait for the others to join them.

'So what happens now?' Owen asks, wishing there was something he could be doing instead of just standing there. He enjoyed taking the lead just now and he's not ready to step away from the spotlight just yet if he can help it. There must be something he can do to smooth the way for them. He's not entirely sure they'll get there without a few nudges from him.

Holloway looks for a moment as if he hasn't heard the question. Then he snaps out of his trance and uses one of the upturned flower pots to scrape the mud from the sole of his shoes.

'What happens next?' he says. 'Well, we've got the bat. We'll send it off to the lab in case there's anything there they can salvage. Doesn't look good but you never know. And in the meantime we do our best to solve a rather interesting little puzzle.'

'Which one?'

'Well, we need to work out exactly how the bat managed to end up in this particular shed of all places. Because that . . . that's a good one.'

A good one? Owen doesn't understand this. Surely it's obvious how it got there. He's always thought Holloway was an experienced officer, more perceptive than the others he's had to deal with. But if he can't see the truth when it's staring him in the face, maybe he's misjudged him. It's Kitchener's shed. Who else does he think put the bat there? He's about to take it up with him but Misery Guts says, 'Hey up', and sure enough here come two of Holloway's colleagues, walking either side of Kitchener. He looks slightly less cocky than a few minutes ago. Not worried maybe, but certainly more serious about things.

He's wearing a thin jacket over a collarless shirt, and if he's not feeling the cold at all that would be a big surprise. The wind is bitter and there's less meat on him than a whippet. He comes over to join Holloway while his two escorts position themselves either side of the group, blocking the path.

Kitchener barely even looks at Owen, which is a bit of a disappointment. He's been hoping for some sort of reaction, like, 'What's he doing here?' He'd like to see surprise. Maybe even a trace of alarm. And that's when he makes the connection, realises what it was that was nudging away at him earlier, asking for a few seconds of his time. He'd pushed it to the back of his mind because there were so many other things competing for space and his senses were buzzing. But it comes back now and he knows it's the other shed that's bothering him: not the fact that Kitchener has got access to it cos there could be any number of explanations for that, but it does strike Owen as a bit odd that Kitchener seemed to be making a point of leading the police away from the one he was painting yesterday. Why would he do that? He didn't know the bat was in there. If he's not looking even vaguely alarmed at the moment, it's hardly surprising because as far as he's aware there's nothing for him to be alarmed about. It shouldn't have mattered which shed he took them to. Owen has to remind himself that Kitchener isn't actually guilty of anything other than being a thoroughly nasty piece of work who deserves whatever comes his way. That being the case, his behaviour in misleading the police like that seems more than a bit odd.

As it is, he looks more irritated than anxious. He wants to know what's going on, why has he been dragged out here for a second time? Maybe if someone would explain what it is they're so anxious to find . . .

'That won't be necessary, Mr Kitchener,' says Holloway. 'We've found what we were looking for.'

He nods in his partner's direction and Misery Guts holds up the sleeve containing the baseball bat. Kitchener peers at it without taking a step towards it.

'Looks like a bat,' he says.

'It is,' says Holloway, hands thrust deep in the pockets of his overcoat. The wind must be pushing the air temperature down below zero. Owen tends not to feel the cold as a rule but even he's got his hood up and finds himself wishing they could have this conversation somewhere other than out in the open. He edges closer to the shed in the hope it might offer a bit of protection.

'Mr Kitchener,' Holloway continues. 'Just now you took us to a different part of the allotments. Why was that?'

'You said you wanted to look in my shed.'

'And the one you showed us . . . let's be quite clear. You're saying that's your shed?'

'Yes.'

'But Mr Hall here,' he says, turning to invite him into the exchange, 'he's adamant that he and Mrs Green came here yesterday to return your house keys.'

Kitchener gives him just the briefest of glances then turns back to face Holloway. He nods.

'That's right. They did.'

'And he says you were staining *this* shed here.'

'I was.'

'But you didn't mention this shed to us just now, did you?'

He shrugs his shoulders.

'Why would I? It's not mine.'

Holloway raises one eyebrow.

'It's not?'

'No. It belongs to a friend of my father.'

'So why were you painting it?'

'A favour. He's a busy guy. Doesn't have a lot of free time so he doesn't get down here all that often. He knew I'd done a good job on ours so he asked if I'd do the same for his if he slipped me a few notes. I was happy to help him out.'

'But even though it's not your shed, you do have access to it?'

'A key, you mean? Sure. He showed me where he keeps a spare one. Looks like you've already found it.'

'And you didn't think to mention this to us earlier?'

'No. Again, why would I? You said you wanted to look at *my* shed. You didn't say anything about any others.'

Holloway nods and points to the bat which Misery Guts is holding.

'And this baseball bat. Have you ever seen it before?'

'Not as far as I'm aware.'

'Can you be more precise than that?'

Kitchener laughs.

'It's a baseball bat. They all look pretty much the same, don't they? Have I seen a baseball bat before? Yes. Have I seen that particular one? Haven't a clue. Not as far as I'm aware, like I said.'

'We found it in this shed.'

'OK.'

'Do you remember seeing a bat in there yesterday?'

'No. But then again, I wasn't looking for one, was I? I was busy painting.'

'And you've no idea how it got there?'

'Well, normally I'd assume it was put there by whoever owns the shed but in this case I'd say that's probably unlikely.'

Holloway smiles, nods again. He's taking his time over this and Owen's starting to get a little impatient. Kitchener's playing with them all and yet Holloway seems happy to plod along at his own infuriatingly slow pace instead of cutting to the heart of the matter. Surely it's not relevant whose shed it is. What's important is that Kitchener knew where the key was. Thought it would be a decent place to hide the bat. Why doesn't Holloway get on with it?

And as if in answer to a prayer, he does precisely that.

'Mr Kitchener,' he says, taking a small notebook from his pocket and flicking through the pages as if trying to find something he'd jotted there earlier, 'what time did you finish here yesterday?'

Kitchener frowns.

'What, finish painting or actually leave?'

'The latter.'

'Well,' says Kitchener, looking up as if the answer might be written in the clouds overhead, 'that would have been around three. It can't have been much later than that cos first thing I did when I got in the car was turn on the radio and get the latest football scores and they'd only been playing for a few minutes. So yeah, I'd say about three.'

'And can you account for your movements after that?'

'Yes. I went straight home, had a bath, got changed. Then sometime around five I picked up my girlfriend and drove her to my parents' house in Bridport. It was my dad's birthday and we wanted to take him out for a meal.'

'And you stayed the night there?'

'No,' says Kitchener. 'My girlfriend and I both wanted to be back here first thing so we drove home late last night. I don't know what time we got back here exactly but it must have been around one fifteen or one thirty in the morning.'

'And where did you sleep last night?'

Kitchener gives a half-smile that Owen would very much like to ram down his throat.

'At her place.'

'And you were together the whole time?'

'Yes.'

'She'll vouch for that?'

'Yes. We were together until you rang my mobile and came to collect me.'

Holloway jots something on his notepad, then looks up and smiles.

'Thank you,' he says. 'I think that will be all for now. If you'd like to go with these two officers, they'll drop you off at your girlfriend's house or back home, whichever is more convenient.'

'Her place would make more sense,' says Kitchener, stepping forward to shake hands with Holloway and Misery Guts. 'My car's still blocking her drive.' He shoots a quick glance at Owen but doesn't offer his hand to him. Instead he winks. It may have been a sharp gust of wind that made him blink suddenly but that's not how it looks to Owen, especially as he's done it with his back to Holloway and his partner so that no one else will see it. Then he turns and starts to walk off down the path with the two officers who escorted him here earlier.

Without a care in the world.

And Owen is raging inside. He knows he's not supposed to say anything but Kitchener is lying. He knows he is. And now it's starting to look as if they're going to let him just walk off without challenging him on any of the detail. He waits for a few seconds, convinced even now that Holloway must have something up his sleeve and when it becomes clear this is not the case he decides he can't stay silent any longer.

'Wait a minute,' he blurts out.

Shut it, warns Willie.

'You can't just let him go like that. Everything he's just said, it's all lies.'

Don't say another word.

'Owen –' says Holloway.

'Mr Hall,' Owen snaps, rounding on him. 'You c-called him Mr K-Kitchener so you can c-call me Mr Hall.'

'Mr Hall –'

'Every time you've questioned m-me you've assumed I'm l-lying and you've pushed and pushed again, trying to find a way to t-trip me up, even though I was telling you the truth.'

'Mr Hall, I can assure you –'

'Then, when it's his turn you just s-smile and say, "Thank you, Mr K-Kitchener," and you let him walk away without even challenging it. Why is he t-treated differently from me?'

'Owen ... Mr Hall,' says Holloway, holding up a hand to tell the others to wait a moment. Kitchener has stopped anyway and is watching the exchange with one of those irritating smirks spread all across his face. 'If you have reason to believe Mr Kitchener is not being honest with us –'

'Of course he's not being honest. He hasn't g-got a girlfriend. He used to have one but she's in Africa for a year and he m-made her come all the way back here just so he could t-tell her he didn't want to see her anymore.'

Kitchener laughs.

'I didn't know you were such an authority on my private life,' he says. 'Haven't you got anything better to do with your time?'

'Mr Kitchener?' says Holloway, inviting him to be more specific in his response.

'He's talking about my *ex*-girlfriend,' Kitchener says, with a dismissive wave of the hand. 'Freja and I finished . . . what, three months ago? Getting on for the end of September, must have been. I've been seeing someone else since then.'

'That's a lie too,' says Owen. 'He hasn't g-got a girlfriend now. If he had, he'd have b-bought the jumper for *her*.'

Shut it, for fuck's sake.

'Jumper?'

'He bought one in Leeds last week. S-so he said anyway. T-tried to give it to Abi just yesterday but she wouldn't take it.'

'So what's your point?' says Kitchener.

'If you had a girlfriend, why would you be trying to g-give the jumper to Abi?'

Kitchener looks at the ground for a moment, shaking his head. When he looks back up, there's a flash in his eyes, something approaching triumph in his expression.

'Abi *is* my girlfriend.'

A sharp gust of wind finally wins its ongoing battle with an empty compost bag which had been weighed down by a slate. It rips the bag out from underneath and sends it skittering along the path. One of the officers instinctively tries to trap it under his foot as it flies past but he's a fraction too slow. Everyone's attention seems to be drawn to it momentarily as it careers off into the distance.

Owen is the exception. He hasn't taken his eyes off Kitchener for one second.

'That's a L-LIE!' he yells, and it's all he can do to stay where he is and maintain the distance between them. One of the officers is obviously on the ball because he moves a little closer to Kitchener to make sure he's in a position to intervene should the need arise.

Holloway puts a restraining hand on Owen's arm and he shrugs it off angrily. He's steaming now. Abi? He shouldn't even be allowed to say the name after what he's put her through recently. And now he thinks it's OK to make up lies about her? To use her to get himself off the hook?

'It's the truth,' says Kitchener and if he's at all rattled by Owen's outburst he gives no sign of it.

'If it's the truth, why d-did she ask me to come here with her to give back your k-keys, eh? Answer me that. I'll tell you why. Abi's scared of you. She's t-told me everything, about how you keep p-pestering her and won't l-leave her alone. She doesn't feel she can trust you anymore. She'd n-never choose someone like you.'

'Well, don't take my word for it,' says Kitchener with a shrug. 'Call her. See what she has to say. Better still, why don't you ask these officers for the address where they picked me up first thing this morning. See if it rings a few bells.'

Holloway nods at one of the two officers who already has his notebook in his hand as if expecting this.

'An address in Bosham, sir. Place called Hedge End in Walton Lane.'

'We've been going out for nearly two months now.'

'You're l-lying,' yells Owen, turning to Holloway for support. 'He's lying,' he repeats, scanning his face for some hint that he at least isn't fooled by this ridiculous web of lies that Kitchener has been spinning. Instead, he sees something else and for one awful moment it occurs to him that it looks a lot like pity. He's buying it.

'Owen –'

'IT'S MR HALL,' he screams, frustration oozing out of every pore. 'How many times do I have to t-tell you?' He's uncomfortably aware that another one of his episodes is imminent if he can't do something about his temper. The last thing he needs now is to start rocking and mumbling to himself. He has to show them what Kitchener is up to. There's no way he and Abi have been seeing each other for two months. For that to be true, she'd have to have been lying as well. What about their dinner together at Prezzo's earlier in the week? The necklace she wore, just to please him? And the gardening project she wants him to go ahead with – does anyone seriously believe that's all a lie? What about yesterday when she asked him to come along and protect her? It doesn't make sense. Why would she do such a thing? Why?

Why?

Penny beginning to drop? You stupid, stupid . . .

Shut up!

Sure! Not like you need my advice, is it?

SHUT UP! I need to think!

Yeah, right. You do the thinking. That's what you're good at.

SHUT UP!!

Owen squeezes his eyes shut, works hard to stave off the episode. Tries to think of nice things but all nice things start and end with Abi and that doesn't feel much like solid ground at the moment. He doesn't feel he can afford to let his thoughts go there just yet. Sometime later maybe, when this has all been cleared up and he can look back on it and even laugh at himself. He takes several deep breaths and finally manages some semblance of self-control.

When he looks up again, Kitchener is walking off down the path, escorted by just the one officer this time as he makes his way back to the gate. The other one has stayed behind with Holloway and his partner. All three of them are watching him closely.

Holloway clears his throat.

'Are you OK?' he asks, and there's genuine concern on his face, or that's how it looks at any rate. Owen isn't sure he trusts his own judgement on anything at the moment.

'You know he's lying, right?' he says wearily. 'You're tricking him, yes?'

'I know you don't want to believe it,' says Holloway, 'but he's telling the truth. About Abi, at any rate. And that leaves us with a bit of a problem, I'm afraid.'

Owen is building himself up to protest again, long and hard. But he decides that can wait. For now the second half of that sentence needs to be looked at carefully.

'What problem?'

'Well, not to put too fine a point on it, *someone* put the bat in this shed. And we know it wasn't either Adam Kitchener or Abi Green.'

'No, you d-don't,' he protests. 'How can you s-say that? He could have p-put it in there any time. It could have been in there already when Abi and I were here yesterday.'

'No,' says Holloway, and there's a certainty about the way he says it that Owen finds a little disconcerting. 'No, I'm afraid it couldn't. You see, we searched this shed yesterday afternoon almost immediately after he left.'

'You . . . why? How could you have? You didn't even know about this shed till I t-told you just now.'

Holloway says nothing.

And speaks volumes.

'He was quite right about the time, incidentally,' Holloway continues. 'It was almost exactly three o'clock when he left and we searched it thoroughly no more than ten minutes later. There was no bat here then.'

'So?' says Owen who now feels there's a corner he badly needs to work his way out of. 'M-maybe he c-came back later. Before he went to wherever he says he went last night. Or even after they g-got back.'

Again Holloway shakes his head.

'No, that's not possible. You see, we had Mr Kitchener under police observation from the moment he left here yesterday after-noon until we picked him up this morning. And the version he gave just now is accurate in all respects. He left here, went back to his place . . . he says it was to have a bath and get changed and there's nothing in the timing to suggest that's not the case. Then he drove to Bosham, picked up Abi Green and then drove to Bridport with one of our cars tailing him all the way. He's been under surveillance the whole time – there's no way he was able to come back here and hide the bat in the shed.'

'No. You're wrong!'

Owen's head is starting to pound. This is wrong. It's all wrong. He needs Abi there, needs to talk with her and get this whole thing straightened out. There's no way she went anywhere with Kitchener last night. She'd die rather than let him sleep over as they're all trying to make him believe. And somehow he must have managed to get here and drop the bat off without their real-ising it. Someone's made a bad mistake. They've lost Kitchener for a few minutes and rather than admit what's happened they've tried to cover it up. There's an explanation somewhere in all this mess if he can just process everything and make sense of it, only there are voices at war inside his head and Willie's screaming advice at him, telling him to shut his mouth and say nothing and he just can't concentrate with all this going on. Why don't they all just shut up and leave him alone?

'So you see my problem,' says Holloway, droning on in that slow, deliberate manner of his. 'If the bat wasn't there and neither Adam Kitchener nor Abi Green had any opportunity to put it there after we last searched it, the only other person who knew about this shed, who knew there was a key and where it was kept . . . is you.'

'No,' he says again.

Shakes his head vehemently.

'As you've just demonstrated.'

'No, no, no. You're f-forgetting something.'

'Forgetting what?'

'Even if he didn't put the bat there himself, he could easily have got someone else to do it for him.'

'He *could*,' agrees Holloway. 'But why would he do that? He either thinks it's a safe hiding place or he doesn't. If he does, as you said just now, he could have put the bat in there any time he wanted. If he doesn't, surely it's the last place he'd put it? And why put himself further at risk by involving someone else?'

'Maybe he knew he was b-being watched. Maybe you weren't as c-clever as you thought. Maybe he sneaked away in the night and the p-people watching him weren't doing a very good job of it. If he knows you've already searched it, it would be the perfect place to hide it. Have you thought about that?'

Holloway nods and for a moment Owen thinks maybe he's scoring a few points here. If he keeps throwing out objections, there's a chance he might blow them off course.

'Just one problem though,' he says, and Owen hates it when he does that. Doesn't matter how many good arguments he comes up with, there's always that one little *but* he has up his sleeve.

'You see,' he continues, 'even if we come up with a convincing explanation as to *how* he managed to sneak the bat in there, we can't get away from the fact that it would be a really stupid thing for him to do. This shed is just about the last place Adam Kitchener would want to hide a murder weapon.'

He senses where this is heading. Doesn't know how to stop it.

'He said ... he said it belongs to a f-friend of his f-father,' he says, increasingly aware of a sinking feeling in the pit of his stomach.

'A bit of an exaggeration, perhaps.'

'So whose is it?

There's a pause and it feels for a moment as if he's being invited to do all the sums himself. And he's almost got there, almost connected all the dots when a voice away to his left finishes the job for him.

'It's mine,' says Misery Guts.

And all he knows right now, as his world threatens to implode, is that there are layers and layers of deceit here that he's going to have to unpick: a sticky web of lies and betrayals he's going to have to smash his way through in order to make sense of what's happening. And somewhere beyond all these layers there's a reality he's going to have to face up to at some stage but now's not the time. Whatever Abi's done to him and whatever her reasons for it, he can't bear the thought of looking too closely at it right now. It's too much.

'So you see,' says Holloway, 'I don't think anyone is likely to believe Adam Kitchener would choose as his hiding place a shed belonging to a member of the team responsible for trying to track the bat down. If that's where it ended up, it could only have been put there by someone who didn't know. Who thought the shed belonged to Kitchener himself. And that person –'

And so he stands there, watching Holloway as he drones on, but taking nothing in. He could be reciting a prayer or the Highway Code for all he knows. All he can hear is the wind, ripping through the allotments, a car horn in the distance, plastic sheeting flapping and crackling as it strains against the restraints keeping it in place. He can't even hear Willie, which is something of a relief. The last thing he needs right now is another lecture, a thousand variations on the theme *I told you so*. But he can see him. He's there right next to Holloway, head tilted to one side, and he's clapping him ... slowly ... sarcastically ... mouthing one word over and over. It's hard to hear above the wind and the maelstrom that's threatening to drag him under right now.

But he thinks he knows what it is.

It sounds like *genius*.

PHIL

'So how long can they keep him?' Anna asked, pushing her dessert plate away and dabbing at the corner of her mouth with a serviette.

He took a sip from his Coke.

'Depends on when the detention clock started,' he said. 'Usually you get twenty-four hours, thirty-six if you get an extension. Any longer than that, you need to apply to a magistrates' court but they'll be hoping to wrap it up long before then.'

'Have they got enough to charge him?'

'Hope so,' he said, leaning to one side to allow the waitress to remove his own dish and asking for the bill while he had her there. She asked if either of them would like a coffee and Anna shook her head so he decided he'd pass as well.

'Most of what they've got is circumstantial,' he continued. 'Depends on how the CPS sees it. I'll know more when I've had a chance to speak to Andy Holloway. Might be a day or two though. He's got a lot on his plate.'

'But they've got the bat.'

'Yep . . . they've got the bat.'

When the waitress brought the bill over, there was a brief wrestling match over who was going to pick up the tab, a struggle he was never going to lose. He liked the fact that she'd offered but the evening had been his idea. He'd asked her out, not the other way round. She thanked him and excused herself for a moment, leaving him to fret for a few minutes over whether he might inadvertently have caused offence. He found it so hard nowadays to know where he stood with things like this. The dividing line between what he'd been brought up to regard as decent behaviour and what was now deemed to be boorish chauvinism seemed to be constantly on the move, perpetually re-forming itself in such a way that he was always on the wrong side of it. He just hoped Anna hadn't taken umbrage in any way.

He entered his code into the machine that the waitress held in front of him and wrapped the receipt around his credit card before replacing it in his wallet. When Anna returned to the table, he half-expected her to start putting her coat on and was relieved when she took her seat and poured herself another glass of water. If nothing else it meant the next step, which had been hanging over him all evening, could be delayed for a while longer.

She asked how he was adjusting to the idea of Abi and Adam. He told her he was coming round to it and realised for the first time that he meant it.

'I won't pretend it was easy,' he said. 'But it's not like Abi owes me anything. She doesn't need my approval. And anyway, he seems like a good lad.'

'And he didn't need to step up to the plate the way he did,' she added.

'I don't think he could help himself,' he chuckled. 'I think he fancies himself as a bit of an actor. Says he did a bit at the Festival Youth Theatre when he was younger. But you're right – he could have walked away from it.'

He noticed she was dabbing at the bruise under her left eye with a tentative finger.

'Sore?' he asked.

'A bit. Does it look bad?'

He leaned forward so that he could get a better look.

'Not really. Not as bad as hers will tomorrow morning. Always worse for the loser.'

'Wouldn't know,' she said. 'Did you really cry when my arm was raised?'

He snorted.

'I said I felt a bit emotional. Never said anything about crying.'

'You did though, didn't you?' she said, aiming a slap at his hand and missing. 'Admit it! It's nothing to be ashamed of. I like the idea of you welling up. It's good that you've got a sensitive side.'

He smiled and played with the salt cellar for a few seconds.

'They've . . . ah . . . they've invited me round for lunch on Christmas Day,' he said, the words springing out of nowhere. He knew the sudden change of subject would sound bizarre but couldn't think of any other way of getting it out there.

She raised an eyebrow and tilted her head to one side.

'What? Who have?'

'Abi. And Adam. They're having it at her place.'

Her place. He could say it at last.

'That's nice.'

'Yes. So, I was wondering –'

'Yes?'

'Well, do you know what you're doing yet?'

She ran her tongue over her top lip while she weighed up what he was actually asking here.

'For Christmas Day? I'm usually at my parents'. Why?'

'I didn't know whether –'

'I'd love to.'

'Only I know you said your family likes to make a big thing of it usually and I didn't want to –'

'I'd . . . love . . . to.'

'OK then,' he said. 'I think it'll be fun.'

'Proof of the pudding,' she said.

'Right.'

'It's in the way we eat it.'

'You could say that.'

She frowned.

'Did I get that right?'

'Close enough,' he said.

OWEN

He's cross. Very cross. He's not about to show it but he's getting more and more irritated by the minute. This all feels very petty to him. Vindictive. Like they can't get him to say what they want to hear, so they're going out of their way to inconvenience him as much as possible. They want to bore it out of him.

It must be getting on for eight o'clock. They've been at it, on and off, since this morning. He gets breaks and meals and water to drink and every so often he wonders whether maybe this is it – they've decided they've had enough and are ready to let him go. But then, every time, they bring him back into this room with no windows that looks like a box and feels like one too. No idea what the weather's like now. It could be pouring with rain or sunny or even snowing and he wouldn't know the first thing about it. Not so long ago he was shivering and complaining about the cold wind that was sweeping across the allotments; now he'd give anything to be out there. Couldn't be worse than this.

It wouldn't be so bad if they asked him different questions once in a while, something to break up the monotony. But they don't, they just keep going over the same old ground, time and time again, and he keeps giving them the same answers. His solicitor seems to think this is a good thing. If they're going to keep asking the same questions, she says, that's a sure sign they've got nothing else to throw at him. They're hoping they'll be able to wear him down, catch him out in a lie, but as long as he sticks to the same answers and gives them nothing to feed off, they'll have to give in eventually. He hopes she's right.

She herself is something of a surprise. It's not like he chose her – she just happened to be the one on duty when he was first brought in. His first thought was that she looked a bit inexperienced. She can't be much older than he is but he's already had plenty of evidence that she knows what she's doing. She's not intimidated one bit by Holloway or his miserable partner. Any time she thinks they're not following the rules, she's quick to pull them up and he likes the confident way she goes about her work. Feels protected. So he's happy to give her the benefit of the doubt.

He was hoping Mr Mitchell would have picked up some really important solicitor, someone who would get him out of here before they'd even had a chance to sit down. But it didn't turn out that way. The moment he heard about the baseball bat something seemed to change in their relationship. He just kept saying, 'Oh, Owen,' over and over again and shaking his head like it was *his* fault or something. Like he'd let him down. He hasn't seen him since early this afternoon and Owen assumed at first it was because he was hard at work, planning the best way to get him out of here, but he hasn't come back. Holloway says it's because Mr Mitchell has had enough, doesn't want anything more to do with him but that's probably just another of their tricks to make him despondent, get behind his defences. He's learning about Holloway. You have to watch him like a hawk. 'All smiles and sharp teeth,' his mother used to say. He's asked if there's anyone else Owen would like to call instead but he's happy with this young lady as it happens. At least she seems to be on his side.

Unlike Willie. He hasn't heard a peep out of him since they were at the allotments but, if he's honest, he thinks that's no bad thing. More a relief than anything else. Willie can be unbearable when he has the chance to say *I told you so* . . . and he'd be in his element here. Owen's been working hard at shutting him out recently. Maybe he's taken the hint at last and decided to leave him alone. He hopes so. Good riddance.

Owen finds it interesting that his solicitor hasn't asked him if he killed Callum. Not once. He doesn't know if it's because she'd rather not know or because she doesn't think it matters either way. She's more interested in how he's going to explain away the baseball bat being found in that particular shed. So he's told her – it's quite simple. He'll tell the truth. He put it there. And he'll make no apologies for having done so because that's precisely what was done to him. He's told her he found it late on Saturday afternoon in his own shed and realised immediately what it was and why it was there. He's not stupid. He worked out pretty quickly someone was trying to frame him. He was going to take it into the police station but changed his mind because he knew they'd never believe him. They'd use it against him instead. It's been obvious for weeks that they think he's the one who attacked Callum and they've resorted to all sorts of underhand tricks to try and catch him out. The whole Julie business was just one example of how they'd tried to get under his skin in the hope that he'd make a mistake. So no way was he going to hand them the murder weapon on a plate. He might as well sign a confession at the same time and have done with it.

Instead he sneaked the baseball bat into Adam Kitchener's shed the first chance he had. And again, he's not about to apologise for that. It's only fair. He's pretty sure it was Kitchener who passed it on to him in the first place. Who else was it going to be? Even Abi thought there was something iffy about the fact that he'd arrived late at the pub and then misled the police about the time. And if Kitchener wanted to point the finger at someone else, who better than the very person the police were desperate to pin it on? No-brainer.

The solicitor – Kristen – is happy with this. She likes the fact that there's another possible suspect who can be used to draw attention away from her client. *Her client.* He likes the sound of that. It's a shame he's had to lie to her but he can't exactly tell her the truth, can he? And what matters is it's a good lie. Holloway and his partner have been battering away at it for some time now and they haven't made any sort of dent in it. It's holding up well. And he knows from his mother's example that sometimes a good lie is much better than the truth.

Kristen's asked him questions about Abi as well but he's shied away from answering most of those. It's not that he thinks it's none of her business. He knows she's only trying to help. It's just that he doesn't understand what's been happening with Abi recently and doesn't want to look too closely at it either. Not just yet. She's obviously been tricked by Kitchener and everyone else into turning against him. There's no way she'd have lied to his face and led him on like that if she was thinking straight, but he knows from his own experience how hard it can be to see things as they really are when you're being squeezed from all sides. What she's done is wrong but he's confident she'll see that for herself eventually. And he doesn't want to start talking about all this with someone he's practically only just met, thank you very much. Personal is private.

He does like Kristen though. She seems to understand him and has his best interests at heart, which is what really counts. She says the police are a long way from being able to prove anything and they're not going to appear in a very good light once their harassment of him is made public. To her, this whole investigation screamed entrapment. They can claim as much as they like that Julie's disappearing act was nothing to do with them, but no one's going to believe that if it ever comes to trial. And the way they tricked him into giving up the bat . . . there's more than a whiff of the unethical about that too. They're claiming there was no need for an appropriate adult at the allotments because they were questioning Kitchener, not Owen, and anything he might have said came of his own volition, even though they'd repeatedly told him to say nothing. She uses words like that: *Volition. Sophistry.* He can tell she's on top of things and she's managed to convince him he'll be out of here before long.

She's taken the trouble to explain how the detention clock works but it's all gone in one ear and out the other to be honest. It bothered him at first that he couldn't keep it all straight in his head but he's past caring now. It's a distraction he doesn't need. All he has to focus on is these questions. If he sits tight, answers them all exactly as he has done till now and doesn't try to be clever, there's nothing they can do. They'll have to let him go home.

She says they'll be searching his house, garden, shed, truck . . . everything. That's why they wanted the bat. They've now got something called probable cause and can start to apply more pressure. He's told her he's not worried. Let them search. There's nothing for them to find. He says it in such a way, with such confidence, that he thinks she'll take this as further proof that he had nothing to do with what happened to Callum. As long as they don't have anything to link him with the crime scene they can come up with whatever theories they like, she says. It's all circumstantial and not even very convincing at that.

As for the bat, that's not going to be a problem. If it turns out there are blood traces, so what? Everyone knows it was the murder weapon. If it has his fingerprints, why wouldn't it? He's admitted he put it in what he thought was Kitchener's shed. As for why he had the bat in the first place, there's nothing to disprove his version. It's his word against Kitchener's. And after the way he's been hounded for the past three months, any jury will see this for the witch hunt it is, which is why it will never get to trial in her opinion. The CPS has to be so careful nowadays. They won't go for it. That's what Kristen says and that's more than good enough for him.

So it's just a question of keeping his nerve and waiting them out. They've been gone for a while now. There's a camera in the corner of the room which they told him about earlier because they've been filming and recording every interview. They're probably watching him right now from another room near by, trying to decide when will be the best time to come in and have another go at him. He's seen it all before in films. He knows what they're trying to do. And even though he's desperate to get out of here and take a few gulps of fresh air, he's not going to let them see it.

He can wait as long as he needs to.

The clock's ticking.

And time is on his side.

'Sorry to keep you waiting,' says Holloway, when they finally come back in. 'Just a few more things we'd like to go over.'

He ignores them. Says nothing. He's seen criminal lawyers on TV before, knows what they'd say in a situation like this: *Is there a question in here somewhere?*

Answer – no.

'You know Estelle Roberts, Owen?'

'Who?'

'It's a shop, not a person. Jewellers. In Arun Valley.'

'No.'

'Never been there?'

'No.'

'OK. Not surprised. Neither had I until recently. Bit pricey for me, to be honest.' Holloway smiles, like maybe he can persuade Owen this is nothing more than a friendly chat. Get him to drop his guard. Not going to happen. Owen is watching him like a hawk.

'Anyway, about a week ago . . . Friday, fifth December, to be exact,' he adds, glancing down at his notebook on the table in front of him, 'the manager of Estelle Roberts phoned Abi.'

Wait for it.

'Abi Green.'

He hates it when Holloway does this. The more he gets to know this man, the more he's convinced it's deliberate. It happens too often for it to be just coincidence. All he needs to say is *Abi* – they all know who he's talking about. But every time he says her name there's this pause and then he tacks the surname onto the end as well. Owen knows why he's doing it. It's not just to hurt him by reminding him that she chose Callum. It's because he knows how Owen's mind works. Knows he won't be able to help himself.

Abi: total = 12, multiple of 3. Owen: total = 57, multiple of 3. *Safe. Happy.*

Abi Green: total = 61.

Prime number. *Danger.*

He does it to unsettle him and it's not going to work. Owen says nothing.

'You want to know what it was about? No? Well, I'll tell you anyway because we were really quite excited when we heard about it. DS Horgan here nearly broke into a smile, didn't you?'

Horgan's expression hasn't altered since he came into the room. He's sitting across the table from Owen, eyes drilling into him, as if they've decided that's the best way to rattle him. *Well, if that's the best they can do . . .*

Holloway consults the sheets on the table in front of him before looking up and smiling. Owen has seen enough of it now to know he needs to be on the alert. Can't believe he was ever taken in by it before.

'Funniest thing,' he says. 'She got this phone call and she was making a cake at the time. You know what it's like when you're busy and your mind's on other things? You can't wait to get the other person off the phone, can you? And just to make matters worse, the call wasn't even meant for her anyway. This woman wanted to talk to Callum about some customer-satisfaction survey they were doing and Abi's still a bit sensitive, as you can imagine, so she more or less put the phone down on them and went back to her cake.'

Owen's been watching him closely while he talks. He hasn't noticed it before but he has this curious habit of wiping his mouth with the palm of one hand after every couple of sentences. He wonders where this strange mannerism comes from, whether it's something he picked up in childhood. Imagining Holloway as a child is beyond him. Some people look as if they've been fifty all their lives.

'Anyway,' he continues, picking up his biro and doodling on the notepad, 'once she got back to the cake she found she couldn't concentrate and at first she thought it was because she felt bad about being a bit brusque on the phone, but now she wonders whether maybe subconsciously she knew there was something funny about the call. Something she couldn't quite put her finger on. So she rang them back.'

From where he's sitting Owen can see quite clearly what Holloway is drawing on the notepad – a 2 first, then a 3 underneath it, followed by a 5. Next will be a 7 . . . and sure enough, here it comes, slightly larger than the others and with a bar across the vertical stroke, the way some people do so you can see it's not a 1. It's pathetic.

'You've forgotten eleven,' he says.

Holloway frowns as if trying to make the connection. Then he realises what he's referring to and looks down at the notepad where he can see he's skipped from 7 straight to 13. He smiles and squeezes the number 11 into its rightful place.

'Well spotted,' he says. 'You can see maths never was my strong point.'

'Is that supposed to make me nervous?' Owen asks. Kristen's puzzled by this exchange so Owen explains and she aims a look of disgust in Holloway's direction before jotting a note inside the impressive-looking folder which she has in front of her.

'Just doodling,' says Holloway. He lays the biro carefully alongside the notepad to demonstrate he's finished with it. Leaves the notepad open. With the numbers still there.

'Anyway, I was saying. She spoke with the manager at Estelle Roberts and this woman was really embarrassed about it all. She explained the only reason she'd rung was because Callum had bought a necklace a while back and then had to return it because of a faulty clasp. She claimed Head Office was looking at their existing refunds policy and they were phoning recent customers to get the data they needed. Only there was a bit of confusion about the whole thing. Really odd, this.'

Odd is not the word Owen would have chosen. He knows where Holloway's going with this. Ever since he casually lobbed the word *necklace* into the conversation, he's been onto him. And he's not worried. He's way ahead.

'You see, according to their records, Callum returned the necklace on . . .' He picks up the notepad and flicks through to the previous page. 'Thursday, eleventh September.'

He puts the pad back on the table with the page of prime numbers still showing.

'Nothing odd about that, you might think. Apart from the fact that Callum had been dead for over a fortnight by then. I'd say their record keeping needs as much attention as their refunds policy, wouldn't you?'

This is all news to Owen. He knows nothing of any refunds. He gave the necklace to Abi on her birthday which was two days after this refund was supposed to have taken place. What Holloway is saying doesn't make any sense at all and he senses a trap of some sort. More lies and tricks.

'Anyway, that wasn't the only thing that got Abi Green's attention. You see, the date Callum was supposed to have bought the necklace was Monday, twenty-fifth August. That ring any bells?'

Owen swallows. Shakes his head without meaning to, then reaches across and turns the notepad over in his irritation with himself.

'It's the day he was murdered. How about that, eh? Time of the transaction, according to the manager when we rang her earlier . . .' He consults the pad again, then puts it down with the numbers hidden. Leaves it like that for a couple of seconds, then slowly turns it over, that maddening smile playing at the corner of his lips.

'Seventeen-thirteen. And I promise that's the time they gave us over the phone. I know they're prime numbers but I can't help that. So at 17.13 Callum Green was buying a necklace and something like a couple of hours later he was dead. Which sort of got us wondering – what happened to the necklace?'

He pauses for a moment, clasps his hands on the desk in front of him.

'I mean, Abi's first reaction – Abi Green,' he continues, 'she was really upset when she heard about it because this was some expensive necklace and she's pretty sure *she* wasn't the one he was buying it for. They weren't on the best of terms at the time, as you probably know, and given that she now knows Callum was planning to spend the week in Bournemouth with Hannah Reid, she feels it's logical to assume that he'd bought the necklace for her instead. And I have to say I agree with her. In which case, it would have made sense for him to have the necklace with him in the car when he drove over there to pick her up. You with me?'

He is. He'd rather not be but he is. And he's saying nothing just yet.

'So that raises a pretty crucial question – what happened to the necklace? It's not in the car. He didn't get the chance to give it to Hannah Reid – we've checked with her, incidentally. And he didn't give it to his wife. So where is it?'

Owen knows it has to be now. He can see where this is going and they need an alternative explanation to keep them off balance but he's already got his exit strategy lined up. He's still way ahead of them.

'Maybe the killer took it,' he says.

Holloway holds up a corroborating finger.

'That's what we thought too,' he says.

'Have you asked Adam K-Kitchener what he knows about it? Maybe he can help you . . . given that he's the one who had the b-bat all along.'

'Ah yes, Mr Kitchener,' says Holloway. 'No, we don't really need to question him about it, do we? You see, we now know where the necklace is.'

'Where?'

'She's had it all along. Abi Green. You see, we asked the manager at Estelle Roberts to email across a photo of the necklace Callum bought back in August and she sent it through. And Abi recognised it at once.' He pauses and there's no smile now. 'It's the one you gave her for her birthday.'

He's shaking his head. Kristen reaches across as if to suggest maybe he shouldn't answer but he pats her hand with his own. *It's OK*, his eyes tell her. *I've got this.*

'I don't understand,' he says. 'Why would she say that?' He's pleased to notice that his hands are just fine and there's no trace of a stammer at the moment. He feels he has this under control.

If he starts down the 'No comment' road, they'll find a way to use that against him later. They need to see he has nothing to hide.

'Are you saying you didn't?'

'Of course I didn't.'

'So she's lying?'

'I don't know.'

'What do you mean, you don't know? She's said in a sworn statement that the necklace came from you. Abi . . . Abi Green is lying about something as important as that? Even though she knows what that will mean, the difficult position it will put you in?'

'She's under a lot of pressure right now,' says Owen. 'She's been through a lot. And that man has obviously turned her head.'

'That man being Adam Kitchener?'

'You don't know what he's like,' says Owen and he has no difficulty whatsoever in summoning a convincing scowl to show how he feels. 'He has this hold over her – she'd say anything if he asked her to.'

'And why would he ask her?'

Owen tuts, gives a brief shake of the head to express his irritation. Does he have to spell everything out for them?

'Because he killed Callum, just like I've been telling you all along. He killed him, took the necklace and then gave it to Abi for her birthday. Why can't you see it? It's not difficult.'

'So you're saying it wasn't you who gave her the necklace?'

'Right.'

'I just want to be clear about it.'

'I didn't give her the necklace.'

Holloway sits back, then snaps his fingers. Horgan responds immediately, taking a photo from a file on the desk. He passes it to Holloway who slides it across the table until it skids to a halt in front of Owen.

'This is the photo the manager at Estelle Roberts sent us. Take a good look at it. It's a very distinctive necklace. You still stand by your story?'

'Yes. I didn't give her this or any other necklace.'

'You were at Abi Green's house on her birthday, weren't you?'

'Yes.'

'Did you give her a present?'

'Of course. I gave her some mints.'

'Mints?'

'Chocolate mints – they're her favourites. She has a sweet tooth,' he adds with a sly smile.

'Did you see any of her other presents?'

'No. Yes,' he corrects himself. 'Her father-in-law drove over to see her. He gave her a book and a DVD.'

'Did you see this necklace at all that day?'

'No,' he says. 'I've *never* seen it.'

'Never?'

Owen pauses before answering. Thinks it might be better to backtrack a little.

'Not that I can remember,' he says. *Better.* Doesn't pay to be any more specific than you have to.

'So what's this?' Holloway holds out his hand and Horgan passes him another photo. The moment Owen sees it, he's surprised at how much it hurts to look back to that evening in the restaurant, Abi reaching across to rest her head on his shoulder, the necklace nestling in the V of her dress. So much has happened in the past few days . . . and he's so tired. But they're getting to the bit that really matters now. He needs to concentrate.

'That is the same necklace, isn't it?' asks Holloway. 'The one you've never seen before?'

He shrugs.

'Obviously I was wrong. I don't remember it.'

'Well, I have to say, I find that very surprising, Owen,' says Holloway, throwing himself back in his chair. 'I mean, I know it was taken on Abi's phone but when I checked your mobile a few moments ago I found the attachment she sent you . . . which you've saved in a collection labelled *ABI*. I've no idea whether our lab boys have a way of checking how often you've gone to that collection and stared at the photo but I'm willing to bet it's pretty damned often.'

'I don't take much interest in jewellery,' he says with a sigh. 'She might have been wearing rings and a bracelet that evening as well. I couldn't tell you what they were.'

We're nearly there, he tells himself. He knows exactly where they're going with this. Has known all along. Let them.

'Now you come to mention it though,' he says, looking at the photo again, 'maybe I do remember this one.'

'You do?' Holloway can hardly keep the disbelief out of his voice.

'Yes. At the end of the evening, when we were getting ready to leave. I was helping Abi put her coat on and she'd got her hair caught in the necklace and she asked me to undo the clasp at the back for her. I remember now – I held it while she sorted her hair out.'

'You held it for her?'

'Yes. For a few seconds. I mean, I wasn't paying much attention to what the thing looked like.'

'So that means if we were to find your fingerprints on the necklace, there would be a perfectly innocent explanation for it, I suppose?'

'Yes.' And what he means is *Yesssssss!* because he can see from the quiet smile of resignation that Holloway flashes at his partner that he wasn't expecting this. But he keeps it all under wraps for now. Plenty of time to celebrate later, once they've let him go and he can get back home. It must be nearly bedtime. He's so tired.

Holloway must be feeling crushed. He'll be every bit as tired as Owen. He's spent not just the past twenty-four hours but weeks and weeks trying to find a way to catch him out and he must have thought he'd got him with this necklace business. He's sitting there, tapping the table with his biro, a weary smile on his face.

'That's very good, Owen,' he says, and Owen is feeling so elated he doesn't even bother to pick him up on the inappropriate use of his Christian name. 'That's really very good.'

'It's the truth.'

'No ... it's not. But it's very good. I'll admit it. We really thought we had you there. I mean, everything we've thrown at you, you've found a way to wriggle off the hook. It was getting to the stage where I thought we'd never catch you out.'

He looks Owen in the eye.

'But I'm afraid we have.'

And Owen is seized by a sudden urge to get to his feet and give the man a good shake. What is *wrong* with him, for Heaven's sake? Doesn't he know when to quit?

'What do you mean?'

Holloway picks up the notepad and closes it. Then he takes the pen, clicks it shut and clips it to the spine of the notepad.

'It's the fingerprints, Owen,' he says. 'We knew all along they were going to be the key to it. The only thing that worried me was that you might come up with some clever reason for having the necklace. DS Horgan here, he was betting you'd say Callum called round on his way home and asked you to look after it for him for some reason. Rubbish, of course, but it might have been difficult to disprove. But the moment you insisted it wasn't you who gave Abi the present, we knew we had you. Because of the fingerprints.'

'But I told you . . . she asked me to undo the clasp in the restaurant. I held the necklace for a few minutes.'

Holloway shakes his head.

'It's not the necklace, Owen,' he says.

'What do you mean?'

'It's not the necklace.' He holds his hand out and Horgan passes yet another photo to him. 'It's the box.'

'The –'

'The box the necklace came in.' He slides the photo across the table. 'The one that the necklace came in, and which has your fingerprints all over it. From when you took it out of her wardrobe to get another look at it. From the time you took it out of Callum's car and opened it up to see what was inside. Those fingerprints, Owen. They're the ones. You see, you may well have handled the necklace at the restaurant, but I can't think of any innocent way you would have handled the box. The only way you could have done that would be if she'd taken it to the restaurant for some reason and then put the necklace on, only we know she didn't do that –' Holloway reaches across and taps the photo for emphasis. 'We know because you met Abi for dinner on Thursday, eleventh December, and we've had the box in our possession since she brought it to us on the day of the phone call. And that was six days earlier. So you see, we've known for some time. It was just a question of whether we could prove it.'

And his thoughts are whizzing around like firecrackers in a tin can. In his head, he's running down a hallway and into one room after another, desperately searching for a door or a window that will offer him a way out of the building, only every opening is blocked off and he feels as if he's been bouncing off the walls for an eternity now. He needs to sit down and rest. Needs it so badly. But there's nothing there . . . nothing he can think of that will explain this away.

And now . . . now of all times, Willie's back. Only it's not the Willie he's been talking to and frequently rowing with for the past twenty years or so. Instead it's Owen's six-year-old twin, clear as daylight, even though it makes no sense. Can't be happening. And he's sitting in the corner, taking no notice of what's going on around him. He's not remotely interested in what Owen's going through at the moment, won't be offering him any help at all. What possible help could a six-year-old give anyway? Instead, he's playing with Owen's toy Bugatti. He recognises it instantly, even though it's years since he last saw it. He knows that if he were to go over and take it from Willie, he'd see the tiny figure behind the wheel, complete with goggles and flying scarf, and the chip in the paintwork where he threw it at Willie when they'd fallen out about something. Can't remember what now. Doesn't matter.

And then Willie turns and looks at him.

And smiles.

And puts the toy car into his pocket as he walks away.

AUTHOR'S NOTE

Last time I looked there was no huge shopping centre called Arun Valley or anything else resembling it on the A259 between Chichester and Bognor Regis. It is a product of my imagination, although it wouldn't be a huge surprise to see something of the sort springing up along that stretch of road at some stage in the future.

Hopefully any readers familiar with the Chichester and Bognor area will take pleasure from recognising the various locations used in the novel, all of which are authentic, including Honer Lane in South Mundham. I'd like to make it quite clear though that no one living there is portrayed in the book and even the vaguest resemblance to Hannah Reid should be seen as entirely coincidental.

As for the Bellamy brothers and Ezra Cunningham, if this area has its own real-life equivalent, may I be the first to apologise. Profusely.

Don't miss

THE HIDDEN LEGACY

ONCE YOU KNOW, YOU CAN'T FORGET

Ellen has received a life-changing inheritance. If only she knew
who had left it to her . . .

1966. A horrifying crime at a secondary school, with
devastating consequences for all involved.

2008. A life-changing gift, if only the recipient can
work out why . . .

Recently divorced and with two young children, Ellen Sutherland
is up to her elbows in professional and personal stress. When
she's invited to travel all the way to Cheltenham to hear the
content of an old woman's will, she's far from convinced the
journey will be worthwhile.

But when she arrives, the news is astounding. Eudora Nash
has left Ellen a beautiful cottage worth an amount of money
that could turn her life around. There's just one problem –
Ellen has never even heard of Eudora Nash.

Her curiosity piqued, Ellen and her friend Kate travel to the
West Country in search of answers. But they are not the only
ones interested in the cottage, and Ellen little imagines how
much she has to learn about her past . . .

Available in paperback and eBook now

ACKNOWLEDGMENTS

I am just as indebted as last time around to the usual group of suspects who have done so much to make it possible for me to produce a second novel. I hope they will forgive me for not naming them all here, which is a convenient way of ensuring that, if I've forgotten certain individuals, they will never know.

I would, however, like to offer a few specific thanks to:

- Gemma, for coming up with the Estelle Roberts scam – would never have happened on her watch!
- The Ginger Cat Cakery (visit the website!) for expert guidance – never made a cake in my life!
- Darren, for help with security at Arun Valley.
- Faz Chitima and everyone at Ockley ABC, for taking time out to talk to me and making me welcome when I visited them. You're not in the novel, Faz, but your spirit and devotion certainly are.
- A whole host of bloggers and reviewers who have taken the time and trouble to give such positive feedback on my debut novel, *The Hidden Legacy*. I said in a blog on my website that you are the lifeblood of the industry – I stand by that.
- Everyone at Bonnier Zaffre and The Ampersand Agency, especially Joel and Peter – you know why.

- The amazing group of debut authors who started at Twenty7 with me and who have been indefatigable in the support they've offered to each other on social media – who said writing was a selfish, cut-throat business?
- Family and friends, for constant support and encouragement. I'd love for Mum to be able to read this one to Dad.
- Elaine – say no more.

Want to read
NEW BOOKS
before anyone else?

Like getting
FREE BOOKS?

Enjoy sharing your
OPINIONS?

Discover

READERS
FIRST

Read. Love. Share.

Get your first free book just by signing up at
readersfirst.co.uk